FOUR STEAMY LOVE STORIES IN WHICH FOUR WOMEN'S MOST SENSUAL DESIRES ARE FULFILLED.

"A Dance On the Edge"
Anne Avery

When interior designer Marlis Jones battles with architect Jack Martin over e-mail, they discover a love powerful enough to blow their circuits.

"Toss the Bouquet"
Phoebe Conn

After her boyfriend falls short of the altar, bridal florist Regan Paisley spends her vacation days at the beach alone. Then she meets a seductive Italian cyclist who pedals his way into her bed—and her heart.

"Heart Craving"
Sandra Hill

Nicholas DiCello is desperate—his wife Paula plans to divorce him. So when a fortune-telling floozy in a flowered dress swears the only way to win back his wife's love is to discover her heart craving, he listens.

"My One"
Dara Joy

When Lois Ed pleads with the cosmos to help her through her hard times, she never expects her cry to be answered— by a hunk of an alien with the wildest sense of passion she's ever experienced.

Other *Leisure* and *Love Spell* anthologies:

ANNE AVERY, PHOEBE CONN, SANDRA HILL, DARA JOY

LOVESCAPE

LEISURE BOOKS   NEW YORK CITY

A LEISURE BOOK®

July 2004

Published by

Dorchester Publishing Co., Inc.
200 Madison Avenue
New York, NY 10016

ISBN 0-8439-4052-2

Visit us on the web at www.dorchesterpub.com.

A Dance
On the Edge

ANNE AVERY

This is for my e-mail buddies, who are living proof that friendships really can flourish through the miracle of modern telecommunications. Thanks for being at the other end of the line!

Jones@tel.com

Dear Ms. Jones:

I received your E-mail. The one with suggestions for the interior of the lodge I'm building for Frank.

Sorry to say this, but you've got it all wrong. Your ideas are totally inappropriate for a timber-and-stone lodge set in the middle of upstate New York wilderness.

Now, I'm not questioning your qualifications as an interior designer. Frank showed me photos of the work you'd done for him on those big commercial projects in Manhattan. It's obvious you know what you're doing in a multimillion-dollar office building.

But frankly, Ms. Jones, that kind of slick sophistication just isn't appropriate for a lodge that will be a second home for Frank and his family. Silk upholstery in a house with a six-year-old who carries her pet frog in her purse? Come on!

I'll be honest. I told Frank I thought he was making

a mistake in hiring you for this project. He insisted.
But *silk?* That's plain ridiculous!
Jack Martin

Martin@tel.com

Dear Mr. Martin,
Just because we are constrained to communicating
by E-mail doesn't give you the right to be rude. You
architects seem to think that a building is the concrete
and glass you slapped together, and anything else is
mere useless decoration. You forget that people are
going to live and work inside all that concrete. Real,
live people. They can't sit on your precious architectural vision!
Marlis Jones
PS. You also appear to have forgotten that you're
building this lodge for Frank *and* Pat. Wives are part
of the deal too, you know!

Jones@tel.com

Dear Ms. Jones:
Interior designers have their place, but if, like you,
they can't grasp the difference between a mountain
lodge and a Manhattan office, they're better off stick-
ing with the office.
Silk, for heaven's sake!
Jack Martin
And I didn't forget Pat—*or* her penchant for knick-
knacks.

Martin@tel.com

Mr. Martin:
From rudeness to outright insults. If we were in the
same meeting room, I'd be tempted to throw your

8

blueprints in your face! I should have stuck to my guns and refused Frank's request that I work on this project with you.

However, I agreed to do my best, and if that best includes trying to educate a thick-headed architect, so be it.

There is silk, Mr. Martin, and there is silk. I am not referring to the fabric used in a woman's scarf, but to the heavier raw silk which can be combined with other fibers to make beautiful and very durable fabrics that are perfect for the lodge. Fabrics that glow with color, yet are tough and easy to care for.

The lodge can't be all rough wood and raw stone, as you seem to think. The beauty of such crude materials can't really be appreciated until they are contrasted with their opposites.

Much as it irritates me to explain such elementary principles, I am sending you some fabric swatches, color photocopies of the watercolor sketches I've worked up for the entry, and a hand-blown glass vase that will show you what I mean. (The vase is similar to the glassware that Pat collects and it is *not* a knick-knack!

If you can put your personal biases aside long enough to really *look* at them, that is!

Marlis Jones

Jones@tel.com

Dear Ms. Jones:

The box you sent arrived over a week ago.

It's taken me that long to admit you were right and I was wrong. And that I owe you an apology.

Much as it galled me to do it, I set the vase on a rock shelf I built near the fireplace in my office and tossed those swaths of colored silk over the pillows on my leather sofa. I have to tell you I felt damned silly, because I'm not a flower vase and silk pillows kind of guy.

After a week of living with them, I find I'm thinking about recovering the sofa and looking for some decorations other than the welded steel sculpture of an eagle that I've had in my office since forever.

Not that I want to get rid of the eagle, you understand.

More than that, the photocopies of your watercolor sketches made me rethink some of my original plans for the lodge. I've already talked to Frank about the changes, and he's all for it.

Providing I work with you.

Clever guy, Frank. He obviously figured out I was behaving like a jerk. Which might be due to the fact that he's known me since grade school.

He also knows I prefer to take complete control of a project, inside and out, top to bottom. Which is why he had a hard time convincing me to work with you in the first place.

I'd call you up to offer my apologies personally, but since you insist on communicating via E-mail, the best I can do is say I'm sorry. And that I'd like to start over in terms of our working relationship, if you'll agree.

Jack

Martin@tel.com

Dear Mr. Martin:

Your apologies are accepted. And I'll apologize for my own quick temper. It seems we're both going to have to learn a few things about E-mail etiquette!

I'm really not trying to change your plans for the

lodge. I feel very strongly that my role as an interior designer is not to hide or make over a place, but to discover the soul of a structure, the central force of its creator's vision, then bring it down into more human, accessible terms. To complement, rather than cover or conceal.

But this lodge is something new for me. When Frank first approached me about working on it, I turned him down. I've handled some of his biggest development projects here in Manhattan, but this just seemed far too intimate and personal. Too risky, really, although that word sounds absurd, under the circumstances.

I think I might have continued to turn him down if he hadn't shown me photos of some of your previous projects.

The incredible variety and integrity of the buildings appealed to me. They all seemed to spring so naturally from their surroundings, as if you had somehow sensed their presence hidden deep in the earth and magically brought them to life. Then Frank showed me the photos of the site and your plans for the lodge.

I decided right then and there that I wanted to be a part of this project. So I guess we're struck with each other.

Maybe both of us will learn something here.

Marlis Jones

Jones@tel.com

Dear Marlis,

Now that we've both apologized, I guess we can get on with the job.

If you don't mind, I'd prefer you to call me Jack. And I'll call you Marlis. Computer E-mail is already too impersonal. We don't need to make it worse by professional formalities.

I'm sending you some samples of the materials we'll be using on the lodge, both inside and out, so you can get a clearer idea of what the finished building will look like. I thought it might help as you're developing your own ideas. Please let me know if there's anything else you might need.

Jack

PS. I really do regret that crack about the silk.

Martin@tel.com

Dear Jack:

I received the samples of stone and wood you sent. I have to admit, when I picture a whole building made of such powerful elements, I find them almost intimidatingly masculine. Raw, like the earth they've come from, yet beautiful in their own way.

The lodge is going to be breathtaking, but I'm not sure I would ever feel comfortable living there. It's so *elemental.* So much a part of the wilderness that surrounds it that I think I'd feel lost and overwhelmed.

I guess I'm just more of a city girl than I thought.

I hope you're not offended by my comments. I'm actually awed by your talent, but you live and work in a world that is completely foreign to me. I feel like I'm venturing out into the unknown. Which is scary and exhilarating, all at the same time.

Marlis

Jones@tel.com

Dear Marlis,

I wasn't offended by your comments, but I *am* bemused.

No, that's not completely true. I'm downright confused.

Natural materials like stone and wood are intimidating? The lodge is overwhelming? I can't see that at all.

I spent my youth roaming these hills, shinnying up trees and climbing on rocks and wading through streams as cold as ice. The lodge is simply an extension of that world. The world I've always known. The world Frank grew up in, just like me.

I see architecture as a way of melding our created environment—our homes and shops and offices—into the natural world around us. It isn't masculine, it's *real,* and that's what I'm aiming for.

And I hope I haven't offended *you* by saying that. Cities like New York are a separate creation altogether!

Anyway, that's not the real point of this post, which is to tell you that the contractor has begun excavation at the site.

I wish I could be there to see it, but that just isn't possible any more. Not that it really matters. I've worked with this crew in the past and know I can depend on them to do things right.

If you have the opportunity of visiting the lodge once it's closer to completion, you can tell me what you think.

Jack

Martin@tel.com

Dear Jack,

It's a good thing you understand this natural world of yours. When I look at the photos of the site, all I can see is raw stone and an undisciplined tangle of trees and bushes. It's not until I compare the photos with your drawings that what seems a shapeless hillside takes on a form and a life I wouldn't have imagined possible.

It's never been quite so difficult when dealing with the professional buildings I usually work with. You can't even begin to imagine a skyscraper being a part of its surroundings, as your lodge will be. Skyscrapers create their own world. Dwarf them, really. Unlike the lodge, they're never on a human scale—they wouldn't be skyscrapers if they were—and that's what I like most about them, their sense of being apart, of standing alone. I confess, I'm more comfortable with them than with your smaller, more intimate structures, which are so closely tied to the earth they spring from.

I guess I'm too much a city kid. I was born in Manhattan. This is my home and I can't imagine living anyplace else. I like the energy. I like having everything I want right here when I want it—the museums, the art galleries, the bookstores. I like knowing that I don't have to be bothered with my neighbors if I don't want to, that I can shut my door against the world and have my own carefully ordered sanctuary. And I like knowing I can open that door when I'm ready and see everything still there, waiting for me.

This lodge is the first thing I've ever worked on that was intended to be lived in. Besides my own apartment, of course.

I was very hesitant at first—I think I told you that already—but I'm finding it an interesting challenge, especially since your style and mine are so different in so many ways.

I'm delighted to hear the crew has begun work already. I won't be visiting the lodge itself. I don't know if Frank told you, but that was one of the essential conditions for my agreeing to take on this job.

My work is mostly here, you know, and what with everything—well, I just said I couldn't make it on site.

I'm a little surprised to hear *you* won't be overseeing the construction, however. I assumed you'd be keeping a pretty close eye on it since you and Frank are old friends and you seem to be so passionately connected to the project.

Not that it's any of my business, of course. We haven't even met, for heaven's sake!

> Marlis, who should get back to work instead of sticking her nose in other people's business.

Jones@tel.com

Dear Marlis,

We may not have met, but somehow I feel I know you.

Funny, isn't it, how you get to feel that way about the person at the other end of an E-mail connection?

Frank sent me some promotional brochures for that new complex he's been working on. I spotted the picture of you right off. Marlis Jones, well-known interior designer, it said. But you probably know that all ready. You worked on the complex!

Somehow, I figured you'd be bigger and—I don't know—tougher-looking, I guess. I certainly wasn't expecting to see a petite strawberry blonde in high heels! Must have been my built-in wariness of big city folk kicking in, I guess.

I don't think I could stand to live in New York like you do. When I used to go into the city, I'd wander around the streets if I had free time. The place terrified me. Still does, actually, though it's been a couple of years since I spent much time there. It's an exciting place, but it's not *natural*. Even its parks and open areas are carefully cultivated and thought out. There's no sense of discovery or wondering what nature will spring on you next. In fact, the only thing you worry about New York springing on you is a thug out to grab your wallet!

That, and being deafened by the constant racket in the streets. The noise in the city is enough to drive a sane man mad, and my friends don't consider me sane. I prefer the rustle of leaves and the sound of the wind through the grass.

Anyway, that's neither here nor there. Back to business.

The contractor called this morning to tell me they've started pouring the foundations. That's always an exciting stage for me, the first real step in transforming an idea into reality. Wish I could be there. Guess we'll just have to settle for some photographs every now and then.

I'm looking forward to seeing more of your sketches!

All the best,
Jack

Martin@tel.com

Dear Jack,

Sorry it's taken so long to get back to you.

I've been visiting the design showrooms to look at furniture and fabrics and what not. I've pulled a number of fabric swatches and am sending samples to you later today. I especially love the raw silk blend with its cool, slick texture and the subtle imperfections of its surface. Like rock under water, I think.

You probably think that's a silly comparison, but I have to tell you how foolishly I behaved.

A Dance on the Edge

After I'd found the fabric in all those gorgeous autumn colors, I stuffed the samples in my purse and rushed off to a meeting in another building. But I got side-tracked by a fountain in the atrium. It was huge. The fountain, I mean. Made of natural, uncut stone very similar in color and texture to the stone you plan to use in the lodge.

I don't know what got into me, but when I saw that fountain I thought about the rocky hillside where the lodge is being built, and I thought about you and how you roamed those hills when you were a boy. I could just see you clambering on rocks and plunging your hands into those icy streams you talked about.

Some crazy imp must have taken possession of me, because right then and there, without paying any attention to the stares from the passersby, I took off my heels and climbed up on the rocks and ran my hand through the water spilling over the stones. I've seen kids doing that, but I've never even dreamed of trying something that—undignified.

It felt wonderful. Absolutely wonderful! The water was cold and battered my fingers, and the rock underneath was slick, yet retained its rough texture, just like the silk. For the first time I got a hint of how you must feel when you're climbing around those hills. It helped me understand a little more clearly your vision for the lodge and your reasons for choosing the materials you did.

I admit, I got a few strange looks when I showed up at my meeting five minutes late with wet spots on my hose and my hands feeling like ice. But the experience was worth it, despite the damage to my reputation.

It certainly convinced me that the silk is the best choice as the central upholstery material. We can make throw pillows and cover sofas and chairs in that exquisite range of colors, with the fabric texture itself, its relationship to your stone and wood and stucco walls, the unifying touch. I really do think it will work well!

The furniture I'm less certain about. Nothing I've seen so far seems to fit, not even the "rustic" styles, but I will keep looking. I know what I want, and I find it's often more difficult to work that way than if you're just waiting for something to catch your eye.

I haven't even started looking at carpet, but my little adventure on those rocks got me thinking about the possibilities of making even the carpet echo the experience of being in a forest.

When you were a boy, did you ever go barefoot through the woods? What does it feel like to have the grass and the fallen leaves and the cool earth between your toes? I relished my climb up those rocks and paddling my hand in the water, but I couldn't quite bring myself to walk barefoot in the garden planters!

Now I'm getting absolutely silly. That's not like me. I suspect something about this E-mail breaks down the normal barriers between people. I feel like I'm talking to you, but it's safer, somehow, because you can't touch me or see me. And I can't touch, or see, you.

Silly, as I said. I'd best get moving. I want to send those swatches to you today, and I'm going to miss the mail if I don't hurry up.

> All the best,
> Marlis

Jack Martin cursed and pushed away from his desk so violently that he ran into the black Lab sprawled across the floor behind him. Julius grunted and scrambled out of the way, then sat down a safe distance away and stared at him reproachfully.

"Sorry, old fellow." Jack couldn't stand to look at

Julius's accusatory stare, but he couldn't stand to look at the computer screen in front of him, either.

He'd found it difficult to write of his youthful explorations in the woods, even harder to read her description of her scramble over the rocks in that building in Manhattan. But to have her ask him what it felt like to have the earth and the cool grass beneath his feet . . .

God! Could any question have been crueler . . . or more innocent?

With one hard, angry shove, Jack swung his wheelchair around, then rolled it over to the wide wall of glass at the far side of his office.

Outside, just beyond the deck, wildflowers painted bright splotches of blue and pink and yellow among the tall meadow grasses. A wild tangle of trees and brush at the far edge of the clearing marked the beginning of the forest that lay beyond.

How many hours had he spent staring out these windows during the past year? A hundred? A thousand? He didn't know and didn't want to figure it out. Even going out on the deck could be torment because it was an ever-present reminder of the new boundaries that hemmed his world.

But to be reminded that he would never walk through the meadow again, never hear the soft crunch of gravel beneath his feet, or dangle his feet in a brook until his toes felt cold enough to drop off . . .

If he had any sense, he'd move away. Either that or put a tall fence around the deck—do *something* to stop the hurt of staring out at those woods day after day.

The trouble was, he didn't know if he could endure living anywhere else. At least from this office he could watch the slow change of the seasons. He could lie in bed at night and listen to the soft rustling of the leaves and the hooting of the owl that had made its home in a massive old oak nearby. Here, at least, he wasn't completely exiled from the wilderness he'd loved for as long as he could remember.

Marlis couldn't have known what raw nerve she'd touched, and he wasn't about to spoil the rapport developing between them by bringing up his disability or the anger he felt about it. Especially not when he was beginning to feel the same strange sense of intimacy in this electronic exchange that she evidently did. If her comments inadvertently triggered unpleasant memories, he was just going to have to learn to live with it, just as he was having to learn to live with everything else.

Jack glanced at the computer with its insistently blinking cursor. Nothing frightening there. Nothing he couldn't handle.

Nothing, that was, if he could ever come to terms with the limitations that now shaped his life.

He hesitated a moment longer; then, ashamed of his fear, he abruptly swung his wheelchair around and rolled it back to the computer.

Jones@tel.com

Dear Marlis,

I can imagine your business colleagues' shock at seeing you march into that meeting with wet legs and cold hands. Your photo in that promotional brochure certainly doesn't make you look like anyone who would ever consider climbing on a fountain in the middle of Manhattan!

On the other hand, it probably made them wish they'd had the courage to do something like that. Too often we get ourselves trapped in rigid expectations about who we are and what we can and should be doing in life. I'm beginning to think it's a good idea to try out something different every once in a while. That way, when life forces us into a different path, it's not quite as difficult as it would be otherwise.

If that makes any sense, which is probably doesn't.

Never mind. I'll be looking forward to seeing those swatches.

Jack

Jones@tel.com

Dear Marlis,

Remember, in your last post, you said something about the carpet "echoing" the experience of walking in a forest?

You probably don't. It was a throw-away comment, I know. The kind of thing a person says without thinking about the broader possibilities. But it got me thinking.

What if the lodge were designed to "echo" the world in which it's placed? Not just physically, or in terms of texture—which is what you were referring to—but in terms of sound, as well?

The small fountain that will divide the lodge's entry from the living room will sound like a brook tumbling down a steep hillside. The entryway is paved with stone, so it will "echo" the sound of footsteps on a rocky path. But surely there must be other things that might bring the sounds of nature indoors.

Trouble is, I can't think what those would be. Carpet that, instead of muffling sound, repeats the shush of bare feet across grass? A decorative mobile that sounds like autumn leaves rustling in the wind when it's touched?

I've always considered sound as an enemy, something you work to eliminate by designing thicker walls and adding extra insulation. This would be different.

Of course, we'd have to be careful not to make the sounds overwhelming or annoying, just soothing and natural. But the idea offers so many intriguing possibilities that I'd like to explore it a little further.

Any ideas or suggestions?

Jack

Martin@tel.com

Dear Jack,

Please forgive my long delay in responding to your last message. I've been trying to come up with the right words to explain my situation.

No, that's not true. I've been trying to find the courage to tell you that I am deaf.

I don't remember ever having heard autumn leaves rustling in the wind or the sound of water falling on rocks. I don't know what footsteps on stone sound like, or how that's different from the sound of footsteps through grass. I can't imagine these sounds as a backdrop to human conversation, because I have a hard time remembering what human voices sound like.

I wasn't always deaf. I lost my hearing when I was six. I'd been sick with one thing after another, which led to repeated severe ear infections that the doctors couldn't control. Eventually, I lost the ability to hear.

I remember the sound of traffic, the honking of horns, and the roar of cars and trucks going past. I remember laughter, a little. But I can't remember what human voices in conversation sound like. I certainly don't remember any of the natural sounds you're talking about even though I must have heard them whenever my mother took me to the park or the zoo or whatever. In my memories, those kinds of sounds were long ago drowned out by the noise of the city.

I had to be taught to speak again. It isn't as hard to learn for those who were once able to hear as it is for those who are born deaf or who lose their hearing before they start talking, but that doesn't mean I sound like a person with normal hearing. I know I don't, and I know that it can make others very uncomfortable.

I can read lips, but I usually arrange to have a translator present if I'm in a meeting with more than two other people. One of the reasons I climbed up on those rocks that day was because I was putting off the meeting I had to go to.

I hate being in a group, but not part of it. I hate sitting at a conference table knowing that everybody around me is busily engaged in conversation and I can't follow most of it. I don't know who will be speaking next so I can't turn to watch their lips. If several people are talking at once, I'm totally lost.

I prefer sign language to lipreading or speaking, but not many hearing people have ever learned it, and usually then only when someone in their family is deaf and they're forced to.

That's why I like working alone, why I like having my apartment where I can shut out the world. And that's why I like the city. Because the little I remember of sound is a part of the city, the racket and roar and rumble. It's what hearing people hate but I cling to, because the memory of it is still there, echoing in my head.

I don't remember what a forest sounds like. I can feel a forest. I can smell it and see it. But I can't hear it. I can't even imagine hearing it. And so I stay away, just as I'm staying away from the lodge. I stay here, in New York, where I know the world and the sounds it makes.

I'm sorry. I'm going on and on and you don't care about any of this. It doesn't have much of anything to do with this project.

It certainly doesn't have anything to do with our professional relationship because we can do everything by E-mail, where it's only words on a screen and you don't have to be frustrated because you can't understand what I'm saying and I don't have to be frustrated because you forgot I can't hear and looked away so that I couldn't read your lips.

It's not self-pity. It's not! It's practical. It's knowing that things are so darned difficult because I can't hear and the hearing world has a hard time accepting that or adapting to it. To me. And so I concentrate on my work and I use E-mail and watercolor sketches and swatches of fabrics and glass vases to speak for me, instead of trying to speak for myself.

I'm sorry. I can't help you with your questions about repeating the sounds of the natural world in the lodge. But just because I can't help in that respect doesn't mean I can't do a good job or respond to the changes you'll be making in the design. I'll work around it. I always have.

Marlis

Martin@tel.com

Jack,

Please, please, please. Delete that last post. Please. It was late and I was tired and I should never have sent it. Would never have sent it if my day hadn't been so frustrating. Trying to work with a client who has been nothing but trouble since we started because he seems to think my deafness is some sort of incredible handicap and he's being kind to the handicapped this week by hiring me.

He's like so many people. He feels guilty, somehow, because he can hear and I can't. The trouble is, he doesn't like feeling guilty or uncomfortable, so he either over-reacts by trying to talk slowly and simply, as if I were an idiot child, or by forgetting I'm there and looking away so I miss what he's saying.

I've worked with people like him before. It's difficult and immensely frustrating, but it's also part of the job, just like working with people who change their minds every time you turn around, then blame you if a project goes over budget or isn't ready on time.

I usually cope pretty well with such frustrations, but after a whole day of it, I just wasn't ready to get your post about using sound as part of your design. I'm afraid I went a little overboard. I certainly didn't mean to. I thought I'd waited long enough so I could make some sort of cool, rational reply, but I couldn't. The minute I started talking about it—all right, writing about it—it all came pouring out.

I've never done that before. Certainly not with the people I work with. Something about this electronic relationship we have came between me and my common sense. I felt like I could share all that with you, and now I'm embarrassed that I did.

So, please, delete that message and forget about it. Okay?

Marlis

Jones@tel.com

Dear Marlis,

To quote you, "please, please, please" forget about it.

No, that sounds rather patronizing. No, that *seems* rather patronizing.

And if this seems rather stupid, forgive me. I never before realized some of the unfortunate associations that come up with words. "Sounds" to the deaf, questions like "See my point?" to the blind. So much we take for granted, without ever thinking there might be another way to look at it. And I didn't even think about that "look" until after I wrote it.

I suppose you're used to that kind of verbal clumsiness. I'm just beginning to find out about it.

And I'm saying all this because I'm finding it hard to tell you—*write* you—that I understand at least some of what you're feeling because I'm confined to a wheelchair and have been for the past year. Ever since an auto accident left me paralyzed from the waist down.

I'll never walk again and I've had—still have—a very hard time accepting that fact.

Does it ever get any easier? You've been deaf most of your life. Do you still find yourself wondering what if? What if someone, somehow, had done *something* so you wouldn't be deaf?

It's a waste of time and energy, I know, yet I play that game over and over and over again. And still I find myself getting furious with those well-intentioned people who either bend over backward to ignore the fact that I'm confined to a wheelchair, or make it impossible for me to forget by being so damned solicitous that I want to hit them. Just ball up a fist and paste them one, right in the snoot.

My physical therapist tells me I'm going to have to live with it, that their discomfort is their problem, and my discomfort with their discomfort is *my* problem. If that makes any sense.

I guess none of this is making any sense, but I still

haven't straightened it all out in my mind. And you're the first person I've ever talked to about it. *Really* talked to about it, I mean. I didn't much like the psychologist I was sent to at the first, so I just stopped going. I've mentioned some of my frustration to my doctor, but she just tells me that frustration and anger are normal. And I don't want normal, damn it! Not in that way. I want things back the way they were.

Oh, hell.

If I had any sense, I'd delete all of this, but I'm not going to. If you have the guts to admit that your deafness can be frustrating, I guess it's okay for me to admit that I'm not being very grown-up about *my* problem.

Jack

Martin@tel.com

Dear Jack,

I've started this message a dozen times and deleted every attempt. I, of all people, ought to know the right words to say, but I don't.

I never told you, but Frank, when he was trying to convince me to work on the lodge, gave me a bunch of articles about you and your work. There were the usual things from *Architectural Digest* and *Country Living* or whatever, but the article that caught my eye was one that *Newsweek* did on you. There was a picture of you, standing on an outcropping of rock, grinning that lopsided grin that seems to fit on your face so easily. Your shirtsleeves are rolled up, the wind's ruffling your hair, which needs a trim, and there's dirt on your hands and your khaki pants. You don't look very dignified, but you do look happy. You look as if you're ready to leap off that rock and right into whatever adventure lies ahead.

No one would guess that the adventure was trying to learn to live life in a wheelchair.

I won't offer my sympathy. You don't want that.

But I do offer all my understanding.

Marlis

Jones@tel.com

Dear Marlis,

I know the article—and the picture—you're talking about. We were looking over a really rugged site that was being considered for a college research center. Even though I was supposed to be working, I couldn't resist the temptation to climb the rocks that would be the backdrop for the building. A friend took the picture after he'd hiked up the back of the formation.

Climbing, hiking, camping—those have been an important part of my life ever since I was a boy. They're at the heart of my work, because whatever I've learned by my ventures into the mountains has affected my professional vision, too.

I tell myself I should be grateful for having had all those years of physical freedom. That adjusting to this damned wheelchair is just a matter of learning how to explore the world in a different way.

God knows I'm trying to adapt, but every time I look out my office window—which is about a hundred times a day—I see the woods out there. A couple hundred yards away, maybe.

They might as well be in another world.

Friends tell me I ought to have a path made around my property. That I should get one of those cross-country wheelchairs they make these days because there are a lot of trails being built that will accommodate people in wheelchairs and that I should take advantage of them.

Makes sense. Any sensible adult, any sensible human being, would say it makes sense.

But it doesn't make sense to me. It makes me angry all over again. Angry at the drunk who swerved in my path. Angry at the doctors who couldn't keep me from being crippled. Angry at my friends who try to understand.

And most of all, angry at me, that I haven't been able to handle it better.

Double hell. I just keep on blathering, don't I?

You're right. There's something about this sort of communication that makes it easy to say things you wouldn't otherwise. You can't see me in my wheelchair thumping my fist against the glass doors in the middle of a temper tantrum. I can't see you frowning at my cry-baby whining.

It's crazy. This computer is just a glorified typewriter, really. A telephone with no sound transmission. So why am I doing this? Why am I saying things I haven't said before, discussing things I haven't discussed before, not even with people I've known for years?

Jack, who wonders if he's going crazy.

Martin@tel.com

Dear Jack,

You're not crazy. Most of the time I don't even think about my deafness because I've learned to work around it. But every now and then I'll get so frustrated that I want to scream or throw something or kick someone. Anyone!

Not because being deaf is so terrible, but because it's so hard for the people around you to accept it and adapt to it, and that reminds you that you're not quite like everyone else, and they can't always accept that fact.

Sometimes it's the little things that hit the hardest. Like when a friend is excited about a song, and you can't share the excitement because you can't hear the music.

I'm sure you've experienced the same sort of thing. And you've had a lot less time to adapt to it than I have.

At least through E-mail, neither of us has to deal with any of that. Here, we're equals, you and I.

I don't mean professionally, though we are. I mean—oh, I don't know exactly what I mean. Or at least I can't find the words to say what I mean. But I know you understand. We wouldn't be having this crazy, deeply personal, and totally unprofessional conversation if you didn't.

I think I'll give up right here, before I make a total fool of myself.

Marlis, who really does understand.

Jones@tel.com

Oh beautiful lady who understands,
    Thanks.
    And I mean that.
    Really.
    Actually, I had a tasteless joke here, but I erased it. I'm being flippant because it's less embarrassing. And I'm embarrassed.
    I don't usually take my petulance and self-pity out for a walk. Sorry about that.

And that's three sentences that begin with "I." Guess it's time to get back to work.

Jack

Martin@tel.com

Jack,

I'm not quite sure how to say this, so I'll just come right out and say it: Your last post was rude.

You admitted you were being flippant, but it was more than that.

What you were really saying is, Whoops! I made a big mistake. I told a woman I don't even know how I really felt. How terrible! I can't trust her to understand. She might think I'm not a big, strong he-man! She might think I'm human!

And, boy! wouldn't *that* be a terrible thing to happen! After all, a *real* man's not supposed to be human, is he? He's a *man!*

Frankly, I don't think much of that attitude.

And that's putting it as politely as I can.

Marlis

Jones@tel.com

Marlis,

You're right. I owe you an apology for my last post. I said I was being flippant, but even *that* admission was—well, flippant.

In case you didn't know, one of the unwritten rules in the he-man code of honor is that it's better to have people think you're a jerk than that you're vulnerable.

You deserved better.

Anger is so much easier to admit to than vulnerability. I told you I'd mentioned my frustration and resentment to my doctor. That wasn't completely true.

31

I've grouched at her. Shouted at her. Raged at her for things she couldn't do anything about. But I've never really admitted I'm afraid.

There. I said it. I honestly don't know why, but I felt that I could say it to you.

Hiding behind the computer, I guess.

At least you'll understand what I'm saying and not hold it against me. And if you think I need to grow up and get on with life, I hope you won't tell me. It's surprisingly comforting to admit that I'm neither as brave nor as adult as I'd like to think I am.

> And by the way—thanks for listening. In spite of my bad manners.
> Jack

Martin@tel.com

Dear Jack,

I'm glad you sent that last post. I *did* think you were being a jerk. On the other hand, I understand all about hiding behind anger.

I remember being scared. I remember when I was about seven or so waking up in the night and screaming, then being even more frightened because I couldn't hear myself scream.

My mother and father would come rushing in to quiet me. They'd turn on the light and they'd hold me and try to tell me that it was all right. But it wasn't all right because I couldn't hear their words of comfort. And then they'd start to cry.

I think sometimes it was because *they* were angry. Angry at me for being deaf. Angry at themselves because they hadn't been able to protect me. Angry at the doctors and fate and the world in general.

And I felt exactly the same.

32

Sound familiar?

It's going to take time for you to build a new life for yourself and for you to feel comfortable in that life. You have a right to feel angry and afraid right now. Honest.

Just don't take it out on me.

And don't pretend you're not feeling any of that. Not with me. Okay?

Take care,
Marlis

Jones@tel.com

Dear Marlis,

I'm sorry it's been so long with no reply, but I've been busy.

Your message made me do some hard thinking about anger and frustration and about how I haven't been dealing with either too well lately.

Used to be, I'd work it out by going for long hikes. That's obviously not going to work any more, so I figured I needed to find something else that would work as well. Took me a while, but I think I found it.

For the past few days I've been trying to clear the path through the meadow behind my house. I haven't used it for over a year—not since the accident, anyway—and it had almost disappeared under the grass and the wildflowers that have grown over it.

In those first few months after the accident, I didn't care because I didn't much want that particular reminder of how much things had changed. But after talking to you, I suddenly found I felt differently. Don't ask me why. I'm not sure I could explain it if I tried, but then I don't imagine you need an explanation.

Anyway, I dug out an old machete, the one I used to use to keep the honeysuckle under control, and started hacking my way through that grass. I quickly found out that's not something you do from a wheelchair! Eventually I abandoned the chair and worked my way forward on the ground. It wasn't much for dignity, but at least I had room to swing the machete.

I've been working out there every day since, clearing and broadening the path. Can't say I'm progressing very quickly, but at least I *am* progressing. My goal right now is to clear the path all the way to the edge of the woods. Once I reach the woods . . .

Well, I'll worry about that when I get there. Right now, I'm just enjoying being out there every day, doing something physical, something constructive.

While I was clearing that path, I finally decided to do what friends have been urging me to do for months. I ordered a lightweight wheelchair designed for "off-road" use, so to speak—a jazzy little go-buggy in fire-engine red and black. It's not like having two good legs, but it should be better than the Model T I'm driving now.

With a wider path and a more versatile wheelchair, in a couple more weeks I'll even be able to manage a guided tour of the meadow for city slickers who can't tell raspberries from ragweeds.

I can see myself now, showing guests around the place, very much the master of the manor in my brand new chariot, expounding on the propagation of, say, *helianthus annuus*. (That's common sunflower to the botanically challenged. I looked it up this afternoon . . . he says with a smirk.) I can easily imagine that some of those guests would be working on a project with me. Say, an interior designer, for instance. A petite blonde from Manhattan, for a special instance.

Which is a roundabout way of saying I'm inviting
you up here for a visit.

Remember your post a while back, about climbing
on the rocks of that fountain and wondering what it
would be like? Well, why not find out? I can't take
you everywhere, but I can show you where to start.

There's a guest room waiting and a whole mountain behind my house, if you care to give them a try.

> Jack, who isn't too great with
> giants, but who's death on weeds,
> for sure!

PS. I promise not to take my bad temper out on you
in the future. Cross my heart and hope to die.

Martin@tel.com

Dear Jack,

I cheered your last message and laughed out loud
when I got to that part about death on weeds. But I'm
a city girl, remember?

What in the devil would I do on your mountain?
Marlis, the Manhattanite

Jones@tel.com

Dear Marlis,

Ditch Manhattan, girl! There are hundreds of things
you could do around here. Thousands! Wade in the
creek, climb a tree, pick flowers.

I didn't tell you I've been keeping that blue glass
vase of yours filled with flowers from my meadow,
did I? Every day I bring them in fresh. And every
day I think about how much more I'd enjoy picking
them if you were here to enjoy them, too.

Getting up here's easy. Just grab the train. I'll pick
you up at the station.

If you need an excuse, just tell yourself we'll be working on Frank's lodge. We might really work on it, too—if we can find the time! (It's going so well, maybe we won't need to bother!)

Jack

PS. You realize, don't you, that you're not getting your vase back unless you retrieve it personally????

Martin@tel.com

You're an unscrupulous wretch, Jack Martin!

Threaten to hold my vase hostage, will you? Well! If I had the time, I'd storm your little fortress—and redecorate your office while I was at it!

Ruffles, I think. Lots of ruffles. All in pink. And a few lace throw pillows, just for good measure. (Picture me grinning here!)

Unfortunately, I can't get away. One of the down sides to success is that you get busier and busier and busier and . . .

But thanks for the invitation. Just sniff a few flowers for me, will you?

Marlis

Jones@tel.com

Marlis,

If there's going to be any flower sniffing done, you'll have to do it yourself. And I'd be willing to wrestle you on that redecorating plan. Best three throws out of five.

Actually, I wouldn't mind a little intramural wrestling, period.

These past few days when I'm outside working, I find myself picturing you out there with me. I can see you in short shorts and a T-shirt running through the

36

meadow or wading in my creek or picking my black-berries.

Did you know you look very good in short shorts and a T-shirt? It's the truth.

> Trust me. My imagination never lies.
> Jack

Martin@tel.com

Jack,

I'm curious. Just what is it you're raising in that meadow of yours, anyway? Seems like you're getting livelier by the hour.

In fact, after your last post, I have strong suspicions that instead of sunflowers, you might be indulging in some sort of—ummm, controlled substance. If you get my drift.

You're obviously off in fantasy land.

> Marlis

PS. I don't own any shorts, short or otherwise.

Jones@tel.com

Dear Marlis,

I'm disappointed in you. No shorts? Not even one skimpy little pair with patches in strategic spots? What a waste. It ought to be a crime!

I can dig out a pair for you in the stores around here, if you like. Size six, right?

> Jack, the ever helpful.

Martin@tel.com

How'd you know about the size six?

Jones@tel.com

My dear Marlis.

I'm disappointed in you. All these years working with architects, and you still haven't figured out we have a *very* good eye for dimensions? Tsk, tsk.

Size six it is, then.

Jack

PS. It's so gratifying to always be right.

Martin@tel.com

Jack.

Don't you *dare* buy me a pair of short shorts! That's . . . well, that's indecent!

Besides, do you have any idea what all that prickly grass and stuff would do to my legs? I'd be a mass of scratches and welts before I'd gone ten feet. Not to mention the sunburn.

And didn't you mention blackberries? Have you forgotten they have thorns? I'm just a city kid, but even *I* know that!

Marlis

Jones@tel.com

Marlis, my dear,

Don't worry about the scratches on your legs. When I was little, my mother showed me how to handle things like bumped knees and scratches. You just kiss it and make it better.

Now, I'll admit my mother isn't always around—she and my dad have a little farm farther upstate—but I'd be happy to stand in for her as chief kisser. Honest. Even in that stodgy business suit of yours, it's clear you have great knees.

Though I want to stress that I wouldn't do it for just anybody.

As for the blackberries . . .

I wasn't thinking about the thorns. I was working more from the angle of the berries, you see. Sweet and plump and warm from the sun. Perfect for eating right there in the berry patch. If you've never tried them, you don't know what you're missing.

Now, I'll grant you that the thorns are a problem. You can wear jeans for the berry picking, if you like. Nice, snug, size six jeans. Yes, sir. I can picture it now. Jeans would be just fine, too.

And, yes, blackberries do tend to stain. Fingertips and lips, especially. But I had some rather specific ideas about how I'd help you deal with that little problem.

Care to find out what they are?

Jack

Martin@tel.com

Jack, Jack, Jack, Jack, Jack.

That's the best I can do for shaking my head in despair. But please consider it being shaken.

Even assuming I was crazy enough to raid your berry patch (and that's a pretty wild assumption!), what makes you think I'd need your help in dealing with those berry stains? You mentioned a creek, as I recall. Water ought to work just fine, thank you.

Marlis

Jones@tel.com

Marlis,

Ahhh, darn. I didn't think you'd hit on that part of my plan.

39

You're right. Water—especially ice-cold water like the creek—does wonders. Especially when T-shirts and beautiful women in short shorts are involved.

> Jack
> Who is trying *very* hard to be
> helpful.

Martin@tel.com

Jack,

I read your last post and you know, I swear I could hear you laughing. I told you, didn't I, that I can remember the sound of laughter? Well, I heard you laughing and I couldn't help it. I burst out laughing myself.

Thank heavens there wasn't anybody around but the geranium to hear me. They'd have thought I'd gone off the deep end.

Which, come to think of it, is probably what you had planned for me as far as that creek goes. Just put me in that T-shirt and shove me in over my head . . .

Which is exactly where I am right now. Over my head.

This exchange is getting downright . . . dangerous.

> Marlis, who is going back to work
> *right now.*

Jones@tel.com

Marlis, you clever lady, you!

I hadn't planned on dunking you in the creek, but now that I think of you and that T-shirt and lots of cold water . . .

I'm glad I made you laugh. If you can only have a few memories of what things sound like, then one of the sweetest has to be the memory of laughter.

But you know, the more I think about you up here, roaming around my meadow and ravaging my wildflowers, the more I think it's exactly what you ought to do. You'd like it, if you'd only give it a chance. You'd find yourself laughing from the sheer joy of it.

Come on. What do you say? This Friday on the 4:38 train. Is it a deal?

Jack

PS. You're a city girl. How come they always have silly times for trains like 4:38? What's wrong with 4:30? Or 4:45?

Martin@tel.com

Silly Jack,

4:38 trains are always scheduled for 4:55. If you arrive early, that is. They leave at 4:30 if you're running late and not going to be at the station until 4:37. It's an unbreakable Law of Life.

Not that it matters, because I am not going to be on it, regardless of when it actually gets going.

I told you. I'm a city girl. I happen to *like* the city.

In fact, I've got a great idea. You come here and I'll show *you* all the things you seem to have missed around here. (You had to have missed them, or you wouldn't avoid New York like you do.)

Bring that new hot-rod wheelchair of yours. I figure the best place to start is at the top of the Guggenheim. Just think of it. I give you a good running start and away you go down all six floors of that crazy spiral. If you get up a good enough head of steam, I bet you could sail right on into Central Park!

Let's see you try and top that!

Marlis, who is making plans.

Jones@tel.com

Dear Marlis, who is planning.

The Guggenheim is good. *Very* promising, in fact.

But that's not the point. I've been to New York. You haven't been up here.

And I asked first.

So . . . What do you say? Quit trying to change the subject and just say yes. Yes. Y.E.S. Yes.

You can do it, can't you?

Jack

Martin@tel.com

Dear Jack,

Honestly, I really can't get away right now. Don't push it, will you?

Marlis

Jones@tel.com

Dear Marlis,

Package on its way. Details at ten.

Jack

The package contained one pair of size-six jeans shorts and one extraordinarily lightweight T-shirt. The kind you could almost see through even if it *wasn't* wet.

Marlis stared at them in their nest of gold tissue in the expensive gold-foil and ribbon-wrapped box that Jack had sent them in. The ribbon she'd ripped off in her haste dangled from her fingers like a heavy gold chain that bound her to the box and its contents. Bound her to the man who had sent the shorts and the T-shirt in full awareness of the message they conveyed. The message he'd intended her to receive.

She let the ribbon slide from her grasp as she carefully folded back the tissue. The glistening paper was smooth and cool beneath her fingers. Like water from a creek, she thought, only this was something she could hang onto. If she dared.

She pulled out the shorts first. They were indecently abbreviated. The kind that revealed the soft curve where thigh merged into buttock, even when the wearer was standing up. Marlis's cheeks grew warm at the thought of what would be revealed if she ever bent over to pick one of those fat, juicy blackberries Jack had teased her about.

With deliberate care, she refolded the shorts and tucked them back into the box, then started to fold the tissue paper over them.

The T-shirt stared up at her mockingly, as if daring her to hide it away in its ridiculously inappropriate wrappings.

Marlis stared back at the T-shirt. It didn't move. She chewed on her lower lip, worrying the question of whether or not she was brave enough—or foolhardy enough—to accept Jack Martin's challenge.

Silly question. It was just a T-shirt, after all. It didn't have to mean anything she didn't want it to mean.

Marlis snatched it out of its shiny gold nest and held it up by the shoulders. ''The Berry Best'' it said in lurid purple lettering above an oversized blackberry with a bite taken out of one corner.

She frowned, studying the art. The crude design could just as easily have represented an oversized, misshapen, dark purple pinecone—assuming people ever snacked on pinecones.

Purple? For a blackberry? The corners of Marlis's

mouth twitched, then spread wide in a silly grin.

With sudden decision, she dropped the T-shirt and started unbuttoning the blouse she wore. Her tailored skirt, pantyhose, and, after only a moment's hesitation, lacy pink bra followed until she was standing in the middle of her living room clad in a pair of high-cut, pink silk underpants and not one stitch more.

She tugged the T-shirt over her head. It wasn't nearly as tight as she'd thought it would be. It wasn't baggy, either. The thin cotton-knit fabric clung to her, soft against her skin. All except for the front, just above her breasts, where the fabric paint had hardened. Jack had applied the paint with such enthusiastic liberality that the fabric was stiff enough to rub against her nipples.

Marlis could feel her nipples peak at the slight irritation. Or was it at the thought of whose hands had applied the paint and what the artist had been thinking when he did it?

Don't think about it! Marlis chided herself. It was just a T-shirt. A joke. A silly gift designed to tease her, nothing more.

Well, it was teasing her, all right, but her reaction didn't feel like any joke. The muscles in her back and belly and buttocks tightened at the intimate roughness against her nipples, the soft caress of cloth along her sides. Jack had chosen this silly shirt, painted it, sent it to her. She could almost imagine his scent lingering in the cotton. Which was absurd, of course. Absolutely absurd.

The shorts were a tad tight. Tight enough so she had to take a deep breath to zip them up and fasten the metal snap at the waist, but not so tight that she couldn't move once she had them on.

Marlis didn't move. She stood frozen in the middle

of her normally well-ordered living room, heedless of the untidy heap of discarded clothes at her feet. Not once had she ever worn anything this . . . indecent, this revealing.

It wasn't just the roughness of the painted cotton against her breasts. The very air in her apartment felt unexpectedly cool on her exposed thighs and the lower curve of her buttocks, cooler than it had ever felt even when she was stark naked and fresh out of the bath. The shorts were taut across her belly, stiff where the zipper and placket traced a direct line from waist to crotch.

Marlis's cheeks flamed. What was she thinking? She closed her eyes and pressed her palms against her cheeks. As if that would make her unsettling thoughts go away.

With sudden ferocity, she tugged at the T-shirt where it was tucked beneath the waistband of her shorts, then stopped just as abruptly. Before she took off these absurd . . . garments . . . she wanted to see what she looked like in them. Wanted to see what *they* looked like on *her*.

No, that wasn't quite true. What she really wanted to know was what, exactly, Jack would see if she were ever foolish enough to dress like this in front of him.

She turned toward her bedroom.

Not there. Not with that broad bed reflected in her mirrored closet doors.

The entryway, then. She'd covered both walls of the tiny space with mirrors to make it seem larger and lighter than it really was. The entryway was safe.

Wrong again. The shorts and T-shirt were even more indecent than she'd thought. Magnified by the double reflection, they were . . .

Marlis groped for the words to describe her appearance, but nothing came. Silently, she stared at herself, shocked by the wide-eyed wanton who stared back.

This woman with the tousled hair and the revealing T-shirt wasn't her. Marlis Jones was a serious career woman, a skilled interior designer, a *professional*. She would *never* appear in public in shorts that covered rather less of her than some of her sensible underpants did. She wouldn't wear these shorts in the privacy of her own apartment, for heaven's sake!

Yet here she was in her own foyer, twisting around to check on just how much of her fanny hung out beneath the bottom of the shorts. Bending, just a little, to see if her underpants showed. They did.

And Marlis, to her dismay, couldn't help wondering if she ought to buy one of those thong thingees, or if Jack would prefer the line of shocking pink that was almost more depraved than the shorts themselves.

Worse, she found herself taking inordinate pride in the way her breasts gave a decided bounce to the tacky T-shirt and her torso curved in to a tiny waist, then flared out again to hips that, thanks to good genes and lots of exercise, hadn't an ounce of excess fat on them. Indecent the shorts might be, but there was no denying she filled them in all the right places and in all the right ways.

What had Jack said? That he had a good eye for dimensions?

Well, he'd gotten hers down to the quarter inch, and Marlis couldn't repress a feeling of shock at the admission. The trouble was, she wasn't sure what she should do about it.

She knew what she *ought* to do, what she *ought* to say . . . and none of it bore any relation to what she *wanted* to do. .

And that was the most shocking—and frightening—part of all.

Jones@tel.com

Marlis,
   Well? Did you get my package? Do they fit?
Tell the truth now.
                                    Jack

Martin@tel.com

Dear Jack,
   Yes, I got the package. I haven't the slightest idea
whether they fit or not. You really didn't think I was
going to try on anything as absurd as those shorts,
did you? In your dreams!
                                    Marlis

Jones@tel.com

Marlis,
   Actually, those shorts *were* in my dreams. And in
my waking fantasies, as well. Some of them, anyway.
Some of my fantasies didn't involve shorts. (He says
with a leer.)
   No, forget I said that.
   Don't wear the shorts.
   But don't use them as an excuse not to come!
   I'll behave myself, I promise. Scout's honor.
                                    Jack
PS. In case you were wondering, I was a *very* good
Scout—and I have the merit badges to prove it!

Martin@tel.com

Dear Jack,

You might have been a very good Boy Scout when it came to things like chopping wood and lighting fires and that kind of stuff, but I have serious reservations about the honor part now that you're supposed to be all grown up.

Very serious reservations.

Marlis

PS. And I have serious doubts about the all-grown-up part, too!

Jones@tel.com

Marlis, Marlis, Marlis.

You're just trying to dance around the real issue, which is that you're afraid to come.

You said it yourself. You know the city. You remember the sounds of horns and traffic. You know the racket that a million people make, but you don't remember the sound of the wind in the leaves or of water running over rocks.

So what? Does that mean you can't see and feel and smell and touch and taste? Does that mean you can't try to fill in the little bit that's missing—the sounds you can't hear—through imagination?

Come on. Give it a try. Give *me* a try!

If nothing else, do it out of pity for me. I need to show off my meadow to *someone* who can really appreciate it. The leaves are just starting to turn and the wild asters are blooming like crazy. In a couple of weeks it's going to be knock-your-eyes-out beautiful around here.

Jack

PS. If you wait too long, it will be way too cold to wear those shorts.

A Dance on the Edge

Martin@tel.com

Wait a minute, buster. Fall leaves. Asters. Have you been conning me? Trying to get me up there on false pretenses?

A couple of weeks ago you were talking about blackberries. I just remembered—they don't grow this late in the season, do they?

And don't try to lie to me. Even if none of my city-bred friends know beans about berries, I have ways of finding these things out. Trust me on that!

Marlis

Jones@tel.com

Marlis,

Now that's not fair. Expecting me to trust you when you won't trust me.

If you won't belive me, why don't you come up here and find out for yourself?

You'll never get a better chance to model those shorts, you know. Or find a more appreciative audience.

Jack, who never claimed to be a botanist.

Martin@tel.com

Dear Jack,

You want to know what your problem is? You need to get back to work. I mean *really* get back. On site. Right in the middle of it. Maybe have a good shouting match or two with a construction foreman or a supplier or something.

Forget asters and blackberries and those darned shorts.

Get to work!

> Marlis
> Who is getting to work!

Jones@tel.com

Ms. Marlis.

I'm hurt. Get to work? What do you think I've been doing? Twiddling my thumbs?

As proof, I'm sending you the photo the construction foreman on Frank's lodge sent me. It's really a lodge—and I think it's beautiful!

A dream is taking shape up there, and we're responsible for making it real. You and me. That's a good feeling, isn't it?

> Jack
> (And there's that path through my meadow . . .)

Martin@tel.com

Dear Jack,

It's a beautiful feeling, and a beautiful lodge.

So when are you going for an inspection? I thought architects were always on site at this stage.

> Marlis, who really wants to know.

PS. *You* aren't afraid, are you?

Jones@tel.com

Marlis,

What! Me? Afraid of facing a construction crew from a wheelchair? Hah!

Nervous, maybe, but what's a few nerves between friends?

I finished clearing the path through the meadow this afternoon. All the way to the edge of the woods. Nice and broad and not too bumpy, considering. Should work just fine for that racy new wheelchair I just got.

In celebration, I picked an especially big bunch of wildflowers and stuffed them in that vase you don't seem to want to retrieve. The flowers add a nice spot of color to my office, but I have to admit the arrangement looks a little ragged.

Why don't you show me how it should be done? In person.

Jack

Martin@tel.com

Jack,

Are you just naturally persistent, or are you trying to annoy me?

(You're definitely succeeding on the annoying part.)

Marlis

Jones@tel.com

Marlis,

Actually, I was hoping that if I persistently annoyed you, you'd come up here and let me have what for.

But if that's not going to work, can I tempt you with a visit to our lodge instead? ·

I've set an appointment with the contractors for the day after tomorrow at three in the afternoon. That way, I know they'll be there, and you'll have plenty of time to catch the morning train so I can pick you up and we can drive up together.

What do you say?

Jack

(Whatever you say, don't you dare say I set that appointment just to prove you wrong!)

Martin@tel.com

Jack,

I'd never say something like that.
Think it, maybe. But I'd *never* say it.

Marlis

Jones@tel.com

Dear Marlis,

This is your last chance. Do I pick you up at the train station tomorrow morning or not?

Jack

Martin@tel.com

Dear Jack,

I can't possibly get away, but I want to hear all about it when you get back. Everything. The lodge. How far they've gotten on finishing the inside. How great it was to be out there again. When you're planning on going back.

I'm betting I'll have to wait for days for you to come back down to earth and get on the computer!

Marlis, who's cheering for you.

A Dance on the Edge

Jones@tel.com

Marlis.

So you want me to tell you about it, huh?

I've got one easy word for it. Humiliating.

I should never have listened to you, damn it! Why did I listen to you? You, who keep so nice and safe in your city and your private little world. What do you know about humiliation? I mean, what do you *really* know about humiliation?

I can tell you about it. I've just had a bellyful.

I'm sitting in my car parked in front of the lodge. Drove up this morning. Hour and a half—the longest drive I've managed on my own since I got out of the hospital.

Impressive, huh?

I used to do that just to pick up a hamburger from my favorite greasy spoon.

Found out my new little go-buggy doesn't do too well on a construction site. I hadn't been here a half hour when I rolled off the edge of one of the outdoor walkways they'd just finished laying.

It was just a five- or six-inch drop. Not even worth thinking about . . . if you have two good legs. Wheelchairs don't like six-inch drops. Especially when you hit them crooked and there's soft ground at the bottom to grab the wheel and twist it.

Jack Martin, architect extraordinaire and all-around tough guy, fell out of his chair like any two-year-old.

Not on my ass. I was already sitting on that. Flat on my face.

Every architect should fall on his face in front of a construction crew. Makes him seem like one of the guys, don'tcha know? Even better if he ends up flopping around on the ground like a stupid fish out of water. Then everyone can have a good laugh about it.

Of course, everybody was *much* too polite to laugh in my face. No! They rushed over and asked if I was hurt and could they do anything. A dozen maiden aunts couldn't have been any more concerned for my welfare.

I couldn't even get back in my chair without their help. And doesn't that make a sweet picture, the crew having to pick up the project's architect and put him back in his wheelchair, just like a baby that fell out of its high chair? Very dignified. Very professional.

Like hell!

Next time you go getting any great ideas, just keep them to yourself, okay? I don't need any help making a fool of myself.

Jones@tel.com

Marlis,

It's two o'clock in the morning and I can't sleep.

I was a jerk. Go on. Say it. Jack Martin is a jerk. You can even put it in all caps if you want. JACK MARTIN IS A JERK!

I'd suggest a whole bunch of more appropriate terms, but you don't seem to be able to write the word damn, so I don't imagine you'd do very well with the words I'm thinking of. What's worse is, I remember promising never to take my frustrations out on you. That's one promise shot all to hell, isn't it?

At least lying in bed staring into the dark gave me lots of time to think about this afternoon and the way I reacted and that damn message I sent you.

Actually, it gave me too *much* time to think about that message.

I know. I should have thought *before* I sent it.

That's the trouble with laptops and modems and cellular phones. If you really want to be a jerk, there's nothing stopping you. Just sit in your car, plug in your phone, and have at it. No waiting. And no thinking required.

Ah, the wonders of modern technology.

You *were* right. I *did* need to get out on the site. I'd almost forgotten what paint and new lumber and raw earth smell like. I'd forgotten the sounds. Hammers pounding and saws buzzing and workers' footsteps echoing on bare floors.

Actually, it was the sounds that got me in trouble.

I was out there on that path, drinking in the autumn sun and the breeze and listening to the construction noises coming from inside. And I was thinking about you, and how I would describe those sounds to you, and wondering what you would see that I was missing. I was picturing the breeze tossing your hair about your face and into your eyes. I was wishing you were there with me, sharing in the excitement.

And because I was thinking about you and not paying attention to what I was doing, I rolled right off that damned sidewalk and onto my nose.

There must have been times in my life when I've made a bigger fool of myself, but I can't remember ever *feeling* more like one. Of course, I dealt with the situation in an eminently mature fashion—I took it out on you.

So kick me. I deserve it. *I'd* kick me if I could get out of this wheelchair to do it. But to get a fair swing at me, you'll have to come up here.

If you think about it, you'd realize that's not such a bad idea. You can clobber me for being an obnoxious, self-centered, self-pitying so-and-so, and then you can let me show you around the lodge.

It's almost finished, ready for your touch to bring it to life. And it *is* beautiful. Afterward, you can let me take you to lunch at a really expensive restaurant I know of less than an hour away.

I *am* going back, you know. And I'm going to keep on going back. The way I figure it, if I could survive this afternoon's humiliation, I can survive anything. And so can you.

So, what do you say? Will you come?

Or are you looking for a manual on boxing so you can take a *really* good swing at me?

> Jack, the jerk
> who is very, very sorry for it.

Jones@tel.com

Dear Marlis,

Have you decided to punish me by refusing to talk to me? You know I didn't really mean those things I said.

Please come. I'm going back to the lodge tomorrow, and the day after that, as well. We could go together.

I promise to be on my very best behavior. Scout's honor, remember?

> Jack, who is giving away his laptop
> and modem, first chance he gets.

Jones@tel.com

Damn it, Marlis, talk to me!
> Jack

Jones@tel.com

Marlis? Marlis! Please. Talk to me. Swear at me. Call me every filthy name you can think of, then call me a few more. I had no right to say those things and I know it. But don't cut me out of your life. Not like this. I won't *let* you cut me out. If I have to drive into New York and camp outside your door, I will. I'll drive your neighbors crazy. I'll drive your doorman crazy. I'll drive *you* crazy until you break down and talk to me and tell me you forgive me.

Please say you'll forgive me.

Jack

Jones@tel.com

My beautiful Marlis,

It's almost four in the morning and I've scarcely slept in the past three days, waiting to hear from you.

It's been a long wait.

It's even longer in the dark, lying in a bed that's far too big for just one person. Thinking of you.

Wanting you.

Does that sound strange? Another one of my self-indulgent fantasies? It isn't, you know.

Just because I can't walk doesn't mean I can't make love to a woman. Whatever else I lost in that accident, I didn't lose that.

It might have been easier if I had.

I've lost track of the number of times I've wakened in the night, hot and tormented from dreams of you. Every time I look out my office window I can see you there in the meadow, your arms heaped with flowers and your hair blowing in the wind. It doesn't matter that the meadow's empty or that you're lost in the racket of New York.

You're here with me because I want you to be here. I want to touch you, kiss you. I want to make love to you, over and over and over again.

I want you here in my bed and in the tall, sweet grass and in the midst of a thousand wildflowers in my meadow where I've cut a path for you to come to me.

I want you now. Today. This minute. And I want you tomorrow, and the day after, and the day after that.

I could teach you, show you. Oh, so much! And you could teach me.

Teach me, Marlis. I want to learn how to drink in all the color and taste and smell of you. I want you hot and hungry and naked beside me. I want to hear your little cries of pleasure and your sighs as you drift into sleep afterward.

I want . . . everything. Everything!

Is that so impossible? We are so much alike, you and I. And yet we both have so much to give the other, if only we try.

I want to try. I want to give you my world—the world you gave me the courage to go back to. And I want to share in yours. If only you'll let me.

Meet me. Here, at the edge of my meadow.

Will you come? Will you let me make love to you? And will you make sweet love to me?

Ah, Marlis! I'm sure you didn't want to hear any of this. So ignore it, just as you've ignored all my other messages. It's easy, isn't it? Just a couple of clicks on a couple of keys of the keyboard and you can make all of this—all of me—go away. Poof! Just like that.

Don't you wish the rest of life were that easy?

Nothing. Not even a short message to say, "Drop dead, jerk."

Jack barely stopped himself from hitting the monitor. Trashing an eleven-hundred-dollar, wide-screen monitor wasn't the smartest way of eliminating its "No messages waiting" message. He settled for snapping off the computer's power, but even seeing that faint phosphor glow disappear brought no comfort.

How long had it been since he'd made an obscene fool of himself? Two days? Three? And still no word from Marlis.

She was probably still too scared to touch the computer for fear of what she might find waiting for her—and all because he hadn't been able to keep first his temper, and then his damned fantasy sex life in control.

What kind of insanity had possessed him? Since when had he become a computer sex fanatic?

Since he'd fallen in love with Marlis.

Jack froze.

Love?

He jerked his chair back from the computer and just missed running over Julius's tail. Julius lifted his head, blinked, then sighed and went back to sleep.

Jack's hands clenched on the cool steel of the rim of his wheelchair.

He was in love with Marlis.

Why hadn't he realized?

His mouth twisted in a grimace. Because he was a thick-headed lunk, that was why.

But Marlis might forgive him for that. She'd forgiven him for a whole lot worse. Up until now, that was.

With sudden desperation, Jack stretched to reach the power button for the computer, too impatient to roll his wheelchair back into place first. While the computer cycled through its warm-up drill, he drummed his fingers impatiently on the keyboard. The minute his communications software blinked ready, he started typing.

Jones@tel.com

I love you, Marlis.
                    Jack

Still no answer.

He had sent his simple message every hour for the
past two days. He'd even wakened in the night to
send it again. And still no answer.

Marlis wasn't going to respond. Not now. Not ever.
He could chase her into New York, camp outside her
apartment as he'd threatened, hound her like the mad-
man he was, but he couldn't call back the words that
had frightened her away.

Suddenly caught between anger and despair, Jack
spun his wheelchair away from the computer and
rolled it to the open patio door and the bright fall sun
that was pouring in across his floor. He stopped, just
at the edge of the deck, staring across the expanse of
wild grass and fall flowers toward the trees in their
lush autumn foliage.

The sun felt good against his skin, hot with the last
wild heat of a dying summer. The faint breeze stirred
the grass, making the drying stalks and stems of the
meadow rattle slightly. A lost cricket chirped somewhere from beneath the deck, taking advantage of the
warmth. In the trees, birds chattered, and from far
away he heard the sharp cawing of a crow.

He closed his eyes, listening to the soft sounds. For
her. He would have to tell her . . .

His hands tightened around the rails of his wheels,
and his face scrunched up against the pain.

She wasn't coming. She'd received his messages
and deleted them, too angry with him to answer.

He forced his eyes open, but this time the autumn
world looked blurred and out of focus. It took him a

minute to realize it was because he was crying and his eyes couldn't focus through the tears.

He blinked, angry again, and forced himself to shut out the sounds, forced himself to stare at the forest that was so near and yet so very, very far away.

At first he thought he was imagining her. She stood at the edge of the meadow, half hidden in the shadows, and stared across the grass at him. Her arms were full of wildflowers and branches heavy with bright autumn leaves. She was dressed in jeans, but Jack could swear there was a patch of bright purple on the T-shirt she wore, just visible above the mass of foliage she held.

She started to move forward, then stopped abruptly and tilted her head up and to the side so she could stare into the spreading, fall-drenched branches above her.

His heart skipped a beat, then started pounding in his chest. His hands trembled on the wheel rails. The binoculars were there on the table where he always kept them, but he didn't reach for them. If he was dreaming, he wanted the dream to last just a little while longer.

He wasn't dreaming. Her head came down and she turned once more to face the house.

That's when she saw him. Across the sweep of dying grasses and autumn flowers, their eyes met and held, and his tears spilled over his lids and down his cheeks unheeded.

And she was no longer standing still, no longer hiding at the edge of his narrow little world. She came walking, slowly at first, then faster and faster, as though with each step she left behind the doubts that had kept her in the shadows.

Jack rolled his wheelchair out onto the deck. He started to maneuver his way toward the ramp, then stopped suddenly and set the brake on his chair instead. It had taken enormous courage for her to come so far. It would take even more to cover these last few hundred feet that separated them, because they both knew that she was doing far more than crossing a flower-strewn meadow. She was crossing the meadow to *him*.

Beside him, Julius started barking—that loud, deep, terrifying bark that drove away unwanted visitors and delighted the children who loved him. She didn't heed the barking, of course. She simply came walking through the meadow with her red-gold hair drifting around her face in the breeze, glorious as the sunshine.

She was the most beautiful thing Jack had ever seen, the creature of his dreams . . . and more. So much, much more.

Her arms were filled with the gifts she brought— cattails and the branches of oak and scarlet maple; red sycamore leaves mingled with purple-blue asters and the heavy, golden fronds of a dozen wild grasses. Heavy in their massed radiance, they dipped and bowed and bounced in her arms with each step she took, precious treasure stolen from a horde he'd thought forever beyond his reach.

She, who had never before ventured out of the city on her own, had brought his lost world back to him.

And then she was there at the foot of the ramp leading up to the deck, then climbing the ramp. Not once did she take her gaze off him, not even when the breeze blew her hair into her eyes.

She stopped a short distance away from him, just far enough that he couldn't reach her unless he rolled forward. He didn't move.

For the longest while, she neither moved nor spoke.

The wind caught her burden, fluttering the leaves so they clattered and shushed against each other, ruffling the delicate asters and setting the cattails to bobbing. She merely clutched her booty closer against her chest, as if it were the anchor that kept her safe against the tempest.

"You were right," she said at last, softly, hesitantly. There was a curious flatness to her tone, yet Jack thought he had never heard a sweeter sound. "I was afraid."

Her chin came up as she said it. Just a little.

"I'm still afraid, but I thought . . . if you could go back, then I could try . . . that I could . . . I wanted . . ."

Her words trailed off and floated away, lost on the sighing autumn breeze. Her grip on the branches tightened even more and she pressed her lips together tightly. Then she swallowed and said, very clearly and firmly, "I wanted to hear you say the words you wrote me."

He could see the quick, subtle movement of her eyes as she shifted her gaze from his eyes to his mouth and back again.

Jack smiled and opened his arms and said, "I love you, Marlis." His smile faded into an intense frown of concentration as he carefully made what were, to him, the most important of the signs he had learned with such care over the past few weeks.

With the fingers of his right hand tucked in except for the pinkie, which stood up straight, he brought his hand toward his chest. *I.*

Both hands closed, he crossed his arms over his chest as if hugging himself. *Love.*

And then he pointed at Marlis. *You.*

I love you.

A frozen instant, no more, then she gave a quick,

glad cry and dropped to her knees in front of him, heedless of the tears in her eyes or the awkward, rustling bundle she held. It didn't matter. Jack's arms were more than long enough to enfold both her and her treasure.

He leaned forward eagerly, drawing her as close to him as he could before he claimed her mouth in a kiss that had no need of words, nor ever would.

Dear Reader,

When my editor first asked me if I'd be interested in writing a story for this anthology, a story about a romance that developed through an exchange of E-mail messages, I was . . . well, doubtful is a good word, I think.

Not that I doubted the power of modern technology to help people connect! I know a very happily married couple who first met through E-mail, and I myself treasure some very supportive friendships with people I have never met in person, but with whom I correspond regularly via computer.

No, what worried me was whether I'd be able to find a story that could be told though the medium of E-mail. I shouldn't have worried. Marlis and Jack showed up one afternoon while I was doing dishes. They were very insistent that their story be told because theirs was a tale about what lies at the heart of any strong relationship, even one that developed over

E-mail. It was a story about honesty, compassion, courage, and the power of love to overcome even the greatest obstacles that life can throw at us.

Those same qualities lie at the heart of another love story. In December, *The Snow Queen,* a story based on the fairy tale by Hans Christian Andersen, will make its appearance. The difference is, this story is set in Colorado Springs, Colorado, in the 1890s.

Hetty Malone has crossed half a continent to marry Michael Ryan, the man she has loved since childhood. But two years is a long time to be separated, and Hetty soon discovers that although Michael still loves her, he has a new passion in his life, a passion that may destroy the future they had hoped to build together.

As a boy, Michael's life was shattered when his mother died of tuberculosis. Now, as a doctor, he is deeply troubled not only by the physical destruction, but the emotional devastation the disease leaves in its wake. He has dedicated himself to a search for a cure to the dreaded disease, no matter what the cost. What Michael has forgotten is that there is far more to life than surviving.

It is up to Hetty to teach him just how much greater than the power of science is the power of the human heart.

I very much enjoy hearing from readers. My address is P.O. Box 62533, Colorado Springs, CO 80962-2533. A self-addressed, stamped envelope would be appreciated.

Sincerely,
Anne Avery

Toss
the Bouquet

PHOEBE CONN

Chapter One

Working with swift confidence, Regan Paisley added the last sprig of star-shaped stephanotis to the bridal bouquet. Fashioned of stephanotis, roses in a delicate blush shade, and soft white phalaenopsis orchids, it was one of Regan's most exquisite designs. After attaching ivory satin streamers, she held the stunning floral creation at waist height to assess its symmetry in the floor-length mirror at the end of her work bench.

Taking scant notice of her own harried appearance, she studied her handiwork. Against her forest-green apron, the bouquet's subtle perfection stood out in vivid relief. Certain it would thrill the bride for whom it had been created, Regan quickly crossed the air-conditioned room to place it in a tissue-lined box.

"Is that the last of the bridesmaids' bouquets?" Regan called to her assistant.

Mary Claire Finch tucked an errant chestnut curl back into the blue-and-white scarf tied at her nape and nodded. "Yes. Thank God. I swear, when I get married, I'm going to have a maid-of-honor and that's it. Not that I don't have eight 'dear' friends, who would love to be attendants, but this is more work than anyone ought to have to do."

Regan blew her wispy blond bangs out of her eyes and reached for a dozen white carnations, three pink roses, and lacy baby's breath. Then, with an exuberant white satin bow, she fashioned the bouquet the bride would toss to her unmarried friends before leaving on her honeymoon. The gorgeous bridal bouquet carried in the wedding ceremony was too precious to be lost in that farewell gesture and was scheduled to be preserved as a tangible memory of the blessed occasion.

"The larger the wedding party, the more money we make, Mary Claire. I'll be happy to give you a generous discount, so go right ahead and have eight bridesmaids if you want them."

Mary Claire's knife slipped from her hand, and she bent down to pick it up from the leaf-strewn linoleum. "I probably ought to wait until I have a fiancé to plan the nuptials. Besides, you're sure to get married first. It wouldn't surprise me if Charles proposed while you're on vacation next week."

An intensely private person, Regan shared few details of her personal life, but a shy smile gave away her faith in her vivacious assistant's prediction. After a relaxed, two-year courtship, she was comfortable with Charles. If he weren't the most exciting man on earth, he was dependable to a fault, which meant a great deal to her. At twenty-nine, she owned her own successful florist business, and she wanted an equally successful marriage.

"It's time," she agreed thoughtfully. "We've both worked really hard this summer and I think Charles is looking forward to our getting away together as much as I am.'' After completing the final bouquet, she used a sponge to wipe the top of her workbench clear of stems and leaves.

''Karl already has the flowers for the altar and the reception on the truck, so as soon as the bouquets are loaded, you can go on home.'' Regan checked the order form one last time to make absolutely certain they hadn't overlooked anything. They had begun working at seven o'clock that morning to make all the bouquets, corsages, arrangements, and center-pieces for three elaborate weddings, and her memory had begun to blur. ''You made the boutonnieres?'' she asked.

Mary Claire called over her shoulder as she washed her hands at the sink. ''I did them first. They're already on the truck with the corsages you made.''

''Perfect,'' Regan replied. ''You have the telephone number for my Aunt Madeleine's house in Santa Barbara, but I'm certain you and Karl can handle whatever's needed next week on your own. The flowers have already been ordered for next Saturday's weddings, and I'll be in early that morning to work.''

Mary Claire peeked out the shop's rear door to make certain Karl was still standing by the delivery truck. ''Why don't you go on home and pack?'' she suggested brightly. ''I'll ride to the wedding with Karl and make certain everyone gets the proper flowers.''

Always careful to plan ahead, Regan was already packed, but she was in desperate need of a quick nap; Mary Claire's offer was tempting. She went out on wedding deliveries whenever possible, but her shop produced work of such exceptionally high quality that she had never encountered a problem, and she knew Karl and Mary Claire wouldn't have any difficulty with the delivery. Still, she wasn't easily fooled.

"I don't suppose this sudden burst of helpfulness could have anything to do with the way you've been eyeing Karl lately?" she replied.

Embarrassed that her motives were so transparent, Mary Claire blushed deeply as she removed her apron. "What with working here and attending law school at night, Karl might not have much time to date, but he could at least notice that I exist."

Anxious to leave, Regan grabbed the broom from the corner and with brisk strokes began sweeping up the cuttings littering the floor. "I'm sure he's noticed you, but it couldn't hurt to give him another chance."

"Then it's all right if I ride with him?"

"Yes. Have a good time."

Mary Claire let out an ecstatic squeal, prompting Regan to add a caution. "Just don't forget to take these bouquets," she reminded her, "and make the client feel as though she, not Karl, is your primary concern."

"Yes, ma'am."

Mary Claire skipped out with the last of the flowers, but it wasn't until Regan heard the delivery truck pull away that she allowed herself to envy her assistant's exuberance. Then she began to wonder why Charles had never inspired that same sweet, tingling excitement in her.

At thirty, he retained the wholesome good looks that had made him popular in high school and college. Fair-haired and blue-eyed, he was the quintessential yuppie, who not only subscribed to *GQ*, but actually dressed as well as the models in the magazine. He was bright, honest, and had an excellent job with a major computer firm. He was precisely the type of solid, stable man Regan wanted for a husband, and if his kisses didn't make any bells clang, she was more than willing to overlook that minor defect.

As if keyed to her thoughts, the chime on the front door sounded, and Regan looked up to find Charles walking her way. Located in Pasadena's fashionable Old Towne, Paisley Flowers shared a Victorian house with a hair salon and an expensive boutique. Because the major portion of her business consisted of weddings, which took appointments to arrange, and orders placed over the telephone, she hadn't bothered to lock the door as she swept up. Quickly leaning the broom against the workbench, she wiped her hands on her apron as she started toward the front.

"Hi, honey," Charles greeted her. "We need to talk a minute, and I didn't want to do it over the telephone. Where is everybody? Are you finished for the day?"

He was in his shirtsleeves, but hadn't loosened his tie. At first glance he didn't appear ready to leave on vacation. Disappointed to think something might have caused a delay, Regan stopped by the glass refrigerator case where she displayed fresh flowers. Late Saturday afternoon, other than a few spindly gladiola stalks and half-empty vases of lemon leaf and fern, the case was bare.

"Mary Claire and Karl are delivering the last order, so I'm definitely finished," she said, feeling more than a little wilted. "What about you?"

Charles fidgeted with his neatly patterned silk tie, then smoothed it down against his pale blue Oxford cloth shirt. "First, promise me that you won't get angry."

"That's a peculiar way to begin a conversation. I sure hope it doesn't have anything to do with our vacation."

Charles looked as though he were about to become ill, and swallowed hard. "Something's come up," he began. "I'm sure you remember my mentioning

73

Sharon, the girl I dated all through college?''

Flooded with bitter disappointment, Regan crossed her arms over her chest. She had never met the woman, but Charles mentioned her so often, she felt as if she had. ''Don't tell me that she wants to come along with us.''

Charles forced a laugh and jammed his hands into his pockets. ''Hardly. She and Bob—that's her husband—have been having some serious problems lately. She's flying in from San Francisco this evening and wants to stay at my place for a few days while she sorts out her options.''

Regan knew exactly what was coming and was so disgusted, she had to glance down at the toes of Charles's highly polished loafers before she could compose herself enough to look him in the eye. ''So leave her a key,'' she suggested flippantly.

''She's all broken up over this, Regan. I can't abandon her.''

It had been a long and tiring day, and Regan gave up all hope of holding on to her temper. ''What about me? Do you think nothing of forcing me to go alone on the vacation we've planned for months?''

·Charles reached out for her. ''Oh, come on, Regan. Don't put it that way. You needn't be jealous of Sharon. She married my best friend. I'd never want to be the one to come between them.''

Regan was so angry that she didn't even know where to begin. ''When did you hear from Sharon?''

''This morning,'' Charles admitted reluctantly, ''but I knew you had several weddings to do, and I didn't want to come over earlier and interrupt your day.''

''How considerate of you. So in other words, Sharon called, and rather than admit how her request would interfere with our vacation plans, you leapt at the chance to hold her hand. I'd really thought this vacation was something we'd both counted on. Didn't it even occur to you that you ought to have discussed this with me before you gave Sharon the okay?''

''Hell. I'm disappointed too,'' Charles countered, ''but Sharon really needs a friend right now.''

''And I don't?'' Regan already knew the answer to that question. Charles had always said how much he admired her ambition and the fact that she owned her own business. He frequently complimented her independence, but she sure didn't feel self-sufficient now. She simply felt cheated, and hot tears of shame stung her eyes.

''We had plans,'' she reminded him. ''When Sharon called, you should have told her how sorry you were about her problems, but that you were going to be out of town. I'll bet that didn't even occur to you, though, did it?'' When Charles blanched slightly, Regan had her answer.

''Go on, get out of here,'' she said. ''I'm leaving for Santa Barbara, and I'm not going to waste another second standing around here listening to you whine about 'poor' Sharon.''

Charles turned sullen. ''I knew you wouldn't understand,'' he muttered.

''But you went right ahead and invited Sharon to come for a visit? I'd say what you think of me is shockingly plain. Like Rhett Butler, you just don't give a damn.''

''It's not that way at all!''

''It sure as hell is! Now go on, get out of here.'' Regan cut around him and made it to the front door in three long strides. ''Hurry up. I want to lock up.''

''You're making a big mistake,'' Charles argued. ''Sharon will be gone in a couple of days, and I can join you then.''

Feeling betrayed, Regan shook her head. "Don't bother. I'll not settle for being second choice, if I'm even that high on your list."

Charles's eyes narrowed. "Sharon's just a friend, not your rival. You're blowing this all out of proportion and you'll surely regret it."

"You're wrong. My only regret is that I ever wasted five minutes of my time on someone who's more concerned about the feelings of a woman he dated years ago than mine." The fire in Regan's eye made it plain she was unlikely to soften her opinion any time soon, and after regarding her with a final glare, Charles strode out the door. Regan locked it behind him, turned out the lights, and left without bothering to sweep up another leaf.

When she got home, she showered, changed her clothes, loaded her car with her luggage and supplies, and was gone in fifteen minutes. Seeking peace of mind rather than speed, she chose the leisurely coast route to Santa Barbara. The scenery was breathtaking as the setting sun turned the Pacific Ocean to liquid amber, but not being able to share the romantic view with the man she loved was heartbreaking.

She and Charles had studied guidebooks of Santa Barbara and made lists of all the things they hoped to see and do. Knowing just how awkward she would feel sightseeing alone, Regan revised her plans as she drove. She would simply relax on the beach and read. Just because this wasn't going to be the vacation she had dreamed of didn't mean it couldn't at least provide a much-needed respite from work. Her aunt's vacation cottage was located in a secluded cove just south of Santa Barbara, and if all she could do was rest, then it was the perfect place for solitude.

The lazy summer twilight was fast disappearing, and as Regan turned down the cove's narrow road she had to strain to read the house numbers on the garages. Like the other homes, her aunt's shingled cottage had been built to capture a magnificent view of the sea. The front window was framed by a luxurious magenta bougainvillea, but the garage was all that was visible from the street.

When Regan at last sighted the familiar number, she swung into the driveway. In the same instant, she felt, as well as heard, a horrible thump.

"Oh my God!" she screamed. Slamming on the brakes, she cut the engine and leapt out of her car. Terrified that she had stuck a child, she raced around the back of the Volvo station wagon praying that she hadn't killed him.

Marco Tomasi had been riding his bicycle and minding his own business when Regan made a sudden right turn in front of him. This wasn't the first time he had fallen while riding, nor was it the worst accident he had ever suffered, but in his view, it was certainly the most senseless. Badly shaken, he picked himself up off the asphalt, then had to reach out and grab for the side of the Volvo when his right knee buckled.

He began to swear in a long burst of colorful insults that the mellow tones of his native Italian language did not disguise. He was ready to rip off the driver's head and hurl it down the street, but when his assailant proved to be a willowy blonde rather than the husky man he had been eager to punish with his fists, he had to modify his means of attack.

"Have you just learned how to drive?" he sneered. "Look what you have done to my bicycle, and to me!" He yanked off his helmet, freeing an unruly thatch of black curls and gestured toward the expensive titanium racing bicycle. The front wheel had been crumpled so badly that it no longer bore any resemblance to a circle. Still, it could be replaced. The true disaster was the damage done to the bicycle's light-weight frame.

"I didn't see you," Regan whispered apologetically. Grateful the man was angry rather than comatose, she attempted to bargain with him. "Please come inside with me. There are sure to be some first-aid supplies we can use on your knee, and then I'll give you a ride home. As for your bike, I'll take it in to be repaired first thing Monday morning."

"I am Marco Tomasi," he hissed through clenched teeth.

"How do you do? I'm Regan Paisley, and I'm so sorry we had to meet under such unfortunate circumstances."

Marco eyed Regan coldly, waiting for a glimmer of recognition to brighten her glance, but anguish remained her only visible emotion. He could not even recall the last time he had encountered a woman who had not deliberately set out to meet him. Despite the painful throbbing in his knee, his anger began to subside.

"Yes. It is a great pity. Now, because I can neither ride nor walk away on my own, I will have to come inside with you. Give me a hand so that I do not fall again."

The instant Regan's fingertips brushed Marco's arm, she felt the sinewy toughness of him as well as an almost magical tingle, as though his whole body were charged with the force of his personality. She drew back slightly; then, thinking she must be imagining the peculiar sensation, she took a firmer hold on him. "I'm not feeling all that steady myself," she revealed. "Please give me all the help you can."

Marco wrapped his left arm around her shoulders

and, still holding his helmet in his right hand, took a cautious step. He was badly bruised, and his right knee was scraped raw, but his gloves had protected his hands. "Go slow," he ordered.

Regan slid her arm around his waist. Charles belonged to a health club and worked out to remain fit, but Marco's body was as lean and muscular as a whip. On Sundays, packs of sleek young men raced their bicycles down the street where Regan lived, and from what she could discern in the fading light, Marco was the same type of superbly conditioned athlete. She was five-foot-eight and judged him to be a couple of inches above six feet in height. It was horrifying that she had failed to see him.

"I am so sorry," she repeated. "I haven't been here in a while. I was searching for the house number and just didn't see you. Were you traveling awfully fast?"

"Of course," Marco replied with a derisive snort. There were no lights on in the house, which intrigued him as much as Regan's naïveté about cycling. "This is not your home?"

As they inched their way across the driveway, Regan debated how much to reveal. After all, she knew nothing about Marco, or how eager he might be to sue her. There was a huge dent in her car door, but that was a slight concern. "The house belongs to my Aunt Madeleine," she finally confided, not wanting him to believe she owned expensive beachfront property he might wrench from her in a lawsuit. "I'm just visiting for a week while she's away."

When they reached the back door, Marco leaned against the house. The sun had set, and the temperature was falling rapidly as the breeze off the ocean cooled the air. He was dressed in spandex shorts and a close-fitting T-shirt, which wasn't nearly enough to keep him warm after his vigorous ride.

"Oh, damn. I've left the key in the car," Regan cried. "I'll be right back."

Marco shot her an ironic glance. "I will not go far."

Regan raced back to her car on unsteady legs. Not wanting to leave Marco's bicycle where it had fallen in the street, she opened the garage door and carried it inside. She then drove her car on up the driveway and returned to the house with the key. As soon as she had unlocked the door, she reached in to turn on the porch light. Now able to take a look at Marco in a brighter light, she was sorry to see he still wore a forbidding frown. It did nothing, however, to detract from his dark good looks.

His eyes were the color of bittersweet chocolate, and framed with thick black lashes and gently arched brows. His nose was straight and his mouth, despite its present downward curl, had a tempting fullness. In all, he possessed the classic beauty of a Roman god, but his long hair gave him a wild, reckless appearance. It wasn't until Regan noticed that he was regarding her with an equally inquisitive stare that she realized what she was doing and grew self-conscious.

"Forgive me. Let's go on inside." She switched on the interior light, and after again wrapping her arm around Marco's waist, guided him into the kitchen. There was a maple table near the window, and she quickly pulled out one of the captain's chairs. She watched as Marco eased himself down into it and was relieved when he did not cry out in pain.

"Just give me a minute," she begged, "and I'll see what I can find."

Regan's eyes were more violet than blue, and Marco was touched by the concern he saw mirrored in their troubled depths. Her hair was gathered atop her head in a frazzled ponytail, and her sweater and jeans were too loose-fitting for his taste, but he had always been attracted to women with her delicate, porcelain prettiness. He definitely preferred a more civilized way of meeting them, however. "A wet paper towel would be useful now."

"Oh, yes. Here you are." Regan grabbed one off the roll next to the sink and dampened it slightly before handing it to him. "I hope the sight of blood doesn't make you as queasy as it does me."

"Only when it is my own," Marco said. He pressed the paper towel to his skinned knee and grimaced slightly. "May I use your telephone?"

There was an extension on the wall within easy reach of the table, and Regan passed him the receiver. "Make as many calls as you like. I should have realized you'd have people who'd be worried about you." Not wishing to eavesdrop, she left for the bathroom, where she hoped her aunt would have suitable supplies. Before opening the medicine cabinet, she paused to splash water on her face; it was all she could do not to cry.

She had really been looking forward to spending a week with Charles just having fun and making love. Instead, she now wondered if they had any relationship left, and to make matters worse, she had nearly killed a gorgeous Italian. The accident had been entirely her fault, and he would be well within his rights to sue, which could easily ruin her.

"Stop it!" she scolded, before her imagination stripped her of everything she had worked so hard for. She did not even want to think about what else could go wrong that day. She was relieved to find that Madeleine had a tube of antiseptic cream and a box of large Band-Aids.

As she started back toward the kitchen, she overheard Marco talking with someone in a low, insistent voice. His attorney, she feared, but he was speaking Italian again and she could not be sure. She waited in the hallway until she heard him hang up the receiver; then, feigning a confidence she didn't feel, she walked into the kitchen.

"This ought to be all we need."

Marco held up his hand. "I would like to shower first, or we will just be rubbing dirt into the wound."

"Shower?" She supposed it was a reasonable request, but though she was eager to offer comfort, she didn't want Marco to make himself completely at home. Then again, if she pampered him now, he might not sue her later. "All right. That's probably a good idea. There's a bathroom just down the hall."

Regan took a deep breath before helping Marco from his chair, but this time she was certain there was something unusual about the feel of his skin. Perhaps it was some exotic European brand of sunscreen, she thought, refusing to believe it was simply his own personal magnetism. They moved more smoothly side by side, and she hoped that meant he was walking more easily.

She released her hold on him at the bathroom door. "My aunt frequently entertains guests and keeps plenty of toiletries in the drawers for their use. Please help yourself to whatever you need."

The bathroom was painted a cool sea green, and fluffy white chenille towels hung on the racks. After a quick glance around, Marco appeared satisfied that he could manage on his own, and nodded to dismiss Regan. As soon as he closed the door, she wished she had asked if someone was coming to drive him home. Her offer to take him there had been sincere, but hitting him had left her so badly shaken, she would rather he left on his own with a friend.

Too anxious to sit down, she went out to her car and carried in the food she had brought from home so she wouldn't have to waste more than a few minutes of precious vacation time in a grocery store. Next she unloaded her luggage and took it upstairs to the spare bedroom. Her aunt had suggested that she use the regal gold-and-white master bedroom, but Regan did not want to intrude upon her aunt's privacy.

Besides, she preferred the sunny yellow bedroom. It had a comfortable antique iron bed painted bright green and a yellow-and-green floral print quilt and linens. The whole room was a riot of jungle colors, and in her view, the perfect choice for a florist. Leaving her belongings on the bed, she went back downstairs to put away the food. She had had each day's menu planned, but without Charles, she doubted she would bother to prepare many of the meals.

She heard the bathroom door open and thought Marco might need some help, but he appeared in the doorway before she had taken a step in his direction. Upon leaving the shower, he had simply tucked a towel around his narrow hips and left his chest bare. His body was a smooth golden bronze, and a single glance at the superb definition of his stomach muscles made Regan wish she had thought to provide him with a robe.

Then again, she hated to offer one when he looked so damn good half-naked. She had never gone to Chippendale's to watch male strippers perform, but she doubted their dancers looked any better than this. She had always been drawn to Nordic types. Charles fit that description, as did Karl Swenson, who handled her shop's deliveries. But Marco Tomasi was such a perfect example of masculine perfection, she thought she might change her preference.

"You'll need clean clothes," she finally recalled.

Regan had such an expressive face that Marco had enjoyed observing her observing him. That he was handsome was something he had taken great pride in at sixteen, but seldom thought of at thirty-two. "My trainer is bringing some. We need to settle something before he arrives."

Here it comes, Regan thought, but she still had to make an attempt to convince him not to sue. "I have an excellent insurance firm. It will cover your medical costs and repairs to your bicycle."

Marco turned aside her offer with an emphatic shake of his damp curls. "You must not contact your insurance company, nor file an accident report with the police."

Regan was astonished by his demand. "I just renewed my driver's license, and I know what California law requires," she insisted. "There's at least $500 damage to my car, and your bicycle is probably worth that too. That means I'm required to file an accident report within ten days."

Water trickled down Marco's forehead, and he raised his hand to wipe it out of his eyes. "The bicycle is worth thousands, but I will handle it, and also pay to have your car repaired. Get an estimate on Monday, and I will give you the cash to cover it."

Regan leaned back against the tile counter. Marco was obviously a foreigner and perhaps unfamiliar with California's laws, but she did not understand how he could possibly believe the repairs to her car were his responsibility. She was relieved that he had not mentioned a lawsuit, but she wouldn't take advantage of his ignorance, nor resort to trickery, to avoid one.

"I caused the accident, Marco, and I'll have to cover the repairs. I had no idea racing bicycles cost so much, but as I said, my insurance will cover it."

Marco limped toward her. "You still do not understand who I am, do you?"

Only one possibility came to Regan's mind, and her fair complexion paled. "Good Lord, you're not some Mafia don, are you?"

Marco began to laugh in low rolling chuckles, and had to reach out for the edge of the counter to steady himself. When he noticed Regan looked as frightened as when he had picked himself up off the pavement, he raised his hand to plead for a moment to compose himself.

"No, Regan. Not all Italians have Mafia ties. I am merely a man who races bicycles for a living, and I do not want my competition to learn I have been injured. If you file an accident report, it will no longer be a secret."

His burst of laughter had caused his towel to slip dangerously low on his hips, and Regan had a difficult time lifting her gaze from the line of dark curls below his navel. "I'm sorry I didn't recognize your name, but I don't follow any professional sports. Although I do know the French sponsor an important bicycle race."

Marco nodded slightly. "The Tour de France. I have had the honor of winning several times, and I can not allow anyone to suspect that I won't be just as strong the next time I race."

He did not appear to be severely injured, but that her carelessness could have easily ended his career made Regan sick to her stomach. She pushed away from the counter and dove for the chair he had used at the table.

"I'm sorry, but this has been one of the worst days of my life and I certainly don't want to do anything more to jeopardize your career. I can't allow you to pay for all the repairs, though. If insurance is out, I'll have to find a way to do it on my own."

"No," Marco argued calmly. "I will pay for your car. Call the money rent if it will make you feel better."

Completely confused, Regan watched in rapt fascination as Marco retucked the corner of the towel around his waist. "Rent has to be the wrong word for what you have in mind," she said in a failed attempt to sound as though everything about Marco Tomasi wasn't unsettling. "Rent is the money you pay to live in a house or apartment."

The doorbell rang, and Marco turned toward it. "Yes. That is precisely what I meant. I will have to stay here with you this week, or news of the accident will get out."

"Stay here?" Regan shrieked. "But that's impossible."

"Why? How many people do you have coming?" Regan gestured helplessly. "Well, none, but—"

"Excuse me. That will be my trainer with my clothes. I must answer, unless you would prefer me to wear only this towel all week?"

Because she had nearly killed the man, Regan found it impossible to throw him out, but no matter what he wore, she was afraid she was going to be in very deep trouble. Though she had known Marco less than an hour, she was positive nothing about him was ever predictable.

"No," she answered hesitantly. "I would prefer you wore clothes."

"Good. You must make a list of everything else you would like, and I will see that you have a memorable week."

He had to use his hand to brace himself along the wall as he moved toward the back door, but Regan did not doubt that he meant that teasing threat. She almost wished Charles were going to join her later in the week just to see his face when he found she hadn't been moping around her aunt's place all alone. Her next thought made her face burn with an incriminating blush, but she had already promised herself that she would not take advantage of Marco Tomasi, and that was a vow she intended to keep.

Chapter Two

Marco's trainer arrived, took one look at Marco's knee, and began to swear angrily. He was a big, burly man, with wavy gray hair and a frog's down-turned mouth, who dismissed Regan with a single threatening glance. Feeling out of place, although she was the one who had the right to be there rather than he, she left him to tend to the cyclist's injuries and let herself out the front door.

A thin layer of sand covered the flagstone patio, giving her footsteps the breathless whisper of snare-drum brushes, but the sibilant sound was lost in the Pacific's roiling roar. She crossed the patio quickly, then climbed up and over the seawall of ragged sandstone boulders heaped to protect the cove's residents from the ravages of high tide.

Once her feet hit the sand, she slipped off her shoes and wiggled her toes. The coarse-grained sand still held a hint of the day's warmth, but the receding tide had left the path cold and damp. At the water's scalloped edge, Regan played chase with the foamy waves, then scooted backward as soon as the tips of her toes got wet.

The sea reflected the moonlight in a thousand starry sparkles, surrounding her with a magical glow and buoying her spirits immeasurably. She inhaled the delicious salty scent of the breeze, and then, tired of her solitary game, she strolled the length of the cove and back. The weekend after Labor Day, most of the houses stood dark, but here and there a light shone in a front window. Regan could not recall the first time her family had brought her to Madeleine's, so she knew she must have been no older than two or three. The beach was a fabulous playground for children, and she had loved every minute she had spent there.

Madeleine was her mother's younger sister, and she had married well—a fact Madeleine never mentioned, and Regan's father never forgot. Still, the family had vacationed here for years, until the wrenching fights between her parents had finally been silenced by divorce. Now her mother was happily remarried, while Regan did not even know where her father lived, let alone his current marital status.

Growing cold, she retrieved her shoes, found the familiar footholds in the sloping seawall, and climbed up to her aunt's patio. The trainer was still standing in the kitchen, and having no wish to go inside, she sat down on the end of a chaise longue, wrapped her arms around her knees, and looked out to the sea. Almost immediately she flashed on a distant memory: a glorious day when her father had lifted her to his shoulders and carried her into the breaking waves. It was proof, however remote, that her childhood had once been happy.

Feeling a hollow, painful ache, she refused to dwell

on the bittersweet memories of her youth, but with her present life a melancholy mess, there was nothing to fill her soul save the changeless beauty of the sea. She closed her eyes and drank in the rushing noise. Tomorrow she would swim, but tonight she wanted simply to sit and build new dreams.

The front door opened. "It is too cold now for you to be outside. Come in. I have lit the fire."

Marco was silhouetted in the doorway. He was dressed in a black polo shirt and khaki shorts, and wore an Ace bandage wrapped around his knee. "Well," he prodded, "come inside."

"Has your trainer gone?"

Marco's voice softened slightly. "I am sorry if Antonio frightened you. He was concerned about me, but he should have greeted you more politely. He spends too much time alone, and lacks charm as a result; but he did not mean to be rude."

"While that's all very interesting information, you still haven't answered my question. Has he left?"

Marco held on to the door, but limped forward and extended his hand. "Yes, and he took my bicycle away to be repaired. Now come inside with me."

That a stranger feared she might become chilled while Charles cared so little for her comfort caused Regan another painful burst of inner torment. The emotional hurt Charles had inflicted still lingered as a gnawing ache deep within her, and she hugged herself as she rose to her feet. "I still doubt the wisdom of your staying here, but I hadn't planned to take up residence on the patio to avoid you."

Marco flashed a sly grin. "I am so relieved. Do you like pepperoni pizza? I would have asked your preference before I ordered one, but Antonio simply brought one for me."

Marco's fingers were long and slim, making his

every gesture graceful. When he reached out for her a second time, Regan slid her hand into his and gasped at the resulting jolt. Had it merely been static electricity, she wondered, or some far more exotic thrill? She turned to stare up at him as they entered the house.

Marco closed the door. "You feel it too," he mused aloud. "It is a most pleasurable phenomenon."

Yanking free of his grasp, Regan hid her still tingling hand behind her back. "I've no idea what you mean."

Marco moved sideways to block her way into the kitchen. "I am talking about the special magic men and women make together. It is happening now. I can see it in your eyes."

He looked highly amused, but he was overestimating his allure. He was definitely attractive, but Regan was positive she wasn't drooling. "I'm sure all you see is that my eyes are bloodshot. Now, I appreciate your offer, but I don't usually eat pizza. It's just too high in fat content. I'll open a can of soup instead."

Marco responded with a sweeping shrug. "Eat whatever you please. But I insist that you join me in front of the fire."

Regan glanced toward the inviting blaze. "Fine. Why don't you sit down? I'll bring the food."

"You need not wait on me," Marco stressed. "I am not that badly injured."

"Perhaps not, but I'll not risk having a slice of pizza land upside-down on my aunt's carpet."

The living room was carpeted in a pale, creamy shag that brought the sandy color of the beach indoors. Marco could easily envision a large triangular stain marring the beauty of the rug, and did not want to take that risk either. "It never hurts to be cautious," he agreed, and moved by her into the living room.

Thinking that she and Charles might want soup with lunch, Regan had brought several varieties and chose her favorite, a hearty tomato with vegetables. The pizza was still warm, and she cut several slices, placed them on a dinner plate, and carried them in to Marco. He had pulled a comfortably worn brown leather armchair up close to the coffee table and had his feet resting on the matching ottoman.

"Would you like something to drink?" she asked. "I don't have wine, but I did bring soft drinks."

"A glass of water would be nice."

He was nestled down in the chair, and looked so at home that Regan thought, despite his protest, that he probably loved to have women at his beck and call. From now on, she would serve meals at the kitchen table. She returned with water for them both, then her bowl of soup. She placed it in the middle of the coffee table and sat down cross-legged on the floor.

For several moments, they ate in silence, and then Marco spoke. "You intrigue me."

He was watching her much too closely, and after the absolutely rotten day she had had, Regan doubted there was all that much to see. "I can't imagine why," she answered between spoonfuls of soup.

"You are joking. You are a very beautiful woman."

Regan shook her head. "Are you certain you didn't hit your head when I turned in front of you?"

"No," he swore emphatically. "Of course, you need a new hairstyle. You should have your hair cut short and feathered around your face."

"I thought you raced bicycles for a living. Are you a hairstylist as well?"

Marco enjoyed her teasing. "I am a man of many talents. After dinner, I will be happy to cut your hair free of charge."

"How kind of you, but no thanks. This hasn't been the best day of my life and I don't want to tempt fate."

"It is only hair. It will grow back."

"Is that what you tell the women who take you up on your offer?"

Marco could not recall the last time a woman had made him laugh as easily as this one, and it was most beguiling. "No, but it is a thought. Now tell me why you came here alone. Where is your lover?"

The audacity of his question stopped Regan in mid-swallow and she nearly choked. "Excuse me? That's really none of your business." Not satisfied, Marco arched a brow to restate his question and Regan's temper got the better of her. Before she knew it, she had spewed out the whole humiliating story in one long, bitter burst.

Marco's eyes widened in disbelief. "No! He chose to stay with an old girlfriend, another man's wife, rather than come here with you?"

Regan raised her right hand. "I swear every word is true." Embarrassed to have lost control of her emotions, she used her napkin to wipe incipient tears from her eyes. "I'm sorry." No longer hungry, she started to rise, but Marco leaned across the table to touch her hand, creating an exquisite caress that kept her in place.

"You must not apologize," he stressed. "You have been badly betrayed and have every right to feel abused. I watch Oprah. I know these things. It is important to be in touch with our feelings."

Disbelief lit Regan's teary gaze. "I had no idea Italian men would even admit to having them."

Marco sat back in his chair. "Of course I have feelings, and expressing them is one of my many talents."

Regan watched a teasing smile spread across his lips. His teeth were very even and white, giving him a seductive grin. Fearing she was again observing him too closely, she took another sip of soup. She took several before she realized the lonely ache inside her had begun to subside. Marco's dramatic looks made him a distracting companion, but his words had impressed her too. She did have a right to her feelings, and just acknowledging the fact had improved her mood.

"I intend to have a nice vacation even without Charles. I suppose I ought to be grateful Sharon presented a test of his loyalty before we got married rather than after. That would have been an even worse blow."

Startled, Marco leaned forward. "You were engaged?"

"No, but I thought we would be by the end of this vacation." She glanced toward the crackling fire, and the dancing flames coaxed forth another long-forgotten memory. "We used to toast marshmallows over the fire," she murmured softly. "I haven't done that in years."

"Do you have some?"

"No. I'd forgotten how much fun it was."

"Go to the store in the morning and buy some. It would be nice to have some ice cream too."

"My aunt might have some in the freezer."

"Good. I don't drink, but I do love ice cream." He winked at her, as though he had just confessed to having a terrible vice.

He did not look as though he ate many sweets, but she supposed he must ride a couple of hundred miles a week and that would keep him in shape regardless of his diet. "When is your next race?"

"This Saturday."

Regan sighed fretfully. "Will your knee be well enough by then for you to ride?"

Marco caught a dripping string of mozzarella and twirled it back atop his slice of pizza. He had always healed quickly and expected to again, but if he made that boast, Regan might insist that he leave before the week was out. She was such an appealing waif that he did not want to go. He affected a pensive frown before he replied.

"I hope so."

He appeared doubtful, and Regan blamed herself. "Perhaps you should be under a doctor's care."

Marco navigated the tricky course between his usual confidence and feigned doubt. "Thank you for your concern, but no. A skinned knee and a few bruises do not require one. All I need is time."

"I hope you have enough."

Marco caught her gaze and held it. "So do I."

His voice was honey smooth, and Regan doubted he was referring to his knee. She quickly focused her attention on her soup. Then, after growing increasingly uncomfortable, she realized she was holding her breath, and inhaled deeply. It calmed her slightly, but not nearly enough.

"Please don't do that," she begged.

"Do what?"

Regan found it difficult to believe he didn't understand the nature of her plea. "Come on to me," she stated clearly. "You're very attractive. I imagine you must have groupies who stand at the finish line of races eager to throw themselves into your arms, but what I want is love, not some casual affair with a celebrity."

Regan's expression was so pitifully forlorn, Marco knew she was not merely playing hard to get. "Cyclists do indeed have groupies, although there are more fans in Europe than here. I will admit to enjoying their attentions when I was younger, but memory has blurred their faces. I cannot race forever. It is a young man's sport and even if you had not hit me, this may very well be my final year."

His attention appeared to be focused on the last bite of pizza, but his expression had turned thoughtful, and Regan believed him. "What do you plan to do then, open a hair salon?"

"A what?" Marco thought the question absurd until he recalled he had offered to cut her hair. "I have considered it, of course," he teased, "but my family manufactures shoes, some for the world's finest fashion designers, others for sports. We even make army boots. When I was twenty, running the company held no appeal, but now"—he paused to smile—"I have mellowed, or perhaps merely grown up, and following in the family tradition does not seem so bad."

"Do you have brothers and sisters?"

"No. You could say I am the sole heir."

He winked at her, and after a slight hesitation, Regan caught the joke. The only son of a shoe magnate would indeed be a sole heir. "A man of your charm will undoubtedly do well in any profession."

"True, but Italy is filled with charming men, and we cannot all do well. Now you must tell me about yourself. You said this is your aunt's house. Are you from a large family?"

"No. In addition to Madeleine, who's widowed, there's just my mother, stepfather, and me."

"Your father is no longer living?"

Regan shrugged. "I've no idea if he is or not. He left us years ago."

Marco nodded sympathetically. "And now Charles has left you too. That's why you are so sad. It is an old hurt, as well as a new one."

Marco Tomasi was easily the most remarkable person Regan had ever met. "Is psychology one of your interests?" she asked.

"Of course. People have such a terrible time understanding each other, everyone should study psychology. I cannot take credit for that insight, however. I heard David Viscott say it to a woman who had called in to his program."

Regan knew of the popular psychiatrist, but she preferred working to music rather than listening to talk shows. "Well, whatever the source, I'm sure it's accurate. Would you like more pizza?"

Marco had eaten the last bite of crust and was no longer hungry. "No, thank you. Are you trying to distract me? I want to know more about you. What work do you do? If blood makes you queasy, you cannot be a nurse. Are you a teacher?"

"No. I'm a florist. I own my own shop in Pasadena."

Marco seemed surprised. "When you are dating a man, does he ask you to send yourself flowers for him?"

Charles had made a joke about that once, and Regan laughed before recalling he was history. "Let's just say that giving me flowers is like shipping oil to the Saudis."

"You prefer big boxes of chocolates?"

"Well, I do have a weakness for chocolate, but doesn't everyone?"

"Probably. Tell me more about what you do."

Now totally relaxed, he leaned back in his chair and appeared to be ready to listen as long as she wished to speak. Though flattered to have his undivided attention, Regan did not have that much to tell. "I'm happy for any order, but I specialize in weddings. They are such joyous occasions, and I try to tailor my designs not merely to the bride's color scheme, but to her personality as well."

"You would suggest big, bright, bold flowers for one bride, and sweet clusters of dainty buds for another?"

"Yes, that's precisely how I work." Regan was genuinely pleased that he understood. "Flowers can be chosen and combined to express a delightful array of sentiments."

"Very much like shoes," Marco added.

"Shoes? Why yes, the perfect pair of shoes can enhance any outfit." She was wearing a worn pair of white eyelet tennis shoes with ribbon laces, which were hidden beneath the coffee table. They went perfectly well with her old jeans and sweater, but that didn't mean the whole outfit was worth wearing.

Marco studied Regan's preoccupied expression and wondered where her thoughts had strayed. "I would choose white orchids for you," he confided softly. "You have the same quiet elegance."

His compliment caught Regan completely off guard. Charles had not been unappreciative of her charms, but he had never paid such an extravagant compliment, and she had never been in more need of one. Tears welled up in her eyes, and she bit her lip in a valiant attempt to stem them. "Thank you. That was such a sweet thing for you to say."

Had he not taken such a bad spill, Marco would have left his chair, scooped her up off the floor, and carried her upstairs to bed. Too sore to accomplish such a romantic gesture, he had time enough to realize Regan Paisley would not be likely to welcome such a spontaneous burst of affection. No, indeed. She would have to be tenderly lured into bed.

"I will sit up with you all night if you need me," he offered. "If not, where do you want me to sleep?"

Regan blotted her eyes on her napkin. There was no trace of his earlier provocative tone in his question, and she found herself surprisingly disappointed. "There are two bedrooms upstairs, and you're welcome to use my aunt's room," she explained. "Or the sofa makes into a bed, so you can stay down here if you'd rather."

Marco had not expected her to invite him to share her bed, but he did not want her to feel crowded and made what he considered the wisest choice. "I do not want to have to deal with stairs, so I will stay here. I am a gentleman, Regan, and you need not fear I will bother you tonight, or ever."

"Thank you." Regan got up to clear away their dishes. Marco's promise had been made in too serious a manner to mistake his sincerity, but there was a lock on her bedroom door and she intended to use it. The sad thing was, she thought she would probably be locking herself in rather than him out. It was still early, though, and when she checked the freezer compartment in her aunt's refrigerator, she found two pints of Häagen-Dazs ice cream: Chocolate Chocolate Chip and Bailey's Irish Cream. She read the fat grams and shuddered, but this was a vacation after all, and she could afford to splurge.

"I found some ice cream," she called. She grabbed a couple of bowls and spoons and carried the pints back into the living room. "Do either of these appeal to you?"

Marco knew the hollow of her belly would make a delightful bowl for any treat, but held his tongue. "Give me the chocolate chip, please."

Regan scooped him out some, took the Bailey's for

herself, and returned the pints to the freezer before sitting down. "I think you would like my Aunt Madeleine. She's very sophisticated, and has done a great deal of traveling. She might even own some of your family's shoes."

"I am sure I would like your aunt even if she went barefoot," Marco assured her.

Regan let a spoonful of the rich, creamy ice cream melt in her mouth and nearly moaned with pleasure. "Are you always so agreeable?"

"Only with beautiful women."

Regan was sure he was teasing her again. "There must not be many blondes in Italy."

"Not many as naturally beautiful as you."

"What makes you think my hair is natural?"

"Your pretty violet eyes and peach-toned skin. You are the authentic variety, not an artificial one. Just like your flowers, I do not believe there is anything fake about you."

Amazed by his comparison, Regan held out her close-clipped nails. "No. It would take too much effort."

"And be unnecessary. Charles is an idiot. Does he really call himself Charles rather than Charlie or Chuck?"

Regan opened her mouth to defend Charles, then thought better of it and slipped in another bite of ice cream. "I prefer to think of him as reserved rather than stiff, and Charles fits him."

Reserved struck Marco as the perfect word to describe Regan as well. He could easily picture her and Charles spending Saturday nights in the library reading, or seated at a long table sorting dusty stamp collections. She deserved better.

"Make Charles suffer. Return home with a more sparkling image. Let me cut your hair. It is always best to begin a new look with a change in hairstyle."

His dark curls brushed his collar, but Regan liked his hair too much to suggest he could use a trim himself. "Something you learned on Oprah?"

"Probably." Marco finished the last bite of his ice cream and set his dish on the coffee table. He then sat up and pushed the ottoman out of his way. "Go wash your hair. Then find us a comb and some sharp scissors. If you sit right here on the floor in front of me, I can make you look like a princess in a matter of minutes."

Regan tightened her hold on her ice cream. "I realize this might not be the most attractive hairstyle, but it keeps my hair out of my eyes while I work."

"That is a pitiful excuse, Regan. Think a minute. If you have short hair, it will not fall in your eyes either, and it will show off how pretty they are. Besides, cutting your hair will help you to break with the past and begin anew."

It was his last argument that Regan found the most compelling. If Charles came into her shop after she returned home, hoping to smooth things over, he would know at a glance that she had changed. "Okay," she agreed. "Give me a minute."

"Take as long as you need. Bring me a wastebasket too."

Regan nodded, and after putting their dishes in the dishwasher, she went upstairs and washed her hair in the bathroom sink. This bathroom was pale blue, but had the same thick white towels as downstairs. As she wrapped one around her head, she had a moment of doubt, but by God, her life had changed, and a visible sign of it wasn't a bad idea at all. She took the small blue wastebasket, her comb, and a pair of sewing scissors with her as she returned to the living room.

Marco had been glancing through Madeleine's magazines, seeking inspiration. "Here. What do you think of this model's look?"

She was blonde, with a pixie's impish twinkle in her pale blue eyes. Her bangs brushed her eyebrows, and soft curls hugged her cheeks. It was an attractive cut, and Regan had often thought a more sophisticated look might impress clients. "Yes. That's nice. Let's go for it."

She sat down in front of Marco, facing the fire, and folded her hands in her lap. When he scooted toward the front of his chair, his knees brushed her shoulders and it was all she could do not to shiver with delight. Then he slid his fingers through her hair, gently combing the wet strands in a leisurely search for its natural growth pattern.

Regan had never been to a male hairstylist, nor had a boyfriend ever brushed her hair, and she was shocked by how sensuously appealing the gesture was. Her breath caught in her throat, and she quickly brought her hand to her mouth and coughed to cover the incriminating gasp.

Marco leaned down to catch her eye. "Have you changed your mind?"

Flooded with desire, Regan longed to slip her arm around his leg and rest her cheek against his bandaged knee, but she would never have admitted that, nor done it. Quaintly prim, she focused on the fire. "No. Go ahead."

Marco occasionally trimmed his own hair, and that of his teammates, simply by following the direction of the curl. That had been his intention with Regan, but her hair was like spun silk. Soft and completely straight, it spilled over his hands without the slightest crimp or wave. He slid his hands down to her shoulders and began to knead them gently as he tried to decide what to do.

"You are tense," he said. "Let me help you relax."

Fearing that if she became any more relaxed, she might simply collapse, Regan leaned into his caress for a mere fraction of a second, then straightened up. "I'm fine. Get on with it."

Disappointed that she had not given him more time, Marco picked up the magazine and studied the model's hair more closely. It had been softly tapered to conform to the bone structure of the young woman's face and the gentle roundness of her head. Believing the splendid results could not be all that difficult to achieve, he reached for the scissors and comb. Taking care not to make such deep cuts that he could not correct a mistake, he began to snip and trim, but Regan's hair felt nothing like his and he soon feared he had made a grave error in pretending to know more about hairstyling than he did.

The fire was dying down, and Regan again wished for a marshmallow, but it was difficult to think at all with Marco's fingertips brushing her scalp. He might describe the sensation as merely the magic men and women made together, but she had never found another man whose touch was so incredibly arousing. She could not help wondering how his fingertips would feel if he were to stroke her breast or inner thigh, and she shivered from the joy of the thought. Licking her lips, she pretended her tongue was his and could not help wanting more.

Her sweater was becoming much too warm, and she was sorry she had not changed into a T-shirt when she had had the chance. She closed her eyes to shut out the flames' erotic glow, but that only served to enhance the stirring effect of Marco's touch. He was snipping away with an easy rhythm and catching each shorn lock before it dropped to the floor.

"Your hair reminds me of lemon meringue pie," he chuckled.

"Why? Is it sticky?"

"No. It is the pale golden color of the meringue after it has been toasted in the oven with some sweet, lemony highlights."

Regan tried to visualize the pie, and believed she had found the proper mental image. "Thank you. I'll bet you come up with really creative compliments when you speak Italian."

"Would you rather I spoke Italian with you?"

"No. I couldn't understand you then."

"Men and women have so much difficulty communicating, it might help us to know from the beginning that we are not speaking the same language."

"I understand you," Regan replied.

"Then we should have a good week. I think your bangs are fine as they are, but turn toward me a minute so I can check." Regan swung around toward him and, startled, Marco was hard pressed to hide his dismay. Rather than the casual elegance he had been striving to achieve, Regan's hair hung in uneven clumps. She looked unkempt rather than superbly coiffed, and he struggled to find a way to correct the problem short of sending her to a professional hairstylist in the morning.

"Your hair is very fine and could use more body. Do you have some styling gel, or mousse?" he asked as calmly as he could.

"I'm sure my aunt must have something in the guest bathroom." She noted the heap of blond hair in the wastebasket, shook her head, then ran her fingers through what was left of her hair. "There's no reason to bother with it tonight, though, because it will just be a mess again in the morning.''

"I did not say it was a mess," Marco protested, but he was enormously relieved; she had improved his results just by tousling her hair a bit. "Look in the mirror and tell me what you think.''

Regan stood up and took care not to brush against his injured knee as she moved away from his chair. There was a mirror above the fireplace, and she took a step toward it. Marco had definitely cut her hair short, but he had left a couple of wispy tendrils at her nape, and the deep fringe of bangs made her eyes appear enormous. When he stepped up behind her, she smiled at his reflection.

"Thanks. It looks great. I should have cut my hair short a long time ago.''

That Regan actually liked what he had done astonished Marco. Believing her taste in hair and clothes must be as bad as her taste in men, he nevertheless forced a smile. "I am happy to have pleased you.''

A teasing smile tugged at the corner of his mouth, and Regan quickly turned away. "Let's check to make certain there are sheets on the sofa bed, and then I'm going upstairs. I assume you can keep yourself entertained.''

"Only as a last resort," Marco replied.

Regan pretended not to understand what he meant, but she blushed all the way to the roots of her newly styled hair. She was elated to find sheets on the bed, and then, hoping it would not inspire another risqué comment, she wished him sweet dreams and went up to bed.

Marco watched Regan nearly run from the room. In motion, her hair had fallen neatly into place. He blew out his cheeks in a restless sigh and prayed that his luck with her would hold. He leaned down to pluck a long strand of blond hair from the wastebasket, drew it slowly through his fingers, and then, wrapping it into a lazy curl, slipped it into his pocket as a souvenir.

The day had not ended as he had planned, but even if it had cost him all the skin on his knee, the evening had been very entertaining. He was tired and sore, but with Regan upstairs, he did not think he would get much sleep. Then again, he knew he would be wise to rest now and hope that on other nights, she would keep him awake until dawn.

Chapter Three

Regan came downstairs Sunday morning and found that Marco had not only gotten up and remade the sofa bed, he had also set the table and poured juice. She had packed nice clothes for her vacation and had taken extra time getting dressed in a pair of rayon slacks in a soft floral print and a pale peach sweater. She had fluffed out her hair and added an extra layer of mascara in hopes of disguising eyes still badly swollen from tears. Self-conscious with her new look, she greeted Marco shyly.

"Buon giorno," he replied. He swept her with a quick glance and was clearly pleased with what he saw. "You look so very pretty. You should always dress in pastels."

"Thank you." Regan would have worn shorts, but she planned to go into town to pick up a few things before going out on the beach.

That Regan owned more attractive clothes than he

had seen the previous evening thrilled Marco almost as much as the fact that she had somehow taken his sadly amateurish haircut and, with what appeared to be a few careless brushstrokes, made it flattering. Enormously relieved, he wondered if perhaps he might not possess more talent than he had thought.

"I would have begun preparing breakfast," he said, "but first I wanted to ask what you wish to eat."

"You like to cook?" Charles was not a male chauvinist, but he had never offered to do more than stay out of her way while she prepared an occasional meal for them.

Marco gestured smoothly. "I love to eat, so I learned to prepare my favorites. I make an excellent omelet. Would you like one?"

Regan seldom ate eggs, but doubted that having a couple now would do any harm. "Yes. What can I do?"

Marco tucked her hand in his elbow and escorted her to the table. "Simply sit down and provide my inspiration." Bowing slightly, he brushed her hand with a light kiss.

It was so easy to lose herself in the warmth of his chocolate gaze, and Regan again found it difficult to remember to breathe. Doubly flustered, she gave only the less revealing response. "I can't recall the last time a man cooked for me."

Marco squeezed her hand lightly before turning away. He had already surveyed Madeleine's kitchen implements and found the perfect pan. He pulled it from the cupboard in a fluid arc. "Charles could not turn on a stove?"

Regan smoothed her fingers over the back of her hand, tracing the lingering tingle of his kiss. "He could turn one on, or at least he knew how to microwave frozen entrées, but it never occurred to him to fix something special for me.''

''That is a great shame. Women love to be pampered, and men should not be too stubborn to do it.''

''Is that more wisdom gleaned from Oprah?''

Marco laughed. ''No. That is my own observation.'' He opened the refrigerator and removed a bell pepper and onion, which he began to dice into tiny cubes. ''I usually make my own sauces, but lacking the opportunity today, I will be forced to improvise. Would it spoil your menu plans if I used a spoonful or two of the spaghetti sauce I found in the cupboard?''

Regan glanced out the window. The morning was slightly overcast, and the sea glowed slippery silver. A solitary woman in a frayed straw hat was walking along the shore, scanning the wet sand for shells. ''No. I've forgotten what I'd planned now,'' she remarked absently.

''Should I take that as a compliment?''

He was again dressed in the khaki shorts and black shirt, and except for the bandage on his knee, looked extremely fit. He had definitely scrambled her thoughts, but she had brought the food to prepare Charles's favorites, not her own. ''You'd like that, wouldn't you?''

Marco moaned, feigning deep disappointment. ''Of course, but I do not want to have to coax kind words from your lips. They must be spontaneous.''

''Frankly, I'm still shocked that you'd want to speak to me at all.''

Marco removed the carton of eggs from the refrigerator. ''Why? Just because of the accident? I am recovering, so there is no need to be angry with you.''

''Perhaps, but you were very angry at the time.''

Marco set the eggs aside and turned toward her. ''I will admit to having a temper, but I never remain angry for long. It takes too much energy, and I prefer to save myself for better things.''

His enticing expression promised a great deal, but Regan had begun to believe she was simply seeing his usual performance with women and doubted she ought to be overly impressed. Still, she longed to believe his every word was sincere. ''I'm sure that's wise.''

Marco cocked his head slightly. ''How did you sleep?''

She had used her pillow to muffle the sound of her tears, but there was no reason to fool him now. ''Rather poorly, I'm afraid. I don't usually stay angry long either, but it's difficult to get over being hurt when it was so completely unexpected and undeserved.''

Marco nodded sympathetically, but for once had no advice and turned his attention to the omelet. Despite a pronounced limp, he moved about the kitchen with a chef's economy of motion and in a matter of minutes produced a fluffy omelet laced with sautéed vegetables and smothered with the chunky commercial spaghetti sauce. He divided it between two plates, and did not protest when Regan came to the stove to carry them to the table.

''This is a perfect morning,'' he exclaimed. He took the seat beside hers. ''We have delicious food and an enchanting view.''

''Yes. I do love the sea,'' Regan replied before taking her first bite. ''Oh, this is good,'' she told him. When she looked up, she found Marco had yet to sample his omelet, nor was he appreciating the serenity of the Pacific. He was simply observing her with a surprisingly tender gaze. ''What?'' she whispered.

Marco reached out to clasp her hand briefly, then picked up his fork. ''I was merely enjoying the moment. It is nice to be here. Thank you for inviting me to stay.''

Regan sat back slightly. "That's not the way I recall it.''

Marco shrugged. "All right, so I invited myself to stay, but you have been very gracious about it and I thank you. It is so nice not to be lodged in a hotel, and last night the sound of the waves made a tender lullaby.''

Horribly embarrassed, Regan rushed to apologize. "I didn't ask how you slept and I should have. I didn't even offer aspirin, and I know you must have been in pain.''

In truth, Marco had barely noticed it, but he tried to appear stoic. "I did not suffer too greatly to sleep. I thought I would sit out on the patio after the sun comes out. What are you going to do?''

"I'd planned to spend the day on the beach, but first I need to go into town to buy a few more groceries. Is there anything I can get for you?''

Marco frowned slightly. "I have a small list of things I wished to have delivered. Perhaps you can purchase them for me. We could also use more ice cream, and a Sunday paper would be nice too.''

He had made the word *we* sound natural, but Regan reminded herself that they were merely occupying the same space temporarily, nothing more. She had thought guilt, if not love, might have prompted Charles to telephone her last night or this morning. Clearly he was too busy with Sharon to have a moment for her. The omelet was good, but after a few more bites, she felt full.

"I'm sorry. I don't usually eat this much in the morning.''

"I am not insulted,'' Marco assured her. "I will just finish yours too.'' Before reaching for Regan's plate, he pulled a scrap of paper from his pocket and handed it to her. "Can you read my writing?"

Regan was not certain what to expect, but doubting it could be an affectionate poem, she quickly glanced over the note and found it was merely his shopping list. "Balsamic vinegar?"

"You have not heard of it?"

Regan was not even tempted to pretend to be a gourmet cook. "I'm afraid not."

"Producing it is an ancient tradition in Modena and Reggio. It was once believed to be an excellent cure for many ailments, but now most people simply enjoy the subtle perfection of the taste in cooking."

"I'll look forward to it then."

Marco had asked her to purchase rice, butter, cheese, salad greens, extra-virgin olive oil, and pine nuts. He had also listed chicken, steak, and French bread. Anticipating an expensive tour through the market, she was still running a mental tally when he handed her two crisp hundred-dollar bills.

"That should cover everything," he assured her.

Regan hesitated to accept the money. After all, Marco would not be stranded there had she not struck him. Then again, she did not want to offer to cover all of his expenses and set a dangerous precedent with a man who probably had extravagant tastes.

"It sounds as though you're going to create some delicious meals," she hedged. "Because I'll eat half, I ought to pay for half of the groceries."

Marco laid his fork aside. "Absolutely not. You are providing this lovely home. The least I can do is supply the meals."

A determined glint lit his gaze, and it was not unlike the first fierce glance he had given her. "You don't like to be crossed, do you?" she observed.

"Of course not," he admitted with a ready chuckle,

"but it is an asset, the mark of a champion. It is why I am so difficult to beat in a race."

He was making a teasing boast, but it filled Regan with a renewed burst of regret. If he lost his next race, it would be because of her carelessness, which was an awful feeling. It also made an argument over expenses trivial in the extreme. "All right then," she replied. "I'll let you pay for food."

She remained with him while he finished eating; then, because he had cooked, she insisted upon cleaning up the kitchen. "Thank you again. I won't be away long."

Marco had remained at the table, and with his injured leg now propped on her chair, appeared to be lost in the view. "Take all the time you need. This is your vacation, after all, and you should not have to rush for me."

Regan went upstairs to get her purse, but as she passed the kitchen on the way out, she paused a moment. Strangely reluctant to leave him, she called out softly. "Are you certain there's nothing else you need?"

Marco glanced over his shoulder. "You could kiss me good-bye."

Regan laughed as though he were teasing her again, but she feared that if she kissed him good-bye, she might not be able to leave.

Once Regan had left the cove, she expanded her errands to include a stop at the Earthling Bookstore in downtown Santa Barbara. She was positive they would carry an assortment of magazines devoted to cycling, and she hoped at least one would mention Marco Tomasi. The spacious bookstore had ample seating for patrons who wished to peruse a selection prior to purchase. Choosing a secluded corner, Regan made herself comfortable before she opened the first of the cycling magazines.

She flipped impatiently through the feature article on Miguel Indurain of Spain, who had won the 1995 Tour de France, but was elated when it was followed by brief sketches of previous winners. Just as he had claimed, Marco Tomasi was among the multiple winners. The accompanying photograph showed him waving to the crowd at the end of a race, and the brightness of his rakish grin affected Regan as strongly as it had in person.

She checked the other magazines and found references to Marco and an occasional photograph of him hunched down over his handlebars at the height of a race. What she could not find, however, was any information on his private life. Clearly he was a celebrity in racing circles, but whether he lived simply or had the wild habits of a playboy wasn't revealed. She was disappointed that she had learned little about the man. Convinced she would have to study him on her own, she bought the first magazine she had opened, returned the others to the racks, and finally headed for the grocery store.

Once the coastal haze had burned off, the day was gloriously bright. When Regan returned from shopping, she was eager to get down to the beach and left Marco relaxing on the patio. Though the Pacific wasn't truly warm, she slowly adjusted to the temperature as she waded in carrying a lightweight Styrofoam board. Too fair to expose her skin to the sun's rays for more than a few minutes, she had donned an old T-shirt over her swimsuit, and with her short hair, she was indistinguishable from the dozen or so men and boys who were also enjoying the surf.

A native of Milan, an inland city, Marco had nevertheless vacationed at some of the world's finest resort beaches. He was not nearly as confident of Regan's swimming ability as his own, however, and the fact that she strode right into the water and swam out past the breaking waves alarmed him greatly. The first time she lay on her board and rode a wave to the shore, she turned and waved to him, but when she swam out again, he lost sight of her among a group of teenagers.

He sat forward on the chaise, then stood and hobbled to the edge of the patio to get a better view, but still he couldn't locate her. The cove wasn't nearly as crowded as it had been in August, but several families were scattered along the beach picnicking and building sand castles. Children ran in and out of the surf, and beyond them, swimmers with brightly colored Styrofoam boards like Regan's caught and rode the waves. It was an idyllic scene, but Marco simply could not find Regan among all the activity.

When the telephone rang, he went inside to answer only because he hoped it would be Charles finally calling to beg Regan's forgiveness. Marco wanted to tell the other man what a colossal fool he was. It was Antonio, though, and Marco quickly reassured him that he was mending rapidly and returned to the patio. He raised his hand to shade his eyes, then wished he had a pair of binoculars. Once he thought he had found Regan riding the waves, but it was a young man who stood up at the shore.

Then he spotted someone floating way out past the others. The lonely figure was merely drifting with the current parallel to the shore. Regan had seemed so eager to get down to the beach that Marco had not questioned her motives as anything more than a simple desire for the lively fun the water afforded. Now he was terrified that she might be so despondent over the miserable way Charles had mistreated her that she had simply ceased to care what happened to her.

What if she planned to drift out of sight and disappear beneath the waves? he agonized. He searched the shore, but the cove was private, and there were no lifeguards. Forcing himself not to overreact, he waited a few minutes, but Regan, if it even was Regan, was clearly floating farther away.

Stretched out on her four-foot board, Regan rocked with the ocean's gentle swells. She covered a yawn and continued to drift while she studied the cove's newest addition. An imposing two-story home with decorative elements chosen from classical Greek architecture, the modern pink stucco structure was handsome, but she preferred the older, more modest homes like her aunt's. They possessed a mellow charm she doubted the new formal house would ever project.

Intending to paddle along the cove, she turned her board with a lazy kick, and inadvertently swung right into Marco, who had swum within two strokes of her. "Marco!" she gasped. "Should you be swimming?"

The saltwater had stung his knee as he limped into the surf, but he had been too worried about her to notice more than the initial bite. He grabbed hold of the end of her board and began to tread water. "You are too far from shore," he insisted, "and it is much too dangerous."

Regan raised herself slightly to gauge her distance from the beach. "I may be the farthest one from shore," she answered, "but there's no undertow here and I'm in no danger. I can't believe that you thought I was."

She appeared to be highly amused, which infuriated Marco all the more. "This is the ocean!" he stressed. "And it is a very long way to Hawaii."

"Indeed it is. Did you really think that's where I was bound?" Regan couldn't help laughing. She came to the cove every summer and felt as safe there as in a backyard swimming pool.

Marco had not heard Regan really laugh, and on any other occasion her infectious giggle would have captivated him; but he had truly feared she was in danger. That she would find his rescue not merely unnecessary but hilariously funny infuriated him clear through. He could think of only one way to silence her. Reaching up, he held either side of her face, pulled her forward, and smothered her mouth with his. It had been a deliberately dominating gesture, but the instant their lips met, the heat of his anger flamed into searing desire.

Caught off guard by Marco's demanding kiss, Regan grabbed for his shoulder to keep from sliding off her board. His touch had always crossed her skin with an electric sizzle, but his devouring kiss grazed her very soul. She clung to him, and his first kiss blurred into a dozen before either felt the need to breathe. Even then, they parted reluctantly and swiftly came together again.

It wasn't until Regan slid off her board that they realized pursuing their passion in the Pacific might very well put them both at risk of drowning. "Get back on your board," Marco ordered, "and I will hold on and return to the shore with you."

Drugged by desire, Regan could barely focus her eyes, let alone swim, but she followed his directions numbly and they soon reached the cresting waves, then caught one that carried them up to the shore. Regan stumbled as she got to her feet, but Marco took her arm and guided her to the seawall. She tossed her board up on the patio; then, needing all the concentration she could muster, she found the footholds and climbed shakily up to the patio.

Marco was right behind her, his sleek body glistening with saltwater droplets and his shorts barely clinging to his hips. He again took Regan's arm and propelled her across the patio. "Unless you want me to make love to you out here, hurry and get inside!" he urged.

Regan's conscience whispered a small warning she was in no mood to heed. It did not matter at all to her that she was on the rebound from Charles, or that Marco Tomasi's stay in her life would undoubtedly be brief. She wanted him desperately, and for now, it was enough.

They peeled off their clothes in the downstairs bathroom, then entered the shower. As soon as Marco had turned on the water and adjusted the spray, he pulled Regan into his arms. He crushed her against him, molding her supple figure to the hard planes of his while the water cascaded over their shoulders and ran down their legs.

The glass-enclosed shower stall filled with steam, but Regan felt only Marco's heat. One moment he framed her face for a deep kiss; the next his hands were cupping her breasts, then exploring the fair curls between her legs. Weak with longing, she wound her fingers in his thick black hair and leaned into his magical caress.

Regan was wet, inside and out, and Marco would have taken her right there had he not been afraid his knee would not hold them both. He was never clumsy, and not wanting to take that risk with such a vulnerable woman, he raised his hands to Regan's waist, and then turned off the water. When she looked up at him, her expression filled with a dazed disappointment, he wanted to laugh, but dared not.

"I am not stopping," he assured her, "but we need a bed."

He had left her stranded on the aching edge of release, and Regan had to hold tightly to his arms to remain on her feet. "Upstairs," she begged, but when they left the shower, Marco was not in too great a hurry to use a plush white towel to blot her body dry.

"You have an exquisite figure," he murmured admiringly. "Pale perfection," he added before leaning down to draw a delicate pink nipple into his mouth. He circled his tongue around the tip, then drew the bud through his teeth. "I want to taste all of you."

Regan wasn't sure she could manage the stairs, but Marco drew her along beside him and when they reached the top, she chose her aunt's bedroom with the king-sized bed. Before leaving the bathroom, Marco had grabbed condoms from his shaving kit, and he dropped them on the nightstand before yanking back the snowy spread and pulling Regan down on the bed. "I will take good care of you," he promised between kisses.

Regan wrapped her arms around him and ran her foot down his leg. Their bodies fit together so perfectly, she felt as though she had come home. Marco was no amorous stranger; he was the embodiment of love and she arched against him, encouraging all he could give. He kissed her with the same passionate abandon he had shown her in the sea, and she returned his fervor in equal measure. Teasing, testing, exploring each other's bodies, they shifted positions without ever breaking the spell that flowed so easily between them.

When Marco moved lower to lave her breasts, Regan slid her fingers through his curls to press his face close to her heart. She had never found simply being held so wildly pleasurable, and like a cat, she rubbed against him silently pleading for more. Obligingly, he lapped at her navel, coaxing throaty giggles that swiftly turned to soft sighs of surrender as he parted her legs.

A generous lover, Marco spread sweet kisses up the soft flesh of Regan's inner thighs before using the full length of his tongue on her tender folds. Warm and wet, he caressed her tenderly, dipped into her slippery sweetness, then used the tip of his tongue to tease her most sensitive nub. Already hovering on the brink of climax, her response was almost immediate, but rather than release her to seek his own fulfillment, he stroked her up and over another stunning peak.

Regan had always been slow to reach orgasm, and there were times when it didn't happen at all, but nothing was as it usually was with Marco. With a flick of his tongue he had ignited a wondrous profusion of sensation, and her whole body came alive. Awash in the exquisite rush, she felt cherished, more a part of him than she had ever been of another man. He truly was her missing half, and she could not bear to think she might never have found him, might never have known how glorious making love was really supposed to feel.

At last, enfolded in Regan's slender arms, Marco slid into her with short, teasing thrusts. He was big, and she was tight, making caution a necessity, but having to go slowly made probing her core all the more exciting. She had an almost virginal sweetness he wanted to honor, and it made having her all the more intensely pleasurable. With each stroke he dove deeper, but his rhythm remained smooth and tender until his own fiery need grew too demanding to be so closely controlled.

Not nearly as delicate as her fair coloring made her appear, Regan rose to meet Marco's thrusts, rocking him with her passion as surely as he had inflamed hers. She drew him down deep, then let him soar high until, with a final hoarse shudder, he surrendered his very soul. Afloat on the bliss of their union, she kept him locked in her embrace, silently memorizing the width of his shoulders and the smoothness of his golden brown skin.

Any lingering uncertainty about her future with Charles was definitely settled now. After Marco, returning to Charles was unthinkable. Charles was such a good man in so many ways, but having tasted true passion, she would not condemn herself to living another hour without it. She slid her fingers through the curls at Marco's temple and relaxed her breathing to match his.

A long while passed before Marco moved aside. He cradled Regan's head on his shoulder and hugged her. "I knew we would be very good together, but I am still surprised."

Regan turned toward him. "Really? At what?"

Marco's fingertips wandered over her breasts in languid circles. "That a woman with such a cool facade could be like fire inside. You ought not to hide your passion."

"I don't think I did," Regan replied. His face was now achingly dear to her, and she reached up to trace the line of his brow.

Marco caught her hand. "Listen to me. I have watched you retreat into yourself—it could destroy you."

Regan silenced his dire prediction with a kiss that made the fiery source of her passions unmistakable. She wanted him again, and even if he made love to her a thousand times, it would still not be enough. Slipping free of his grasp, she moved astride him, luring him to dare even more of himself this time. She was no danger to herself, or him, but if the heat of their passion destroyed them both, then she would perish happily in the flames.

Chapter Four

"Don't move."

It was an imperious command rather than a polite request, but in Marco's arms Regan was far too content to turn rebellious. Stretching languidly, she curved her spine to press her shoulder blades against his chest and bent the angle of her knees to match his. His body radiated a delicious heat and she savored every simmering degree.

"What are you thinking?" she asked.

Marco nuzzled her nape. "I am trying very hard not to think."

Regan yawned widely. "Good plan." She was happy simply to enjoy his company with no worries from the past or anxiety over the future. It wasn't like her to lose sight of the big picture, but lying in Marco's snug embrace, her usual cares had blurred blissfully out of focus.

Marco slid his palm over Regan's hip in a smooth,

circular motion. "Your skin is softer than an angel's wing," he murmured, his voice husky with desire.

Regan placed her hand over his. There was no softness in Marco's body, but that was exactly as it should be. "Have you known many angels personally?"

Marco laced her fingers in his, then raised their hands to cup her breast. "Yes, and if you brush against their wings, their feathers tickle."

"Are they beautiful white feathers with a soft pink underside?"

"Ah, precisely. You must have seen them too. When they spread their wings, they glow with the perfection of dawn. I would love to have wings. Wouldn't you?"

Regan could not recall ever seriously contemplating the issue, but immediately found a problem. "It would be glorious to be able to fly, but wouldn't wings be in the way when we make love?"

Marco laughed and tightened his hold on her. "No. We would make love the way eagles do, soaring above the clouds."

It was a fascinating concept, and Regan closed her eyes to appreciate it fully. She had never had a lover who liked to cuddle and talk after making love, and she was thoroughly enjoying Marco's fanciful conversation. She had heard that swans mated for life, and wondered if eagles did also. Then a truly horrible possibility occurred to her. Raising herself on her elbow, she turned to look at Marco.

"Are you married?" she asked.

Marco's eyes widened in amazement. "How can you ask such a thing?"

Regan thought she recognized a diversion when she heard one; she sat up and pulled the sheet over her breasts. She raised her hand in a plea for silence.

"You needn't apologize for not telling me. I'm an adult. I could have asked before now."

Deeply insulted, Marco moved with his characteristic speed and agility to shove Regan right back down into the soft feather pillows. "The answer is no," he insisted firmly. "Do you honestly believe I am so lacking in character that I would neglect to mention something so vital as a wife?"

Regan had seen that same hot gleam in his stare after he had picked himself up off the pavement. It had frightened her then, and it still did. All too aware of Marco's strength and the weight of his nude body, she licked her lips and tried to find a way to apologize that wouldn't add a further insult.

"I've not known you a full day as yet," she reminded him. "Please forgive me if I leap to wrong conclusions, but people who don't want to give a straight answer are often evasive, and I—"

Marco silenced her halting amends with a demanding kiss that stole her thoughts as well as her breath. Her only fear then was that he might simply be making a point before abruptly leaving her; she raised her arms to encircle his neck and held on with a commanding fury. They were too finely matched a pair to allow mere words to separate them, and her supple body spoke to his with the clarity of an ancient language.

With her blatant encouragement, Marco seized the opportunity to make love to Regan again. In his mind, they were swift, graceful birds of prey, who dipped and soared with a speed that seared the heavens. He poured his passions into her, marking her as his own. When she at last fell into an exhausted sleep, he was confident that when she awoke, all her doubts would be forgotten.

* * *

Marco used the balsamic vinegar in a dressing sweet-
ened with brown sugar for the tossed green salad.
Regan had never once made her own salad dressing
and just watching him assemble and simmer the ingredients wore her out. She kept out of his way as he
cooked the *risotto in bianco,* but by the time they
were ready to dine, the savory aromas from the classic
rice dish had her mouth watering. Wanting to prolong
the afternoon's romantic mood, she lit a fire and carried their dishes into the living room.

Once they were seated, she quickly sampled the
salad. "I've never had pine nuts on a salad, but
they're really quite good," she complimented Marco
sincerely.

Marco responded with a lazy smile before taking
another bite of the crisp greens. "I hope you will find
all our adventures as pleasurable."

Regan gave an appreciative hum when she found
the rice laced with freshly grated Parmesan cheese
was almost as delicious as his kiss. The flames lent a
coppery glow to his curls, and she had to caution
herself not to stare. It was difficult to believe anything
that had occurred over the last twenty-four hours was
real. When she reached out to caress Marco's hand,
he felt warm and solid, but that someone with his
dramatic good looks and forceful personality could be
equally fascinated with her was much too good to be
true.

Marco paused to study Regan's expression. "You
are wearing your private smile," he observed. "It is
more thoughtful than your others. Is it only the food
that pleases you?"

Marco was a perceptive man, who noticed signifi-
cant details, and that he could analyze her smiles so
expertly did not surprise Regan. Still, it made her self-
conscious. "Your cooking is superb," she remarked

easily, but she kept the rest of her praise to herself.

"Only my cooking?" Marco pressed her.

"You swim well too." Regan was beginning to enjoy teasing him. "Although I imagine cycling is your best sport."

"True, but until we find a tandem bike, you cannot go with me."

The mental image of the pair of them pedaling around town on a bicycle built for two brought a bubbling laugh to Regan's lips. "Would you let me ride in the front?"

"Of course."

He was smiling, and Regan could not help being flattered by the admiring light in his eyes. He had put on a tan polo shirt and black shorts to cook dinner while she was wrapped in one of Madeleine's silk robes. This was the first time she had dined with a man in such a luxurious state of undress, but she wasn't surprised by how much she liked it. When in the next minute the robe slid off her left shoulder, she made no move to adjust its fluid drape.

With Marco's attentive company and such a delicious meal, Regan considered the evening perfect. She could hear the ocean's rhythmic roar above the crackle of the flames and felt surrounded by a sensuous cocoon. Whenever she glanced up, Marco was wearing the same sly smile, and she felt certain his thoughts matched hers. This was what a honeymoon was meant to be, she realized suddenly—necessarily brief, but while it lasted, splendid in every respect.

They each had second helpings of the rice, then left their dishes in the sink and stretched out by the fire. Marco combed Regan's hair with his fingertips. "Do you really like the way I cut your hair?"

"Yes. I'm sorry you won't be around when I need a trim." The instant the words left Regan's mouth, she regretted speaking them. Marco frowned slightly, and she feared she had hurt him. "I'm sorry. I didn't mean to spoil the magic."

Marco slid his hand inside her robe. "You cannot break the spell when we create it so easily."

He sent a light caress wandering over her lush swells and gentle dips. He watched her reaction and gauged his motions to the fluttering beat of her heart. He understood a woman's body well and knew that she was sensitive all over rather than only in the most obviously erotic spots. Slow and sweet, his hand brushed over her pale skin in stirring swirls, gently tracing the map of her body and embedding it in his memory.

"I do want to make time to toast marshmallows," he murmured absently.

Regan caught his hand and brought it to her lips. "Later," she promised. "For now, all I want is you. It's warm here by the fire, and the rug is thick. Take off your clothes and you'll still be comfortable."

Because Marco had warned her not to hide her passions, he could not object to her request. He removed his shirt and shorts with a couple of easy tugs. He then tossed them onto the leather chair to get them out of his way. "Yes. It is warm here, but I fear it is going to get much too hot if we are not careful."

"If I had been more careful, we'd not have met," Regan teased, but she took care not to touch his bandaged knee as she moved between his legs. "You have a perfect body. Do artists beg you to pose for them?"

As she began to spread teasing kisses up the insides of his thighs, Marco reached out to tousle her hair. "Yes, but their intentions are never honorable and I have always refused."

Regan licked the velvet-smooth head of his sex before peering up at him. "I hope you don't mistake my intentions," she purred smoothly.

Since they met, Marco had seen such a remarkable transformation in Regan that he found it impossible to predict what she might say or do next, but he was confident it would please him. She had the sweetest mouth, and as her lips returned to their task, he lost interest in witty conversation. He trusted Regan to be precisely what she seemed—an endearing creature with an unlimited capacity for love.

He leaned back and gave himself up to her tender attentions. The heat of her mouth rivaled that of the fire, and he felt as though he were being licked by bright flames. Enjoying each blissful caress, he let her coax him to the brink of rapture, then pushed her away while he still could. "Upstairs," he breathed out in a tortured sigh.

Sharing his sense of urgency, Regan left her silk robe where it lay and led him up the stairs. The instant they reached the bed, he grabbed for her with a fierce grasp, but there was no violence to the act, only a deep and consuming passion. She gripped his shoulders and silently enticed him to reach for the limits of his endurance while he plumbed her own with deep, driving thrusts.

She arched up against him as all too swiftly a shattering climax burst over her with an intensity so sharp it bordered pain. She gasped for breath, but couldn't fight it. The molten heat of their union flooded her mind as well as her veins. Making love was too gentle a phrase for what they shared, but Regan knew no other words profound enough to describe it.

Marco felt Regan shudder beneath him, and abandoning himself to his own pleasure, he stretched out over her to possess her fully. Her hands were in his hair, and her frantic kiss lured him still deeper until no space remained between their bodies or their souls.

He was lost in her then, captivated by the sweet woman-child with the fiery passion that matched his own. Afterward, unwilling to release her, he cursed the weakness that made his body crave sleep when he wanted her a thousand times more.

Equally drained, Regan went limp in his arms and doubted she would ever want to leave their bed. As she fell asleep, she hoped that in the morning Marco would still possess the strength to cook for her and bring water, or she feared she was in real danger of dying right there in Madeleine's bed. It was a surprisingly peaceful thought, and she hoped all the angels in heaven were as handsome as her dear Marco.

Missing the newfound joy of Marco's presence, Regan awoke in the pale, silent hour before dawn. She looked up and found him leaning against the wall by the windows, staring out at the sea. She would have spoken, but his pensive frown demanded a respectful silence. She could not help wondering what had driven him from her arms and prayed it was not the memory of another woman's love.

She also hoped he was not worried about Saturday's race, but even that was preferable to whatever misgivings he might hold about her. He had not bothered to dress, and as always, just observing his finely sculpted body filled her with a heady sense of pleasure. She longed to call him back to her side, but dared not intrude on his thoughts when clearly he had sought solitude to work out some problem.

When he suddenly glanced her way, she had no time to feign sleep, but he did not appear disturbed by her scrutiny. ''The route of a race is carefully plotted, but life is full of unexpected turns. One brought us together, and I do not want to disappoint you.''

Regan sat up to face him. He was favoring his

bandaged knee and his posture was slightly twisted, but his expression was easy to read. "I doubt you ever could," she assured him.

Marco shook his head sadly. "There are more ways than you can imagine."

Regan raised the sheet to invite him back into bed. "This will surely be the most incredible vacation of my life, but you needn't offer promises of more. It's too early for you to be awake. Come back to me."

Marco hesitated briefly, then pushed away from the wall. "Antonio will return in the morning. He is afraid I will get soft if I miss more than a day of training."

"Impossible." Regan sighed as his side of the bed dipped under his weight. Then he pulled her into his arms and Antonio's fears ceased to have any meaning. Rather than make love again, Marco simply held her, but just touching him provided such a glorious sensation that she needed nothing more to feel complete.

Wanting to be away from the house when Antonio arrived, Regan headed down to the beach right after breakfast. The children who had built sand castles the day before were in school, and other than a brief glimpse of the woman with the frayed hat who was searching for shells, Regan was alone. Dressed in shorts and a T-shirt over her bathing suit, she had brought along part of the Sunday newspaper she had not had time to read, but once she sat down on her beach towel, simply watching the sea proved to be far more entertaining.

She scooped up a handful of sand and let it drift through her fingers. Marco had been his usual cheerful self that morning, and she had not wanted to ask him to elaborate on his pre-dawn comment, but she had not forgotten the anguish in his voice. In the time they had spent together, he had shown her a fascinating array of moods, but she sensed there were still more he kept hidden.

What had she hidden from him? she wondered. Nothing that she could recall. It was so easy to confide in Marco. With Charles, it had taken her far longer to feel comfortable enough to share her feelings. "Charles," she murmured absently. A great many hours had passed since she had last thought of him. Rather than feeling guilty, she considered it ample proof of just how little she missed him. That she had expected him to propose that week now struck her as ludicrous, but that she would have accepted was downright appalling.

By the time Marco finally appeared, Regan had begun construction of a sand castle of her own. Lacking a spade or bucket, she had been forced to scoop out the moat with her hands, and pat the resulting mound of sand into a gentle dome, but she thought it showed promise. Then Marco knelt beside her, and the darkness of his expression cast a shadow of doubt across her own.

"What's wrong? Is it your knee?" she asked.

"Yes, and no. Antonio called me lazy and insisted that I move back into the hotel with the rest of the team."

The sound of the surf swelled to a deafening roar as Regan fought to shut out his words. She wanted what was best for him, of course, but that the week she had thought they would share had just shrunk to two days was more than she could bear with a stoic calm. She made no attempt to project a sophisticated indifference and simply stared at him numbly as tears began to blur her vision.

Marco reached out to grasp Regan's shoulders.

"You should have more faith in me," he urged, but then his voice softened. "I am nothing like Charles. I do not care what Antonio calls me. I will be ready to race on Saturday whether he works with me or not, and I am not leaving here. Now what are you building in the sand? Is it a castle, or a circus tent?"

Embarrassed by her tears, Regan wiped them on her arm, and leaned forward to give Marco a gentle kiss before she replied. "It was supposed to be a castle, but I'm afraid it looks more like an Indian burial mound than anything else. Can you help me?"

"I would love to. We can use one of Madeleine's wastebaskets for a bucket, and her garden tools will make it easier to dig. I will get them."

"No," Regan insisted. "I'll go up to the house. You stay here." Before Marco could argue, she sprang to her feet and left. She needed to get away and not simply to run the errand. When she reached the house, she went into the kitchen to splash water on her face, but her heart was still pounding with fright. She had never believed in love at first sight, but it seemed the only explanation for how quickly she had fallen for Marco.

That he had chosen to stay with her overwhelmed her completely. She was elated one moment, and in the next feared that he might be hiding the full extent of his injuries from both her and Antonio. What if he knew he would not be able to race no matter how hard he trained that week? What if she truly had ended his career?

She got herself a drink of water and slipped into her chair at the table. Down on the beach, she could see Marco leaning back on his elbows. He appeared to be perfectly relaxed, but she was a tortured jumble of nerves. She was adept at arranging bridal bouquets, but felt hopelessly out of place as the companion of an internationally known sports star.

Marco turned to look up at the house and waved, prompting Regan to hurry before he returned to the house to check on her. She thought she had seen a trowel stuck into the ground by the hose, and grabbed the bathroom wastebasket on her way out. In past years, she had replanted her aunt's flower beds with ice plant, which grew well in the sandy soil and provided a brilliant touch of color. Her hands shook as she picked up the trowel, but by the time she reached Marco, she had succeeded in seizing control of her erratic emotions. She wondered if she could maintain that control once Marco was gone.

Chapter Five

"Get a grip," Regan scolded herself, but Marco didn't hear her frantic plea above her giggles. She ran across the sand to get another wastebasket of sea water. She could not recall the last time she had had so much fun. Since opening her own business, she hadn't allowed herself the opportunity to do something as frivolous as building a sand castle. That failing struck her as absolutely tragic now.

She quickly dipped the wastebasket into the oncoming waves. Full, it was heavy as she started back toward Marco, but her mood remained effusively buoyant. "Adults don't allow themselves nearly enough time to play," she exclaimed, and deliberately splashed him as she poured the water into the narrow trench encircling their multi-towered creation.

Laughing, Marco welcomed the refreshing spray. He had found a bit of driftwood to serve as a drawbridge and laid it in place over the moat. "I have said that same thing myself a great many times,'' he replied. Then, wanting to prove his point, he grabbed for Regan's legs and pulled her down into his lap.

"Why should children have all the fun?"

Regan rested her hand on his shoulder. "There is a type of fun children don't even know exists," she reminded him coyly.

Marco curled his lips and growled seductively. "Animals do, though," he teased. "Wings fascinated us yesterday. What should we pretend today?"

Taking up his game, Regan glanced out at the shimmering sea. "With all this water, I can't help thinking of fish, but I don't consider them much of a romantic possibility."

Marco tightened his hold on her. "What about an octopus?"

"Hmm." Regan wished Marco did have eight arms to hold her, but because he didn't, she took their play in another direction. "Being a mermaid would be fun, but what could you be?"

Marco slid Regan off his lap, rose, and pulled her to her feet. He turned her around and gave her a push toward the sea. "Go on. Get in the water. I will think of something exciting while you swim out."

Regan paused to remove her shorts; then, after adjusting the fit of her swimsuit, she again ran down to the surf. She did not care what Marco wished to be in their game; she knew he would make it fun. The water held an invigorating chill, but she strode right into it and began to swim.

Marco gave Regan a head start, but he was swiftly overcome with the same prickling anxiety he had experienced on Sunday. She swam well, but the ease with which she sliced through the waves with long, clean strokes was not the issue. Their game forgotten, he followed her into the sea. With no one else sharing the waters of the sheltered cove, he pursued her easily. After dipping below the surface, he came up behind her, looped his arms around her waist, and pulled her back against his chest, where they could both tread water comfortably.

"The mighty Poseidon would build you a coral palace," he whispered against her ear. "Captain Nemo would entertain you on board the Nautilus with marvelous organ concerts. Godzilla would burst out of the waves and carry you along on a splendid tour of Tokyo. But I think I would just rather be myself," he finally confessed. "I want a mermaid of my own."

Floating in his arms, Regan turned toward him. She had expected a teasing smile, but his expression was as serious as it had been before dawn. Suddenly, pretense lost its appeal, and she gave him such an enthusiastic kiss that they both slipped underwater before they remembered where they were.

Regan came sputtering to the surface and waited for Marco to flip the water from his curls. "I wish Madeleine had a sunken tub," she exclaimed.

Marco shook his head slightly. "I think we are lucky that she does not."

Water droplets glistened on the tips of his eyelashes, brightening his gaze. He wore a glorious smile, and Regan was relieved to have banished his frown. For the first time, it occurred to her that he must need a vacation as desperately as she. That such a privileged man could share her sense of wonder pleased her deeply, but she lacked the eloquence to put her thoughts into words.

"Let's just swim a while," she suggested, and breaking away, she swam along parallel to the shore. Marco swam with an easy rhythm at her side, and feeling perfectly comfortable, she doubted that it mattered what they pretended to be when they were so delighted simply to be together.

Rejoicing in the beauty of the day and deliriously happy with her company, Regan threw out her arms and moved into a slow, rolling back flip. As she came up for air, she barely skimmed alongside Marco, then swiftly dived out of sight. She curled around him with a languid grace, then swam away before he could reach out to catch her.

As she surfaced, her laughter sparkled above the surf's tumbling harmonies. Taking up the challenge, Marco used a powerful stoke to close the distance between them, but Regan again eluded him and disappeared beneath a cresting wave. Dark and cool, the Pacific became a sensuous playground where Regan felt free to find new ways to tease her handsome lover. She wound a slender strand of seaweed around his shoulders, then swam away trailing the kelp streamer.

Marco grabbed for the sturdy vine and tried to reel her in, but Regan let go of her end and left only a sparkling spray as she dove out of sight. Marco turned, searching for a bubbling trail, but he found only the ocean's gentle swells rolling past him. Nearly a minute went by, and frightened, he began to tread water with a furious kick.

"Regan!" he yelled.

Regan surfaced behind him and tapped him on the shoulder. "You called?"

Marco sprang with a lunging twist, dunked her deep, then yanked her up by her T-shirt. He held on tightly to keep her within reach. "Enough," he cried.

Regan had not meant to scare him, but the anger blazing in his eyes was convincing evidence that she had. Rather than attempt to escape him again, she relaxed and treaded water. Wet, his black curls formed a gleaming cap, adding a dark frame to his scowl; but in the next instant, a fierce yearning came over his face. Stunned by the change in his expression, Regan glimpsed the truth in his heart and knew, even if this were the only show of love he ever gave, it would be enough to power a lifetime of memories.

The sun swept the sea with rays of molten gold, and awash in the magical light, Regan was as exquisitely aware of Marco's emotions as of her own. Her soul filled with a desperate longing to spend eternity floating in that splendid sea of love, but with her next heartbeat she ached for even more.

"Enough," she repeated in a throaty invitation, and Marco softened his grasp on her arms.

Feeling very foolish, Marco broke into an embarrassed smile. "You swim as beautifully as a mermaid. There was no need for me to be afraid." Yet even as he spoke, the powerful need to protect her made him urge her toward the beach. He wished their sand castle were real, and that he could take her inside to a fabulous bed draped in satin and silk. It was all so clear in his mind, and he hung on to the exotic image as he raced Regan across the sand and climbed the rocky seawall to reach her aunt's comfortable house.

There was no pain at all in his knee, but he prayed Regan was far too distracted to notice how easily he chased her up the stairs. Their wet clothing went flying in their eagerness to be together, and as their lips met in the first frantic kiss, Marco reveled in the salty sweetness of Regan's taste. He drank it in, desperate to fill a bottomless well of desire.

Falling across the bed, he moved over her, savoring the cool dampness of her skin, and the grace with which she mirrored each of his motions. She was a treasure worth guarding behind the highest castle walls, but for now, he could not bear to have any separation between them. In his mind he saw the marble hallways of a palace, but the woman in his arms was wonderfully real.

He had her caught now, and she could not escape him with playful teasing. He pinned her to the wide bed, his hands locked around her wrists and his hips pressing her down into the tangled sheets. The tangy scent of the sea filled the room, mingled with their own fevered passion, and sent his spirits soaring even higher, He hovered over Regan, then dipped into her with a shallow thrust. For him, this moment of complete surrender was best, for it held the promise of all they would soon share, and he moved slowly to prolong the exquisite tension that filled them both.

The first time Regan touched Marco, she felt the jolt of a stirring force previously unknown and yet achingly familiar. Now the boldness of his touch sent her senses reeling. She hungered for his kiss and rocked her hips to lure him deep. She wanted to be completely filled, to hold all of him in the secret recesses she had never shared with such abandoned joy.

With an expert's flair, he stroked her to a radiant climax that sent pleasure throbbing throughout her body. But even at its height, their intangible bond held, and she felt his rapture as deeply as her own. It mattered not at all how they made love. Tender or wildly passionate, the reward was precisely the same, a bliss that made words unnecessary. The exhausted sleep that followed was incredibly sweet.

At Marco's insistence, Regan did get an estimate for the repairs to her car, but she adamantly refused to accept his money to pay for them. It was their one argument and continued all week, but each time the topic surfaced, Regan succeeded in distracting Marco with such blatantly seductive gestures that he would soon seek to cool his temper in her charms. That she had such power over him gave her a heady rush, but she never forgot how fleeting their liaison would be or that their every shared moment was precious.

When Friday night at last arrived, she looked back on the week with a fondness that barely kept the imminent pain of their parting at bay. Marco had roasted a plump hen liberally seasoned with rosemary and garlic to again create a delicious meal. They were enjoying it as they had his others, seated in front of the fire.

"I think it's a good thing we spent so much time swimming," she said, "or I'd surely have gained several pounds by now."

Marco splashed a drop of balsamic vinegar on his chicken and enjoyed it fully before he replied. "I would credit our other form of exercise for keeping us slim."

Regan could not dismiss making love as mere exercise, but let his comment slide. She wanted to thank him for giving her the best week of her life, but because the words would come so close to a fervent good-bye, she dared not speak them for fear of dissolving in tears. There would be plenty of time to weep come Sunday, but she could not break down now and spoil their last night together.

Regan smiled slightly. "Whatever the cause, you certainly look fit enough to race. I hope you truly are."

Marco shrugged. "Of course I am. If for no other reason than to make Antonio apologize. No," he swiftly corrected. "I should not have said that. Tomorrow, I want only to make you proud."

Her heart already beginning to rip, Regan spoke in a husky whisper. "I'll be proud of you no matter how well you do."

Marco laughed at her pledge. "Yes. You would be

proud if I came in dead last, but I intend to win."

Regan chose not to consider his prediction a boast, but merely the confidence of a born champion. "Where's your next race?"

"Antonio keeps track of the schedule; my job is just to ride."

That he did not even know where he would be next week made Regan wonder how long he would recall the days he had spent with her. Quickly shoving the maudlin thought aside, she promised to pay more attention to the sports section of the *Los Angeles Times*. "I like staying in one place," she remarked absently.

"Yes. Like your beautiful flowers, you need roots." He finished his last bite of chicken and set his plate aside. "Leave room for marshmallows. I do not want the week to end without having tasted a single one."

That each evening he had preferred to taste every inch of her brought a bright blush to Regan's cheeks, but she also had an inexplicable craving for toasted marshmallows. "Let's turn out the lights and pretend we've gone camping."

"Whatever you wish." Marco got up to carry their plates into the kitchen, returning with the bag of marshmallows and two long-handled barbecue forks. He moved the fireplace screen aside and switched off the lights. The fire lent the room a cozy glow, and he liked the way Regan's fair curls caught the light.

"Do you still like your haircut?" he asked.

"Yes, very much. You were right about making a new start. I'll keep it short for a while."

Regan deliberately kept the conversation light as they toasted the marshmallows, and Marco gave no indication that he was leaving anything unsaid either. She knew it was better this way, and laughed with him while they licked the stickiness from each other's fingers. "Three is my limit," she insisted, but reluctantly let him talk her into toasting a fourth.

"I've a couple of big weddings tomorrow," she finally revealed. "So I'll have to leave early to get home in time."

"Antonio will be here at six," Marco replied.

Regan sat staring into the fire. For their last dinner together, she had worn nothing under the soft silk robe she had come to regard as her own. She intended to take it home with her and send Madeleine a replacement. She toyed with the fringed belt as the silence between them grew uncomfortably long.

"On the beach in bright sun, or here, in golden shadows, you are so very beautiful, Regan."

While she had had a difficult time accepting Marco's compliments at first, she believed in his sincerity now. "Thank you." She meant to compliment him too, but didn't find the words before he moved close to kiss her.

"*Ti voglio moltissimo,*" he swore as he pulled open her robe.

Regan could not understand his words, but his intentions were plain, and she slid her fingers through his thick curls to press his face close to her heart. They had several hours until dawn, and she vowed not to waste a single one. She called Marco's name in a fervent plea and arched against him. She saw the fire's glowing embers reflected in his eyes and could not even imagine enjoying another such appealing blaze without longing for him to share it. Though he might not remain with her physically, he would live forever in her heart, and she celebrated that certainty with every breath and sigh.

* * *

Phoebe Conn

When, long after midnight, Marco fell asleep in Regan's arms, she dared not close her eyes for fear of losing the last few deliriously happy hours she might ever live. She had already packed her things, but left her bags out of sight so Marco would not guess just how early she planned to leave. She knew she lacked the courage to tell him good-bye, but leaving him while he slept was the most difficult thing she had ever had to do.

She waited until he was so deeply lost in his dreams that he did not stir as she left the bed. Then, with a silent step, she crossed the hall to the bright yellow-and-green jungle bedroom she had used only once. After turning on a single lamp, she pulled on the clothes she had laid on the bed and carried her bags downstairs. Trusting Marco to lock up the house on his way out, she hurried outside and nearly flung her gear into her Volvo.

The master bedroom was on the opposite side of the house from the garage, but without a car of his own, Marco would be unable to follow her even if the sound of her engine awakened him. "Not that he would," she murmured to herself. He had a race to win and his own dreams to pursue.

Dense fog off the ocean made the scene eerie as Regan turned onto the main road, but she refused to allow thoughts of Marco to distract her on the drive home. One accident had been more than enough for her, and she would not risk having another. She turned on the radio and found a rock station whose blaring music kept her from sinking into melancholy. After all, she had work waiting, and two lovely brides who deserved the best her shop had to offer.

Marco had compared her to an orchid, but on the lonely drive home, she had none of the exotic flower's serene elegance. She could block her sorrow from her

144

mind, but her body refused to overrule her heart. She missed Marco with a steady ache that grew increasingly more intense with every passing mile. Marco had not been a mere fling she could dismiss lightly, but as true a love as any her intricate bridal bouquets were made to honor.

As she rolled into her driveway, she was seized with a sudden inspiration to include a memento of their brief romance in every wedding bouquet she made, but just as quickly she realized it might take a great deal of thought to devise something truly worthy of it.

Chapter Six

Marco slammed his fist down on top of his travel clock to silence the nerve-jangling alarm, then turned toward Regan to apologize for waking her so early. When he found that her side of the bed was not merely empty, but held no trace of her warmth, he called her name. No answer came from the adjacent bathroom, and he assumed she must be downstairs preparing breakfast for them.

He never ate before a race and grabbed a pair of shorts before going down to the kitchen to stop her. The first floor was as silent as the second, however. Marco searched all the rooms before he was forced to accept the sorry fact that Regan just wasn't there. His apprehension growing, he stepped out onto the patio, but the fog off the water hid the beach under a thick veil of mist, and he did not think Regan would have been out walking that early even if the weather had been clear.

Toss the Bouquet

The surf provided a constant murmur, but it was Regan's voice Marco longed to hear, and he simply could not believe that she had abandoned him while he slept. No woman had ever walked out on him, asleep or awake. How could someone as dear as Regan have deserted him so callously? If she had no consideration for him, he fumed, what about her aunt?

Last night, they had sated their passions rather than give Madeleine's house a final cleaning. Regan had been so careful with her aunt's possessions, he did not understand how she could have left their supper dishes in the sink and failed to change the linens on the bed. Of course, she could not have changed the bed with him in it, and apparently leaving with the stealth of a cat burglar had been her goal.

Fighting his growing anger, Marco went back through the house and out to the garage to confirm his awful suspicions. When he found Regan's Volvo gone, he slammed the garage door shut with a force that shook the whole structure. He swore an ugly oath, and then tore back inside the house to pack. If Regan could not spare a minute to tell him good-bye, then he did not want to spend an extra second in the house they had shared.

By the time Antonio arrived, Marco had channeled his rage into a fierce desire to win the day's race. He was far too proud a man to tell the stern-faced trainer how Regan had treated him, but in his heart he knew another victory would be a poor consolation for the loss of the only woman he had ever loved.

When Mary Claire arrived at Paisley Flowers that morning, the first thing she noticed was Regan's new hairstyle. Though she welcomed the flattering change, she refused to allow her employer to shrug it off as a vacation whim. She tied on her apron, then confronted her.

"It would be silly for me to pretend that I don't know what happened. Charles came by here last Wednesday hoping that I'd heard from you, so I know you didn't spend the week together. He made some mumbling excuse about an old friend, but it didn't make any sense to me."

"Nor to me either," Regan agreed. "Why don't you start with the spider chrysanthemums for the bridesmaids?"

Mary Claire leaned back against the workbench. "Just a minute. I made all the bows yesterday, so we can spare a few minutes to discuss what really happened. When Karl and I left here last Saturday, you were so eager to get away with Charles that I don't understand how you could have gone to Santa Barbara without him."

Regan shot her assistant a warning glance. "That's ancient history, Mary Claire, and the Castañeda wedding is at eleven o'clock."

Consumed with curiosity, Mary Claire refused to be intimidated and continued to regard Regan with a puzzled frown. "It's not only your hair that's different. You've a few new freckles, but something else about you has changed. I can't decide exactly what it is yet, but I will before the day is out."

Although Mary Claire was a perceptive individual, Regan sincerely doubted she would ever understand how profoundly meeting Marco Tomasi had affected her. Her physical appearance could not possibly provide sufficient clues, and she would never confide such a remarkable personal experience in her assistant. No. Meeting Marco was a delicious secret she intended to keep all to herself and savor.

"The Castañeda bridesmaids can't walk in without

their bouquets," Regan repeated in a louder tone. When Mary Claire again failed to begin work immediately, Regan turned inquisitor. "What about you and Karl? Did he find time for you in his busy schedule?"

Mary Claire let out an ecstatic whoop. "Did he ever!" She shook her head as though it were impossible to describe, but the width of her smile said it all.

"Well, good for you," Regan said, but her assistant's open delight did not compare with her own grief at the end of her bittersweet holiday.

"I'm worried about getting all of the arrangements finished in time for the reception. As soon as you complete the attendants' bouquets, please start on them."

Knowing she had to get busy, Mary Claire was about to turn toward her end of the workbench when she noticed the delicate sprigs of ivy Regan had begun threading into Lorena Castañeda's bridal bouquet. "The ivy's a nice touch. I've not seen you use it before."

A lush profusion of the hardy vine grew alongside Regan's apartment building, and when it struck her as the perfect substitute for a strand of seaweed, she had picked some before driving to the shop. The attractive plant had Marco's tenacity, and because the emerald leaves blended so well with almost any flower, it was a good choice for the memento she had been seeking.

"I'm glad you like it," she answered absently. "I thought the pointed leaves provided a nice contrast to these gently rounded rosebuds."

"Of course," Mary Claire agreed. "You have an artistic principle behind each of your choices. That's why you own the place and I just work here."

Regan had not thought she would have to justify her choice of greenery, but she was grateful such a believable explanation had occurred to her when in truth, the ivy was merely a heartfelt token of love. Mary Claire went to the refrigerator case to get the chrysanthemums, and there was no further opportunity to chat as they assembled the bouquets and arrangements for the first of the day's two weddings.

When they had finished them, Regan sent Mary Claire with Karl to deliver the flowers to the church and hall, while she kept working on their next order. The Seacrest wedding wasn't until five o'clock, but it was going to be an elaborate affair at the beautifully appointed Valley Hunt Club and required every bit of Regan's concentration. Karl and Mary Claire brought her a turkey sandwich, which she ate while still standing at her workbench. Then, engrossed in creating a magnificent arrangement of white gladiola and deep purple iris, she was startled when Charles called her name.

"My God," she squealed. "You frightened me."

Uncertain whether he liked her new hairstyle, Charles stared at her for a long moment. "You like your hair that way?" he finally asked.

Regan grabbed another iris and sliced the stem to the correct length before plunging it into the papier-mâché basket that would later fit into a wicker stand. "Yes. I absolutely adore it."

"Well, then. That's all that matters."

"Isn't that the truth." Regan could not believe Charles had not thought of a better opening if he had been by himself since Wednesday. Had he greeted her with an astonishing show of wit, however, she still would have responded with a marked lack of enthusiasm. "As you can see, we're really busy."

"I can wait." Charles leaned back against the

counter side of her workbench and crossed his arms over his chest. He glanced at her over his shoulder. "I took the afternoon off."

"If you're not well, you ought to go on home."

"I'm not sick," Charles argued. "I just need to talk with you."

"This isn't the time," Regan insisted. She turned the stunning arrangement and, satisfied it was complete, added an exuberant white satin bow. She placed the bouquet on the cart with the others, picked up a pencil, and checked it off her list. "We've got a lot to do in the next couple of hours, and you'll have to forgive me, but I just can't fit in a heart-to-heart talk with you."

There was no hint of regret in her voice, but Charles could be as stubborn as Regan any day. Mary Claire was feigning great interest in the dainty basket she was decorating for the flower girl, but it was obvious that she was paying closer attention to him than Regan was. That annoyed him no end, but because he felt compelled to explain, he simply ignored Mary Claire and began what he had come to say.

"Sharon spent Saturday night and all of Sunday crying buckets of tears," he said. "Monday she spent the whole day on the telephone with Bob, and Tuesday she flew back to San Francisco to be with him."

Regan did not even look up. "Am I supposed to be interested in that pathetic little melodrama?"

"I don't care whether you're interested or not. I just want you to know that I didn't spend the whole week with her."

Regan at last looked him in the eye. "You didn't spend it with me either, though, did you?"

Charles raised his glance to the ceiling. "After the way you threw me out of here last Saturday, I didn't think I'd be welcome."

Regan could not help but laugh. "You're right. You weren't." She checked the clock. It was already three, but they were on schedule. Mary Claire had set the beribboned basket aside and begun working on the corsages for the mothers of the bride and groom. It was time for Regan to begin the bridal bouquet. She wiped her hands on her apron and went to the refrigerator case to fetch the white roses and stephanotis.

Charles watched her closely as she walked back to her workbench, and Regan wondered if he could discern the difference spending the week with Marco had made. She wasn't certain it even showed in her appearance, but inside she still felt a delicious warmth all the way to her toes. Concentrating on her task, she cut several lengths of wire, wrapped them around the stems of the stephanotis, and covered them with white florist's tape.

Charles continued to observe her with a narrowed gaze. It was difficult to believe that this time last week she had actually thought she loved him. Now she felt so detached from the serious young man standing opposite her that it seemed more like a century.

A deep, rumbling hum signaled the arrival of a low red sportscar out front at the curb. Intrigued by the distinctive sound, Charles turned to look and Regan followed his gaze.

Charles let out an admiring whistle. "That's a Lamborghini. It's a small fortune on wheels, but damn it if it isn't a beauty."

"The driver ain't bad either," Mary Claire added, then quickly glanced over her shoulder to make certain Karl wasn't within earshot.

Regan had never expected Marco to come after her. When he came striding through the front door, her breath caught in her throat. She had to grab the edge of her workbench for support. He was dressed in an elegantly tailored black silk shirt, black slacks, and black loafers. He had a shoebox in one hand and yanked off his sunglasses with the other.

"How did you think I would feel when I woke up this morning and found you gone?" he shouted as he came toward Regan.

"My God!" Charles gasped. "Who is this man?"

Marco spat out his name, then dismissed Charles with a searing glance and slapped the shoebox down on the counter. "Well?" he prompted. "Were you in too great a hurry to leave to consider my feelings?"

Regan tired to catch her breath and wet her lips with a nervous lick. She had dressed for work in a comfortably worn T-shirt and jeans, while Marco looked as though he had just stepped out of Georgio Armani's showroom. She had never expected him to be this furious with her and did not even know where to begin.

"How was the race?" she whispered.

"The race?" Charles echoed. "Are you *the* Marco Tomasi?"

"Who's Marco Tomasi?" Mary Claire asked.

"He races bicycles." Charles leaned around Marco to explain. "He's one of the best in the world."

"The best," Regan assured him. She heard Karl come through the back door and hastened to assure him she was in no danger. "It's all right," she called to him. "Marco's a friend of mine."

Marco swore in Italian before asking, "Am I no more than a friend?"

Grateful he wasn't the only one with some explaining to do, Charles broke into a wide grin. "I can't wait to hear the answer to that, Regan."

Marco didn't look his way. "Is he Charles?"

Regan managed a slight nod. Marco had an energy

that charged the air in her shop with a tingling excitement. Though Charles was only a couple of inches shorter, he looked very small and pale beside Marco.

Still concentrating on Regan, Marco lowered his voice. "Did you really leave me for him?"

"Now wait just a minute—" Charles argued.

Marco turned toward him with menacing speed. "I never give more than one warning. Shut up or get out."

Charles raised his hands and took a cautious step backward. "Hey. There's no reason to vent your temper on me. I'm not the one who walked out on you."

Regan saw the muscles tighten in Marco's jaw and wished Charles had had sense enough to leave. "If either of you throws a punch, I'm calling the police to have you arrested, and I won't put up your bail either. Now stop yelling at us, Marco, and tell us what happened in the race."

Marco swept Charles with a last disgusted glance, then turned back toward Regan. He struggled not to swear again, took a deep breath, and then spoke more calmly. "I almost did not ride because I did not want you to think winning yet another race meant more to me than you do. Then I thought if I did not ride, you might believe it was because I could not, and blame yourself. I did not want to risk that, so I rode and won. We have a strong team, though, and they would have won without me."

Marco waited for some reaction from Regan, but she offered only a sad, sweet smile. "It was only a race, Regan. Now why did you leave me?"

Regan felt not only Marco's intense gaze, but the heat of Charles, Mary Claire, and Karl also studying her closely. The radio was tuned to a classical station and the melancholy melody was the perfect accompaniment to the moment. She felt as though she were starring in the final scene in some intense Russian play, but somehow she had failed to learn her lines. It wasn't like her to be unprepared, but she was at a complete loss for what to say.

"I didn't leave you," she finally said. "It was merely time to go."

"Oh, that says a lot," Charles muttered under his breath.

Marco ignored him. "What are you saying? That your vacation was over and it was time to go home?"

When he put it that way, it didn't make much sense, but Regan could not have begged for more than he had already given her. "You had planned to leave today too," she reminded him.

Marco shook his head. "No. It was only the race that was today. Did you really think that I would leave you after what I said last night?"

"This is getting better and better," Charles swore, but he took care to edge his way over toward Karl and Mary Claire before he spoke.

Confused, Regan looked down at the white roses and then up at the clock. "It's getting late, and we have to deliver the flowers on time."

"Answer me," Marco demanded.

Mary Claire took Karl's hand. "You owe him an answer, Regan."

Regan remembered eating the roast chicken, toasting marshmallows, and making love, but she didn't recall any of Marco's comments as being particularly special. Because it was obviously important to him that she did, she had to stall for time while she fought to remember. "Look. Amelia Seacrest has a lovely wedding planned, and I'll not disappoint her. First, I have to finish the flowers, and then we'll talk."

Adopting a thoroughly businesslike attitude, Regan plucked a rose from the counter and picked up a piece of wire. "I have to be finished by four o'clock. Why don't you go out for a walk and come back then?"

"A walk? I have had more than enough exercise for one day," Marco scoffed, but when he saw her flinch, he instantly regretted having been so curt with her.

Regan had forgotten about the race. Feeling very foolish, she lost her concentration and fumbled with the rose. "I'm sorry." There were several chairs grouped around a table where she usually sat with prospective clients to display her portfolio. "Please have a seat. Would you like something to drink?"

Reluctantly, Marco forced himself to be patient. "Water if you have it." He crossed to the table and took a chair facing Regan.

Without being asked, Mary Claire dropped Karl's hand, dashed to the refrigerator in the back room, and brought Marco a bottle of spring water. As she handed it to him, she bent down and whispered, "Hang in there."

"Grazie," Marco replied, but his smile made it clear he was referring to her advice rather than the water.

"Is that thanks?" Mary Claire asked, and Marco nodded.

Regan's head came up with a jerk. Marco had said something to her last night in Italian, but its meaning had escaped her. Could that be what he was talking about? Desperate to believe it must be, relief flooded down her spine and loosened the tension making her so clumsy. She picked up another rose and continued shaping a spectacular bouquet.

Charles walked over to the table and took the chair opposite Marco's. Marco eyed him coldly. He was not used to having to compete for a woman's affections, but he had already dismissed Charles as unworthy of the label of serious competition. He took a long drink of water, then set the bottle aside and went back to the counter.

"I could help," he offered.

As always, Regan lost her heart in the depth of his gaze. Her throat tightened, and a threat of tears stung her eyes. She quickly blinked them away. "Do you arrange flowers as beautifully as you cut hair?"

"Yes, my sweet orchid. I am sure that I can."

"He cut your hair?" Charles howled. He bolted out of his chair and walked toward Regan. "Look. I'm willing to take full responsibility for last week's fiasco. You were absolutely right. I should have told Sharon that I already had plans, but damn it all, she really needed a friend, and you're so damned independent that you never need anything from me."

"'Damned independent'?" Regan gasped. "I've always thought my independence was what you liked best about me."

Marco leaned toward Regan. "Shall I tell you what I like best?"

His engaging grin made his preference plain, but Regan was surrounded by people she did not want to include in such a private revelation. She made a valiant attempt to focus her attention on the bridal bouquet rather than the maddeningly attractive Italian. "Later, please," she begged.

She was blushing a most becoming shade of pink and Marco was tired of waiting. He sidestepped Charles, circled the workbench, passed between Mary Claire and Karl, and removed the bouquet from Regan's hands. He took a firm grip on her waist, picked her up, set her down on the leaf-strewn workbench, and stepped between her legs.

Alarmed, Karl took a step toward them. "Ms. Paisley?"

Flustered, Regan couldn't decide where to put her hands, then finally rested them on Marco's arms. His enticing heat came through his silk sleeves and flooded her whole body with desire. It was all she could do not to wrap her legs around his waist and throw herself into his arms. She heard Charles exclaim that she ought to consider whether she wanted to spend the rest of her life with some hot-tempered cyclist or with a rational man who was clearly the better choice for a partner.

"It's all right, Karl," she answered weakly. Charles had failed her in an important way he still did not understand, but it was the best thing he could have done for both of them because it had allowed her to meet Marco, and she was positive that was what fate had had in store for her all along.

She spoke without turning toward him. "Find someone else, Charles." Marco inclined his head to kiss her, but she raised her hands to his shoulders to hold him back. "Wait a minute. You're going to have to remember to speak English when you say something important, because I didn't understand what you meant last night."

Confusion marred Marco's seductive glance for only an instant, and then he began to laugh. "*Ti voglio moltissimo* means I love you very much, but do you really need the words to understand how I feel about you?"

Mary Claire sniffed away her tears and reached for the unfinished bridal bouquet. "I'll work on this. It's high time you let me do one myself."

Charles began to back away. "I don't believe any of this."

Marco shot him a challenging stare. "Call Sharon and tell her that now you need a friend."

Charles's face filled with fury, but as he came forward, Karl intercepted him and shoved him toward the front door. "You were just bragging about being rational," he scolded. "A rational man knows when to quit."

Charles yanked free of Karl's grasp and bolted out the front door. He paused briefly, then spat on the Lamborghini and strode off down the sidewalk.

"I hope that was all right," Karl apologized as he closed the front door.

Regan had begun the day in utter despair, but she was elated now. "Yes, it was, Karl. Thank you."

Grateful to be rid of Charles, Marco moved close and kissed Regan with a slow, sweet abandon. Her slender body melted against his, but fully aware that he could take his passion for her no further in her shop, he reluctantly broke away and handed her the shoebox. "You have not opened your present. I knew just where to look on Rodeo Drive."

Dazed by his lavish kiss, Regan could barely make her fingers work well enough to remove the lid. Inside, she found a beautiful pair of white satin pumps decorated with lace and pearls. They were from his family's company and clearly meant for a bride. A huge tear escaped her lashes and rolled down her cheek. "I thought we'd only be together for a week."

"It was the best week of my life, Regan. Make it last forever."

"This is just like Cinderella!" Mary Claire announced. "Well, maybe not exactly, but it's a wonderfully romantic proposal. Aren't you going to say yes?"

Regan could not even imagine another reply. Still holding the exquisite shoes, she broke into a burst of effervescent giggles, and grabbed Marco in a boistrous hug. They had so much to decide, so many plans to make. But for now, all that truly mattered was just how dearly he loved her. It was more than enough.

Wanting no more misunderstandings, Marco framed Regan's dear face with his hands and asked his question in English. "Was that a yes?"

"Oh, yes, my darling. It most definitely was."

Happier than she had ever been, Regan complimented Mary Claire on the way she had completed Amelia's bridal bouquet, but in her mind she had already begun designing her own—with a cluster of stunning white orchids entwined with trailing sprigs of ivy.

Heart Craving

SANDRA HILL

To all women, regardless of age or culture or background, who yearn for those ethereal things men do not understand: "heart cravings."

To those good men who try, but just don't get it.

And especially to those men who try and do get it. Their women are the luckiest of all.

Chapter One

Nick DiCello pounded on the apartment door with one fist. The other clutched the legal document he'd just received from the subpoena server he'd been dodging for weeks.

"Paula! Paula, are you in there? Answer the door!"

The only response was the wild barking of a dog.

He took a key out of his back pocket and tried, unsuccessfuly, to open the door. "Damn! She must have changed the lock."

Nick pressed his forehead wearily against the cold wood of the door frame, then stiffened with determination. Paula wasn't going to hide from him this time.

A locked door. No problem.

Pulling a flat leather pouch from the inside pocket of his sport coat, he selected a small tool. Within seconds, he was inside.

He braced himself for the sound of her security

alarm, but silence greeted him. The same old Paula! he thought, with disgust. He closed the door after him and checked the keypad. Yep, despite his nagging, she'd forgotten once again to turn on the alarm system.

The dog leaped forward then and almost knocked him to the floor. Backing him up against the wall, the huge German Shepherd stood on its hind legs and put its lethal front paws on his chest.

"How ya doin', Gonzo?"

The dog lapped his tongue across Nick's face in reply.

He pushed the dog aside with an affectionate ruffle of his fur and walked around the familiar room, checking the door with its numerous locks, the windows, and the high tech, direct-link police security console—unplugged and obviously never used.

Satisfied that everything was okay, Nick dropped down into a chair, planning to wait for Paula's return. He flicked on the remote for the TV and surfed the channels, stopping at Oprah.

Lord, what do women see in this broad?

Oprah was interviewing a bunch of psycho psychics who claimed they could help people improve their love lives.

"Hah!" he remarked to Gonzo, who sprawled at his feet, adoringly. It was nice to have someone show a little appreciation for him. Even if it was only a dog.

Pointing to the TV, he told Gonzo, "Women believe all this relationship crap, you know, but we men know better."

"Woof!" Gonzo agreed.

"If women would just tell men what they really want, instead of expecting us dumb schmucks to figure it out on our own, there wouldn't be any need for scam shrinks. Or divorce,'' he added bleakly.

Gonzo gave him one of those male looks that said "Women! Go figure!"

"So, how's your love life, boy? Better than mine, I hope."

Before Gonzo had a chance to respond, Nick heard water running in the bathroom down the hall. The shower. *Uh-oh!* Paula was home, after all.

Briefly, he considered joining her for a quick one. *Nah, she's gonna be mad enough that I've broken into the apartment.*

On the other hand . . .

He couldn't stop picturing Paula. He knew exactly how'd she'd look. Her shoulder-length auburn hair slicked back wetly. Soap bubbles covering the nipples of her full breasts, sliding down her flat belly, through silky curls, onto her long, long legs.

Oh, hell!

His heart slammed against his chest wall, and he swallowed hard, forcing himself to look back at the TV, where another loony bird was now advising that men should find out what women crave.

Nick tried to listen, but he was unable to stop thinking about Paula in the shower. Remembering. And a long-neglected part of his body—the one with no common sense at all—jump-started into a full-blown, mind-blistering hard-on.

It had been *way* too long.

He slipped off his loafers, then his socks. Just testing, he told himself. He wasn't *really* stupid enough to try joining her in the shower. Mentally patting himself on the back for his great self-control, he decided, like brain-dead men throughout the ages, to test himself just a little bit more by removing his slacks and jacket and shirt.

And the intelligence cells in his brain melted.

Testosterone took charge.

"Maybe Paula wouldn't really mind my company. Maybe she's as horny as I am."

Gonzo rolled his eyes. That was doggie for, "It's your funeral, buddy."

Paula stood under the shower, her face raised to the warm spray. She'd been there a long time, but still the tears kept coming.

Her lawyer had called a little while ago to tell her that the divorce papers had finally been served on Nick. Their hearing would be in one week.

"So, it's finally over," she said aloud.

"Never!" a harsh voice said, and Paula jumped with shock.

Nick opened the shower doors and stepped inside, totally, gloriously nude. At first, relief flooded over her that it wasn't a stranger who'd broken into her apartment. But her relief soon turned to outrage.

"Nick, get out! You know our lawyers said we shouldn't be talking."

"Actually, it wasn't talking I had in mind." He smiled at her crookedly, his black hair already wet, beads of water rolling down his neck onto his broad shoulders.

Paula recognized the gleam of passion in his pale blue eyes, and it was impossible to ignore the powerful arousal standing out from his body—what Nick used to call a "blue steeler," a particularly virile erection.

"No, Nick. My lawyer says we should stay away from each other. Let alone . . . you know." She backed up against the tile wall and Nick followed. A predator, dangerous and out of control.

"What do lawyers know?" he murmured, pressing his body up against her, rubbing his crisp chest hairs against her sensitive skin. He moaned huskily with appreciation. "You're my wife. I'm your husb—"

"No! We haven't been husband and wife for a year," she cried out and pushed against his chest, to no avail. "You creep! The last time I saw you was at Casey's Tavern a month ago. You were three sheets to the wind and your arm was wrapped around Sheila Zeppenzipper."

"Zapper," he corrected, putting his hands on her waist and nuzzling her neck.

"Huh?" Paula's mind was fast turning fuzzy as Nick's hands cupped her bottom and lifted her, parting her legs in the process. He fitted her to his hardness, and moved against her rhythmically.

"Zeppenzapper, not zipper." He lifted her higher so her breasts came level with his mouth, her toes barely touching the floor.

"Aaarrgh!" Paula wasn't sure if she groaned over his semantics, or the excruciating pleasure of his mouth suckling her.

"And the reason I was drinking"—he explained with deceptive calmness, deliberately teasing her by pulling away, aware that she didn't want him to stop—"is that I saw you on the other side of the room with your friends. And you were ignoring me. And I wanted to make you jealous."

"Jealous! You're a fool."

"I know." He appeared contrite with his black hair plastered to his head and water dripping down the fine bones of his face, like a little boy, but his innocent look was belied by the expert fingers working their magic between their bodies.

"You were trying to make me . . . oh, my . . . ah . . . jealous?" Her knees grew weak and she tilted her hips forward, reflexively, accommodating his intimate caresses. "After punching Jerry Sullivan . . . stop that''—she slapped his hand away, only to have it move to another equally erotic place—''in the nose . . . the week before? Just because he delivered some . . . some . . . legal papers to my . . . uh . . . apartment?'' She knew she was blabbering incoherently. She couldn't help herself.

Paula hated her weakness. After refusing to see or talk to Nick in person the past year, how could she suddenly succumb to his advances? It must be because he'd caught her off guard, she told herself. And because, with the delivery of the divorce papers today, the clock had begun counting down the final hours of their marriage. Only seven more days.

''There's a perfectly good explanation.'' He brushed her lips with his, back and forth, coaxing her to open for him.

She jerked her head aside. ''Huh? What explanation?''

He chucked her under the chin, knowing the effect he was having on her, and loving it. ''An explanation as to why I punched Jerry Sullivan, honey. I thought he was your date.''

''Oh, you are incredible! He's my lawyer, for God's sake! But even if he was my date, you had no right to hit him.''

''I know. I know.'' He closed his eyes on a deep moan as he lifted her once again, wrapping her legs around his waist.

She could barely hear over the roar of blood in her ears.

Taking his erection in his own hand, he placed himself against her.

''What did you say?'' she choked out.

''I . . . don't . . . know,'' he whispered on a gasp. Before he'd barely entered her body, she began to convulse around him. "That . . . feels . . . so-o-o . . . good."

It was her turn to gasp.

Trembling with hard-fought restraint, Nick imbedded himself in her with one long stroke and began to push her against the shower wall. The stall shook with the force of his thrusts.

Her orgasm never stopped.

Over and over he moved inside her, hard, violent plunges into her woman's center.

The small spirals of her climax widened, becoming harsher, longer in duration.

Nick seemed to grow larger inside her body's sheath, reaching for her very womb.

It was over in minutes.

His neck arched backward with a guttural growl of masculine release.

Paula felt him jerk inside her and she shuddered once more with a violent internal convulsion.

Drawing in deep draughts of air, Nick finally pulled away and let her feet slide to the floor. The shower continued to pelt them both with its hot spray.

Leaning back against the opposite wall, fighting for breath, he said, "I love you, Paula."

Then he grinned with typical male self-satisfaction.

He probably expected her to swoon and say, "Oh, Nick, you are so wonderful. I forgive you everything."

Instead, she swung her arm in a wide arc and punched him in the stomach.

Fifteen minutes later, Paula padded into the living room in her bare feet, having donned only jeans and a T-shirt. She was still drying her hair with a towel.

"Nick, I told you to leave," she said testily.

He'd combed his thick black hair off his face, but

it was still wet from their shower. She tried to shut off her sensual awareness of him, but memories assaulted her. How many times, over how many years, had she seen him looking just like this?

She had trouble swallowing over the lump in her throat.

He was sitting in front of the television, fully dressed in khaki, pleated slacks, open-collared Oxford shirt and navy blazer, watching Oprah.

Oprah? Nick?

His long fingers were idly stroking Gonzo's fur. The traitorous beast sat at his feet, making doggie sounds of slavish ecstasy. A lot like she had a short time ago.

Oh, Lord!

"We have to talk, Paula." He waved the divorce papers at her angrily.

"Like we just did in the shower?"

"I didn't plan that. That's not why I came over here."

"Hah! The devil made you do it, then?" She threw down her towel with disgust and finger-combed her hair back off her face.

"Nah, it was some other . . . being," he countered, and winked, looking down between his legs.

Well, she'd stepped into that one. But she'd had enough of his foolishness.

"Listen here, you big jerk. Don't ever, *ever,* break into my apartment again and assault me. Because, believe me, I'll have you arrested. And don't think I can't."

"Assault! Hey, you're suffering a memory lapse here, babe." His strong chin lifted with affront. "You wanted it as much as I did."

She felt her face flame. "Yeah, well, it's not going to happen ever again. I'll get a restraining order if I have to. I mean it. This marriage is over." *So, why do I feel like he'll always be mine?*

"If you think a restraining order would stop me, you've got another thing—"

Holding up a hand to halt his bitter words, Paula tried another tack, "While you're here, Nick, there is something I wanted to tell you." Her voice softened. "I got my master's degree last week. Finally."

"Oh, Paula, that's wonderful!"

She knew that Nick's enthusiasm was genuine. She'd been an elementary school teacher, attending college at night the past three years to get a master's degree in social work. He, more than anyone, knew how much time and heart she'd put into her studies.

He stood and opened his arms for her, to hug her in congratulation. She ducked and stepped away. No way could she risk the temptation of his touch. Again.

Suddenly, he seemed to think of something, and an emotion like fear transformed his handsome face. "You're not . . . oh, no . . . don't tell me. You're not quitting your job, are you?"

"Yes, I am. I have a couple of interviews set up, including the Patterson Projects, as a youth activity coordinator."

"No! That's a DMZ, the most dangerous section of the city. You can't!"

"Yes, I can, Nick, and there's nothing you can do about it. And while we're on the subject, I want you to stop having patrols go by here every night. I'm a grown woman, not a baby. I can take care of myself."

Nick cringed as all the old arguments resonated between them. This was not the point of her telling him her news.

"Paula, honey, let's not fight."

"Don't you honey me. And fighting is the only thing we do well anymore."

"Not everything," he reminded her gently.

"O-o-oh! It's just like you to think a quick romp in the shower is the answer to everything. Wham-bam, and I'm the cream in your coffee again. You are so predictable."

He flinched at her uncharacteristic crudeness. Nick hated it when she used street talk. He always wanted her to be up on this impossible nice-girls-don't pedestal.

"Give me another chance. We can work things out."

"Nick, don't do this," she cried. "You and I have talked till we're blue in the face. It's over. Dammit, it's over." Her voice cracked with the last words.

Nick's face flushed with angry resolve. He wasn't a man who accepted defeat easily. "Over? Never! I've made mistakes, but—"

"Nick, stop it. Stop it right now."

"Paula, I love you . . ."

She started to cry.

". . . and I think you love me, too . . ."

She hiccupped.

". . . let me just hold you, sweetheart . . ."

She blew her nose.

". . . and maybe we can discover what your . . . ah, problem is . . . what you really want."

She could tell by the stunned look on his face that he immediately regretted his poor choice of words.

"My problem?" she shrieked, her mood changing like quicksilver. "You think I have a problem?"

"That's not what I meant, honey."

"Let me tell you something, Nick—you're right. I do have a problem. I crave things you will apparently never understand. And that's what this divorce is all about. How can a guy who's so smart be so dumb?

I'll see you in court in one week, you turkey. Be there!''

Seconds later, standing out in the hall with the door shut behind him, Nick shook his head. He felt like he'd been blindsided with a sucker punch.

Women!

He didn't need a crystal ball or a psycho psychic, like the one jabbering away on Oprah, to realize he'd screwed up again. But he didn't exactly understand where he'd gone wrong, either.

One week. Seven lousy days.

Maybe he needed some outside help.

Chapter Two

"Crazy . . . out-of-this-world crazy . . . that's what I must be."

Nick continued to mutter as he stepped gingerly up the rickety staircase of the faded yellow structure, wondering whether the rotting planks would hold his 210 pounds. Hell, it would serve him right if he fell and cracked his thick skull. It would be just payment for the stupidest damn thing he'd ever considered doing in all his thirty-five years.

Nick looked furtively back over his shoulder at the busy highway, hoping no one would recognize him entering such an establishment. He'd never live it down. Never.

Grimacing with self-disgust, Nick knocked on the door before he lost his nerve. Tapping his foot impatiently, he studied the hand-lettered sign in the grimy window: MADAME NADINE: FORTUNE TELLING, LOVE POTIONS, MIRACLES. And in smaller letters at the bottom: HAIR WAXING AND TATTOOS, BY APPOINTMENT.

He should turn around and go home.

But the prospect of another night, alone, turned his blood cold. Besides, he had only seven days left until . . . until . . . oh, God!

Nick took a deep, painful breath. He felt like a vise was squeezing his heart.

This time he rapped harder and the door was jerked open.

"C'mon in, honey. I been expectin' you."

Nick's mouth dropped open incredulously, but not at the words of invitation.

The woman standing before him—only a few inches shorter than his six-foot-one—had stuffed her big-boned, overweight body into a tight purple dress covered with huge yellow sunflowers. Lots of sunflowers. So bright they made his eyes water.

A cigarette hung from her crimson lips, its long ash threatening to fall onto her mammoth bosom at any moment. Its acrid odor filled the air, and smoke streamed about in misty, eerie clouds.

"Whattaya mean, you've been expecting me?" Nick finally choked out.

"You been drivin' by every day for weeks, too proud to ask for my help." She flashed him a toothy, gloating smile. "Guess you weren't desperate enough . . . till today."

Yup, desperate, that's me. Desperate and nuts.

Nick followed the floozy into a bright sitting room with windows on three sides and dozens of pots filled with flowers of every variety imaginable. Outside, the heads of sunflowers the size of hubcaps peeped over the window sills. He raised an eyebrow in question,

175

and Madame Nadine—he presumed she was Nadine—raised all six of her chins defensively. "We don't got flowers where I come from."

Where's that? he wondered. Probably prison.

"Are you a gypsy?" he asked suddenly. Weren't gypsies supposed to be especially good at fortune-telling and stuff? If she was a gypsy, maybe she really did have some talent that could help him.

The blowzy babe flashed him a look of utter disbelief. "The only gypsies I know are moths. You want a gypsy psychic, you better call one of them 900 numbers."

Nick barely heard her. His eyes kept coming back to the growing ash on her cigarette, amazed that it still held on.

Noticing the direction of his gaze, the fortune-teller added, "We don't got cigarettes where I come from, either." She put her hands on her hips belligerently. "Any objections?"

"Nah, I used to smoke myself."

"I know."

"Huh?"

"Sit down," she ordered, shoving him rudely into a straight-backed chair drawn up to a round table in the center of the room. Immediately, three cats slithered up and rubbed themselves sinuously against his pant leg. He shivered. Lord, he'd hated cats ever since he was a kid in the projects and the super's answer to rat control was cats. Every time he saw a cat, he remembered . . . well, he remembered too much.

He raised his eyes mutinously to the woman who was easing her ample rear into the chair opposite him. Two more cats ambled in and jumped up onto her wide lap.

"Let me guess. You don't have cats where you come from, either." When she didn't answer, he

176

NAME: _____

ADDRESS: _____

_____

_____

TELEPHONE: _____

E-MAIL: _____

_____ I want to pay by credit card.

___ Visa   __ MasterCard   __ Discover

Account Number: _____

Expiration date: _____

SIGNATURE: _____

Send this form, along with $2.00 shipping and handling for your FREE books, to:

Historical Romance Book Club
20 Academy Street
Norwalk, CT 06850-4032

Or fax (must include credit card information!) to: 610.995.9274.
You can also sign up on the Web at <u>www.dorchesterpub.com</u>.

asked, "Do you charge extra for cat hair?" *Damn, I'll be covered with hair when I get home. Probably smell like cat, too.*

"You've got a smart mouth on you, boy. Be careful or I won't help you."

His eyes widened hopefully. *Oh, please, God, I need help so bad.* "Can you help me?"

"Do angels have wings?"

"I don't know. Do they?"

Ignoring his sarcasm, Madame Nadine reached under the fringed tablecloth and pulled out a round glass ball, open on one side. She dusted it off on the hem of her dress and plunked it ceremoniously in the center of the table. It was the most pitiful-looking crystal ball he'd ever seen—more like an upended fish bowl, or a ceiling light globe.

"So, what's your problem, sonny? Want a tattoo? Or a body waxing? Yeah, I bet that's it. You're one of them Fabio guys, right? You want your chest hairs removed so you can pose for a romance novel?"

He slapped a hand to his chest defensively. "You're not pluckin' anything from my body. No way!"

"Fortune told?"

"Well . . . maybe." Nick could feel his face flame. But he never blushed. And he'd never been shy about expressing himself before, about *anything*. What was wrong with him? "I was thinking more on the lines of . . . well . . . oh, hell . . . a love potion."

Madame Nadine's ash finally fell into the cleavage of her dress, and she immediately lit up another cigarette. He watched, fascinated, as she blew a waft of smoke his way, which hovered in the air, then swirled about the glass globe, finally filling it with a murky sheen. Then she turned her attention back to him, studying his face with disconcerting thoroughness.

"A love potion ain't gonna do you diddly squat, sweet cakes. You need *big* help."

Tell me about it! "How do you know?"

Madame Nadine shrugged. "You are one screwed-up hombre. But maybe you're not hopeless yet. Start from the beginning, and let's see if we can unravel this mess you've made of your life."

This was ridiculous. He'd been a fool even to enter this rat trap. The chick was a scam artist if he'd ever seen one, and he ought to know. He stood abruptly and threw a few bills on the table. "Thanks for your trouble, but I've changed my mind."

He hightailed it for the door.

She called after him, "Don't wait too long, sweetie. You only got seven days left."

The fine hairs stood out on his neck as he pivoted slowly. "What did you say?"

"You only got seven days till your divorce is final, hon." She was leaning back in her chair, blowing smoke rings with studied casualness. "If you want to save your marriage, you better not dawdle."

"Who . . . are . . . you?" he asked, spacing his words evenly, as he plopped back down into his chair.

"Madame Nadine. The answer to your prayers. So, you better start showin' some respect."

He pressed the fingertips of one hand to his eyes, closing them tiredly for a second. Paula refused to see him, or take his phone calls. How could he save his marriage if she wouldn't talk to him? Despair enveloped him like a shroud. He had nowhere else to turn.

When he unshuttered his eyes, Madame Nadine patted his hand compassionately. He could swear he felt a tingling sensation where her skin brushed his.

"Tell me what happened, and let's see what we can do," she advised and lit another stinking cigarette.

Nick surprised himself by spilling his guts, giving her a brief capsule of his problem, finally ending, "So, even though Paula and I have been separated for a year, the divorce doesn't become final until next Wednesday."

"How long you been married?"

"Five years."

"Why did you split?"

"She left me," he admitted bleakly.

"And you just let her go? And you waited till now to try to get her back?" She looked at him as if he was the most brainless, ass-backwards blockhead in the world.

He was. It must show on his face.

"Just like a man. Dumber'n a doornail." She made a tsking sound of disapproval. "Do you love her?"

His throat closed over, and he had trouble speaking. Finally, he answered in a raspy voice, "Yes."

"And does she still love you?"

"Yes . . . no . . . damned if I know." He blinked rapidly, feeling his eyes begin to water. It must be the damn cigarette smoke. "Paula said that in the end love wasn't enough."

Madame Nadine nodded as if she understood perfectly. He wished he did.

"And now you want her back?"

"Desperately."

"Desperate is good." She ground her butt into an ashtray and studied the cloudy fish bowl, waving her long fingers over it with a practiced flourish. Then she raised her two hands in a *voilà* fashion. "It's simple."

"What's simple?" he asked, frowning. Had he missed something here? Maybe his brain was becoming numb from nicotine and cat breath.

"All you need to do is find your wife's heart craving."

Some memory flickered at the back of Nick's mind. Hadn't that psycho shrink on Oprah said something about men needing to discover what women craved? And, holy cow, the last time he'd seen Paula, she'd said he didn't have a clue as to her *cravings*.

"Heart craving? What the hell is a heart craving?"

"That's for you to discover," Madame Nadine said with a mysterious smile. Then she added dismissively, "That'll be twenty dollars. Shut the door on your way out."

Stunned, Nick watched as Madame Nadine waddled toward a beaded curtain on the other side of the room.

"But I don't understand. What kind of craving? For food? Like chocolate? Or sex? Or kids? What?"

But Madame Nadine was gone. The only thing left was her cigarette smoke—and about two zillion cat hairs on his dark trousers.

And the words, "Heart craving, heart craving, heart craving . . ." echoing in Nick's puzzled brain.

Three hours later, Nick was at the bookstore in the mall, doing another really dumb thing.

He'd decided to seek some reference materials.

When the sales clerk stepped away for a moment, he punched "craving" into the computer, and about two hundred entries came up, most of them in the "human sexuality" section. He wondered idly if that was different from the "unhuman sexuality" section.

So, the craving thing did refer to sex, after all. Well, he could handle that.

Not that he didn't know his way around the block, and then some. And not that he and Paula had ever had sex problems. But . . . *Hmmm,* maybe there was something he'd been missing all these years. Or, rather, something she'd been missing.

Women were always examining things to death— reading how-to books, trying to make their relationships better. They watched too much Oprah, in his opinion.

But he had an open mind. Maybe something new had been invented in the sex department recently that he hadn't heard about yet.

And, frankly, he was willing to try anything at this point. *Anything.* Yeah, he was cool with this stuff. He was a nineties guy. He was willing to learn.

Aliens must have stolen his brain.

Still, Nick gave himself a mental push and headed toward the sex books.

An hour later, a dozen books lay at his feet, and Nick was bug-eyed and gape-mouthed with amazement. "Who reads all this stuff?" he muttered.

"My wife," a skinny guy of about ninety answered with a groan. His trousers were hiked up practically to his armpits, and four inches of white socks showed at the ankles. "Lorna—that's my honey—Lorna says she wants to spice up our lives. I think she's tryin' to kill me." He grinned with lewd satisfaction.

"Get outta here!"

"It's the truth." The gray-haired codger pulled a paperback from the shelf and handed it to Nick. "This is Lorna's favorite."

Nick turned the slim volume over in his hands and read the title aloud: *How to Make Your Baby's Motor Hum When Her Engine Needs a Tune-Up.*

"The diagrams are pretty good, I must say." The old coot winked suggestively.

God! Against his better judgment, Nick flicked through the book till he came to the illustrations. Turning his head this way and that, he tried to figure out just where the "spark plug" was on this particular model.

"I think you have it upside down," his newfound friend informed him.

"I don't believe this," Nick said when he finally figured out the drawings.

"I'm partial to the chapter on lube jobs."

"Did you get a look at this dipstick?" Nick exclaimed, with a low whistle. "This guy must need a wheelbarrow to haul his equipment around."

"Lorna calls me Mr. Eveready—"

Nick slanted him an incredulous look.

"—but, I must say, that fella musta invented the expression 'hung like a horse'."

Nick slammed the book shut with disgust and put it back on the shelf. Then he gathered up the pile of books at his feet, wanting to put as much space as possible between himself and this old-age pervert.

Just before he turned away, the guy added, with a chuckle, "And, I must say, the book has good advice on how to prime her starter."

Yep, I'm going off the deep end.

"Was that guy bothering you?" a teenage girl at the checkout asked as he stacked the twelve books he'd chosen on the counter. "The manager says he's harmless, but I think he's a pre-vert. Do you want us to call security?"

Nick shook his head with amusement. "Nah, he's okay."

Cracking her chewing gum loudly, the girl began to call out his purchases as she rang them up on the register, *out loud,* in a grating, sing-song voice.

"*Women's Sexual Fantasies,* $4.95."

"Miss, do you think it's necessary—"

"*Two-hour Orgasms,* $10.99."

"Can you keep your voice down?"

182

"Huh?" She stared at him blankly, then went on, "*The All-Time, Most Spectacular Sexual Position in the World,* $34.50. Criminey! $34.50? I hope it's worth it."

"I hope so, too," Nick murmured.

"*Women Who Ejaculate,* $15.95."

The man in line behind Nick craned his neck over his shoulder and whispered, "Where'd you get *that* one?"

Nick pointed and the man, along with two others, left the line and headed back toward the section on human sexuality.

"Listen, can you just hurry this up?"

Ignoring him, the girl yelled to a clerk on the other side of the store, at least a mile away, "Hey, Hank, can you look up the price on this one? *G-Spots and Love Knots.*"

Every single person in the store turned to look at him. Nick thought he'd like to put a knot in the big-mouth's tongue.

That night, Nick ordered pizza and sat down in his living room, surrounded by his purchases, planning a long night of "research." He was going to save his marriage, or die trying.

The high school student who delivered his pizza an hour later scanned the room while Nick dug in his pockets for a tip. The kid snickered over the titles, boasting, "I know everything in these books."

"Yeah! You wish!"

The teenaged Casanova picked up one paperback, exclaiming, "Hey, I read this one. *A Thousand Ways to Kiss Your Lover.*"

"Go away," Nick said, shoving the money in his hand. First, he got advice from a senior citizen, now a pimply-faced adolescent.

Walking away, the know-it-all called over his

shoulder with a laugh, "You oughta try the slide kiss. The women melt every time."

"You wouldn't know melt if it hit you in the face." Nick slammed the door shut. "Smart-ass," he added to the closed door.

Then he couldn't resist. He picked up the book in question, turned to the index and moved his fingertip until he found "slide kiss." He read the brief chapter. *Wow!* A few moments later, he added "slide kiss" to the list on his notepad.

It was midnight before Nick finished the last book. He studied the voluminous notes he'd taken and saw a common thread in many of the books. In fact, he'd written an exact quote from one of the texts: "In their hearts, many women crave sexual fantasy."

Hearts. Crave. Sexual Fantasy.

Hell, that was a definition for heart craving if he'd ever heard one.

Nick leaned back in his chair, crossed his hands behind his neck and grinned. He had the solution to his problem.

Paula didn't stand a chance.

Chapter Three

Day Two

Paula kept glancing toward the entrance of the diner, half expecting Nick to stroll in. She'd avoided him all last night and today, but she suspected he wouldn't give up easily.

She took another sip of coffee and scrutinized the woman sitting across the table, her good friend, Kahlita Simmons. The short, energetic black woman had slicked-back hair and horn-rimmed glasses that said a lot about her no-nonsense attitude toward life. Paula needed some no-nonsense advice on how to handle Nick's persistence.

Paula peeked at her watch anxiously. "I only have ten more minutes until my appointment with my lawyer."

"You're signing the papers today?"

Paula nodded. "Nick refuses to sign the ones that

were served on him yesterday.''

"Skip says he's acting crazy.'' Kahlita was engaged to Skip Bratton, a Newark policeman, and a good friend of his.

"I know. He called at least ten times last night and left the most touching messages on my answering machine. I can't listen without crying.''

"Paula, the man clearly loves you. And you love him. Isn't there any chance you can work this out?''

"No. I wish there was. Nick and I have been separated this past year, but you know, Kahlita, it's not the first time we've split. And I can't tell you how many times we've tried to work it out. Counseling. Separations. Arguments. Over and over. The man just can't change. He wants to, I think. And he tries, but he just can't change.''

"And you can't live with him the way he is?''

"Could you? He's obsessed.''

"There are a lot of women who would grab him in a nano-second. In fact, Skip fixed him up one night with . . .'' Her words trailed off as she saw what must look like horror on Paula's face. "Oh, God, I'm sorry. I didn't think—I mean, I thought you knew.''

"Nick's been dating?'' she asked in a shaky voice. "Who?''

"Well, not exactly dating. See, Skip fixed him up with this stripper—''

"Nick went out with a stripper?''

"No, but Skip introduced him to one, and she's only a stripper on the side. Actually, Laura Bishop—her stage name is Jezebel—attends Harvard Med School. Anyhow, before he even finished one drink, Nick went to the men's room and never came back. He told Skip later that she was too mud-ugly for him.'' Kahlita laughed softly at some memory. "Skip told me that Laura is a former runner-up for Miss New Jersey.''

Paula shouldn't have been relieved, but she was.

"And Lizzie Phillips, that new police trainee, has had the hots for Nick for months. Guar-an-teed, the ink won't be dry on the divorce papers before she launches a frontal attack. And believe me, she could do it with those bosoms of hers.'' Kahlita put two cupped hands in front of her chest to demonstrate.

Paula had met Lizzie, and she was actually a very nice, very attractive young woman. Her heart ached to think that Nick would soon be free to date other women, even if he hadn't already. Then she glanced up at Kahlita with suspicion. "I know what you're doing. You're trying to make me jealous so I'll get back with Nick.''

Kahlita ducked her head sheepishly.

"If I thought there was even the remotest chance of Nick changing, I'd be back in his arms in a flash. It just isn't going to happen.'' She sighed deeply with resignation and stood. Shifting her shoulder bag into place, she laid some money on the table and added, "It's time to get on with my life. And Nick, too. I'm sure that once we're divorced, I'll start to get over him. All the old cravings will go away, eventually.''

Brave words, she thought, as she entered her lawyer's building down the street, *but I'm deathly afraid Nick is the only man I'll ever crave.*

Two hours later, Paula was cruising down the highway, dabbing at her eyes with a tissue. In the orange glow of the setting sun, she could see the final legal papers she'd picked up at her lawyer's office sitting on the passenger seat. A reminder of everything wonderful she'd had in her life—and lost.

Oh, Nick! Why can't you change?

Sighing with regret, Paula glanced idly in the rearview mirror. And saw the blinking red-and-blue light.

Immediately, she checked her speedometer, and groaned. She was going fifteen miles over the speed limit.

"Great! That's all I need today. My life is going down the toilet, and now I get a speeding ticket, besides. What next?"

The berm of the highway was too narrow, so she veered off at the next exit and drove a short distance down a rural road before she could find a large enough area to pull over. The marked police car followed close behind.

Muttering with self-disgust at her carelessness, she had her license, registration, and insurance papers ready before the uniformed cop walked up. Rolling down her window, she handed him the cards.

"Where's the fire, lady?" a gruff voice asked.

"I wasn't really going *that* fast, officer. Only—"

"Step out of the car, ma'am," he cut her off in a stern, muffled voice. Paula glanced up, but all she could see was a strong male jaw and a flash of suntanned skin, shaded by dark sunglasses and a hat. Before she could look closer, the tall, rangy figure turned his back on her and began examining her cards. Over his wide shoulders, he asked, in an extremely deep, gravelly voice, "Is that Miss or Mrs. DiCello?"

She swallowed hard. With the divorce pending, she suddenly realized . . . oh, Lord . . . in six more days, would she be Miss once again? She wasn't sure, but for now, she replied, "Mrs."

He nodded, as if pleased by her answer. "Any outstanding warrants?" His head was averted, looking down at the small clipboard in front of him as he wrote.

"No."

"Last speeding ticket?"

"Two months ago, but I can explain. It was a reduced speed zone and—"

"Save it for the judge, sweetheart."

She thought she heard a smile in his voice. He probably heard hundreds of excuses every day. In fact, Nick once told her about a lady who, when caught speeding, said she was ovulating and had to get home to make love with her husband before her body temperature changed. She smiled to herself as she recalled how she and Nick had spent that afternoon in bed as well, making slow, delicious love. And definitely raising some body temperatures.

There she went, thinking about Nick again. Paula forcibly brought her thoughts back to the present.

"Drug convictions?"

"Absolutely not."

"Prostitution?"

"I resent this questioning. I just came from my lawyer's office. I'm going to call him right now." She turned, about to open the car door and get her cellular phone.

"Put your hands on the roof of the car and spread your legs," the policeman snapped.

"Not on your life—*oompf!*" The cop had put his palm on the center of her back and shoved her up against the car. Her breasts, covered by a silk tank top, pressed into the driver's window. Her belly, under a long, gauzy skirt, flattened against the warm metal of the door. "Hey! Who do you think you are? You can't do this."

"Wanna bet?" With one deft movement, he forced her arms up and over the top of the car. A knee between the back of her legs quickly separated and spread her legs.

This can't be happening to me. Not after all the

years that Nick warned me about all the dangers out here and the precautions to take. She prayed that another car would drive by soon, take in the situation, and stop. But she realized with dismay that not one car had approached the lonely spot thus far.

The officer's large hands brushed over the filmy fabric covering her buttocks, and alarm bells went off in her head.

"Is this the kind of outfit a *lady* wears to her lawyer's?"

"That's none of your business."

His hands continued on a slow, frisking path along her sides. Over her waist. The sides of her breasts. Her armpits. And higher, over her shoulders and along her arms.

"What do you think you're doing?" she cried out in panic. She tried, futilely, to squirm free from his imprisoning arms and legs.

"Full body search."

"For what?" Skepticism and outrage had turned her voice shrill.

He hesitated, then murmured, "Contraband."

"I'm going to report you," she warned.

"Go right ahead,"

"This is not standard operating procedure. Believe me, I know lots of cops."

He chuckled. "I'll bet you do, honey."

Paula felt his breath against the back of her neck. The hard ridge between his legs pressed against her bottom. The fragrance of a woodsy aftershave drifted around her. Hauntingly familiar, yet different. Evocative of forbidden, secret delights.

The back of her neck prickled as an elusive memory tugged at the back of her mind.

Paula pressed her cheek against the roof of the car and spread the palms of her outstretched arms. Perhaps if she didn't struggle, this whole sordid experience would be over in moments and she could just go home.

She watched, mesmerized, as the long fingers of his hands skimmed the surface of her bare skin from shoulders to elbows to wrists. For a second, the hands paused, then lay over hers, gently, dwarfing them with their size. Dark skin against light. A leather watchband. A gold wedding band.

Wedding band!

Paula blinked and looked again at the hand that rested intimately over hers, then moved to the side. Two gold wedding bands, side by side. Identical.

Tears filled her eyes as recognition hit her.

She struggled in earnest now. "Let me go."

"Never."

"You bastard!" Paula let loose with a number of expletives then, too furious to curb her tongue. She couldn't stop looking at the two matching wedding rings.

The cop just laughed softly with appreciation. "I love it when you talk dirty, honey."

"Is it worth losing your job?"

"Yes," he said without hesitation.

Paula's heart skipped a beat at that one simple word. What did he mean?

Then she couldn't think at all.

Outrageously, the policeman swept the long strands of her hair behind her ear, exposing her neck to the nuzzling of his warm lips. He bit the lobe of her ear, softly, and inserted the tip of his tongue in its crevices.

"Just what kind of search is this?" she choked out.

"Cavity search," he growled—a hungry, masculine sound, both threatening and tantalizing—then traced the sensitive whorls with expert precision.

Paula groaned. Sweet, erotic tingles spread from the teasing movements of his tongue in her ear to her breasts, which swelled and peaked. A dull ache began to grow at the vee of her legs.

She was no longer frightened of a strange cop. She was frightened of herself and her unwilling surrender to the dangerous, erotic fantasy.

"You're going to get arrested," she gasped as his fingers found her nipples and played with them.

"Probably." He didn't sound at all concerned.

Impatiently, he tugged her shirt from the waistband of her skirt and his hands moved up over her bare skin to her lace-covered breasts, molding them to fit his palms, tugging at the nipples, rolling them between his fingers. All the time, he whispered sexy, explicit words in her ears about what he would like to do to her, what he intended to do to her.

"O-o-oh!"

Paula's thighs grew heavy and weak. She almost swooned with the sheer agonizing pleasure that rolled over her body in waves.

This was some wanton creature Paula did not recognize. It couldn't be she, undulating her hips against his hardening erection, arching her back to give him greater access to her aching breasts, her flat stomach, and lower.

She'd been so lonely since Nick had left. Yesterday's lovemaking in the shower had only whetted a hunger she'd thought long dead. That was the only excuse for her body's betrayal.

Determined male hands bunched the fabric of her skirt in gathering fists, lifting the hem higher and higher, up to the sides of her bikini panties. Then, in one hard jerk, they ripped away both sides of her underpants. The silky fabric fell to the ground, exposing her still widespread legs to exploring fingers.

One hand moved back up to her breasts, fingering them lightly. The other hand found her wet heat.

"My God!" he exclaimed behind her, his lips pressed against the pulse beat in her neck. Then, "Sweet. Oh, baby, you are so sweet."

She almost fainted. Then she bucked back against him, trying to break free, to no avail.

He nipped her shoulder with his teeth, asserting his controlled aggression.

She pressed her forehead against the car roof, barely able to stand as his expert fingers found her pleasure points and played a tortuous game of fluttery music.

Just then she heard a car motor approaching.

"Holy hell! Don't move," he ordered, shielding her body with his own as the pick-up truck slowed, then continued down the highway past them.

Paula barely noticed. And yelling for help was the last thing on her mind.

She started to look back at him over her shoulder. The rasp of a zipper stopped her.

Then her hips were being lifted and tilted backward into the cradle of a hard male body. Her sandaled feet barely touched the road.

In one long stroke, he entered her, and Paula couldn't suppress the keen of pure ecstasy. Her body welcomed him with rippling convulsions that seemed to make him grow inside her, harder and thicker, filling her to excess. And more.

He moaned, low in his throat. A raw, savage noise.

When her first climax passed, he lifted her hips higher, penetrating her even deeper. Then he began to move. Long, slow thrusts, accompanied by seductive murmurs. Forbidden words. Scandalous thoughts. Fantasies, imagined but never spoken aloud.

"Do you like that, sweetheart?"

"Oh . . . oh, yes!"

"And that?"

"Please . . ."

"Can I touch you there?"

She put a restraining hand on his wrist, shocked, then lifted it in sweet, reckless surrender.

"Would you like to be handcuffed?"

"I don't know. Maybe."

"You're my prisoner."

"Yes."

"You can't escape."

"I know."

"You have to do what I say. Everything."

Hot, sensual images flashed through her mind. Wicked. Dark. Taboo. She licked her lips. "And if I don't?"

"I'll stop. Do you want me to stop?"

"Never."

When his strokes turned short and hard, Paula became mindless, incapable of thought or talk. A hot tide of molten sensation engulfed her. She fought her orgasm, and raced toward it, out of control.

The twilight air resonated with the sounds of crickets from the nearby woods, and heavy breathing. His and hers. Melded. In rhythm.

When the final climax came—a shattering explosion of the senses—he drew back one last time and slammed into her, his thighs braced rigid with tension, the sinews of his arms roped with muscles. They cried out their release, together, and gasped for breath as her searing sheath continued to caress him with smaller and smaller spasms until, whimpering, she could bear no more. And he wilted with the intensity of his release.

Softly, he kissed the back of her neck.

After a long moment, he pulled out of her and let

her feet slide to the ground. But his arms continued to hold her from behind, one around her waist, the other gently stroking her arms and shoulders and hair. She could feel his heart thudding wildly against her back.

Finally, he turned her in his arms, still pressed against the car. He must have removed his hat and sunglasses before making love with her. His short-clipped hair was as thick and black as a moonless night.

His eyes held hers for a long, poignant moment in question, perhaps wondering if she was angry, or pleased. Blue pools of passion surrounded by thick, black spidery lashes. So beautiful.

Slowly, he lowered his head. With tenderest care, his full lips brushed her mouth. A pleading caress. No demands here. A lover's kiss.

Then he drew back and grazed his knuckles along her jaw and tilted her chin upward.

Paula could see the sexual satisfaction in his misty eyes and parted lips. And she saw the silent sadness on his face, as well.

"Come home, Paula," he pleaded huskily. "Please, come home."

Chapter Four

"Come home?" Paula repeated.

Time seemed to stand still as Nick waited for Paula's answer. Surely, they would reconcile after what had just happened between them.

He couldn't believe his plan had gone so well. Hell, satisfying this heart-craving business was going to be a snap. And more damn pleasure than he'd ever imagined in his hottest wet dreams.

Now, all he had to do was get Paula to come home with him, and he'd spend the rest of his life fulfilling every sexual fantasy—every heart craving—she could ever have. And then some.

Who was he kidding? He'd forgotten his plan the moment she'd stepped from the car. He couldn't have stopped himself from touching her if his life depended on it. He'd been celibate for so long—a year, in fact, until yesterday.

And he had to admit, she'd surprised the spit out

of him. He had never been so demanding in the four years they'd been together. Or suggested such exotic sexual activity. And, hot damn, she'd liked it. A lot.

He brushed several strands of silky auburn hair off her face, and she swatted his hand away. That was his first clue that fantasy island was fast becoming a mirage.

The second clue came right after that, when he rubbed the pad of his thumb over her passion-swollen lips, and she bit him, hard.

"Ouch! Why'd you do that?" He stepped back, sucking on the sore appendage. With a sigh, he then adjusted himself inside his pants and zipped up. The cold, angry glitter in her green eyes did not bode well for sexual seconds.

"Are you crazy?" she lashed out, smoothing down her silk tank top. Her still-aroused nipples stood out like sentinels, and he couldn't help the slow grin that pulled at his lips.

She looked down and grunted with self-disgust, then folded her arms across her chest. "You are a toad."

"Yeah. You wanna check out my warts?" He reached out for her, but she ducked under his arms. "Or we could play leap frog."

"Aaarrgh! Would you stop kidding around?" She reached down with a groan of dismay and picked up her torn panties, stuffing them into her skirt pocket. Turning back to him, she asked tiredly, "What did you hope to accomplish here—no, let me guess. You figured a quick screw on the side of the road, and I'd drop the divorce petition. God, you must have a low opinion of me."

He cringed at her vulgar assessment. "We made love, Paula. And you're just mad because you enjoyed it so much."

"I did not," she said, raising her chin defensively.

"Liar."

"And stop grinning at me."

He shrugged and grinned even wider.

"You are such a rat."

He jiggled his eyebrows. "And that would make you the cheese. Would you like me to eat—"

"Don't even say it!" She began pacing back and forth along the length of the car. "Nick, you caught me in a weak moment, but it's not going to happen again. Ever! You've got to give up. It's over."

"No. No, it's not. If you'd just come home, we could talk—"

"Like we 'talked' just now? Like we 'talked' in the shower yesterday?"

"Why are you being so difficult?"

"Why can't you understand that our marriage is dead? And sex can't resurrect it."

He closed his eyes briefly on that painful thought.

"What are you doing in uniform anyhow? You haven't been in uniform since you made detective ten years ago. I'm surprised it still fits."

"It didn't," he admitted sheepishly. "Skip loaned me his."

"Skip? Oh, you are too much! Dragging other people into our affairs." She blushed as a sudden thought occurred to her. "You didn't tell him why you wanted the uniform, did you?"

"Nah, it's our secret. Listen, honey, it's getting dark. Let's go back to our apartment—I mean, your place—and talk. I promise I won't touch you again. Unless you want me to."

She flashed him a look of utter disbelief. "I'm not going anywhere with you, Nick. And we're getting a divorce six days from now." Tears filled her eyes as she gazed up at him bleakly.

Heart Craving

"I love you, Paula. Doesn't that count for anything?"

"Oh, Nick. Of course, it does. But we've been over this a hundred times before. Your love suffocates me."

He flinched at her harsh words. "I can change."

"No, you can't. You've tried. Many times. But you can't stop smothering me with your obsessiveness."

"I only want to keep you safe. What's wrong with that?"

"Nick, I hated that high-rise prison we lived in."

"It was a maximum security complex," he corrected. "That's why we moved there in the first place. And I got us another place, just like you wanted."

"No, Nick, like *you* wanted. Not me." She shook her head wearily. "A low-rise apartment building with bars on the windows is not my idea of home."

He drew himself up, affronted. "They aren't bars. They're security grills."

"Why couldn't we have lived in the suburbs? All I wanted was a little house with a backyard and an apple tree."

"Uh-uh. Too unsafe, especially close to the city."

She made a clucking sound of disgust. "And my car? I asked for a Volkswagen convertible, and you bought me a Volvo sedan."

"Honey, soft-top cars are an invitation for burglars. For chrissake, you could be attacked at a stoplight, even with the doors locked."

"And Gonzo! Lord, I asked for a Cocker Spaniel, and you gave me a small horse."

"A German Shepherd is one of the best guard dogs." He looked wounded at her lack of appreciation. "I thought you liked Gonzo."

"I love Gonzo. *Now.* But he's not what I wanted."

"So, you're pissed off because of a house, a car, and a damned dog?"

"Aaarrgh! Listen to me for once, you stubborn fool. Those things were just bricks in the wall you were putting up day by day. What hurt the most the last couple of years was your refusal to talk about your work."

He braced himself, knowing what was coming next.

"I had no idea what kind of cases you handled. Sometimes you were so angry, or sad, and you kept it all inside."

"Paula, I'm surrounded by muck in my job. The dregs of humanity. Believe me, you don't want to know about some of the things I witness."

"How do you know what I want, you blockhead? God, you're impossible! And my job—you refused to listen—oh, I give up!" She threw her hands up in the air. "We've been over this a million times."

Nick's pride tempted him to turn on his heel and say, "To hell with it, then." But he couldn't give up without one last salvo, "Don't you love me anymore?"

She averted her eyes.

"Tell me. Say the words, 'I don't love you, Nick'."

A single tear slid down her cheek and she wiped at it angrily.

He felt like a fist was squeezing his heart.

"You know I can't. Not yet," she said on a sob. "But I'm going to learn to stop. And finalizing the divorce is the first step." With determination, she opened her car door and slid behind the steering wheel.

"I have six more days to convince you otherwise," he shouted through the closed window, with equal determination.

"Give it up, Nick. All I crave now is . . ."

Crave? He couldn't hear the rest of her words as she revved the motor and shot out onto the highway. At first, his shoulders slumped with defeat. But then, in the wake of skidding gravel and exhaust fumes, he noticed the oddest thing growing along the road.

A lone sunflower.

Day Three

Nick finished booking the three teenage boys for burglary, carrying an unlicensed firearm, resisting arrest, and possession of narcotics.

"Man, you gonna lock us up again?" the freckle-faced kid with the nose ring whined.

"You bet your stupid ass, I am, Peterman. And this time, I'm asking the judge to send you to Stonegate."

"I ain't goin' to no juvie hall again. Betcha my momma'll have me outta here by tomorrow."

"Not if I can help it! When are you guys gonna learn?" Nick's contemptuous glare took in Peterman, as well as his two buddies, Casale and Lewis. They all wore T-shirts proclaiming the name of their gang, "Blades."

"Learn what?" Casale asked angrily. "You make me puke. You sit in your lily-white houses in your lily-white neighborhood. Whaddayou know what it's like in our hood, Ko-jak?" His intelligent eyes bespoke a deep rage—one Nick, unfortunately, understood too well.

"I know that your way is a dead end street, *Richard.*"

Nick saw Casale grit his teeth at the use of his given name. Somehow, the anonymity of surnames suited these street gangs better. Growing up, Nick doubted anyone ever knew his first name. It was always just, "Hey, DiCello!"

Patiently, in a softer tone of voice, he informed Casale, "Richie, I was born in your hood . . . Patterson Street. I lived in the same project you do, maybe even the same unit." At the look of disbelief on the kid's face, he asked, "Do the halls still smell like spaghetti sauce and urine, all the time?"

Casale blinked with surprise. Then he sneered, "We got us a *crew-say-dah* here, boys. A real Deputy Do-Right. There ain't nothin' worse than a reformed bad boy."

Nick made a blowing noise of exasperation. What was the use? "You do know that the captain wants you guys charged as adults this time?"

A brief spark of fear appeared in Casale's brilliant blue eyes before he masked it with the usual bravado. Of the three, this kid had the most potential to pull himself out of the ghetto dungheap. But he probably wouldn't.

Nick filled in the last of the forms, then motioned for the patrolman at the door to lead them away. Handcuffed and shackled, the trio shuffled down the hallway to the holding pen, arrogant and unremorseful. They knew the way with their eyes closed.

Nick felt a twinge of pity for the stupid kids. Hell, they were only fourteen years old. Yeah, fourteen going on forty! And with rap sheets to rival those of the hardest criminals.

Any sympathy he might have considered died when Lewis looked back over his shoulder and called out, "I'm gonna get you, DiCello. I'm sick of you jerks pickin' me up. Watch your back, you sonofabitch. I got a bullet with your name on it."

Lewis was the most incorrigible gang member he'd encountered in the last few years—a vicious, surly punk with a chip on his shoulder the size of a tomb-stone.

"I'm shivering in my boots," he snapped back.

"Yeah, well, how 'bout your old lady? You even got a chick, you fag?" Lewis asked.

Nick made a low hissing sound.

Seeing that he'd found Nick's vulnerable spot, the creep laughed evilly—how could a kid so young be so evil?—and spelled out graphically, in filthy gutter language, what he could do to Nick's "old lady" to get back at him.

Trembling with fury, Nick started after the hood-lum. But Skip stepped up to him and put a restraining hand on his shoulder. "Let him go, Nick. They all make threats like that. He's just a punk with an atti-tude."

As a final insult, all three delinquents flicked their middle fingers at him.

Nick pressed his forehead against the cold concrete wall, inhaling and exhaling deeply.

And Paula wonders why I don't want to talk about my work. Or why I'm overprotective. Hell!

Finally, his temper cooled. He looked back at Skip—a patrol officer and friend, only twenty-five years old, who worked out of the same precinct. "You off duty now?"

Skip nodded.

"How 'bout going for a beer?"

"Sounds good."

They were about to leave the building when Cap-tain O'Malley called out, "See you tonight, DiCello. Right?" The burly Irishman smirked from ear to ear, then erupted into a deep belly laugh.

Nick felt a flush move up his neck. "Yeah, I'll be there."

"Eight o'clock. The high school gym. Don't be

late." He started laughing again.

"What was that all about?" Skip asked as they walked toward his patrol car.

"I'm going to the prom."

Later, Nick and Skip were nursing their second beers in a neighborhood tavern.

"Stop smirkin' at me," Nick said.

"I can't help it. Geez, I just can't picture you at a prom. Do you even know how to boogie?"

"Boogie? I was thinking more along the lines of dirty danc—"

His words were interrupted by the waitress, who smiled invitingly down at Skip and asked, for the third time in a half hour, "Will there be anything else, sugar?" She totally ignored Nick.

Skip winked. "Not now, darlin'."

Smiling, Nick shook his head at his friend. "Stop flirting with the waitresses. If Kahlita were here, she'd wring your neck. And you're not on stage now, so you have no excuse." Everywhere he went, Skip attracted women. And it wasn't just that he looked like Denzel Washington in an Arnold Schwarzenegger body. Skip exuded sexual charisma without even giving it a thought. *Hmmm. Maybe Skip can give me a little advice.*

"Maybe you ought to moonlight, too," Skip suggested. "Might learn a few tricks to lure Paula back."

Now that was hitting too close to home. Nick winced. "Me? A male stripper? Hardly. Besides, if you're not careful, the captain's gonna hear about your nightclub act. Do you wanna get fired?"

Skip shrugged. "Maybe it would be for the best. The money's better, for sure. And, no kidding . . . Sal is looking for someone to replace Lee as the Indian in the line-up. Lee got moved up to detective. He's working night shift now and had to quit.''

Nick choked on his beer. ''Lee Chin was stripping? As an Indian? Holy hell! He's Chinese.''

Skip grinned. ''Yeah, but the women didn't seem to notice his face. They were lookin' a little . . . lower. Then, too, he can flex his buttocks. I don't suppose you can . . .'' He paused, seeing the look of horror on Nick's face. ''I guess not.''

Smiling, Nick leaned back and sipped at his beer. ''Even if I had the inclination, this aging body couldn't stand the scrutiny of a couple hundred screaming women. I could lift weights till my nose bleeds and still not look like you. Besides, I'm trying to get my wife back, and Paula's not the type to go for male strippers.''

''Actually, Paula and Kahlita came to the club one night. They seemed to be having a good time.'' Skip raised an eyebrow knowingly.

Nick gaped at Skip's grinning face. ''Not my Paula!''

''Maybe you don't know Paula as well as you think.''

Paula had just returned to her apartment that afternoon when the doorbell rang. A delivery man stood there with a stack of boxes imprinted with the name of Bambergers, a popular department store.

At first, Paula frowned with puzzlement when she opened the boxes and peeled away the tissue paper. There was a beautiful, strapless evening gown, white, embroidered with pastel flowers along the bodice and the hem of the full, frothy skirt. In addition, the other boxes contained matching sling-back high heels, sheer silk stockings, and a corsage. *A corsage?*

Paula knew, even before she read the enclosed card. *Nick.*

Sighing, she sank into an easy chair and read. "Will you be my date for the prom tonight? Love, Nick."

Oh, what a low blow! Nick knew that she'd never gone to a dance in her high school days. She'd attended a private Catholic girls' school in the suburbs, which held no such frivolous events. And she'd told him once that it was a part of growing up she'd wanted to experience, but had missed.

Just then, she noticed the red light blinking on her answering machine.

The first call was from her lawyer, reminding her of their court date next Wednesday. *Oh, God! Only five days away. I feel like I have a time bomb ticking away inside my heart.*

Next, her mother invited her to use the beach house at Long Beach Island for the next few weeks. She and her dad planned to visit some friends in Florida.

Finally, Nick's voice came on.

"Paula, don't hang up. Just hear me out. Please, honey, go to the prom with me tonight. Captain O'Malley's daughter is graduating and they need extra chaperons." She heard the chuckle in his voice. *His deep, wonderful voice. The voice she might not be hearing again after this week.* She closed her eyes briefly against the soul-searing pain.

"I know it's not the same, going as chaperons instead of high school seniors. But we could pretend. And, Paula"—his voice deepened with emotion—"I never told you . . . but I never went to a prom, either. And . . . and I really, *really* would like to experience it with you. It's only one night, babe."

"Oh, Nick," Paula murmured, pressing his note against her heart, "why can't you just give it up? Our marriage is over."

"Honey, I know our marriage is over . . ." he said.

206

She jerked to attention. Criminey, was he reading her mind now?

"... but we can still be friends, can't we? And I promise ... I swear to God ... I won't jump your bones."

She smiled grimly. *But how do I stop myself from jumping yours?*

"I'll pick you up at eight. Okay?"

Paula felt her resistance crumbling. She wanted to go to a prom. More important, she wanted to go to a prom *with Nick*. But she shouldn't. If she were smart, she'd take this beautiful dress and send it back to the store. She'd call Nick and tell him she couldn't go.

"Don't try to call me back, hon. I'm driving Skip down to the nightclub. He's gonna teach me how to be an Indian strip dancer. You oughta see me swing my ... tomahawk."

Her mouth dropped open with incredulity.

"Just kidding."

She laughed, despite herself.

"Bye, honey, see you later."

She heard him drop the phone with a loud clatter and a sharp expletive. Then, just before her answering machine clicked off, she thought he muttered something about heart cravings giving him a heartburn.

Chapter Five

"This is not a date, Nick," she said that evening as they were driving to the Montclair high school.

"Right," he agreed, too readily.

Nick flashed her a dazzling smile before turning his attention back to maneuvering the car through the busy parkway traffic.

Just his nearness overwhelmed her. He looked so handsome. She'd never seen him in a tux before. She had to admit that accompanying him to this prom, no matter how foolish, was worth it, just to see him in formal attire. Forget about *Playgirl* centerfolds. Nick in a black tuxedo was sexier than any of the nude models, hands down.

"And we're not getting back together," she asserted. "The divorce still goes through on Wednesday."

His strong hands, lean-fingered and capable, gripped the steering wheel with a vengeance, turning the knuckles white. Staring straight ahead, he agreed, "Right." But there was a gritty tone to his voice.

"And you are most definitely not going to 'jump my bones'."

A grin tugged at his firm lips. "Right."

"No hanky-panky."

He gave her a sideways glance of amusement. "Define hanky-panky."

She laughed. This was the old Nick—the one she'd fallen in love with five years ago. What had changed him into the somber, overly protective, possessive, withdrawn male of recent years? She remembered their early days together when he'd been just like he was now—teasing, carefree, irresistibly charming, devastatingly attractive, sexy as hell. *Oh, Lord, I am playing with fire. This is a big mistake.*

"Did you groan?" he asked.

"No, it was probably the wind." She tossed her head back and let her hair blow in the breeze. "Who lent you the Volkswagen convertible?"

At first, he didn't answer, and she sat up straighter, suddenly suspicious. "Nick?"

"Okay, I bought it for you, but don't get your hackles up. The dealer said you could bring the Volvo in for the trade-in next week. It's not as if it's a gift or anything."

"You traded in my car?" she sputtered. "I don't believe you! You actually traded in my car without asking me?"

"Geez, Paula, you said I never listen to you. Just yesterday, *remember,* you complained that you always wanted a VW convertible and I got you a Volvo."

Tears of frustration smarted her eyes. "You just don't get it, do you, Nick?"

He pulled to a stop in the parking lot of the high

school, flipped off the ignition, and turned toward her, clearly aggravated. "What now? No matter what I do these days, I piss you off. I just can't seem to please you, no matter what. You want a car, you don't want a car. You want a dog, you don't want a dog. You want to move, you don't want to move. Make up your mind."

"Oh, you are a real piece of work, DiCello. Do you really believe our marriage went to hell in a hand-basket over a stupid car? Or a mangy mutt?"

"God knows! Because I sure as hell don't." He got out of the car and stomped around to her side, opening her door with a jerk, almost pulling it off its hinges. When she got out and stood before him, he slammed it shut with a bang. He breathed in and out several times to calm his temper, just the way he always did. Then his shoulders slumped. "C'mon, Paula, let's forget the fighting . . . just for tonight."

She wanted to reach up and smooth the frown from his suntanned forehead, to brush his unruly ebony hair off his face, to erase the look of hurt in his eyes. But all she could do was agree, "Okay. Friends . . . for tonight."

He muttered something foul under his breath about friends.

"What?"

"I said, let's not fight. I didn't say I wanted to be your pen pal." With a grumble of disgust, he took her elbow, leading her toward the school entrance. "And don't be surprised if that VW convertible is stolen while we're inside."

Midnight came too quickly. Time to go home. But Nick didn't want the night to end. "One more dance?" he asked.

"Definitely," Paula said with a sigh. Like a cloud

of her lemony perfume, she drifted into his arms, which encircled her waist. Leaning her head back, she looked up at him dreamily.

She had curled her shoulder-length auburn hair so that it looked expertly mussed and incredibly wanton. Her green eyes appeared misty.

"Thank you, Nick, for a wonderful, wonderful evening. I haven't had this much fun in a long, long time."

"The pleasure was mine, babe," he said, pulling her closer. The band was playing a slow, steamy backdrop to the singer's not-so-bad rendition of "When A Man Loves A Woman."

"I think your captain got a big kick out of you being at a prom," she said with a laugh. Her breath tickled his ear and sent slingshots of white-hot messages to other important parts of his body. "I like him—and his wife, too."

"Yeah. O'Malley's okay. His daughter was a little embarrassed to have her parents here, though."

"Wouldn't you have been, at that age?"

He stiffened with sudden memory. He knew exactly where he'd been the night of his senior prom. And it hadn't been a high school gym. More like the city hospital, watching his mother die of liver failure. Too many years of whatever cheap wine she could scrounge up with her welfare checks. And his father . . . he hadn't seen the worthless bastard since he was five years old.

"Nick . . . Nick . . . what's wrong?"

"Huh?" He forced his thoughts back to the present. Paula was staring at him with concern. "Nothing's wrong. By the way, did I tell you how beautiful you look tonight?"

"Only a hundred times."

She looked so sweet, and seductive at the same

time, in the gown he'd bought for her earlier that day. The strapless top pushed her breasts up, creating a cleavage he'd have liked to sink his hands into. And the skirt billowed out like a froth of white cotton candy, brushing against his legs enticingly as they danced.

No wonder he'd been in a state of blistering half-arousal the entire night.

"You look pretty spectacular yourself, cowboy." She swayed in perfect rhythm with him to the music.

"You think so, huh?" He winked at her. "Does that mean I get to jump your bones?"

She laughed. "Not on your life!"

"How 'bout a drive before I take you home, then?"

"I don't know if that's a good idea," she said dubiously.

He didn't look forward to cramping his body into that motorized tin can, but he'd do anything to keep her at his side just a little longer.

"Aw, c'mon. We're supposed to be pretending this is our senior prom. Don't young kids go out somewhere afterwards? All-night parties. Restaurants. Movies." *Motels.*

"Well, yes, but—"

"Be a sport, Paula. Don't you *crave* a little fantasy?" *Good Lord, I hope so! If not, Madame Nadine is a gold-plated fraud, and I'm the sucker of the year.* "Besides, this might be the last time . . ." His words drifted off. He couldn't voice the possibility that this might be their last time together.

But Paula honed in on the fantasy part. "I think you gave me enough fantasy yesterday to last a lifetime." Her lips parted, reflexively, in remembrance.

You ain't seen nothin' yet, sweetheart. "Just a drive."

Heart Craving

* * *

Nick had driven all the way to Sandy Hook to show her the beautiful sight of a full moon and bright stars shining on the mirrorlike surface of the ocean at low tide. But Paula wasn't fooled for one minute. He'd come here to park and neck . . . and more.

She couldn't be mad at him, though. He'd given her this magical night, a gift to make up for the past year of pain, a special way to end their marriage . . . amicably, without rancor.

They pushed their seats all the way back and arched their necks so they could gaze at the sky. Still, Nick's long legs were bent at the knees, and his tall frame spilled over onto the gear shift. He was definitely not made for a VW.

"Why are you chuckling?" he asked, putting his right arm behind her seat and twirling one of her long curls around a finger.

"I was just thinking that when I asked you for a VW, I never realized that you wouldn't fit."

"Who says I don't fit?" he said, feigning affront.

"I say. Well, at least I'm safe in this cramped space. No way could two people—"

He tugged on her hair, still wrapped around his finger, and pulled her closer. Against her lips, he whispered, "Don't bet on it."

"Nick, you promised," she demurred, faintly, before his lips captured hers, sliding back and forth with exquisite care, teasing, barely touching, just sliding over the wet surface, coaxing.

Finally, she could stand no more. Putting her hands on either side of his face, she held him firmly still and pressed her lips to his.

At first, he made a low chuckling sound deep in his throat, mumbling something about chalking one up for slide kisses. Then he growled and proceeded to take charge of the kiss.

His teeth nipped at her bottom lip. When she opened her mouth to protest, his tongue plunged deep, then withdrew. He devoured her lips in ever-changing kisses—soft, gentle, coaxing caresses, alternating with hot, bruising promises of searing passion.

Waves of longing swept over her, turning her skin hot. Her breasts grew heavy, and the vee between her legs felt molten and damp.

She moaned around his tongue.

He moaned back.

Once, he pulled away, gasping for air. "We're not going to make love," he assured her. "I'll keep my promise."

She nodded, wanting to tell him to forget his promise.

"Just a little necking," he assured her, nuzzling her cheek. "Like two teenagers after their senior prom. A little horny, but not ready to go all the way."

"Are you saying I'm horny?" she asked, trying to sound insulted.

He chucked her under the chin and grinned. "I know I'm horny as hell. Maybe you're just turned on." He put his mouth near her ear and played tongue games with its delicate crevices, whispering, "Are you turned on, babe?"

She thought about lying, then admitted, "Like an oven."

He laughed and, in one expert move, put his hands on her waist and lifted and turned her so that she lay across his lap, breast to chest. Her legs were bent and draped on the passenger seat, and her back pressed into the steering wheel, but she hardly noticed the discomfort because Nick had unzipped the back of her dress and was lowering the bodice of her strapless gown to her waist.

She objected, feebly.

He inhaled sharply, and in the bright moonlight, she could see the hazy mist of want in his half-closed eyes. His parted lips looked thick and swollen from her kisses.

"Oh, Paula, honey . . ." His voice was choked with emotion as he gazed down at her, then touched her nipples lightly with the fingertips of both hands. She keened softly as ripples of intense, almost painful pleasure shot out from her breasts. She threw her head back and arched her chest forward, inviting.

"Show me," he whispered huskily.

And she drew his mouth down.

He cradled the underside of one breast in one hand, pushing upward, then took her hardened nipple, open-mouthed, flicking it with his tongue until she mewled with yearning. Only then did he suckle her in earnest, hard, his cheeks flexing with the rhythm. By the time he gave equal treatment to the other breast, she was gasping for breath.

Nick seemed to have trouble breathing himself.

"So, this is necking, huh?" she teased when he finally looked up at her.

"Well, maybe we've progressed to petting," he admitted, smiling sheepishly.

"Do you suppose teenage girls do this, as well?" she asked, reaching between their bodies and running her palm over the ridge of his erection. She wanted to give as much enjoyment as he was giving her.

He groaned as if in agony, flinging his head back against the seat, as she continued to fondle him in the way he liked best. Suddenly, he stiffened and set her back in her own seat with an abruptness that startled her.

Jerking the car door open, he walked onto the beach and bent over at the waist, clasping his thighs, inhaling and exhaling with labored breaths. Finally, he stood and just stared out over the ocean, a bleak, lonely figure.

Confused, Paula adjusted her gown and stepped out of the car. Putting her hand on his arm, she asked, "Nick, what's wrong?"

"I promised I wouldn't jump your bones tonight."

"Well, maybe . . . well, maybe I changed my mind."

"About the divorce?" he asked hopefully.

"No, of course not. Just about . . . you know."

His jaw clenched angrily. "Well, I want more than a quick lay."

"Nick, don't ruin tonight by arguing. It was a wonderful evening. I didn't know how much I had craved this kind of thing. It was like a fantasy come true."

"You craved the fantasy?" he said with decided interest, his face no longer so despondent.

"I guess I did. Deep in my heart."

He said the oddest thing then, "Thank you, Lord . . . and Madame Nadine. At least I'm on the right track."

Day Four

"Ouch! I thought you said this wouldn't hurt."

"No, darlin', you asked me if getting a tattoo might fulfill your wife's 'heart craving', and I said it probably wouldn't hurt. It's not the same thing."

Sitting on a high stool, Nick tried to peer back over his shoulder at Madame Nadine, who was working with concentration on his right shoulder blade. Or at least as much concentration as she could muster with that blasted cigarette hanging out of her mouth, cats meowing all over the place, and flowers sucking all the oxygen out of the air. Or did flowers give off oxygen? He couldn't remember in the midst of his pain.

"Ouch!" he said again.

"Stop moving. I can't see."

Hah! He didn't know how she could see anyhow in the glare of her bright orange dress embroidered all over with neon yellow sequined sunflowers. The broad did have a thing about sunflowers.

"Watch you don't burn me with that damn cigarette," he grumbled as her two-inch ash grazed and crumbled against the back of his neck.

Madame Nadine mumbled something that sounded an awful lot like "Up yours." But he was probably mistaken.

Just then, her needle hit a particularly sensitive spot and Nick almost shot out of his chair. "Are you sure you didn't work for Hitler in another life?"

"Tsk-tsk! No pain, no gain," she remarked blithely.

"Easy for you to say! What kind of tattoo are you putting there anyhow? It better not be one of those hokey snakes. Or a skull and crossbones. I want something to impress Paula, not gross her out. How about two linked hearts?"

"Puh-leeze, I'm an artiste. I am creative. I am—"

"—a fraud," he muttered under his breath.

"I heard that, young man," she said. "Watch your mouth, or I won't help you anymore. And I still think you should have let me put the tattoo on your privates. It's the latest thing, you know."

"Get real!"

"Would you consider a genital earring?"

"You're not getting within a mile of these family

jewels.'' He placed both hands protectively over said treasures. ''And you'd better hurry up. I only have another ten minutes left on my lunch hour.''

Finally, she finished and told him how to care for the tattoo over the next few days. He tried to peer at her creation over his shoulder but she kept distracting him, blabbing on about how she'd gotten a ticket the day before for failing to procure a business license and could he fix it for her. He kept telling her he didn't work in that division, but somehow she managed to talk him into seeing what he could do.

After putting his shirt back on and slapping fifty dollars on the table, he asked the question he'd wanted to ask for the past half hour—the real reason he'd stopped by to visit Madame Nadine once again. ''So, how do you think I'm doing on this heart craving business?''

Madame Nadine blew a smoke ring the size of an inner tube his way and, in the midst of his coughing, she said, ''You tell me, sonny boy. Has she torn up the divorce papers yet?''

''No,'' he said on a groan of despair.

''Is she weakening?''

Remembering last night's senior prom fantasy, Nick felt his face grow hot. Since he never blushed, he figured it must be the lack of air-conditioning.

Madame Nadine raised an eyebrow questioningly. When he declined to tell her the intimate details, she smiled knowingly. ''Some progress then, huh?''

''A little, but not enough. The bottom line here is that I have less than three days. Any clues on how I can speed this along?''

She looked down at his crotch, then over to her tray of tiny earring loops.

''Forget it!''

He was already headed for the door, ignoring her

chuckles, when she added, "I don't suppose you'd like to give your wife a cat? Gargoyle's gettin' bored with me . . . seems to be lookin' for a new home."

"No way! Absolutely not! Never!" He looked back at the feline parked on her lap, a tabby the size of a small automobile, and shivered. It was licking its chops and gazing at him with a condescending I-know-something-you-don't cat grin, probably thinking, "What a chump!"

Nick's upper lip curled with distaste. "I hate cats."

"I know."

"Huh?"

"Maybe you should learn to conquer your fears."

"Maybe you should stick to hair plucking and crystal fish bowls. I will never, *ever* have a cat for a pet."

He turned toward the door again.

"Not even if it could help you get your wife back?"

"Not even if my life depended on it." He slammed the door resoundingly and leaned against the door frame, wheezing. The mere thought of living with a cat revolted him. He felt like upchucking.

He closed his eyes briefly and fought the picture of a five-year-old boy in the projects. Rats. So many rats! And all those cats chasing them. And his poor baby sister, Lita, in her crib, trapped . . . oh, Lord!

Stiffening with resolve, he forced the bad memories aside. No, he didn't need any damn cat to remind him of all he'd left behind. Not in this lifetime!

When he arrived back at the station house a short time later, he met Skip coming out. Skip stopped dead in his tracks and gaped at him. "What the hell is that giant furball sitting on your front seat?"

"Gargoyle."

"You mean Garfield."

"No, I mean Gargoyle."

219

"It must weigh fifty pounds. I thought you hated cats."

Nick said a very foul word and stomped past him up the steps, without answering. He was in a cold sweat from having sat next to a cat for the past fifteen minutes. He wanted to go take a shower, brush his teeth, and spray himself with a film of disinfectant.

"Hey, have you given any more thought to that Indian stripper job I mentioned?"

Nick said two foul words, and added a hand gesture.

Chapter Six

By the time Nick quit work that evening, he was in a really bad mood.

His first mission was to unload the cat. So he headed to Paula's.

She declined his gift, graciously but firmly. "Nick, I already have Gonzo. What would I want with a cat?"

In the background, the German Shepherd was barking and growling like crazy, straining to leap through the barely opened doorway. Gonzo hated cats almost as much as Nick did.

Paula refused to let Nick come inside her apartment, reminding him that they'd agreed last night to stop seeing each other altogether and accept the fact that they'd be divorced in three more days.

Nick wanted to point out that he'd never agreed to any such thing, but he had more important concerns. *She's not gonna take the damn cat! Oh, Lord! Now what?* Nick's cold sweat turned colder, and a visible shudder passed over his body.

"What am I gonna do with a cat?" he complained. He stood in the hallway, shifting from leg to leg, his arms aching from holding the monster cat that was gaining weight by the second.

"Take it back where you got it. And stop buying things for me without asking. I'm sick of you making decisions for me. If I want a cat, I'll get one myself."

"Talk about ingratitude!"

She glared at him. "And, Nick . . . don't come back tonight. I won't be here." Her lips trembled and her voice cracked. "Last night was an ending. Give up! I don't know how much more I can take."

He gazed at her bleakly.

She peered closer at the cat then. "Nick, that cat's awfully big. Are you sure it's not pregnant?"

"Come again?" He looked at the giant shedding machine in his arms, which was smirking up at him. "It couldn't be. It's a guy cat. Isn't it?" He lifted it up by its front legs and looked where he thought the evidence should be. Nope, no cat penis, as far as he could tell.

His eyes widened with sudden understanding. Then, swearing a blue streak, he spun on his heel and stomped down the hallway.

"Nick, what's wrong? Where are you going?"

"I'm off to kill a fortune teller."

But of course Madame Nadine wasn't at home. He knocked till his knuckles grew raw. He peered, then shouted through the closed windows.

But no answer.

She was probably out cruising the parkway on her broom.

He thought about leaving Gargoyle on the porch, but decided against that when he looked at the busy highway behind him. Even he wasn't into cat roadkill.

That night he discovered two things. He still hated cats. And Gargoyle loved SpaghettiOs and cherry Kool-Aid, the only food he had in the house.

Day Five

The next morning he discovered two more things. Gargoyle had parked herself at the foot of his bed. And she planned a permanent stay, as evidenced by the hissing noise she made every time he tried to pick her up and take her to his car. Scratches up and down his forearms proved the cat had marked his apartment for her new home.

Well, Nick had a few plans of his own. He was going to Pet Control first thing this morning and get a tranquilizer gun. Then he was going to deliver a package—a very large package—to the psychic from hell.

After he showered, he filled the tub with a week's worth of dirty dishes, squirted on a half bottle of Dawn and turned on the shower again. It was a trick Skip has taught him.

Then he searched the pile of dirty clothes on the floor of his bedroom for a reasonably clean shirt. He was forced to run a streak of white-out along the inside of the collar. Another dumb-men trick Skip had recommended.

Before he left for work, he wagged his finger in the cat's face, warning, ''If you dare to have one single baby while I'm at work, I'm making cat soup. No, cat-and-fortune-teller soup.''

Gargoyle, of course, just ignored him, licking her fur with decided indifference.

''And don't breathe on anything while I'm gone.

And make sure you confine your cat business to that box of rags in the bathroom. I'll have you know I gave up my favorite ten-year-old jockey shorts for your crap.''

Gargoyle shot him a look down her haughty nose that said clearly, in female cat body language, ''You are *so* crude. And dumber than catnip.''

Nick arrived home at four, carrying a shopping bag with a gallon of milk and five cans of cat food. For himself, he had a six-pack of beer, ten more cans of SpaghettiOs and a box of Froot Loops. The cat would have to share the milk.

Pet Control had told him he couldn't tranquilize the cat if it was pregnant. So between assignments that day, he'd driven over to Madame Nadine's, alone. Six times! There was no answer to his repeated pounding on Madame Nadine's door or his shouted threats, although he could swear he saw cigarette smoke through the window.

Before he even unpacked his bags, Nick picked up the phone and dialed Paula's number—for the zillionth time that day. Once again, he got her answering machine and slammed the phone back into the receiver. Paula was avoiding him big time. Apparently, she'd been serious about their not seeing each other again until the divorce hearing.

Well, he would show her he could be just as determined. But first, he had to feed the damn cat, which was rubbing itself against his pant leg and meowing in a disgustingly coaxing fashion. Holding his nose, he opened the can of cat food—''Tuna Milanese''— and dumped the gelatinous mass onto a plate on the floor. *Yech!* Next, he poured a saucer of milk.

Gargoyle lapped up the milk but ignored the cat food disdainfully. Instead, she eyed the SpaghettiOs he was eating cold from the can, washed down with a Bud Light. He tried to ignore her as he put away his purchases, but her eyes followed him accusingly. Finally, he gave up in disgust and dumped the rest of the SpaghettiOs onto another plate and put it on the floor. "I wouldn't eat that tuna, either."

The cat meowed a delicate "Thank You."

"Don't think this means I like you. Or that you're staying."

"Meow."

"Tomorrow you and I are breaking down Madame Nadine's door."

"Meow."

"I don't suppose you did any laundry today."

After showering and gathering together some items Skip had lent him, Nick headed toward Paula's place. He wasn't surprised when she didn't answer the door. *No problem.*

After picking the lock, he hurried to shut off the delayed ring of the security alarm, which Paula had turned on, for once. He quickly punched a series of numbers into the keypad, breathing a sigh of relief. What he didn't need was the police showing up.

Then, checking out Paula's answering machine tapes for the past few days, he got a pretty good idea of where she was hiding out. Her parents' beach house at Long Beach Island.

He grinned with satisfaction. Paula's location worked very nicely into the next item on his fantasy agenda. Yes, indeed! Sand . . . lots of sand. He rubbed his hands together with relish.

Paula, baby, this is going to be a night you'll never forget.

Pulling out his wallet, he found the business card he'd been given earlier that day. "Mr. Saleem? Hi, this is Nick DiCello. Yeah, we're still on for tonight, but listen, Omar, there's been a slight change in location.'' He gave the guy directions to the beach house and told him he'd meet the work crew there in two hours.

''May Allah bless all your plans.''

''I sure hope so.''

''Do you still want me to contact that traveling circus?''

''Yeah. Sure. And don't forget all the props we discussed. The palm trees, brazier, the cushions—lots of cushions.''

''A thousand pardons, my friend, but you've gone over this list with me three times already today.''

Nick could hear a calculator clicking in the background.

''You do realize, Mr. DiCello, that this is going to be a *very* expensive evening.''

''I expect it to be worth every dollar. And then some.'' *Even if it sucks up all my savings.*

''Well, 'tis said Allah put woman on earth for a man's pleasure. Are you sure you don't want me to send a belly dancer for entertainment?''

''Nope. I'm planning my own entertainment.''

Paula had been walking the beach for hours. Nightfall approached as the setting sun cast an orange backdrop to the blue ocean, and still she strolled aimlessly, her bare toes skimming the foamy edge of the cool water.

Her family had purchased the cottage on Long Beach Island for a summer home at her birth, thirty years ago. She knew the shoreline like the palm of her hand. And yet it was ever-changing, like her life.

Thoughtfully, she picked up a sea shell, examining its intricate, beautiful whorls, and remembered with a slight smile how she and her young girlfriends used to search fervently for that one shell that would yield a priceless pearl.

And she remembered as a grown woman once reading some philosopher who likened those pearls to temples built by pain around a single grain of sand.

Like Nick's love. So beautiful, but so much pain surrounding it.

She started to throw the shell back into the water, but then whimsically tucked it into the pocket of her shorts.

A heavy cloak of depression weighed her down, as it had all day. She'd escaped Nick physically, but not emotionally. And she doubted she ever would.

She loved the man—totally. But she couldn't live with him.

Thinking about their divorce made her shudder with hurt. And, more important, she knew that she was hurting Nick, terribly. But she truly believed he needed the divorce to start healing, as much as she did.

Sometimes, walking away is the greatest expression of love.

Nick just didn't understand—she knew that—but he probably never would. Coming from different backgrounds—she, an only child raised in the sheltered, loving arms of a middle-class suburban family; he, one of five kids barely surviving in a one-bedroom ghetto apartment—they would probably never see things in exactly the same way. That would have been okay. In fact, it had been more than okay at the beginning of their marriage.

But in the last few years, his need to protect her had grown into an obsession. Suffocating her. Changing him. The numerous locks on their doors. A guard dog. A need to know her whereabouts every minute of the day. Attempting to control her activities and her friends. Even her choice of employment.

Worse, he drew more and more into himself, refusing to share his troubles or talk about his work.

A prison. For him, as well as her.

Yes, their marriage would have to end, and she couldn't bear the torture of seeing him again. Each time, the pain tore her apart. Being together made their inevitable parting harder for both of them. Two more days until the hearing. Then their marriage would be over.

With a deep sigh, she turned around and headed back toward the beach house.

Glancing sideways, she saw several trucks parked along the road that ran parallel to the beach—Omar's Special Events Catering, two pick-up trucks, and, of all things, a huge animal transport vehicle, with the words CLYDE BEADER TRAVELING CIRCUS stenciled on the side.

She laughed. Someone must be having a party. The residents of this exclusive private beach could afford the most expensive theme parties, and they often tried to outdo themselves with the bizarre.

She turned the bend around a large sand dune that protected against beach erosion and screened their property from the neighbors. Jerking to a quick stop, she stumbled.

At first, she blinked several times, thinking she was seeing a mirage. "Oh, my God!"

A large, low, white tent, its fabric billowing in the slight evening breeze, stood on the beach in front of her house. Torches flamed on tall spikes at each of the corners and near an oasis.

An oasis! Her mouth dropped open in amazement. A portable hot tub had been set up on the beach, surrounded by enormous fake palm trees and exotic flowers.

"GR-ONK, GR-ONK!"

Paula jumped at the loud—very loud—nasal call of some animal. Incredibly, a large beast ambled out from behind one of the palm trees.

A camel!

How could that be? A camel on the Jersey shore? Impossible! Local ordinances didn't permit the littlest dogs on a beach these days, let alone a camel. Her brow furrowed with puzzlement.

Then she noticed the black-haired, dark-skinned man sitting cross-legged in front of the open flap of the tent, staring at her somberly like some desert sultan. Dressed in full Arab dress, from long, black robe to matching head cloth, tied in place with a ropelike piece of material, his shoulders were thrown back arrogantly, with all the pride of the most potent Arab sheik.

Nick.

She was going to kill him. She really was.

But before she could scream out her rage or storm up to the stubborn jerk, two large Arab guards grabbed her from behind. They wore similar flowing robes, covered with concealing burnooses. They quickly tied her hands behind her back and wrapped a silk scarf around her mouth, gagging her. One of them picked her up and carried her over to the front of the tent, dropping her to the soft Persian carpet on the sand. She immediately squirmed upright and tried to stand, but one of the brutes shoved her to her knees in front of the sheik.

"Mrffmfh!" She looked back over her shoulder to glare at the two of them, and her eyes almost popped out with disbelief.

Skip winked at her and grinned with wicked appreciation at her situation. Lee Chin was laughing so hard that silent tears ran down his face. Then they both bowed low in dramatic obeisance before the sheik and salaamed, placing their right palms to their foreheads.

"Master Raschid, we bring you the slave girl, Zara. Will you accept her for your harem?"

The sheik—rather, Zack—studied her insolently, as if he wasn't sure. Paula thought about whacking him with a piece of nearby driftwood, but one of the "guards" still held a hand on her shoulder in restraint.

"We shall see," Nick said, rubbing a forefinger thoughtfully over his upper lip, "if she pleases me."

Me please him? Hah! "Mrffmfh!"

She heard Skip and Lee chuckle behind her, but they stopped immediately at Nick's imperious glare. With a curt nod, he dismissed them, stating, with a hand over his heart, "Peace be to you." And she thought she heard him murmur in an aside, "Now, get lost!"

They returned the hand-over-heart gesture. "And peace to you, *master.*"

Master? Hah! "Mrffmfh!"

Skip remarked to Lee as they walked off, "I'd like to be a fly on that camel's butt when Paula gets her hands free."

"I think Nick's goin' stark raving bonkers, myself," Lee opined. "No woman's worth makin' a fool of yourself like that."

"Do you think he's makin' a fool of himself? No way! Women eat this romance fantasy stuff up like candy. You really oughtta watch more Oprah, Lee."

"I got better things to do than—"

"Betcha didn't know what some couples do on top of a washing machine."

"Huh?"

Skip gave a short, graphic account of laundry room sexual activity, most of it revolving around vibrating washing machines.

Impressed, Lee asked, "And you learned that from Oprah? Wow!"

Paula's face flamed with embarrassment. Good Lord! By tomorrow morning, everyone in New Jersey was going to know about this latest stunt of Nick's. And it would be linked right up there with vibrating washing machines.

She gritted her teeth, closed her eyes, and counted to ten for patience. Finally, she opened her eyes and looked at Nick.

He still sat, cross-legged, in front of her with his arms folded across his chest. He stared at her with blatant sexual interest, not even trying to hide his intentions.

"Mrffmfh!"

"Would you like me to remove the gag, Zara?" he asked in a soft voice.

She nodded vigorously.

"Do you promise not to scream?"

"Mrffmfh!" Her eyes flashed sparks of defiance. Oh, she intended to scream all right. And slap some sense into his silly head.

He laughed, a low, throaty sound. "Ah, then, we cannot allow that. It appears you need to understand your role, my dear. I will, of course, enjoy teaching you."

Her eyebrows shot up at that.

And little tingles of unwanted pleasure rippled across Paula's skin at the erotic promise in his voice.

A slow, knowing grin tugged at Nick's beautiful lips. "I wonder what kind of pupil you will be, Zara."

I wonder, too. Oh, Lord!

"Will you be defiant and resist me, like a proud desert princess? Or will you be compliant and seductive, like an experienced *houri?*"

Every nerve ending in her body leaped to attention at those vivid mind pictures.

He stood and walked behind her, so close that she could feel the soft caress of his robe against her bare leg, the whisper of his breath against her hair. Abruptly, before she could react, he lifted her by both upper arms and propelled her inside the tent, closing the flap behind him.

And the fantasy began.

Chapter Seven

Paula felt as if she had fallen into a black hole and emerged on the other side of the world. It was *Arabian Nights* and a torrid Bertrice Small novel all wrapped up in one.

By the flickering light of candles and tall flame-lit torches, she saw jewel-toned Persian carpets, topped with dozens of satin pillows. Wine cooled in an ice-filled bucket, and succulent Middle Eastern foods warmed over a brazier. Exotic music came from somewhere—a mournful twang reminiscent of hot Sahara nights and dark-skinned Bedouin lovers.

Paula fought the seductive pull of the erotic fantasy Nick was creating for her. She didn't understand why he did it, but she couldn't deny the heightening of her senses—or the lowering of her resistance. She closed her eyes, fighting for control, and groaned behind her gag.

"Did you say something, Zara?"

Nick had come up behind her, silent as a desert bandit, and placed a sharp blade near her throat. She glanced back over her shoulder at him. A shiver ran through her, but not of fear. Nick wouldn't hurt her.

Before she realized what he intended, he cut her oversized T-shirt from the neck band to the end of the short sleeves on both sides. Despite her hands being still bound behind her back, he was able to pull the shirt down till it fell to the ground, exposing her bare breasts. They peaked immediately into telling points of aching arousal. She wore only shorts now, but those, and her panties, soon joined her shirt on the ground.

And she stood before him, naked and vulnerable, like the slave captive he had deemed her.

He circled her in a predatory fashion, examining her body from all angles, as if determining her worth. Nick had always been a good actor. That was why he often got assigned to drug busts or gigs where he had to play a role. He was using all those talents now. If Paula hadn't known him before, she would swear he really was a ruthless sheik who'd captured an unwilling slave girl . . . on a New Jersey beach.

She giggled, low in her throat.

"You find humor in your captivity, do you, Zara?" he asked in a velvety voice, and trailed the dull side of his knife downward, flicking the nipples of both breasts lightly.

She inhaled sharply at the intense pleasure.

He smiled. "I'm going to remove your gag now, Zara, and you are not to speak unless I give you permission. I am the master. You are my slave. Do you understand?"

At first, she remained obstinate. Then she nodded her head. Despite herself, she was curious as to just how far he would go with this charade.

The minute the silk scarf fell away from her mouth, she charged, "Nick, you can't do this."

"Oh, can't I?" he said. "Did I not tell you to remain silent? I am Raschid. It is the only name I will answer to. Or master."

She made an "in your dreams" snort of disgust.

He raised an eyebrow at her in challenge and continued, "And you are Zara . . . my love slave."

Love slave? Oh, my.

"What is this, some kind of middle-aged crazy thing?"

"Middle-aged?" he sputtered indignantly. "I'm only thirty-five. And you're doing a hell of a lot more drooling than I am."

"Pre-middle-aged then. Or post-raging-stud-dom. All I know is, you're acting crazy lately."

"Stud-dom?" He grinned, honing in on that one word. "You think I'm still a stud?"

"Still?" She made another snort of disgust.

"Now, now, sarcasm does not befit a harem girl." He winked and held out a bundle of sheer fabric. "When I release your hands, *slave,* you will put this on," he ordered.

Paula looked down in puzzlement as he shook the fabric out, causing all the tiny bells sewn along its edges to tinkle delightfully. She couldn't help but smile . . . until she realized what he held. A harem girl's outfit—like a belly dancer's—little more than transparent scarves that would reveal more than they would hide. Oh, this was outrageous! And, worst of all, it probably belonged to one of the strippers at Skip's nightclub.

"No."

"No?

"You can't make me."

"Think again, *slave.*"

"Hah!" *I'd like to know how—*

"I could tie you to a tent pole and caress you till your tongue curls."

"Hah!" *He wouldn't dare. Would he?*

"I could lay you on those pillows and slather you with honey and lick you from your toenails to your eyebrows."

"Hah!" *Oh, he is good.*

"I could give you a new lesson in aural sex, talking—just talking—for hours about the things I fantasize about doing to you, until you come, and come, and come."

"Hah!" *Stop panting, Paula, or he'll know you're interested.*

"I could touch myself the way I would like you to touch me, and force you to watch."

Oh, my God!

"I could stick dates in—"

"Stop!" she choked out. "Give me the damn bimbo clothes."

He laughed smoothly and untied the scarf binding her wrists behind her back, then handed her the sheer garment. Turning away, he poured two glasses of wine while she dressed, which didn't take long, considering the small amount of fabric.

The top portion was a red chiffon, bolero-style vest, with no buttons or clasps, ending just under her breasts. The loose pantaloons, also of red chiffon, hung low on her hips, exposing her navel. Tiny bells lined all the gold twining edges of both the top and bottom garments.

Paula felt more exposed than if she were naked.

And she felt incredibly sexy. Especially with Nick still being fully clothed.

She got grim satisfaction when he turned, and his jaw dropped with surprise. He almost spilled the glass of wine he was about to hand her.

"Hot damn!" he murmured under his breath.

She walked closer to him, jingling like a Christmas sleigh—*just call me Tinkerbell*—and reached for the glass of wine.

"Well?" she asked, wanting to reverse the tables on him, to take over the reins in this power play. She experienced an odd thrill in knowing she could turn him on so easily. She felt an even greater thrill wondering how it would feel to play out this tantalizing drama. "Does this fulfill your fantasy?"

A grin teased at his lips. "Allah be praised. You are every man's dream. But this is to be your fantasy, Zara. For your pleasure, if Allah wills."

Suddenly, Paula was frightened of this game, and how easily she had fallen, once again, under Nick's spell. They shouldn't be talking, let alone having sex, with their divorce a few days off. Not only was Nick going off the deep end, but now she was about to take the leap, too. "All right, Nick. You've had your big joke. Now, tell me what this is all about."

"Not Nick. Raschid," he corrected. "And you need not understand the fantasy. Do not fight the fates Allah has foretold."

She put both hands on her hips, stamping her foot.

His eyes flashed blue fire, darkening with passion, as they riveted on her chest.

She looked down and groaned. Her posture had caused the vest to part, exposing a good portion of her breasts. She jerked the sides together and scowled at him.

He smiled, a dazzling display of white teeth and pure Nick charm. She melted. She couldn't stay mad at him when he smiled at her like that. She never could.

That is, until he spoke his next words.

"You will feed me now, *slave*."

"I beg your pardon," she said with disbelief.

He dropped down languidly to a nest of cushions, sipping at his wine, and pointed to the brazier. "A good slave feeds her master . . . with her fingers."

Paula took a long drink of her wine to cool her consternation—and ardor—but it had the opposite effect. The potent beverage rushed to all the nerve centers in her body, heightening their sensitivity. Even the air teased her skin, which had become one large canvas of unending erogenous zones.

"This is the nineties, babe—I mean, Raschid," she snapped, fighting the whirl of her dizzying emotions, "and women don't *serve* men."

Paula knew she'd made a mistake almost immediately. She downed the rest of her glass of wine in a big gulp as Nick rose in one fluid motion and pushed her gently to the cushions. "Of course, you are right, Zara. I will serve you."

And he did.

Half reclining on the cushions, sipping at the second glass of wine Nick handed her, Paula had trouble concentrating. Perhaps it was the effects of the alcohol. More likely, it was the enticing feel of Nick's fingers against her lips, feeding her rice with slivers of succulent lamb, bite-sized pieces of pita bread dripping with honey, marinated olives, sweet dates.

Along the way, somehow, she'd begun to feed him as well. He lay on his side, leaning on one elbow, with a tray of food between them. His expression was hungry and lustful, and she thrilled at the knowledge that food was only the appetizer in this delicious foreplay.

When she placed a pomegranate seed inside his mouth, he held her wrist in place and sucked the pulp surrounding the kernel till she finally removed it from his mouth. Over and over, she repeated the procedure, fascinated by the play of light and shadow on his flexing cheeks, increasingly excited by the abrasion of his tongue on her thumb and forefinger.

"I would like to do the same with your nipples," he said huskily, holding her eyes.

And when she put the next seed in his mouth, she felt each pull in her breasts.

"Do you feel it, Zara?"

She could not answer, but he knew. He knew.

"Bare your breasts for me, slave."

She had probably had too much to drink. That could be the only explanation for her even considering doing as he asked. Sitting up, she watched as he removed the tray between them. Then, slowly, she drew her bolero apart and over her shoulders.

Nick made a low growl of approval.

She lay back down, feeling as seductive as the Bedouin princess she pretended to be. Nick gazed at her like a thirsty man who just arrived at a sand-locked oasis, about to be offered his first cup of water. And Paula realized that the last thing in the world she wanted was to make him suffer.

"Arch your back, Zara, like a cat. Purr for your master. Can you purr?"

She could. And she did.

The Middle Eastern music thrummed around them, exotic and sexually compelling.

All of Paula's blood seemed to center and pump rhythmically in the fullness of her breasts, which she offered to him wantonly. Leaning back on both elbows, she threw her head back with shameless abandon, concentrating all her attention on the pebble-hard tips.

She was no longer Paula. She was a desert princess,

and Nick was her sheik, the answer to her most intimate dreams.

Tossing aside his headdress, he rose to his knees at her side, his adoring eyes raking her body.

With his hands at his sides, he bent forward, and his hot breath fanned her breast as he whispered, "You are my beloved, and I am your slave."

Paula keened aloud then with the intensity of her need and arched higher, forcing her nipple against his lips. He chuckled softly with delight.

"No, I am the slave. I must be a slave to bend to your will so easily," she whispered.

When he kissed the taut buds, then drew on them gently and laved them with his tongue, she began to whimper and tried to pull away. Wave after wave of pleasure mingled with pain washed over her, and Nick put one arm under her back to hold her in the arched position. He would not let her escape now.

For long minutes he played the two hardened "seeds," overt marks of her overwhelming arousal. Alternately, he used his lips and tongue and teeth to nip and caress, suck and blow, flick and press.

Her thighs grew rigid as she strained, fighting against the onslaught of her approaching climax. "Stop. It's too much. Please. Oh. Please."

But he would not comply. "Yield, Zara," he coaxed her in a thickened voice. "Surrender to me."

Then, suddenly, he stopped and stood, pulling her to her feet. The tiny bells on her trousers jingled.

Blinking, barely able to focus through the haze of her inflamed senses, Paula watched as Nick drew away from her and leaned against a tent pole, folding his arms casually over his chest. But there was nothing casual about his pale eyes, glistening like beautiful pools of blue passion, or his full lips, parted sensually.

She couldn't believe he was going to just stop. How could he? Nick had never been so cruel.

"Will you dance for me now, Zara?" he asked in a low, erotic growl.

"I don't know how," she protested weakly, but already her hips swayed seductively to the rhythm of the Arab music. The bells jingled softly as she moved.

She found she *could* dance. For Nick.

Raising her hands to the nape of her neck, she lifted her hair. She looked back at him over her shoulder and saw that he'd shifted back into his role-playing. He watched her intently, his face an expressionless mask, like some caliph viewing a harem girl. And that bothered her. A lot. Hah! She'd show him.

Paula turned and lifted her own breasts. *Oh, Lord, did I really do that?*

A muscle twitched near his lips.

Good! She rolled her shoulders. Slowly.

His lips parted.

So, the caliph isn't a eunuch, after all? She picked up a set of finger cymbals and clicked them in tune with the music.

He gasped softly.

So, he'd like to lock her in a harem, would he? Well, maybe she was more woman than he could handle. She undulated her hips.

He began to smile.

All the time, she held Nick's eyes.

He began to disrobe, showing her how very much he wanted her.

And Paula forgot where the game ended and reality began. The molten heat that had been centered in her breasts gushed in a torrent to all the extremities of her body and pooled in a simmering mass between her legs. She felt hot, and desirable, and all woman. She would do anything for Nick. Anything.

"And does this slave please her master, Raschid?" she whispered, coming up close to Nick, circling him, teasing him with swaying hips, trailing fingertips across his wide shoulders.

When he reached for her, she slipped away, laughing gaily. The second time she approached, he grabbed her by the waist and pulled her hard against his body, chortling triumphantly. Pressing his lips to the wildly beating pulse in her neck, he rasped, "This slave pleases her master mightily." And he took her hand, curling her palm around his "might."

Desire licked like hot flames through Nick's body as his wide palms swept over his wife's bare back. He nuzzled the shadowy hollow of her neck and savored the familiar scent of her lemony cologne.

This was Paula, the woman he loved more than life. And this was Zara, the alluring *houri,* who could enchant a Bedouin raider. They were one and the same.

Slipping his hands into the back waistband of her trousers, he cupped her buttocks and pulled her hard against his erection, lifting her feet off the carpet. "I want you," he rasped.

She undulated her hips against him. "I know." Her eyes sparkled teasingly.

He laughed. "You take to your role very well, slave. I wonder, will you be able to hold my *attention* all through the night?"

"Hah!" she said, ducking under his arm and stepping out of her trousers to stand before him, proud and unashamed of her nudity. "I wonder if you will be able to *hold* your attention all through the night."

Then she amazed him by walking to the bed of cushions and lying down on her back. She raised her hands above her head and parted her legs slightly, posing for him with an abandon he would have never thought possible for his Paula. "I yield to you, my

242

master. You may have your will with me now. Your wish is my command.''

Nick dropped to his knees. Then, nudging her legs farther apart, he moved on top of her. Braced on his elbows, he slanted his lips over hers and began to enter her body, whispering, ''My wish is to make love to my wife. My wish is that you surrender to me . . . everything.''

He saw the brief flicker of fear in her eyes, felt the tightening of her arm and thigh muscles. ''No, no, darling, don't be afraid. All I ask is your complete trust.'' He knew she wondered if she would be surrendering to more than one night's madness. But, gradually, she relaxed and gave herself up to him.

Nick controlled the pace of their lovemaking then. He slowed his thrusts, even as she urged him with throaty cries to end her torture. When her body began to convulse around him, he held himself rigid until her orgasm stopped. Then he began the rhythm again.

''I'm dying,'' she moaned as she writhed from side to side.

''Then we are dying together.'' Desperate and obsessed, Nick fought to make this night last forever. He had to convince Paula, if only with his lovemaking, that they belonged together.

His caresses took on a frantic character. He lay beside her, over her, under her. Touching and exploring every inch of her body. Memorizing. Her heat and the intensity of her orgasms and regenerating arousals enveloped him and spurred him toward his own climax. Relentlessly, he resisted the release.

But the force of his need eventually overpowered him.

Sucking in deep, soul-drenching draughts of air, he hurtled toward a mind-blowing pinnacle. Bracing himself on straightened arms, he threw his head back, feeling the cords in his neck stand out, and cried out triumphantly as he exploded inside her body's convulsing folds.

He must have passed out for a few moments, or slept, from the intensity of his climax. When his brain emerged from its fuzzy state of confused satiety, he felt Paula's hands caressing his shoulders and back, crooning soft words of pleasure and encouragement . . . love words. Even though he lay heavily on her, she didn't protest. Tears burned his eyes, and he blinked them back. He didn't think he could love his wife more than he did at that moment.

He raised his head. "Paula, honey, I love you so much."

"I know, Nick. I know. I love you, too." She brushed a wisp of hair off his brow, sweaty from their exertions. And the gesture displayed as much caring as the most intimate caress.

Hope blossomed like a desert flower in his heart. "Paula, does this mean that—"

"Shhh, not now. No talking," she said. "If we talk, I'll have to think. And I don't want to think. Just feel."

"Well, then, my desert flower, perhaps I can help you feel some more," he said, rolling to his side and propping himself on one elbow, gazing down at her. Lightly, he ran a forefinger from the curve of her neck, down over the peak of one breast, over her belly button, to the damp curls of her womanhood.

She sighed. "I don't think I'm capable of any more feeling."

He quirked an eyebrow. "Ah, that sounds like a challenge to me. We Bedouin warriors have a reputation to uphold."

She giggled.

"You doubt me, wench? Hmmm. Well, since we

have no female harem girls here to serve you, I will have to act as your handmaiden. Turn over on your stomach, Zara. I will minister to your weak body . . . bring it back to life.''

He stood and picked up the beaker that was warming on the far side of the brazier.

''What's that?'' she asked suspiciously.

''Warm oil to massage your muscles, which are sadly out of shape from lack of use.''

''So you think I'm out of shape, do you?'' She stretched lazily, and he felt a part of his body stretch, too.

''No, not you, Zara. Just certain muscles.'' He jiggled his eyebrows as he spoke. ''Lie on your stomach, slave, and stop asking questions,'' he ordered in a mock stern voice.

Surprisingly, she did as he demanded. *Hey, maybe that's where I went wrong. I didn't do enough ordering.*

''GR-ONK! GR-ONK!''

Oh, no!

''What was that?'' Paula asked, her head jerking up with alarm.

''Just the camel,'' Nick said, setting the beaker on the ground.

''Camel! I thought I saw a camel out there. Nick, you're going to get in big, big trouble bringing a camel onto the beach.''

''I am Raschid, and Raschid can do anything in his kingdom.''

''And Long Beach Island is your kingdom?''

''You betcha, baby. Besides, Raschid knows the local sheriff who owes him many drachmas for a favor I granted him.''

''Hmpfh! That probably means you squelched a ticket.''

Under his breath, he muttered something about a poker game.

"Hey, where are you going? I thought you were going to give me a hot oil massage."

He reached down and slapped her playfully on the tush. "Do not be so anxious, Zara. We have all night. Right now, I am off to feed yon camel."

She grinned. "And what do yon camels eat, oh great desert warrior?"

"Damned if I know," he said with a shrug as he stepped through the tent flap, bare-assed naked, uncaring if any of the neighbors could see him.

This night was turning out better than he'd ever expected. Even the huge piles of camel dung that he almost stepped in didn't dampen his enthusiasm. Hell, Paula's mother prided herself on her prize dahlias. Surely, camel dung was no different than cow manure, and farmers used that for fertilizer all the time.

After tending to the camel, he returned to the tent, where he massaged the scented oil into Paula's body, and she reciprocated, followed by their making slow, slow love. They laughed softly at the slickness of their bodies, sighing their pleasure at the exquisitely drawn-out foreplay, crying exultantly in unison at the climax.

Then they washed each other's bodies in the jacuzzi oasis and made love again. When he carried her back into the tent, they drank the sweet Arabic tea, pronounced *shay-hee,* from glasses with peanuts at the bottom. He tried to talk Paula into trying the fermented goat's milk, served at room temperature, but she turned up her nose at the strong, unpleasant odor.

"Nick, what in heaven's name is that on your shoulder?"

He grimaced. "A tattoo."

"You got a tattoo? I can't believe it. It's amazing

that I didn't notice it before.''

"I just got it yesterday,'' he admitted, ''and I suspect you were too occupied to see it last night.'' He flashed her a knowing, very satisfied look.

She blushed in remembrance. ''But why would you get a tattoo?''

''For you,'' he stated flatly.

She frowned in puzzlement.

''You see, there was this fortune-teller, and I was asking for advice, and she said women like these things, but I didn't know she was gonna put a sunflower on my back. I thought it was gonna be something sexy like—hell, I don't know what I expected.'' He took a deep breath after his long-winded explanation.

A frown of confusion still furrowed her brow.

He pinched her bottom playfully. ''Hey, you're lucky I didn't do what she really wanted . . . pierce my genitals and hang an earring there.'' He pointed downward.

''Oh, you!'' Paula said finally. ''I should have known you were just kidding.''

If you only knew, babe!

Smiling, they fell asleep in each other's arms, sated and happy.

Day Six

Morning light already filtered into the tent when Nick awakened to the rustling of fabric. He rolled over lazily and opened his eyes halfway. Paula was dressing as best she could in the revealing harem costume. He decided then and there that he wouldn't return the outfit to Skip's boss. Instead, he'd buy it for Paula, a memento of this fantasy interlude. Maybe they'd take it out every year on this date, an anniversary of sorts.

"Where are you going, honey?" He stretched and his knee and elbow joints creaked. He was getting too old for this stuff. *Yeah, right.*

She looked down at him lovingly and shook her head helplessly. "You are the only man I know who wakes up in a good mood. I love that about you. Did I ever tell you that before?"

"You wake up with that many men, huh?"

"You know darn well you're the only one, you brute. And it's not fair that you can look so sexy first thing in the morning."

Damn, I'm good. "I look sexy? Hmmm. Maybe you'd better come back to bed, sweetheart, and show me just how sexy."

She pretended horror. "Not again, Nick. I can barely walk."

He grinned at her and sat up. "I like that. Come here, you. I want to kiss you good morning." He held out his arms.

She hesitated, then walked over and sat next to him.

"I love you, Paula," he said solemnly as he kissed her lightly.

She grazed her knuckles over his bristly jaw and whispered, "And I love you, Nick. I never stopped."

"We're going to work this out, Paula. Aren't we?"

"I think so . . . I hope so, Nick. It seems like an impossible task, but every time I'm with you, well, it just keeps getting better and better. I'm finding it awfully hard to imagine living without you."

Thank you, God! And God bless Madame Nadine. I think I'll buy her a new crystal ball. Maybe even a new dress. Heck, maybe she'd like a truckload of camel dung for her sunflowers.

Chuckling softly at his whimsical thoughts, he kissed her gently and tried to pull her down to the cushions again. But she pushed his chest playfully and stood up, adjusting her clothes.

"Sorry, Charlie, but I have an appointment in Newark in three hours."

He lay back with his hands folded behind his neck, watching her try to finger comb her sex-tangled hair. If she could only see the brush burns on her face and neck, her kiss-bruised lips, and the languid passion still evident in her limpid eyes, she wouldn't show herself in public today. Ah, well, he kind of liked the marks of his lovemaking being displayed to the outside world. She belonged to him, and he wanted everyone to know.

"What kind of appointment did you say you have?"

"A job interview . . . at the Patterson projects. I've had three other interviews these past few weeks, but this is the one I really want. I'd be working directly with the kids as a youth activity coordinator, and—what's wrong? Why are you looking at me like that?"

He stood up and hunched over at the waist, inhaling and exhaling deeply, fighting for breath. *Oh, Lord, no! Not now! Just when things are starting to go right again.*

"Nick—Nick, what's wrong?"

"Cancel the interview," he said peremptorily. "Don't go."

"Why not?"

"Because I don't want you to. Can't that be reason enough?"

A cloud of doubt, then gradual comprehension, began to transform the softness of her face, turning it cold. "Already . . . *already,* it's starting again, isn't it, Nick?" Her voice cracked with painful regret.

"Paula, please try to understand. You can't work in the Patterson projects. It's just too dangerous. I'm willing to agree to your being a social worker, even let you work with the city kids. But from a safe point. An office in some government building, maybe. Just not Patterson."

"You're willing to *agree?*" she snapped, anger turning her voice shrill. "How dare you suggest I need your permission to do anything, you jerk?"

"Paula, just try to understand my viewpoint. I have my . . . reasons." He gulped hard, clenching his fists against the tide of despair threatening to crush him.

"Why don't you explain those reasons to me, Nick? For once, be honest. Tell me what frightens you so much. Tell me what it is you have buried so deep inside, that's so painful you can't talk about it, even to me."

He tried to speak, but the words wouldn't come. Bleakly, he admitted, "I can't. Not now. Maybe someday."

"No!" she cried, tears welling in her eyes and streaming down her face. "Someday is never going to come for us. *Never.* I was a fool to think you were changing. A fool." She began to weep and turned away from him.

"I can change, Paula. I am changing. Just give me a little more time. A chance to—"

"No!" she repeated on a sob, shoving away the hand he extended imploringly to her. "I have an appointment that I'm not going to miss. And I'm going to accept the job if it's offered."

"That's what you think," he said coldly. "Is your appointment with Lottie Chandler, the social service director?"

She turned abruptly with surprise. "Yes. Do you know her?"

He nodded. "I'll call Lottie. I'll tell her not to give you the job."

"You wouldn't!" she gasped, her eyes swimming with tears of hurt.

"You bet your sweet ass I would. I'd do anything to keep you safe. Anything." *Even if it means losing you in the process.*

"You are a bastard. And I never want to see you again after our divorce hearing tomorrow." Her face flushed with anger as she spat out the words.

He flinched.

Without waiting for a response, she flipped open the flap on the tent and stormed out.

Nick gazed dejectedly through the opening toward the ocean. Last night, he'd had his dreams back, within his grasp, and they'd slipped away once again, just like the sand along the shore. It was hopeless. Hopeless.

A second later, Paula rushed back through the doorway, blushing hotly.

His hopes soared.

"Your camel got loose."

His hopes plummeted.

"There are about two dozen kids on the beach chasing that blasted camel of yours in the surf."

She hadn't come back for him.

"And a man named Omar said to ask if you want to keep the tent for another day. Also," she added, looking down at her flimsy outfit, "he had the nerve to offer me a job as a belly dancer."

Nick started to laugh then, deep belly laughs. Despite the sadness of his situation, despite their impending divorce, despite all that he loved and seemed to be losing, he couldn't help himself.

Paula threw her chin up haughtily and wrapped herself in a soft Persian throw rug, walking out again.

But still he laughed and laughed until tears rolled down his cheeks, and he forgot whether he was laughing or crying.

Chapter Eight

Paula's interview was not going well.

First, she'd arrived fifteen minutes late for her appointment with Lottie Chancellor, the head social worker of the Patterson projects, a huge complex of low-income housing.

It had taken her almost an hour to mask the marks of Nick's lovemaking—whisker-burned face and neck, kiss-swollen lips, and hair so tangled she finally just skinned it back into a ponytail. Paula still couldn't believe that whole Arabian Nights scenario Nick had pulled off, or that she'd willingly participated. *Oh, Lord, the things I did! The things he did!*

Then she'd been unable to find a parking place within a block of the project office. Nick would have a heart attack if he could see the side street where she'd eventually left the little VW convertible.

To top it all off, Mrs. Chancellor—she'd emphasized to Paula from the start that she was *Mrs.*, not

Ms.—kept asking her skeptical questions about her motives in seeking an inner city job. "Ms. DiCello, you have a good teaching position, an important job, molding young minds. I just can't see why you'd want to work here in the projects."

The tall, bone-thin black woman, with tight, steel-gray curls capping the sharp planes of her face, closed Paula's folder on the desk. Her discerning brown eyes probed Paula intently, as if looking for hidden secrets.

Paula squirmed in her seat, her eyes darting nervously about the shabby, but clean, office. Searching for words, she tried to explain. "I enjoy teaching, but it was never what I really wanted. The biggest problems the nine-year-old kids in my class have are whether their parents will buy them a five-hundred-dollar mountain bike or—"

Mrs. Chancellor gave a short hoot of laughter. "And the nine-year-olds in this neighborhood are figuring out how to steal them."

"—or where they'll go on vacation this summer, the shore or the mountains."

Mrs. Chancellor's face revealed infinite sadness. "Most of my kids will never have a vacation. They either die young, or never leave the ghetto."

Paula knew that. Surely, Mrs. Chancellor didn't think she was an insensitive do-gooder with no understanding of the life-and-death struggle urban children faced every day. That was one of the reasons she yearned to help.

Raising her chin stubbornly, she continued to explain herself. "I always intended to go to graduate school right after college, but then . . . well, I got married . . ." *Oh, Lord! When I met Nick, it was like being hit with a Mack truck of sexual attraction. Those were the days! Nick couldn't keep his hands off me. Heck, I couldn't keep my hands off him.*

School was the last thing I was thinking about then.

She gulped and went on, "My plans were put aside for a few years. I worked and went to school at night." She held the social worker's eyes with a level stare. "This is my dream, Mrs. Chancellor. I want to *really* make a difference in young people's lives. Children in desperate need."

"It's not safe here for a woman like you," she said flatly.

Like me? Paula bristled. "If I were black, would it be any safer?"

"No."

Paula tossed her hair back over her shoulder, forgetting it was still in a ponytail. "Because I'm a woman?"

Mrs. Chancellor made a rude snorting sound. "I have just as many women as men on my staff. In fact, sometimes women do a better job reaching these children."

"My age? I am twenty-nine, you know."

She shook her head.

"Then what?"

"Your background. Girl, you have no idea what it's like to grow up in a project. To see death on a daily basis. To hunger for a better life and know it's hopeless."

"I can learn," she protested. "And I refuse to accept that it's hopeless."

"Perhaps." Mrs. Chancellor smiled at her vehemence and tapped her pencil thoughtfully on the desk. "Nick would never forgive me if I hired you."

Paula gasped. So that was the reason for Mrs. Chancellor's attitude. "Nick called you?" she asked incredulously.

"Oh, yes, Nick called. Threatened to have me arrested for breaking some law or other. Challenged my morals for even considering your application.'' Mrs. Chancellor chuckled. ''Said he'd stop volunteering for the youth basketball program.''

''Nick threatened you? Oh, this is too much! How dare he?''

Mrs. Chancellor waved Paula's indignation aside. ''I've known that husband of yours since he was five years old. He doesn't scare me one bit.''

Paula thought of something else. ''Nick plays basketball with the kids? How long has he been doing that?''

''Two years.''

Two years? Before she'd left him. How was it possible that she'd never known? So, all those nights she'd thought he was playing one-on-one at the gym with Skip, he'd actually been down here in the ghetto. Why wouldn't he talk about such an admirable activity?

The answer came to her immediately. He knew she'd want to come along to the projects, and he'd spent years trying to prevent her from doing just that.

''Mrs. Chancellor, Nick and I are getting a divorce. He had no right to call you or—''

''He's worried about you. Don't blame him for caring about your welfare,'' Mrs. Chancellor chastised her sternly. ''Ninety percent of the women in this project have no husbands. What they wouldn't give to have a man—anyone, for that matter—who wanted to protect them! So don't knock the protective instincts of a good man to me, girl.''

Paula stiffened. ''But Nick goes too far. He—never mind, I didn't come here to discuss my personal problems.'' She picked up her purse from the floor and stood. ''I can see now that this interview was doomed from the beginning. You're never going to hire me with Nick breathing over your shoulder.''

"Now, I never said that," Mrs. Chancellor inter-jected quickly with a sly smile. She pulled a set of keys out of her drawer and stood, towering over Paula. "C'mon, I want to show you something." Without waiting for Paula's agreement, she led her through the door of her office, making sure to lock the three dead bolts. Then she walked briskly down a corridor to the stairway, bypassing the elevator. "Half the time the elevators don't work," she ex-plained, "and the smell inside their close confines is enough to gag a maggot."

The smells were pretty bad in the halls, too, Paula thought, recognizing spaghetti sauce and urine and God only knew what other odors. Graffiti marked the walls, and the sounds of crying children and arguing adults echoed through the thin walls of the units.

She felt like crying.

Hurrying to catch up, she followed the energetic woman up one flight of stairs after another, till they got to the fourth floor.

"This apartment is empty right now," Mrs. Chan-cellor told her as she inserted a key in the door and entered, motioning for Paula to follow.

Paula looked around at the small combination liv-ing room and kitchen. The two windows overlooked the dumpsters on one side and the brick walls of the next building on the other. Sun would rarely brighten these drab rooms.

In the single bedroom, two double beds took up almost the entire space except for a dresser with a cracked mirror. The grimy bathroom had only a sink, a toilet, and a tub with no showerhead.

Coming back to Mrs. Chancellor, Paula raised an eyebrow questioningly, unsure what her prospective employer wanted her to see.

"This is the apartment where Nick grew up with

his mother and four brothers and sisters.''

Paula clasped a hand to her heart and tears welled in her eyes. *Oh, no! Oh, God, no! Such a dismal place!*

''Actually, they weren't as crowded as most families here,'' Mrs. Chancellor went on. ''You know, of course, about Lita?''

Paula nodded. Nick had told her his little sister had died when she was a baby.

''Lita passed on when Nick was only five years old. That's why the authorities called me in. Too bad the little one had to die to bring about any change here.'' She shook her head woefully in remembrance.

The fine hairs stood out on Paula's neck. She knew the little girl had died, but apparently Nick had left out a few facts. ''How did her death bring you here?''

Mrs. Chancellor looked surprised at Paula's question. ''You don't know how Lita died?''

Paula hesitated, not sure she wanted to know.

''Rat bites,'' Mrs. Chancellor informed her bluntly.

Paula exhaled loudly with dismay and sank down to the sofa, realizing immediately that it had a broken spring, and moved to the other side. ''Tell me.''

''The old superintendent—Wilson—was skimming money out of the projects for years. One of the areas he stole from was pest control. His idea of rat eradication was to bring in cats, dozens of the rat catchers, which, of course, weren't sufficient to curb the rodent population.''

Cats? So, that's why Nick hates cats. They remind him of the projects. And rats. She laced her fingers together in her lap to stop their trembling.

''Lita was only one year old, sleeping in her crib. Her mother was out somewhere. Drinking, no doubt. And Nick was in charge of the younger children.''

Oh, poor Nick! And only five years old.

Even the hardened Mrs. Chancellor seemed shaken then as she recalled the past. "That summer was especially bad here in the projects. Unrelenting heat. A sanitation strike. And rats." She sighed deeply. "The bottom line is that Lita was bitten repeatedly by rats. Nick didn't understand the seriousness; he was only a kid. And his mother was negligence personified."

"No!" Paula resisted what she suspected was coming next.

"Yes. A rampant infection set in, which wasn't treated for days. Lita died within a week of blood poisoning."

Paula gagged and rushed for the bathroom. When she emerged a short time later, Mrs. Chancellor appeared apologetic. "I shouldn't have told you all that."

"Yes, you should have. Actually, Nick should have told me himself, but—"

Mrs. Chancellor patted her shoulder. "You have to understand the shame, my dear."

"Shame? Why should he feel ashamed? It wasn't his fault."

"I know, I know. But he's a proud young man. The last thing he would want is pity."

Yes, Nick was proud. And stubborn.

"And he felt guilty."

"Guilty?"

"Of course. He'd failed to protect the ones he loved."

Understanding rushed over Paula in a torrent. Now—now when it was too late—she'd been given a reason for Nick's overprotectiveness. A clue to his obsessive behavior. He'd never lied to her about his past, but, oh, he'd omitted so much.

"What about his brothers and sisters?"

"Teresa died of a drug overdose when she was

thirteen. Anthony was killed in a gang fight. And Frankie is in prison for grand larceny.''

"Nick has a brother who's alive?" Paula didn't know if she could take any more shocks like this today.

Mrs. Chancellor nodded slowly. "You really should talk to your husband."

"No, Nick really should talk to me." *And he would. Oh, yes, he definitely would.*

After that, Mrs. Chancellor showed her around the rest of the projects, including the youth activity rooms where Paula would work if she was hired. Her heart wept as she pictured a young Nick in this setting, scrambling about the makeshift gym after a volleyball game, playing checkers with one of the counselors, fighting off the encroaching decay and evil that hovered outside—and within.

Mrs. Chancellor finally told Paula, "We have a desperate need for help here, Ms. DiCello. If you want the job, it's yours. But think about it for a few days. Talk to Nick—now, now, don't get your hackles up—he's in a position to give you good advice. Listen to what he has to say. Then call me."

As Paula walked toward her car, she pondered all she'd seen that morning. She put her fingertips to her lips, still bruised from Nick's many kisses. Her body, as well as her emotions, had been battered the past week. The upcoming divorce. Her job search. Nick's refusal to accept the end of their marriage. His persistent, endearing efforts to woo her back.

Through the mist of her tears, she had to smile, picturing the impossible erotic fantasies he had created for her. Who would have imagined Nick going to the trouble of making an Arabian Nights oasis on a New Jersey beach? Or the Senior Prom dream-come-true? Or the Highway Sex Scene?

Hmmm. A pattern began to emerge in Paula's mind. What was the big lug up to here? Was it merely seduction, trying to get her back? Or something more?

Well, she had more important things to discuss with him now. How dare he call a prospective employer and try to undermine her job efforts? The interference reeked of his obsessive protectiveness. And she planned to put a stop to it *now.* Obviously, their divorce was the only way to convince him of her seriousness.

"Well, well, well. If it isn't Mrs. Dickhead—I mean, Mrs. DiCello."

Paula was jarred from her deep thoughts by the drawling remark of a youth with a red bandanna tied around his head, gang style. He couldn't have been more than fourteen years old, but the deadness of his dark eyes bespoke no youthful innocence.

"Kindly step away from my car," Paula demanded, refusing to show her fear. He half sat on the hood, his long, jeans-clad legs crossed at the ankles, his arms folded over his chest.

Paula wanted to scoot inside the protection of her car's interior—not that the tiny VW, with its soft top, would give her much protection. Oh, Lord, she wished she'd driven that damned, practically bullet-proof Volvo. Pretending a nonchalance she didn't feel, she sidled around to the driver's side, but the boy straightened ominously and stepped in front of her.

"Where you goin', pretty lady?" he crooned, reaching out an arm and pulling the rubber band from her pony tail. Her hair spilled out around her shoulders. She tried to knock his hand aside and his fingers locked on her wrist. "What's that mark on your neck, baby? Your hubby been givin' you hickeys, huh? I didn't think the old man had it in 'im. Maybe the dick has some lead in his pipe, after all.''

His two friends, whom Paula just noticed leaning against a concrete wall, laughed at the crude joke.

He jerked on her wrist and pulled her closer. Paula could smell the musk of body odor and danger on his sweat-coated skin. ''I think I got me a fine piece of tail here.''

She struggled, in vain, and he laughed, enjoying her fear. Raising her other hand, she tried to swing her heavy purse at him, but one of his friends came up from behind and grabbed it, handing it to a third boy, who began to rummage through its contents.

''We gonna do a train on her, Lewis?'' the boy behind her asked, rubbing his hips against her bottom, pressing her closer to Lewis, who was now propped against the driver's door, holding the soft flesh of her upper arms in an iron grip against her rib cage. She was now sandwiched between the two hoodlums.

Lewis leered at her and thrust his crotch toward her. ''Yeah, I think this slut would enjoy a gang bang.''

She gasped.

He grinned evilly. ''Then we're gonna mark her up a bit. I warned DiCello. Maybe this time he'll lis—''

''Maybe this time *you'll* listen, Lewis. Man, we don't need this kinda shit. Let the lady go,'' a harsh, unfamiliar voice shouted behind her. Paula looked over her shoulder to see a gangly, black-haired boy approaching with two friends. They all wore the same red bandannas. And they were wielding ominous-looking knives.

''Stay out of this, Casale. This ain't your problem.'' Lewis stepped away from the car, still holding on to Paula's upper arm. The other hand pulled a knife from the waistband of his jeans.

262

Paula's heart thudded madly. With a spurt of adrenalin, she pulled out of his grasp. But immediately he backhanded her across the face and she landed against the hood of her car, jarring her hip painfully. She tasted blood on her cut lip.

"Don't move," he warned, "or you're dead."

Paula could see that he was serious. He would have no compunction at all about killing her. So she remained still and watched in horror as the six boys, three against three, circled each other.

They struggled, slicing at each other with wary attacks and withdrawals. Harsh, vicious curses and ethnic slurs were thrown into the otherwise silent street. Threats of dire consequences if one or the other didn't back down.

In the end, they seemed to realize they were evenly matched, and there were going to be no easy winners. The fight was over in seconds. Both sides backed away, not surrendering, just putting off the outcome for another day. It appeared there would be no mortal wounds struck today.

Paula exhaled on a deep sigh.

Lewis bolted with his two friends, calling over his shoulders, "I'm gonna get you for this, Casale. And you, too, Mrs. DiCello. I'm coming after you both."

Casale's two friends chased after Lewis, but Paula's rescuer stayed behind. Not out of any concern for her, she realized immediately. He was bent over at the waist in pain, bleeding from a thigh wound, and his bare arms and neck bore minor slice marks from the deadly knives.

"Get in the car," she ordered. "I'm taking you to a hospital."

"It ain't nothin'. And I'm not goin' to no friggin' hospital. Just go."

Paula clucked at his false bravado and looked about

for her purse. It was gone, of course. Well, at least, she still had her car keys in her skirt pocket. She unlocked the passenger door and pushed the youth inside. He was too weak to protest.

Quickly, she scanned the now empty street and walked around the front of the car. Soon she had the car in gear and was driving out of the city toward the hospital.

"I told you, I ain't goin' to no hospital. Besides, I just need to stop the bleeding. I've had worse than this lots of times." The boy had torn open the rip in his jeans, exposing a six-inch cut that was already coagulating. The cut couldn't be very deep. Pulling the dirty bandanna off his head, he wrapped it around the wound and winced.

"Well, it will have to be cleaned and you need an antiseptic. Where's your house? I'll drive you there. Then we'll go to the police to report this crime."

The boy shot her a look of disbelief. "Are you nuts? I'm not goin' anywhere near my . . . place. Lewis will be on the lookout for me. And the police . . . hell, I ain't gonna squeal to no pigs."

Paula started to protest, then decided that taking care of his wound was the most important thing. Looking down at the key ring in the ignition, she realized that she still had the keys to Nick's apartment—the ones he'd given her a year ago in hopes they could reconcile. Making a quick decision, she said, "We'll go to Nick's place. It's nearby. Then *we* can decide what to do. What's your name, by the way?"

"Casale."

"No, I mean your first name."

The boy jerked his head toward her in surprise. At first, he balked, then he admitted in a soft voice, "Richie."

"Well, Richie," she said, turning to him as she pulled to a stop at a red light, "I want you to know that you are my hero. And I'm going to make damn sure no one hurts you again."

He glanced at her as if she'd really flipped her lid. "Me, a hero? No way! And there ain't nothin' you can do to protect me."

"Wanna bet?" She flashed him a secretive smile. Then she ruffled his hair and leaned over to brush a kiss on his adolescent-fuzzy cheek.

He blushed and turned toward his side window, but Paula could have sworn she saw tears in his eyes.

She noticed the oddest thing then. On his left shoulder, just under the strap of his tank top, a blue-and-yellow tattoo peeked out, and it looked an awful lot like that sunflower tattoo she'd seen on Nick last night.

"Where did you get that tattoo?" she asked hesitantly.

He made a low growl of disgust. "Some broad out on Highway 10 talked me into it. I thought she was givin' me a skull, but instead, I got a damn flower. Geez! Can you believe it?"

Right now, Paula was beginning to believe anything was possible.

Chapter Nine

"Take off your jeans, Richie."

"No way! I don't take off my pants for no chick unless I'm gonna boff her." The embarrassed boy raised his chin stubbornly and plopped back down on the closed lid of the toilet in Nick's pathetically tiny bathroom.

Paula thought about telling Richie that, at his age, the only "boffing" he did was in his dreams, but then she bit her tongue. These days, the sad fact was that even outside the ghetto kids engaged in sex at fourteen.

"Listen, sweetie, I've got to clean and disinfect your cut. I can't do it through that little rip in your jeans. I promise I won't look anywhere else. You can cover yourself."

He agreed finally, but he did put a towel over himself, just in case his "assets" were too much of a temptation for her. Luckily, his wounds proved only superficial, although painful, as evidenced by the boy's tight fists and tear-filled eyes.

"Now take a shower," she said gruffly, touched by his bravery. "And put these clean clothes on," she added, shoving a bundle into his hands. "You'll feel better."

A half hour later, Paula sat out on Nick's minuscule, third-floor balcony with Richie. He wore an old Adidas T-shirt of Nick's, along with a pair of his cut-offs, which were way too big, hanging down below his skinny knees.

Her heart went out to the barefooted youth, who continued to be awestruck at being in Detective DiCello's home, meager as it was. Shifting nervously in the porch chair, he could have been any other boy in the suburbs, not the dangerous gang member she'd witnessed earlier that day.

In fact, with his too-long black hair and blue eyes, he looked an awful lot like Nick might have at that age. *I wonder what Nick's son would look like . . . our son. Now that's a dangerous train of thought.*

She smiled then, watching Richie wolf down his second bowl of SpaghettiOs, washed down with a third glass of cherry Kool-Aid. *Blech!* How could Nick eat this swill? It was the only food she'd been able to find in his apartment, aside from a six-pack of beer and a carton of milk in the fridge, a box of Froot Loops in the cupboard, and four cans of un-opened cat food in the trash can.

Speaking of cats . . . Paula looked down at the monster cat sitting imprisoned on her lap, hissing and glaring at Richie for daring to consume what she seemed to consider her personal supply of SpaghettiOs and Kool-Aid.

After all she'd learned that morning from Mrs. Chancellor, Paula now understood Nick's aversion to cats. They must remind him of his horrendous childhood in the projects and the tragic way in which his little sister had died.

Then why did Nick suddenly decide to get a cat?

The answer came to her instantly. *He wanted to please me. He wanted to show me that he's trying to change.* Paula's throat tightened with tenderness for her hard-boiled husband—a real pussycat at heart.

And she had a few other things to consider, as well. She'd almost been raped, and possibly killed, this morning. Those hoodlums had apparently threatened Nick that they would go after his wife. Perhaps other criminals he'd caught had done so, as well. In fact, he probably saw a whole lot of dangers out there everyday in his police work, *real dangers,* and he had legitimate cause to take extraordinary precautions about her safety.

Could Nick's overprotectiveness these past few years have been warranted?

No!

Well, maybe.

Oh, she wasn't saying he hadn't gone too far, but maybe . . . hmmm . . . maybe she needed to rethink some things about Nick. And herself.

Just then, Richie laid the empty bowl on the patio table and the cat made a quick, screeching leap for it.

Assuming the cat was about to attack him, Richie jerked back abruptly, causing his half-empty glass of Kool-Aid to fall from his hand to the concrete floor where it splintered apart.

"Oh, Mrs. DiCello, I'm sorry. Let me—" The horrified boy jumped from his chair and picked up a large sliver of glass.

"No, step back, Richie. You'll cut your bare feet," she warned. She went down on her haunches to pick up the remainder of the glass. Meanwhile, the stupid cat sat on the table, licking the SpaghettiOs bowl clean.

"Get up, Mrs. DiCello. Or you're gonna get cut, real bad."

Nick was in a frenzy as he approached his apartment door. An anonymous caller had alerted police to an attack on his wife earlier that day, hanging up before the desk sergeant could ask for details on whether Paula was safe or injured. He, and practically every policeman and detective in his unit, had spent the past few hours trying to locate her, to no avail.

Finally, Captain O'Malley had sent him home to shower and calm down before returning to the station. "You're not doing anyone any good, going off half-cocked like this, least of all Paula," O'Malley had told him. "Don't come back till you can think rationally."

Hah! I'll never be able to think rationally while Paula is still out there. Maybe raped. Or wounded. Or dead. No! I won't believe the worst until I find her. I've got to think she's okay. I've got to. Otherwise—

Nick stopped dead in mid-thought. A sixth sense rang like a bell inside his head. Something didn't feel right. He turned the key in his lock, and the door pushed open. Too easily.

It wasn't locked. Unlike Paula, he never left a door unlocked. Never.

"Hell!" Reflexively, he reached under his jacket and unbuckled his shoulder holster. Pulling out his gun, he moved toward the balcony where he heard Paula's voice. *Thank God!* Well, that explained the unlocked door. It appeared Paula's lack of concern over safety would never change.

He started to put his gun back in the holster, then

hesitated when he heard a loud crash, like glass breaking. Then Paula's voice. Who was Paula talking to? And in such a frantic tone of voice?

"Get up, Mrs. DiCello. Or you're gonna get cut, bad," he heard a male voice say.

Oh, God! As he approached the open balcony door, he saw Paula down on her knees and some punk leaning over her with a deadly shard of broken glass in his fingers. His heart stopped, with a lurch, and a loud roaring exploded in his ears. The weapon dripped a red substance onto the back of her white blouse.

Blood! Oh, no! Paula's blood!

Then he noticed her face. Fingermarks formed welts on her one cheek, and her upper lip appeared to be cut and slightly swollen.

A boiling haze of fury threatened to blind Nick for that brief second before he assumed a firing position. Unhooking the strap over the hammer of his gun, he spread his legs, dropped into a slight crouch, and took aim, wrapping all ten fingers around the handle of the revolver. With one finger over the trigger, he pointed at the perp's back, dead center.

"*Freeze!*" he yelled in warning. "Police!"

The guy turned with surprise, then stared at him wide-eyed with fear, his eyes riveted on the gun in Nick's hands.

Casale? What the hell is Casale doing attacking my wife?

Nick lowered his gun momentarily in surprise, then raised it again. "Drop your weapon, boy. Slowly. Or . . . you . . . are . . . dead. And, believe me, you slimeball, it will give me great pleasure to be the one to off you."

"Nick, are you crazy? Put that gun away. *Now!*" Paula stood and glared at him.

"Move over here, Paula. It's okay now. He can't hurt you anymore."

Instead of obeying his orders, his contrary wife stepped in front of Casale, protecting him with outspread arms.

"Move, Paula. This isn't a game. It's—"

"I'll tell you what it is, you jerk," she snapped angrily. "It's a big misunderstanding. This boy saved my life today, and you almost killed him. Are you nuts?"

"Saved your life?" he repeated numbly.

"Yes, he chased away some gang members who tried to attack me, and he got hurt in the process. He didn't want to go to the hospital, and your apartment was closer than mine. So I brought him here." She took in a big swallow of air after her long-winded explanation.

"But the blood . . . ?" He glanced down at the puddle on the balcony floor.

"Blood?" She tilted her head with confusion, then made a clucking sound of disgust. "Cherry Kool-Aid, you fool."

"Kool . . . Kool-Aid! But . . . how about those bruises on your face?"

"Lewis backhanded her," Casale interjected.

"Lewis?" Nick blinked as understanding seeped into his thick head, and his heart slowed down to about a hundred and fifty beats per second. He lowered the gun and sank into a nearby chair, his hands shaking visibly. He laid his gun on the table. "Jesus, you scared the hell out of me today, Paula," he said on a loud exhale.

"I scared *you?* Why, you big doofus! Look what you've done to this boy."

Reluctantly, he raised his eyes to Casale, who looked as if he might have wet his shorts with fright.

Then Nick's eyes widened in surprise as he noticed something else. The kid was wearing *his* cut-off shorts. And his T-shirt, too.

Oh, Lord.

"I better go," Casale said, inching his way toward the apartment door.

"No!" Nick shouted.

Both Casale and Paula jumped.

"I mean, I want you to stay. I'm sorry if I overreacted—"

"Overreacted?" Paula snorted. "You almost killed an innocent boy. I'd say that's a hell of a lot worse than overreaction."

Nick winced at her harsh appraisal.

"Sit down, Richie," he said, more softly, deliberately using his given name. "Please. We need to talk."

After a half hour in which Paula and Richie explained what had happened that morning, and Nick told them of his frantic search for her after the anonymous tip, they all relaxed a bit.

While Nick reported in to the police station, Richie ate what Paula told Nick, with a raised eyebrow, was a third can of his SpaghettiOs and the last of his cherry Kool-Aid. He sensed one of her nutrition lectures coming later.

Finally, he told Richie, "C'mon, kid."

"Nick, you can't take him home. Those other gang members will look for him there."

"Paula, this kid doesn't have a home."

"What . . . what do you mean?"

"He lives in a shelter, or the street."

"How'd you know that, man?"

"I know *everything* about you, my friend." Nick turned back to Paula, continuing, "His dad took off a long time ago, and his mother's in prison for theft and possession and sale of a controlled substance.''

''And prostitution,'' Richie added in a flat voice.

Paula gasped, raising tear-filled eyes helplessly to Nick. ''On the streets? Homeless?''

''Don't worry,'' he assured his wife. ''I'm gonna take him someplace where he'll be safe.''

''Where?'' Richie demanded. ''I ain't goin' to no juvie hall.''

''No, I'm not taking you to a reformatory,'' he said, ruffling Richie's hair with sudden affection. His throat choked up as he realized the punk had saved his wife's life. He owed him big time. ''Richie, I'm going to find a better place for you. Just like someone did for me a long time ago. Like I should have done for you before . . .'' He felt a huge lump of emotion grow in his throat, and he couldn't continue.

But Paula and Richie stood with arms folded over their chests stubbornly, refusing to budge.

''Okay, I made a few calls after I booked you the last time,'' he explained to the boy. ''There's this program called The Second Mile that places inner city kids in foster care programs. In fact, I already talked to some people about a vacancy in their residence in central Pennsylvania. They have a home with resident house parents for boys from inner cities. It's run by Jerry Sandusky, the Penn State football team's defensive coordinator.''

Both Paula and Richie listened with furrowed brows to his long explanation.

''So?'' Richie asked finally, trying to sound coolly indifferent, but clearly interested.

''So, it would give you a chance to live in a normal home atmosphere, out of the ghetto. Maybe even go to college someday. Hell, this could be your ticket to a better life, boy. Are you interested?''

Richie shuffled his feet. ''I ain't never been outside

Newark. Are there cows and stuff there? I ain't never
even seen a real cow.''

Nick pressed his lips together to stifle a smile.
''State College is a big town, but there might be a
cow or two on the outskirts.''

''And you say you lived in one of these places
once?''

Nick nodded, ignoring Paula's surprised expression.

Fear and hope fought a battle on Richie's open
face. Hope won out. ''Maybe.''

''All right. I'm going to take you over to the home
of a friend of mine, George Madison. He acts as a
liaison with The Second Mile. You can stay there
tonight, and tomorrow someone will drive you to
State College to visit.'' Nick turned to Paula then.
''Does that meet with your approval?''

She didn't have to answer. The tears in her eyes
spoke volumes.

''I'll be back in an hour. And you''—he pointed a
finger at his stubborn wife—''stay right here. Don't
move from this apartment till I get back. We have
some major talking to do, babe.''

''Babe? You call your wife 'babe'?'' Richie snickered. ''Cool! I didn't think old people did that.'' Then
his eyes almost bugged out as he looked at something
behind Nick. ''Wow!''

Nick turned and his eyes did bug out. His damn
cat was sprawled, big as you please, on his favorite
easy chair in the living room. Popping out baby cats.

Paula helped him make the cat more comfortable
and had to tell him at least ten times to stop swearing
in front of the boy. *Hah!* As if Richie couldn't teach
him a few blue words!

''Hell, what am I going to do with five cats? Oh,
no! There comes another one. Geez! I won't be able

to breathe. There'll be cat hair everywhere. I'll go broke buying SpaghettiOs. Bet there's lice on—''

"Shut up, Nick," she said softly. "I'll help you find a home for them. Relax.''

"Easy for you to say," he muttered.

The last straw came when he was walking out of the apartment with his arm looped over the kid's shoulder, and Paula called out, "Nick, did you know that Richie has a tattoo just like yours?''

"Huh?" He glanced down to where Richie's stretched neckband had slipped over to one side. He burst out laughing. It was probably delayed hysteria.

A sunflower stood out like a beacon on Richie's shoulder. Just like Nick's.

The kid looked at him in question. "Whoa! You have a sunflower tattoo, too?''

Nick nodded, with a sick feeling in the pit of his stomach. "Madame Nadine, right?''

"Yep," Richie said and grinned. "She said it would bring me good luck. She said there was going to be a dark stranger coming to save me, like one of those old knights, and—'' He gaped at Nick suddenly, as if he'd sprouted a suit of shining armor.

"Hell!" Nick exclaimed.

"That's what I said to Madame Nadine." Then Richie seemed to think of something else. "I don't s'pose you got a horse?''

"No, just a cat that looks like a horse.''

Before he closed the door, making sure to secure the locks, he heard Paula laugh and add, "Don't forget the camel.''

Chapter Ten

After taking Richie to George Madison's house, Nick spent some time reassuring the boy that everything would be okay. Actually, Richie and George, a young guidance counselor at a nearby private school, hit it off great. Nick had a good feeling about Richie and his future.

His own future was a lot more shaky.

Nick decided to take the long way home. Thinking. Making decisions.

He'd almost killed an innocent boy today. And that had taught him a screeching big lesson.

He felt like a monster, a cripple, handicapped by his overwhelming need to screen his wife from the dark side of life.

Paula was right. He was obsessed with her safety.

Hell, life was dangerous everywhere today. Even in the suburbs. Even in rural America. He'd been looking for guarantees where none existed. People couldn't live in glass cages to avoid danger, the way he'd been trying to do with Paula. That was no way to survive. No way to live.

How could I have been so blind? Over and over he berated himself with that question as he drove aimlessly.

The big question was, could he change?

Unfortunately, the answer was no. At least, not in the big ways that would matter most to Paula.

I'm going to have to let Paula go, he decided finally.

His heart ached at the thought, and tears welled in his eyes, but Paula had been right about another thing, too. Sometimes, real love meant letting go. As much as it hurt, that was just what Nick resolved to do. For Paula.

I'm going to have to be a hero. Nick laughed cynically at the prospect.

It won't be so bad, he tried to tell himself. *I could always quit my job, give up my dismal excuse for an apartment, and move to the Bahamas. Become a beach bum. Drink beer all the time. Learn to surf.*

He tried to smile, but all he could manage was a grimace.

Hey, I know, I could become a private detective and ask Madame Nadine to go into business with me. We could call ourselves The Psycho Detective Agency.

No, no, no! I've got it. I'll locate that codger from the bookstore, and we'll write a sex advice book together. Sex For the Brain-Challenged, *or, better yet,* Screwing for Screw-ups.

A lump of despair the size of a cantaloupe lodged in his throat. Probably a hair ball.

Speaking of cats. I could always become a cat

breeder. He shuddered with distaste. Now, that wasn't even funny.

Finally, two hours later, Nick let himself into his apartment. He didn't even curse when the door opened too easily. Apparently, Paula had disobeyed his orders to stay put. As usual.

The smells of good home cooking permeated the air. Paula must have gone to the grocery store.

He sniffed appreciatively, leaning back against the door with closed eyes. Marinara sauce. That probably meant angel hair pasta. He sniffed again. Bacon. Aaah! Spinach salad with hot bacon dressing. Two of his favorites.

This is going to be a lot harder than I thought.

"Nick, is that you?"

"No, it's Jack the Ripper. And you left the door unlocked for him."

"Oh." There was a long pause; then she said weakly, "I guess I forgot . . . again."

She stepped out of the kitchen.

And his knees buckled.

He braced one hand on the wall for support. His shattered nerves had sustained a number of shocks today. Apparently, the bumpy road was far from over.

Paula was wearing scanty, cream-colored silk tap pants and a matching camisole edged in lace. And that was all.

He gulped. *Yep, this is going to be a whole lot harder than I thought.*

The racy undergarments were intended to be the ingredients for Fantasy Number Four. Well, that was out of the question now.

She smiled shyly at him and laid some napkins on the table, which she'd placed invitingly before the balcony door. Even a tablecloth had appeared from somewhere. Son of a gun! His tiny apartment looked almost presentable. *Maybe I won't move to the Bahamas and drink beer, after all. I can wallow right here in comfort.*

Then he noticed her toenails. *Pink! She painted her toenails pink. Oh, that's a low blow. She knows how I love her toes, especially in pink polish. I am in bi-i-g trouble!*

Get a grip, DiCello, he told himself. *Your brain is splintering apart.*

"I found these clothes in some Victoria's Secret boxes in your bedroom. I couldn't resist trying them on. I assumed . . . I mean, I probably shouldn't have . . . but I assumed they were for me." Her face flamed with embarrassment.

He should tell her they belonged to someone else. He should say he'd bought them for another woman. "They're for you," he said gruffly, moving closer. "Along with all the sexy things in those other boxes."

She raised an eyebrow at him. "More of your middle-aged sexual fantasy stuff?"

"Yep." He furrowed his brow suspiciously. What was Paula up to here?

Well, whatever it was, he would have to resist. He would have to push her away. Be a hero.

But the unheroic side of his brain disagreed. It forced him to grin, loop a forefinger under one of the tiny straps at her shoulder, and tug, closing the gap between them.

The lemony fragrance of her perfume wafted around him, enticing his senses. *Okay, I know I've got to be a hero, but there's nothing in the hero code that says I can't enjoy the smells before taking off into the sunset.*

His gaze shifted back to her scandalous attire. "A perfect fit, I see." *Or the view. There's nothing wrong with a hero looking . . . one last time.*

"Uh-huh." Her lips parted and she stared up at him through sultry, half-lidded eyes.

His noble decision to let Paula go weighed heavily on him. Being a hero was proving to be real tough. He backed up a step, his eyes narrowing suspiciously. "What are you up to, Paula?"

"Up to? Me?" She batted her lashes at him with mock innocence, then added, "Who did you send into the store to buy this stuff? One of the female detectives?" She began to stalk him. Closer and closer.

He took another step backward, around the table. "I picked them all out myself, babe," he said in a wounded voice. "And I didn't need to ask anyone about sizes, either." He looked her over meaningfully. "I have a perfect memory."

She laughed, a delightful, joyous sound that rippled over his parched soul like rain in the desert.

"You? A macho guy like you traipsing around in a lingerie store? I find that hard to believe," she scoffed, but Nick could see that she was pleased.

He felt confused and disoriented, barely able to follow their conversation.

Yep, this is going to be a whole helluva lot harder than I'd expected.

He steeled himself to be strong and deliberately put the table between them. "One of the clerks asked me if I'd like her to model that outfit," he said, his eyes feasting on her skimpy, delicious attire. It was best if he went for a light mood. It was best if he didn't even look at his wife. It was best if he got the hell out of there.

"I'll bet she did," Paula snapped. Jealousy turned her cheeks pink with chagrin.

He liked that. "But I told her I'd rather see my *wife* do the modeling."

280

Paula blinked rapidly at him.

"Don't you dare cry."

"I'm not crying." She wiped her eyes, nonetheless, and asked, "Is Richie okay?"

Now, this was safe territory. "Yeah. I'll stop by to see him again tomorrow before he leaves. In fact . . . well, I was thinking . . . maybe I'll drive up to see him in a couple of days."

She nodded.

"How about the damn cat?" he asked, floundering for neutral subjects. *Yep, it is definitely best to change the subject. And what better way to cool my ardor than talk about cats.* "How many kittens do I have to blackmail my friends into taking?" he asked, concerned about Gargoyle and her progeny, despite himself.

"Seven. And the mother is just fine." She pointed to a corner of the living room where a large wicker cat bed was situated with the happy family firmly ensconced. Nearby, a litter box stood ready. He raised an eyebrow. Apparently, Paula had done more than a little shopping in his absence.

Then her words sank in. "Seven! I don't know enough people I hate enough to foist seven cats on."

"Now, Nick, I know you don't really mean that."

"Don't bet the farm on it, babe. How soon can I take Gargoyle back to Madame Nadine?"

"You're still going to take her back?" she asked in surprise. "I thought maybe you two had bonded by now."

"Bonded? Are you nuts? I'd rather bond with a barrel of Krazy Glue."

Paula smiled and sashayed around the table. That was the only way to describe the swish and sway of her hips in the revealing tap pants.

He forgot to move. When he did, belatedly, the

back of his knees hit the seat of a straight-backed chair. He plopped down.

"Paula, we have to talk about . . ." he started to say.

At the same time, she said, "Nick, honey, I want to thank you . . ."

Honey? Uh-oh! "Listen, Paula, I've finally realized . . . huh? What do you have to thank me for?"

"For taking care of Richie. He's a good kid. He reminds me of you."

"Hah! No way!" But secretly, now that he thought about it, he agreed. "Besides, it's my job. Actually, it's kind of nice to be able to help a kid once in a while. Mostly, I just lock them up."

"Oh, Nick."

"Don't start feeling sorry for me, Paula. And stop changing the subject. About the divorce. I've decided . . ." He gulped, having trouble spitting out the words.

"Later, sweetheart. Right now . . . are you hungry?"

"What?"

She didn't give him a chance to answer. Instead, she moved in for the kill. With the ease of a siren, she slipped onto his lap, straddling his legs. Looping her arms around his neck, she asked huskily, "Well?"

"Huh?"

"Are you hungry?"

"Oh, yeah."

She squirmed her silk-clad bottom up higher on his lap, and he felt fireworks ignite all over his body. In fact, his rocket practically left the launch pad.

He tried to remember his earlier resolve. Their marriage was over. He was going to let her go. He was going to be a hero.

"Take off your jacket and shirt, Nick," she coaxed as she nibbled his cheek and neck. "Your gun is poking me."

"Which gun?" he choked out, feeling like he was about to explode.

One side of his brain said he should fight his baser urges as Paula laughed seductively and helped him slip out of his coat. His conscience screamed, *Get up and walk out the door. It's over between me and Paula. It has to be.*

But the other, stronger side of his brain argued, *Well, maybe there could be one last time.*

Sighing in surrender, he unbuckled his holster and let it slide to the floor, then watched with fascination as Paula unbuttoned his shirt, pressing gentle kisses along the path of his exposed chest.

He groaned. "I'm trying to be a hero here, Paula," he protested half-heartedly.

"You *are* my hero, Nick."

"Oh, great! Make me feel guilty. Paula . . . could you stop touching me *there,* babe . . . listen . . . I don't believe you just did *that* . . . oh, Lord . . . oh, Lord, this is not a good idea."

"Honey, this is the best idea I've had all day. In fact, all week. Maybe even all year." She moved her hips against him and he almost shot out of the chair. "Don't move," she ordered. "Just let me . . ."

She looked at him through dreamy green eyes, and he knew he was lost.

With a knowing smile, she placed a fingertip on the pulse point in his neck, and his heartbeat accelerated.

She fingered the edges of his hair, brushed his collarbone, stroked his bare arms. And he made a hissing sound of surrender.

Gently, he rocked his hips forward, and a mewling

cry of sweet surprise escaped her parted lips. To his satisfaction, her long lashes fluttered uncontrollably.

Pleasure flooded through him in a violent shiver. He felt like he was catapulting through space. His body ached from scalp to toe.

She put her hands on either side of his face, gently, and pressed her lips to his, whispering throatily, "Nick."

Just "Nick."

But that one word shattered any resistance he had left. His mouth opened under hers, taking her tempting tongue. He grew against her.

She gasped, then drew back slightly. For a brief second, the intense physical awareness resonated between them as their eyes held.

Okay, so I'll be a hero a half hour from now. Hah! Who am I kidding? Ten minutes from now. Then he placed her hand over his sex. He almost passed out from the bone-melting waves of sweet heat that licked over him. He was barely aware that Paula was undoing his belt buckle and unzipping his fly. He watched helplessly as she took him in one hand and used the other to push aside the wide leg of her panties. With a long, drawn-out sigh, she raised herself slightly, then eased down, inch by excruciating inch, onto his erection until he was buried in her hot center.

"Pau-la," he ground out, putting his wide palms on her buttocks to hold her in place. When the first turbulent wave of his arousal had passed, he leaned down and kissed her taut nipples through the silk camisole. Her head reared back and she began to whimper.

"Now," he said, still embedded in her.

She nodded and slowly undulated her hips. Expertly, her slick sheath stroked him, building the fires of his molten desire.

Heart Craving

He wanted to make it last forever.

It was over in minutes.

But they were the best damn minutes of his life.

Breathing raggedly, he wrapped his arms around her waist and feathered kisses over her lips and neck and shoulders, whispering soft endearments between each kiss. His love flowed over them both, and her eyes grew large and liquid with emotion.

When he felt himself begin to thicken again, he stood abruptly, with Paula still riding his sex, and laid her on the table, sweeping aside the placemats and napkins. He climbed up with her and reached down and behind to grip her ankles and pull them up and out. This time, his body hammered its need into her welcoming folds. Penetrating deep, he used his body to show her how very much he loved her.

When the first tingles of his impending climax flash-flooded through his body, he laced his fingers with hers, holding her to the table, and pummeled her with rapid-fire, mind-blowing strokes. Her eyes gazed up at him, unfocused and misty with passion. She made soft, mewling sounds of entreaty, "Please, Nick . . . oh, no . . . oh, yes . . . now . . . *now!*"

He slammed into her one last time, crying out his triumphant release.

And she wrapped her legs around his waist, yielding to the uncontrollable convulsions of her own climax which alternately clasped and unclasped his sex.

When he was finally able to breathe, he rolled off Paula and tucked her under his arm. He kissed her softly, smiling against her lips. "That was some appetizer, babe."

She slanted him a look of disbelief, then answered saucily, "Wait till you see what I have for the main course."

That was when he remembered his good intentions.

There was going to be no main course for them.

But Paula had other intentions.

And Nick's willpower seemed to have taken a leave of absence, he learned, as Paula served him one delicious "main course" after another, each wrapped in a different Victoria's Secret outfit. Nick swore he was going to buy stock in the company first thing Monday morning.

About 2:00 A.M., they finally decided to eat dinner.

"Nick, why is that sock sitting on the kitchen counter?" Paula said as she prepared to put the food on the table.

"It's my potholder," he said distractedly as he soaked in the remarkable view of Paula in a red-and-black bustier and garter belt, bent over the oven where a loaf of garlic bread was warming.

"A potholder!" she exclaimed, peering up at him over her shoulder. She tsked her disapproval when she noticed the target of his perusal—her nicely curved derriere.

"I haven't had a chance to shop lately," he said sheepishly.

She made another tsking sound and placed the bread on the table alongside the pasta and salad. She motioned him to sit down and commented idly, "And how come your jockey shorts look so gray? Not to mention the sheets and dish towels."

"Shampoo." He was already helping himself to a generous serving of the food, realizing belatedly that he hadn't eaten all day.

"Shampoo?" Paula blinked at him with confusion.

"Yeah. I ran out of soap powder; so I've been using Prell in the washing machine. Lord, you should have seen all the bubbles. The building manager told me he's gonna sue me if I ever do it again." He was eating ravenously the whole time he talked. Finally, he glanced up when he noticed the silence. "What? Why are you looking at me like that?"

"Oh, Nick."

"Now what? You look like you're gonna cry. Just because I ran out of soap powder?"

"Because I lo—"

"Hey, it's no big deal," he interrupted in a panic. He couldn't let her finish. He just couldn't. He wanted to believe there was still a chance for them, but he was afraid to hope. And he didn't want to break this precious bond that connected them tonight.

He searched his brain for a way to change the subject. "Geez, if that's what turns you on, maybe I should tell you what I've been using for a toilet brush."

She stared at him incredulously, then laughed. "I don't think I want to know."

"You know, Skip passes on the best tips to me."

"I can imagine."

"Betcha didn't know what you can do with the crumbs at the bottom of a toaster."

"Throw them away?" she suggested.

"Nah, they make great croutons."

They exchanged a smile. Nick wished he could freeze the moment and make time stand still. "God help me," he murmured under his breath.

When they returned to the bedroom, Nick undressed her slowly, worshipfully. With each garment that slid off her body to the carpet, his lips followed the silken path, whispering soft words of appreciation at the beauty of her smooth skin, the sensitivity of her breasts, the flatness of her stomach, the length of her legs.

Dropping his shorts, he stood before her, inhaling her lemony cologne. "Do you know that I bought a sack of lemons one day and squeezed them in bowls all over the apartment just to remind me of you?'' he disclosed as he ran the pad of his thumb over her parted lips.

She leaned closer. ''Oh, honey, I—''

''And once I went into Saks and had the clerk take out one perfume sample after another, trying to find yours.''

A sad smile curved her mouth. ''It's Jean Naté cologne. They sell it in the drugstore, silly. Not Saks.'' She reached up a hand to cup the side of his face.

He took her hand in his and kissed the palm, then the wrist. He felt her pulse jump against his lips.

Feeling dizzy and intoxicated, Nick led his wife to the bed. Frozen in a limbo of love and pure physical sensation, he pushed all logic aside and wanted to believe that anything was possible.

He would never forget a single detail of this night. *Never!*

Forcing her to remain immobile on her back, he paid homage to her body, from scalp to toe.

''Lie still, hon. Let me do the work,'' he implored huskily against the soft curve of her throat.

''But Nick—''

''Shhh.'' His lips moved lower and covered one breast.

''Oooooh, my God!'' she keened and arched her chest up off the bed.

He suckled rhythmically.

And she began to make low, whimpering gasps of need.

He smiled and drew back, examining the wet nipple appreciatively.

''Don't stop,'' she cried out.

He moved to the other breast obediently. ''As if I ever could!'' he said against the hot, turgid flesh.

By the time he had traveled the slow, slow journey

over her responsive body, giving particular attention to the shadowy curve under her arms, the dip of her navel, the backs of her knees, even her delicious toes, Paula was writhing from side to side, begging him to end her torment. "Now, Nick. I want you *now.*"

She tried to reach up for him, but he pushed her back gently and knelt between her outspread thighs. "Uh-uh, babe," he asserted with a low growl. Placing his palms under her buttocks, he lifted her up off the mattress and nuzzled her hair. "You've been providing me with one main course after another, sweetheart. It's time for a feast of another kind."

By the time they were both satisfied, Nick lay depleted on his back, his arms thrown over his head, his legs spread with satiety. Sweat coated both their slick bodies and the only sounds in the deep night were those of their syncopated, ragged breaths.

He pulled Paula into the crook of his arm and kissed the top of her head. "That was sensational, honey."

"Yeah, it was, wasn't it?"

Paula raised herself slightly and brushed the hair off his forehead. "I know about your childhood, Nick."

An icy foreboding rippled over him. "What do you mean?"

"Mrs. Chancellor told me about your sister Lita . . . how she died. And about your brother in prison. Nick, why didn't you tell me? Maybe I would have understood you better. Maybe—"

All of Nick's new-found hopes for their future came crashing down. "Damn her! She had no right," Nick exclaimed, trying to push Paula to the side so he could get up.

She wouldn't let him. "I'm glad she did. At least

now we have some logical point where we can start to communicate.''

Pity . . . Paula had made love with him out of pity. And, oh, God, now she knew how he'd let his family down. How he'd fail her, too. Pain roiled in his head in angry waves. He couldn't think. ''I don't want to talk about my past, or Lita, or the projects, or—''

''I know, I know, but we will. Tomorrow.'' She burrowed closer and chuckled softly.

''What's so funny? You think the things Mrs. Chancellor blabbed to you are humorous?''

''Of course not. I was just thinking that you must have learned a lot from all those books.''

''What books?'' Her change of subject puzzled him.

''When I was looking through those Victoria's Secret boxes, I saw that pile of books in the back of the closet. Since when are you into how-to sex books?''

Then he remembered. *Oops!* ''Since I lost you.''

She propped herself on one elbow and stared down at him. ''You'd better explain that.''

He told her all about Madame Nadine, and Paula's mouth dropped open. ''You went to a fortune-teller to get advice on how to win me back? *You?*''

''Yeah. Dumb, wasn't I?'' He felt his face turn hot. ''But she's not just a fortune-teller. She also does tattoos. And other stuff.'' He rolled his eyes meaningfully, then told her about the character at the bookstore. She laughed till tears ran down her face.

He kissed them away.

Nestling at his side once again, she yawned and said, ''So all these sexual fantasy events were at Madame Nadine's suggestion?''

''Well, not exactly. She told me I had to find your 'heart craving', and I punched in cravings at the bookstore computer, and it came back with all these sexual fantasy titles, and I thought . . ." His words trailed off as he realized how ridiculous they sounded. "Hey, it made sense at the time."

Paula shook her head hopelessly. "You jerk. The only craving I've ever had that you didn't meet was the need to be free of your obsessiveness."

"Free?" Nick felt like he'd been blindsided. "I thought you loved me."

"What does love have to do with it? You're my husband, not my jailer. A wife shouldn't feel like a prisoner."

"I didn't realize . . . you've been miserable, haven't you, Paula?"

"Very," she agreed with a yawn. "Freedom, that's all I ever wanted, but you wouldn't listen. I've been so unhappy for so long. I can't remember what it's like to feel happy—and free—anymore."

Paula didn't know how her words shattered him. She just burrowed closer and yawned again. "We must have a *long* talk in the morning, Nick. I see so many things differently now. You do, too. I know you do." And she fell instantly asleep.

But Nick didn't sleep at all that night. He kept thinking about her words, "I've been so unhappy for so long."

Paula loved him. Nick knew that. And he loved her. Too damn much.

Well, it was time to prove that love.

Toward morning, with tears welling in his eyes, Nick kissed his sleeping wife one last time and rose from the bed. Minutes later, he signed a note, which he left for her on the table. Then he slipped out the door, unable to stop himself from double-checking the lock.

"Be happy, Paula," he whispered in a broken voice.

291

Chapter Eleven

Day Seven

Paula overslept.

When she awakened, the warm sun already streamed through the open balcony door, portending another hot summer day. Maybe she could talk Nick into going to the beach house with her later. In fact, if he had any vacation time coming, they could spend the week there, sort of a second honeymoon.

She smiled and rolled over to the side, opening her eyes.

Nick was gone.

That wasn't really surprising, she decided, despite her disappointment. It must be close to 10:00 A.M., and he usually started his shift at nine. She *was* surprised that he hadn't awakened her to say good-bye, though. Well, he was only being considerate, she concluded.

Stretching languidly, she relished the ache of muscles that hadn't been exercised in a long time—until the past few days. Looking down, she saw whisker burns on her breasts, a bruise on her thigh, even a faint bite mark on her flat belly.

She felt an odd thrill, seeing those marks of Nick's fierce lovemaking on her skin. He'd been so hungry. For her. And that was a powerful compliment, in her opinion.

A hazy memory nagged at her of their conversation before she fell asleep. Something about his past and her heart craving.

But it was the strange, forlorn look on his face she remembered now. Hmmm. Shrugging, she figured it would all be cleared up today.

She swung her legs over the side of the bed. Today was going to be the first day of the rest of their lives *together*. That meant lots of work. She began to make a mental list.

Number one, of course, she and Nick had to talk. Clearly, they loved each other as much as ever. That was the most important thing.

Number two, she had to phone her lawyer and call off the divorce proceedings.

Number three, she and Nick would need to make arrangements to sublet his apartment and sell her condo. She wanted their new beginning to start in a home of *both* their choosing, not just his. Although she would insist on no bars on the windows, she was ready to compromise on some of his safety measures.

Number four, she would call Mrs. Chancellor and withdraw her job application. After her near escape yesterday, she saw the logic in Nick's concern for her safety. They'd both been at fault over the danger issue, but she could make concessions, if he could.

Suddenly Paula realized how much she'd learned

the last few days about Nick and herself. His obsessiveness over her safety had forced her into a corner, but now she saw the reasons for his overprotectiveness.

And he had been trying to change. He really had.

To think that he'd actually gone to a fortune-teller for help! She grinned and shook her head hopelessly. How endearing it was that Nick had staged all those sexual fantasy events just to satisfy her "heart."

The fool! Didn't he know that the only thing her heart had ever craved was his love—an unconditional love, free of obsessiveness? The love had never died, for either of them, and she vowed that in the future there would be open lines of communication between them—no more secrets.

She determined to meet this Madame Nadine, too. She had a lot to thank her for, and not just that adorable cat, Gargoyle.

Okay, first things first. Coffee. She needed coffee to jumpstart the day.

After checking to make sure Gargoyle and her kittens were all right and supplied with fresh food and water, Paula headed for the kitchen. Grimacing with distaste, she began to wash last night's dirty dishes while her instant coffee heated in the microwave.

That was when she noticed the note on the table.

A tingle of foreboding swept her body as she walked closer. With trepidation, she picked it up.

She gasped and pressed one hand over her heart as she began to read.

Paula: I love you. Because of that love, I'm giving you your heart craving—your freedom. It's the hardest, most heroic thing I've ever done in my life. I won't be at the hearing today, but

Heart Craving

I've signed the papers for you.
Be happy, babe. Just be happy.
Love,
Nick

Tears welled in Paula's eyes and spilled over. *A hero? The jerk! Now, after all this time, he decides to be noble.*

Paula sobbed softly, but more for Nick than for herself. She knew how much Nick must love her to have signed these papers. She knew he'd done it for her. Hot tears burned her eyes, streaming down her cheeks.

They should have talked their problems out last night before falling asleep. But she'd been so confident that their marriage was over the biggest hurdle. Why couldn't Nick have understood, without the words?

He couldn't read her mind any more than she'd been able to read his all these years, she immediately chastised herself.

God, I love the man. And, God, how I'd like to whack some sense into his thick skull. He should have talked to me first! How long is it going to take him to learn that communication is our problem, not any "heart craving"?

Wiping the tears from her eyes with a tissue, she stood and lifted her chin resolutely. Oh, she wasn't going to let the numbskull go, but she decided he needed to be taught a lesson. Tapping a forefinger thoughtfully against her chin, she pondered all her choices.

Finally, she smiled.

After canceling the hearing with her lawyer, who was not surprised at all, she called Skip. He listened as she outlined her plan.

"Stop laughing, Skip. I'm serious."

"That's why I'm laughing."

"Are you going to help me?"

"Yeah, I guess so. Can I follow and watch?"

"No."

"Dammit, Paula, you guys are no fun. Nick wouldn't let me stay and watch you ride a camel, and—"

"I did not ride a camel," she said indignantly.

"—or model Jezebel's harem outfit."

Jezebel? I'm going to kill Nick. "Are you going to help me or not?"

"Okay, but I expect a full report from both of you. I can't wait to see what you two come up with next."

Yeah, me, too.

"Are you sure you don't want to try my idea of being a stripper at the club, and Nick an unsuspecting member of the audience? The owner still hasn't found a replacement for Lee."

"Maybe some other time."

Nick had gone into work that morning, but one look at his ashen face and Captain O'Malley had sent him home. Of course, he couldn't go home yet. Paula would still be there, and he couldn't face her. Not today when their marriage would be ending.

Instead, he'd gone to Madison's house and talked to Richie for a long time. Over breakfast at McDonald's, he'd reassured the kid that moving out of the city would be the best thing, that it had worked for him. And he'd promised Richie that he could call him anytime, that he could consider him a friend.

After that, he'd driven to the projects and stood, leaning against his car in the parking lot, watching the everyday activities. Nothing changed here in the ghetto. Nothing. But he should have put all this behind him long ago. Instead, he'd carried his past around like an albatross.

In a way, he was saying good-bye to his sister Lita, as well as Paula, today. The guilt had somehow slipped off his shoulders.

He looked at his watch and sighed. 1:45 P.M. The hearing was scheduled for 2:00 P.M. Another half hour, and he could go home to drink himself into numbness. Then tomorrow, he was going to have to learn how to live without Paula, one day at a time.

But first, he wanted to stop by Madame Nadine's and give her a piece of his mind. Some psychic she turned out to be!

Fifteen minutes later, Nick sat in his car along the highway, stunned.

There was no rundown yellow house. No sign that proclaimed, MADAME NADINE: FORTUNE TELLING, LOVE POTIONS, MIRACLES. And in smaller letters, HAIR WAXING AND TATTOOS, BY APPOINTMENT. No giant sunflowers. No herd of cats.

He hit the side of his head with the heel of his palm and looked again. Nothing. Just an empty lot overgrown with knee-high weeds.

He saw a jogger approaching and rolled down the passenger window. "Hey, buddy, what happened to the house that was here yesterday?"

The middle-aged Yuppie in designer shorts and $300 shoes leaned down, wheezing. "What house?"

"The fortune-teller's house that was sitting right there." Nick pointed behind the jogger.

The guy backed away suspiciously. "There was no house there. I've been running this route every day for the past year, and that empty lot's always been an eyesore. You must be lost."

Yep, I'm lost all right, Nick decided, watching the man lope off. *I've taken advice from a psychic who doesn't exist. I've practically kept my wife prisoner for years with my obsessions. And then I almost kill an innocent kid. "Lost" about says it all.*

Then he thought of something else. How could he have a real tattoo from an imaginary person?

Another mind picture immediately followed, and he frowned. *Gargoyle.* He had the cat Madame Nadine had given him; so, that must mean she existed. Right?

Nick closed his eyes and pressed his head on the steering wheel. The mother of all headaches pounded behind his eyes. He didn't understand any of this. Was Madame Nadine an angel or something? Had she been sent here to help him solve his problems? Or was it all a figment of his desperate imagination?

Nick knew his problems were about to get worse when he heard a motor behind him. He raised his head and looked in the rearview mirror.

A police car.

Great! Now everyone will know what a lunatic I've become.

The car door opened and a female officer emerged.

His mouth dropped open, and his heart started beating like a jackhammer.

Paula, wearing a female police uniform, approached his open car window. Stern-faced, she asked, "What are you doin' here, fella? Admiring the view?" She jerked her head toward the sorry-looking lot.

"Looking for Madame Nadine."

Paula raised an eyebrow.

"She disappeared."

"Oh?"

"It appears she never existed."

That got her attention, but she quickly hid her interest. "It's illegal to loiter along a public highway,

298

mister. I think I'm going to have to take you in.''

"Listen, Paula, I'm not in the mood for games today. And you could get in big trouble impersonating an officer.''

"You did it,'' she reminded him.

"I *am* an officer, dammit.'' Suddenly, he remembered and looked down at his watch. 2:00 P.M. His heart threatened to jump right out of his chest, and his blood began to roar in his ears. "Shouldn't you be somewhere about now?''

She ignored his question and strummed her fingertips on the roof of the car.

He tried to ignore her puffy lips, swollen from his kisses, or the passion mark on her neck. More than anything in the world, he wanted to pull her into the car, on his lap, and tell her how much he missed her . . . *already*.

"I definitely think I'm going to have to take you in for questioning,'' she concluded. "Slide over.''

"What?''

"Move over to the passenger side, mister. I'm confiscating this vehicle.''

"Oh, Lord,'' he muttered, but inclined his head in compliance. He felt something hard brush his wrist and glanced down, his eyes widening with disbelief. She'd handcuffed his left hand to her right one. "Are you nuts?''

"Maybe.'' Then she had the nerve to wink at him. "I'm just making sure you don't escape this time.''

"Escape? This time? Damn, Paula, would you watch where you're driving! You almost backended that car.''

"I'm not used to driving with one hand manacled to a prisoner.'' She took the berm of the road at sixty miles per hour. Gravel was flying everywhere.

"I'm not your prisoner.''

"Think again, buddy," she said, slanting him a seductive look, and yanked his chain.

"Ouch! That hurt."

She zig-zagged in one lane and out another. Car horns blared. But she was smiling with unconcern. "Do you want me to turn on the radio?"

"No, I do not want you to turn on the radio," he gritted out. "Watch the damn road."

"Tsk-tsk." She took her hand off the steering wheel for a brief second and patted his handcuffed one. "Don't worry. I've got everything under control."

He closed his eyes, deciding it was better not to see. "Where are we going?"

She began to hum a soft tune, ignoring him.

He decided to ask the important question hammering away in his head. "Why aren't you at the divorce hearing?"

She flashed him one of those woman looks. The one that said, "Men are so-o-o-o dumb."

He decided to go with the flow and relax.

His eyes swept her body, assessing her for the first time. In a deliberately lazy tone of voice, he said, "You look pretty good in a uniform."

"Yeah, I do, don't I?"

She looked sensational. The shirt hugged her breasts, outlining hard nipples, and the pants gave a clear, enticing view of hips and buttocks. He shook his head hard, mid-thought, and looked again. Yep, hard nipples and no panty line.

"You're not wearing any underwear," he accused her.

She winked . . . again.

He almost swallowed his teeth. Especially when she just missed sideswiping a car in the next lane.

Then, completely impervious to the honking cars

and cursing drivers, she smiled at him. And he felt warm and suddenly full of hope.

"The uniform does look good, but not as good as that black lace thingee," he said, trying to disconcert her, the way she had him.

She blushed. "Teddy."

"Teddy who?"

"Not Teddy who. It was a black lace teddy."

"Oh."

"I went shopping today."

Big deal! My life's falling apart, and she goes to the mall.

"I bought you some new underwear . . . to replace those yellowed, shampooed ones."

"Oh." He tried to sound bored.

"I know you don't like bikini briefs, so I got boxers."

Boxers? Hmmm. That sounds safe. Boring, actually. "Thank you."

"In the daylight, they have NO imprinted all over them, but in the dark they glow fluorescently with YES, YES, YES—all over."

"Oh." Nick looked down and noticed a very unbored part of his body. He hoped Paula didn't notice.

She did. And she winked . . . for the third time.

"And they're silk."

Uh-oh! What the hell was she up to? Before he had a chance to ask, Paula exited the highway into a residential area of Nutley. She drove confidently down one quiet, tree-lined street after another. He frowned in puzzlement. He couldn't remember anyone they knew in this neighborhood.

And, hey, she'd better stop interfering with his hero plan. It was hard enough playing a knight in shining armor.

Stopping before a small Cape Cod with a white

picket fence, she killed the motor, staring straight ahead, suddenly grave.

"I took the VW back to the dealer this morning," she said suddenly, "and got my Volvo back."

"What?"

"I decided you were right."

Now, this is really interesting. Paula admitting I'm right about something.

"It isn't a safe car for the city. Besides, you didn't fit into it. And I want a car you can fit into."

He was afraid to ask what she meant. Instead, he focused on their present situation. Waving his free hand to indicate the quiet street, he asked, "Now what?"

She gulped nervously. "I want to show you something."

"I've already seen everything you've got to show."

"Tsk-tsk!"

"Of course, I wouldn't mind seeing it again."

"Behave, Nick. I'm serious. C'mon, let's get out." She opened her door and pulled him along beside her, roughly.

"Hey, slow down. You're cutting off my circulation."

He thought she said something about wanting to cut off a lot more than his circulation.

They were standing in the front yard of the house. A FOR SALE sign standing in the grass and the curtainless windows announced its lack of occupants.

"How about undoing these cuffs? That guy looks like's he's about to call the police."

Paula turned to see a man walking his dog, gaping at their handcuffed wrists. "I *am* the police," she muttered.

"Hah! And I'm Mickey Mouse."

"If you're Mickey, then I'm Minnie, babe."

"What's that supposed to mean?"

"Figure it out yourself, bonehead." She undid the lock and was about to pocket the cuffs.

"Yoo-hoo! Oh, yoo-hoo!"

He and Paula both turned toward the dog walker at the same time. He came closer, and Nick couldn't believe his eyes. The man sported gray hair spiked to a curly point on top, slacks pulled up to his armpits, and about four inches of white socks showing at the ankles. "Oh, my God, it's the guy from the bookstore."

"Really? The one who gave you the sex advice?" Paula asked.

"He did *not* give me sex advice," he corrected.

"And is that his wife, Lorna?" Paula said.

Just then, Nick noticed the short woman with the orange curls springing all over her head. She wore a mini skirt and halter top with sneakers and bobby socks. And she clung to the old man's arm, gazing at him adoringly, as if he were Mel Gibson or something.

"Aren't they sweet," Paula cooed.

Nick looked at her as if she had a screw loose.

"Hey, good idea!" the old man yelled, pointing at the handcuffs. "Can Lorna and I borrow them later?"

"Oh, Fred, you rascal, you! You really are the bee's knees," Lorna simpered, batting her eyelashes flirtatiously at her husband.

"Durn tootin' I am." Fred-the-lech beamed.

Yep, I'm definitely going off the deep end. Any minute now, Madame Nadine will come flying by on her broomstick, or her cloud.

"So, did you get the lead back in your pencil?" the old coot asked with a chuckle.

Paula giggled and Lorna nudged her husband with

an elbow. Nick just put both hands on his hips and glared at Fred with consternation. "I never had trouble with lead in my pencil."

"Oh. My mistake. Guess you were lookin' for new ways to gas up the old engine. Heh, heh, heh. Took my advice, didja?"

If Fred weren't a senior citizen, Nick might have gone right over and belted him one. Paula latched on to his arm, just in case.

"Engines, huh?" Paula asked, "Did he recommend *that* book to you?"

Nick played dumb.

But Paula persisted, "You know, *How to Make Your Baby's Motor Hum When Her Engine Needs a Tune-Up?*"

He felt his face grow hot. "Oh, all right. Yes, he did," he snapped. "Now, can we drop it?"

Paula smiled and turned back to the couple. "Hey, Fred, not to worry! My motor's humming just fine now."

Nick made a strangled sound.

"We live next door," Lorna informed Paula conversationally. Nobody paid any attention to Nick; he could be choking to death for all they cared. "We're having a hot tub party next Saturday. Why dontcha come over, sweetie? And bring your hubby along."

Hubby? Nick choked even harder, unable to spit out the words, "Absolutely not!"

"Maybe," Paula said.

As the old couple walked off, waving, Nick turned back to Paula. Instead of laughing, as he'd expected, she was looking up at him in question, blinking nervously.

"Well, what do you think?" she said in a whispery voice.

"Of what? Those senior citizen sexpots? You being a police officer? Us being handcuffed? The weather?"

"The house?" she said in a small voice.

"The house?" That was the last thing he'd expected. He examined the building for the first time, and then, slowly, he began to understand. "Oh, Paula."

"Don't say no right off, Nick. I love this house. I've been looking at it for months," she said defensively. "I . . . I want to buy it."

His first reaction was to tell her to forget it. There was no security fence. The bay window in front would be an easy target for burglars. And Nutley was way too close to Newark and druggies out for quick money. But he saw the look of hope in her eyes, and he bit back his objections. "Well, let me see."

They began to walk around the house, and he stopped at his first glimpse of the backyard. *Oh, Lord!*

"What?" Paula exclaimed, seeing the look of horror on his face.

"Look! Look at that!" The whole back fence was lined with sunflowers. Hundreds of them. Bobbing in the sunlight. "Is this a joke?"

"What?"

"The sunflowers. You planted them here to play a joke on me, right?"

"I don't know what you're talking about. Nick, what's wrong? Why do you have tears in your eyes? Honey, don't. I can live without this house if you don't like it. It's just a house. We can move somewhere else."

"*We?*"

She tilted her head in confusion. "Of course, *we*. Did you think I would live here myself?"

He wasn't sure what he thought. He could barely think for the pounding of his heart. "Paula, don't do this to me. Signing those papers this morning was the hardest thing I've ever had to do in my life. I did it because I love you, and—''

''I know.''

''—I realize now that our divorce is for the best. I *am* obsessive. I have—what did you say? What do you mean, *you know?*''

She swung her right arm in a wide arc, like a windmill, and punched him in the stomach.

''Ooomph!'' It didn't hurt much, but it sure surprised him. ''What the hell was that all about?''

''For leaving this morning without talking to me. Our biggest problem hasn't been your obsession with my safety, you big lunkhead. Or my carelessness. It's been your failure to communicate. And it's going to stop right now, babe.'' She jabbed a finger in his chest.

''It is?'' He went still, hope unfurling in his chest like a giant balloon, choking off his air. He was afraid to believe what she seemed to be offering.

''Do you love me, Nick?''

''Of course.''

''Ask me if I love you?''

''I don't have to ask. I know you love me, babe. That was never the iss—''

''Ask, dammit!''

''Do you love me, Paula?''

''More than life.''

He said a quick prayer then and hoped that Madame Nadine would wing it on up to heaven, first class.

Paula took a step toward him.

He took a step toward her.

''Nick?''

''Paula?'' He held open his arms and she jumped

into them, almost knocking him backward. Bracketing her face with his hands, he studied her face, his eyes probing to her very soul. "Are you coming back to me?" His voice shook with vulnerability, but he was too frightened to care.

She nodded and he kissed her hungrily, holding her tight.

She was laughing and crying at the same time.

He was laughing and trying not to cry at the same time.

"God, I should be noble and walk away. I should love you enough to let you go. I should be a hero. I should—"

"Be quiet."

"Right!"

Tucking her into his side, he kissed her again quickly and began to walk toward the back door. "Maybe you'd better show me the inside of this place before we give the neighbors a show."

"Wouldn't this be a great place for all our cats?"

He groaned. He liked the sound of *our*, but then he exclaimed, "Cats! As in plural? No, Paula, uh-uh. Not in this lifetime. I mean, I've learned to compromise, but that's asking entirely too much. Cats! Yech!"

"Now, Nick, don't you think it would be kind of cute to name the kittens Sneezy and Grumpy and Dopey and—"

"Oh, great! Gargoyle and the Seven Dwarf-kits."

She offered him a sweet, arresting smile, and he groaned again.

As they entered the kitchen, he said, "Now give me those handcuffs."

"Why?" she asked, suddenly suspicious.

He looped his arms around her waist and grinned.

"I just had another idea to satisfy your heart craving."

And right there, on the kitchen floor, he did just that.

My One

DARA JOY

"I have always known that at last I would take this road,
but yesterday I did not know that it would be today."
—Narihara

Chapter One

She had called to him.

Not to him precisely, but he was the one who had heard her. He was the One.

It was a most inopportune time. He was just preparing to *imbody* with a very lovely woman he had met at a circuit gathering of Patrollers. It had already gone past the foreplay stages, and she was more than ready. So was he.

The connecting fever was upon them and his lust ran hot. How could he pull back now? The instant he had the thought, he knew the answer.

He must.

He disengaged himself from the protesting woman, apologizing for his rudeness. The woman was not happy. Her curses seemed to follow him through the Substantive Transport to his ship, which was docked now, during his off time, adjacent to Station 12.

He went directly to his quarters in the single-occupant ship. Removing his flight suit, he lay naked on the bunk waiting for the automatic holo-sensor to appear around him, giving the illusion that others were surrounding him in touch.

The senso-image brought him immediate comfort, as it was designed to do; he relaxed into the familiar warmth, knowing that without the comfort of the illusion, Patrollers could not remain alone long in space. He had always seemed even more sensitive to this particular affliction than others of his kind, for he could not bear lying down to surrender his consciousness without feeling the presence of another next to him.

Even with that limitation met, he had never felt truly at peace.

Trystan relaxed into the warmth surrounding him, closing his eyes, breathing deeply. It wasn't long before he achieved the state he was reaching for.

He sent his mind out....

Past planets . . . past entire star systems . . . past the far reaches where no one had ventured before. Still he journeyed. Eons and eons of nothingness; matter dark. Past pockets and anomalies, wormholes, red giants and on . . .

Until he found what he sought: the source of the call. An average, insignificant planet amongst thousands of like planets in the far arm of the galaxy. A place no one would even think to investigate, so remote was its location, so unexceptional its existence.

Though deep in trance, he furrowed his brow in puzzlement. He had never heard of anyone receiving the call from such a distance. In truth, as far as he knew, the linkage only occurred within their own system, amongst their own peoples, scattered throughout the twenty-seven habitable planets in their sector.

Immediately after the thought occurred to him, another, more disturbing, followed. The call had come from an outsider.

Not from their own kind.

What should he do? Interaction with other species not approved by the Joint Councils was forbidden. Upholding that particular law was an integral part of his existence as a Patroller. And yet . . .

The most sacred of their laws held that one must answer the call when it came, for the call was a prelude to wholeness, which all of his kind actively sought throughout their existence. The call superseded all, for it *connected;* it was the very foundation of who they were.

There was no choice to make. He would go.

It was fortunate this particular voice came to him. Another, he realized, might not have access to his ship; another might not be able to respond to her. But he could.

Yes, the distance to her was vast, but he had been known amongst his people as a man who often accomplished what others could not; the superior ship and elevated rank they had gifted him with for exemplary service was proof of it. With the uniquely modified design of his craft and its exceptional abilities, he could manage it—and without having to go into the Sleep, which he detested.

His eyes blinked open. As he sat up, the holo-image of others sleeping around him dissolved.

The optimum course would be intricate, the journey long. He would have to ride the waves wherever he could to conserve ship energy. The return trip would be more difficult; fuel levels would have to be carefully gauged, especially with her added presence causing further drain on reserves.

Nonetheless, he was confident the ship would make it.

And so would he; she had called to him.

Chapter Two

The doorbell rang.

Lois dropped the laundry she'd been folding. It had better be that noaccount plumber—the one who had promised he would be out the next day, three days in a row! Her kitchen sink was backed up and threatening to spill over the counter with the slightest breeze across the standing water.

She had been tiptoeing through the kitchen for days trying to ward off that particular disaster. The last thing she wanted to do was sop up greasy, dirty sink water that had been standing for three days.

No, that wasn't quite true.

The last thing she wanted, *needed* right now, was an enormous plumber's bill. Her shoulders sagged. She had tried everything to unplug the stupid drain herself and had only succeeded in making it worse.

Her only option, other than blowing her small house to kingdom come—an option which appealed mightily at this moment—was to call in a professional. An expense she could ill afford.

Not when her business was on the brink of failure.

Not when, three months ago, her partner-cum-boyfriend of four years had emptied out their joint accounts after charging up a fortune on her credit cards and simply disappeared, leaving her to mop up the disaster.

Not when her entire life had come down to the present, and she didn't know if she was going to be able to endure the coming months of loss and failure on both the professional and personal fronts.

She had never felt such despair in her life.

In one incredibly selfish move, Mark had stripped away everything she had come to value in her life: her good name, her belief in her own judgment, her reality base.

She swore that if she ever got involved with a man again, it would just be a casual, albeit monogamous, relationship. No promises. No deep protestations. No baring one's soul.

Lois knew where baring one's soul got one. A one-way ticket to Palookaville. If she doubted it, all she had to do was remember a night weeks ago, when, in a rare moment of intense internal pain, she had actually sent out a heartfelt plea to the cosmos for help. It was a stupid thing to do, she realized, but she guessed when you were desperate enough, stupid lost its meaning.

Now she chuckled at the silly request to the miasma of space. At least she had managed to retain her sense of humor through this nightmare.

The bell sounded again.

Yes, I am getting there! She threw the door open.

And stared, mouth gaping, at the man on her doorstep.

She just couldn't help herself. He was exquisite. Never in her life had she seen such masculine perfection.

The pure lines of his face came together, forming a picture of sheer beauty—the straight nose, neither too large nor too small; the cleft chin; the strong jaw; lips that begged for a kiss; and eyes . . . eyes that watched her with a strange combination of innocence mingled with age-old knowledge, eyes a clear silvery blue and glittering with . . . *something*.

Her shocked gaze took in a swift inventory; he was tall and well-built. The man had a body many women might be tempted to kill for. Not her, of course. And that hair! Black, thick, silky, it hung loose past his shoulders.

He appeared to be a few years older than she was. Somewhere around thirty, she guessed, although it was hard to tell. He was in that perfect state of grace men achieved between the ages of thirty and forty.

Did he have Indian blood? He might, she thought, noting his high cheekbones and dusky skintone. Now this was a nice visual surprise on a rotten day, week, month, year.

The man's translucent eyes seemed to question her inspection of him, strangely holding no knowledge of the reason behind her blatant regard. She would have expected someone of his appearance to be impossibly vain or very sure of his effect on women. At first impression, he seemed to have neither of those traits. He spoke in a smooth, deep voice, breaking into her assessment of him.

"You called me and I have come."

The plumber! He was a plumber? She would have thought a guy who looked like him would've headed straight to Hollywood at the first opportunity, do not pass go. Instead, this—this *hunk* had chosen to become . . . a plumber? The Norton of the beautiful people?

Her brows slanted down. *Of course he became a plumber, you dolt; that's where the money is! Just think what he's going to charge you for this little fiasco of yours. Who needs television commercials or a lucrative movie contract when you're armed with a plunger and a snake!*

Here it comes, she thought furiously. I'm about to get taken big time, and there's not a damn thing I can do about it! *Men.* Suddenly this one became the focal point for months of suppressed anger at his sex.

She barked at him, no longer in the least awed by his looks. "Well, you took your sweet time getting here!"

Trystan's eyes widened. He looked down at the woman, amazed at her fury. Why was she angry with him? Had he not come to her at once? Crossed endless amounts of space to reach her?

"Don't stand there gawking at me—I know you charge by the hour! Get in here and do your job!"

She gestured towards her kitchen, indicating by a sweep of her hand that he should enter at once or pay the dire consequences. Her no-nonsense approach must have gotten through to him; he gingerly stepped around her into the house. She closed the door with a snap.

"Well?" She crossed her arms over her chest, tapping her foot impatiently. The man was just standing in the middle of the room, staring at her with a dumbfounded expression on his gorgeous face. The jeans and sneakers were fine, she reflected, but that black T-shirt with the fuzzy teddy bears was truly bizarre.

"I—" He cleared his throat. "I am Trystan."

"How nice for you. I'm Lois Ed and, yes, before you say it, my father was Mister Ed. Ha-ha. Seen it, heard it. Now, do you think you could get to work?''

He was confused by her strange words. Since he could make no sense of her speech, he choose to begin by questioning her last word. ''Work?''

''Yes, you know—do what you came to do,'' she answered him sarcastically. These workmen would do anything to waste time and jack up the bill—although, for some reason, he seemed genuinely surprised by what she had said.

''You wish me to—to begin right away?''

She threw her hands up in the air. ''Of course!''

''You are very forward.'' One corner of his mouth lifted in a slow, seductive smile, his low voice vibrating along her nerves. ''I like that.''

If she were any other woman, say one who wasn't wise to the wiles of his kind, that smile might have turned her into a bowl of pudding. Fortunately, she was immune to the pudding syndrome. At least she thought she was, until he began walking toward her. Purposely.

''What are you—''

Before she could finish her question, he had reached her side.

Before she could utter a protest, his hands came up, cupping the sides of her face.

Before she could remember to breathe, those incredible light eyes locked onto hers.

He stared intently down at her, thoroughly examining her. Somewhere, in the background of her mind, she thought she must have the same expression as a deer caught in headlights.

''It will be as you ask, Lois Ed; I will not wait for you to accustom yourself to me. I will *imbody* with you now.''

Her lips parted, but the question was never issued.

A strange prickling sensation seemed to be coming

from his hands and vibrating to the base of her skull. She looked up at him, caught between fear and fascination. *What was going on?*

Trystan observed her carefully. Her eyes were already beginning to dilate with his prelude movements. Good. She was going to be incredibly responsive to him.

The physical touch of her was acutely pleasing. Strange, he had never noticed the physical touch of another as being different or . . . enlivening. But such was the case here. He stroked his thumb along the underside of her jaw just to test the phenomenon. Yes, most pleasing.

He scrutinized her features once again. She had a . . . good face. He enjoyed the beauty of her eyes; she would not know they were gentle for him now, a hazel shade. And he definitely approved of the shape of her mouth; the lips looked soft and full.

He wondered what he was doing.

It was odd he had noticed these things, such considerations being of very little import. But then, she was his One, so perhaps it was only to be expected that this would be very different from any other experience in his past. There would be nothing holding him back. He could delve into her as deeply as he wished.

Trystan had had plenty of time on the long journey to absorb her language so he would not frighten her by having to immediately link with her to gain this knowledge. And yet, she didn't seem frightened of him at all.

On the contrary, she seemed most bold. He approved of her methods. By her minute examination of him, she seemed to favor him in some way he could not name.

Perhaps the ship's facsimilator had done a decent

job with his wardrobe. In his quest to find the proper raiment, he had viewed many male inhabitants on this planet, including a very small one, whom everyone seemed to like.

Trystan had noticed her staring at the copy he had made of the small male's shirt. There was no doubt; she was impressed with his choice.

Now he would know her truly—after these countless years of waiting and wondering if he would be fortunate enough to receive the call. Many did not and were forced to live out their existence incomplete. This would not be his fate. For he had heard her.

His One.

His to imbody with completely. At last, he would be able to unlock the final barrier when he mated. His heart sped with the thought.

He always knew he would desire her, but had never envisioned the depth of his desire until this moment, when he gazed down at her and she stood within his mating embrace. Trystan could taste his passion rising.

It surged up in him, through him, along his arms to the tips of his fingers, which were even now locked about her in the traditional securing position for his initial thrust into her.

His breathing sped up. Hers did too. He would not wait. No, she did not want him to wait.

Lois fell into his eyes.

Those clear, light blue eyes.

She felt as if she were falling, tumbling end over end through a never-ending spiraling tunnel. Multicolored lights swirled past her going faster and faster. Intricate designs of breathtaking beauty continually formed around her, dissolved, forming again. Like being in a 3-D kaleidoscope, she marveled.

What is happening to me? Where am I?

Her descent stopped and the patterns gathered her up, teasing her, lifting her on the crest of paisley waves, as if—as if the waves themselves were reflections of joyous emotion. They began to play with her now, teasing her, tickling her, and she began laughing, caught up in the sheer joy surrounding her.

Then she felt another presence there with her. Or was it the same presence as the lights? She didn't know. But this nebulous presence seemed to surround her now, engulf her. It came over her completely, warmly cloaking her. It felt . . . nice. Soothing, yet somehow, in a way she couldn't explain, stimulating.

Until the presence began pressing in on her.

Suddenly she didn't like this anymore. She tried to push back from the pressure, but she could not stop it from penetrating her.

There was intense pain.

She screamed, lifting her hands to her head.

Trystan snapped the connection immediately, stunned.

The world turned right again and Lois slid to the floor, clutching her throbbing head. Oh, my God! What had just happened to her? Had she suffered some kind of stroke?

Trystan knelt beside her, badly shaken. "Forgive me, my One. I had no idea you were untouched. Had I known, I would have been very careful in my attempt to breech your barrier. Let us try again—I swear you will not feel this pain."

Lois peered at him through bleary eyes. "Wh-what are you talking about?"

His hands cupped her shoulders in earnest entreaty. "I am so sorry. You must know I would not have caused you pain for any reason, my One. Will you let me—"

She slapped his hands away. The pain in her head

was receding rapidly and with it her disorientation. "What are you babbling about? Look, something . . . odd just happened to me. I think . . . could you take me to a hospital?"

He grinned at her! Instead of being properly concerned like any decent human being would be, he was laughing at her!

"You do not need a hospital." He brushed aside a stray lock of dark brown hair that had fallen over her forehead. "I assure you, the pain, though regrettable, is a natural response of the female when penetrated by the male for the first time. Has no one taught you this? Had I known you were unbreeched, I would have attempted a more careful entry to lessen your discomfit."

"Wh-what are you saying?" Lois stared at him, horror-stuck. Was he implying that *he* had caused that—that *thing* to happen to her? That he had somehow entered her mind?

It was too unbelievable to contemplate, yet she had just experienced something very paranormal.

He raised an indulgent eyebrow, which, in any other circumstances, would have irritated her no end. "You are inexperienced. It appears you know nothing of the ways of mating."

He sighed deeply. "I suppose I will have to teach you as we go along."

Trystan contemplated this unexpected development. It might prove interesting. Somehow the idea of her being untouched excited him. He would be the first, the only experience for her. Not just her One, but her *only* man. *Yes.* It made him hot just to think of it.

Lois ignored the man's overbearing, foolish statement, getting straight to the part which was of paramount concern to her. "Are you saying you entered my mind? How could you do that?''

He gave her an extraordinarily sexy grin, as if to say, "need you ask?''

Lois began backing away from him, holding her hand up to ward him off. ''You're not the plumber, are you?''

He began to close the distance between them. ''I've already told you; I am Trystan. Your One.''

She tried backing up some more, but the wall stopped her. Swallowing, she forced herself to look him straight in the eye, which wasn't too easy since he stood a full head and shoulders above her.

''My one what?'' She gulped.

''Your one . . . *everything*,'' he whispered, reaching up again to cup her face.

Lois quickly ducked under his arm. She wasn't going to let him touch her like that again. Not for anything. If a man enjoyed something that much, it was probably wise for a woman to be very careful with it. Besides, it hurt!

''Stay away from me, Trystan! I—I don't want you in my mind.''

The corners of his mouth tightened as if she had insulted him in some way. It was strange, very strange.

He was strange.

Oh, not his looks—they were simply exceptional. It was a certain way he was behaving that just didn't make sense. She would chalk him up as a nutcase if she hadn't experienced that odd *probe* of his.

''Where exactly are you from?'' She was afraid she already knew the answer, but when his silvery-blue eyes slowly glanced skyward, a sinking feeling washed over her. *Oh, my.*

''How did you get here?'' she croaked, clutching a sidetable for support.

He motioned her to the front door. She followed gingerly, staying several steps behind.

When he opened the door, he drew a small flat disc from his back pocket, directing her attention to the sky above the woods surrounding her house. Then he pressed a sequence of some kind onto the disc.

A ship materialized over her woods.

It just hovered there, silently waiting.

Lois grabbed his arm, not even realizing she was doing it. She stared up at the alien craft, spellbound.

Trystan watched her silently, noting her ashen complexion. She had not expected him to come. The insight shook him to the core. She should have had more faith in him!

With a flick of his fingers, the ship dematerialized. He drew her gently back inside.

"You called me and I have come," he repeated, emphasizing the flow of cause and effect for her.

"Oh, my God." Lois sank onto the couch clutching her stomach. "I think I'm going to be sick."

He sat down beside her. She turned to face him. "You—you *heard* me?"

"Yes, I heard you. I am your One."

"You keep saying that. I don't understand what you mean."

He stared intently at her. "I am . . . not One without you. You are not One without me. Together we become One."

She still didn't understand. But it sounded strangely sexual, nonetheless. "Are you coming on to me?" Her voice was tinged with suspicion.

"No." He emphatically shook his head. "I am coming *into* you."

Lois jumped up. "Like hell you are, buddy!"

Trystan smiled indulgently. "It is your inexperience frightening you. You must trust me the next time I *imbody* with you.''

''*Imbody?* Do you mean, enter my mind?''

''It is more, much more. It is joining pleasure in its pure form, and in our case''—his eyes flicked over her in a very male way—''it is a journey we take together, forever, once we—''

''So you want to, like, meld energies or something with me?'' This was weird. Not that she would consider it under any circumstances.

Her question seemed to distract him; he turned away, a dull flush of bronze highlighted his cheekbones. Had she embarrassed him in some way?

''You are very direct.'' He turned back to her, a hungry expression in his eyes. ''Yes, I do.''

Lois jumped at his response.

''But not yet. I see now you are not ready. You are too uncontrolled, too inexperienced—''

Lois began giggling. She couldn't stop herself; it was all so bizarre. ''Are you saying I'm a virgin? Oh, this is rich! I'll have you know, a long-term relationship of mine just recently ended. I admit, I'm no barfly, but I can assure you, after four years Mark—''

''It is pointless for you to try to deny the truth.'' His expression was downright smug. And very male. ''I was there, remember?''

Lois's mouth parted, but nothing came out. It appeared he thought of this mind thing he referred to as *imbody* in a sexual way. Perhaps that was how his species fooled around? Could it be? There was an easy way to find out.

''Tell me, Trystan, have you ever been with a woman?''

He thought of his well-deserved reputation in that regard. His response was a blatantly masculine one.

"I have been with women—many, many women."

At her crestfallen expression, he added, "Surely you did not think I was as untouched as you? Do not think on it, my one; I assure you, the others are naught to me."

As if she cared! Have patience, Lois, you're dealing with an alien mind here. "I mean, have you ever physically been with a woman?"

His answer was a confused expression. She was right! Oh, well. She regarded his beautiful body wistfully. What a waste. "So, in actuality, *you* are the virgin."

Trystan chuckled. "I assure you, it is one thing I have never been accused of, Lois Ed." His superior expression conveyed blatant amusement at her apparent naïveté.

It hit her.

He didn't understand.

He had no concept of physical love. Probably was incapable of it.

She had to laugh at herself. *Now here's just the type of answer I get to any kind of plea I send out. A hunk that can't.*

The situation took on mythological proportions, rather like one of those weird punishments the Greek gods meted out to people who misbehaved—like dangling grapes forever out of the reach of a starving man. She looked at Trystan, seeing a bunch of muscatel. It figured.

Not that she wanted anything to do with men right now.

But in this case, it would have been nice to have had the choice.

Chapter Three

"You wish me to sleep alone?"

The look of utter horror on his face would have been comical if he hadn't just turned a sick shade of pale. You might think she had just told him he was to be executed at dawn! What was the big deal?

"Yes, I expect you to sleep alone here in the guest room." She emphasized "guest" to imply that he was not. "On the foldaway bed."

"I cannot!"

This was getting to be annoying. It was one long, obstinate refusal after another. After she had tried to get him to leave, which he flatly refused, she had tried to get him to understand that he had made a mistake in coming here. He refused to believe that as well. Now he was squawking about the sleeping arrangements.

She released a long-suffering breath, crossing her arms over her chest. "Why, pray tell, not?"

"I must sleep with the touching. We all must. I cannot surrender myself to the sleep state without it."

"Are you telling me you *always* have to sleep next to someone?" When he nodded his head at her, she threw her hands up in the air. "For Pete's sake, this is too much!" What was next? She was only thankful she hadn't gotten a guardian angel out of her request. God only knew what that would have produced!

A possibility occurred to her. "Is anybody else on your ship?"

"No, I come alone."

He appeared a little uncomfortable with his confession. Maybe he had taken off when he wasn't supposed to. Well, if he got into trouble, it was none of her concern. Maybe next time he would think twice before chasing a wrong number across the galaxy.

"Wait a minute—how did you sleep on your journey, if you were alone as you say?"

"There is a holo-sensor imaging—do you know what that is?"

"I can guess," she responded in an annoyed tone.

"It—it simulates the sensation of the touching."

"I scc." *Dammit.* "I don't suppose you could just return to your ship in the evenings?" she asked hopefully.

"No. The repetitive trips through the Substantive Transport would be too draining on my ship's reserves. I have calculated this excursion very carefully; I need to conserve all possible energy."

"All right." Lois threw the towel in reluctantly. She couldn't be responsible for the poor guy suffering sleep deprivation. "Come on."

He eagerly followed her into her bedroom. Too eagerly, it seemed to her. She stopped abruptly, almost causing him to collide with her.

"No imbodying." She pointed a stern finger at him.

He shook his head, earnestly, like a chastened schoolboy. "No, my One."

"Okay, then—why are you taking off your clothes?"

"How else do we sleep with the touch?" He looked at her as if she were missing a few circuits upstairs.

How else indeed.

"You must remove your raiment also."

"No way, José."

"You must. The contact has to be by both. Remove them."

Lois bit her bottom lip. Should she? Did she have a choice? Not if she didn't want to be unnecessarily cruel to him. Okay, so it wasn't like he would pay any attention to her in *that way*. She sighed. Did it really matter? Only to her; it wouldn't to him.

She quickly shed her clothes and dived under the covers. She was right; he hadn't even glanced her way.

But she glanced his way.

The wrapping did not do justice to the package. And even though he seemed oblivious to physical love, he had his share of the proper equipment. More than his share.

Trystan got under the covers, gathering her to him.

"Hey!" She fruitlessly tried to break his hold.

"Shh, we will entwine with each other. You will like it. Already, I can feel a difference with you that I have never experienced before. It will be good." That said, his large palm flattened her head to his broad, toasty chest.

My One

My God, she was lying naked in the arms of a studmuffin.

A sleeping studmuffin. And by the peaceful expression on his face, a damned comfortable one.

The back of his hand stroked the curve of her waist.

Chapter Four

He awoke in the middle of the night.

There was a strange tingling sensation at the base of his spine.

It did not seem to be indicative of any discomfort or illness. He felt perfectly fine.

Better than fine.

For the first time in his life, when he slept, he had felt at peace. He decided to ignore the dull, unaccountable vibration in his lower back.

Trystan rubbed his cheek in a cuddle motion against the soft skin of Lois's shoulder, drawing her tighter into his secure embrace.

Chapter Five

Lois sleepily opened her eyes onto silvery blue ones. In her sleep, her arms had found their way around Trystan's warm neck. His stare was intense, silent, and deep. What was he searching for in her?

Without speaking, he moved one of his hands from around her waist to the base of her neck, under the heavy fall of her hair. There, he massaged her, using his thumb and forefinger, loosening the tight muscles that had constricted under his burning gaze.

How had he known that?

Lois vaguely remembered rubbing her forehead against the strong column of his throat, and the spicy, intoxicating scent of him. She definitely remembered the tender way Trystan had held her all night long and how he had intermittently stroked her in his sleep, as if, subconsciously, he needed to reassure himself of the contact between them.

Her breath caught as his lucid gaze now swept

down to her slightly parted mouth, lingering there. The thick, spiky black lashes made a crescent on his cheekbones; Lois found this intimate view of him utterly sensuous. She was struck anew by the pure beauty of his masculine form.

Raven-black lashes rose slowly, languidly.

Trystan met her dazed look with a palpable intensity. His eyes said he wanted her. His hand, stroking her nape, said it. His body, pressed close to hers, said it. And finally, his husky voice said it.

His low tone caressed the stillness of the morning. "Let me love you."

Let me love you. . . . A little sound issued from her throat. A little sound that seemed to excite him.

He groaned low in response. The bronzed hand still holding her waist trailed up her chest, moved lightly over her breast, to cup her face. Attentively, he positioned his splayed fingers against the side of her face and the base of her head.

A jolt of color flashed across her vision.

Not physical love, she realized. Quickly, she clutched his strong wrists, catching him by surprise and breaking the contact. "No, Trystan, no . . ."

Trystan closed his eyes, remaining perfectly still for several moments. Lois wondered if he were in some kind of pain. Was it similar to an Earth man breaking off at the last moment? Was he trying to bring himself under control?

It seemed so, for he remained in the same position with her for several minutes, her hands clutched to his wrists, his fingers, a hairbreadth away from touching her.

It occurred to Lois that if he wanted to proceed, there was little she could do to stop him from taking her in whatever way he took a woman; the physical strength he possessed was very evident in the highly toned muscles of his perfect physique.

Finally, though, he pulled away from her, breaking all contact.

He rolled onto his back, his sinewy forearm flung across his forehead, his upturned fist clenched. He wouldn't look at her; instead, he stared up at the ceiling.

His voice, when he spoke, was flat, toneless. "Leave me now."

Lois quickly scooted out of bed.

He wanted her consent.

The realization relieved her of her fears. Trystan might try to entice her into this odd communion of his, but he wouldn't force her. She was safe with him.

Chapter Six

That afternoon, when Lois entered the family room, she noticed Trystan in front of her computer, his hands flying across the keys. He was sitting in the chair wrapped in a bed sheet from the waist down. Earlier, he had come out of her shower innocently claiming he could not don the same clothes he had worn previously unless they were first cleaned.

Then he had asked her where her sanitation unit was.

She smiled at the memory. Rather than argue with him that his jeans were hardly dirty after a half-day's wearing, she had simply thrown them into the washing machine. Later, when she had gone into town to do some errands, she had picked up a change of clothes for him, including a couple of T-shirts that didn't have fuzzy teddy bears on them. She still wondered about that.

"What are you doing?" She leaned over him, placing a cup of hot tea on the table for him. Trystan smiled at her over his shoulder, producing one very intriguing dimple in his right cheek. He was so handsome . . . and so unaware of it.

"I'm playing with your computer; it's very primitive. I've made some modifications." He took a sip of the tea. "This is very soothing; what is it?"

"Tea. What do you mean, modifications?" she asked, alarmed. Her computer was her livelihood. Or what was left of it after Mark had run out.

"Watch." His finger hit the option key. The graphics display jumped four inches out of the screen in a holographic projection. Lois's mouth dropped open.

"How did you do that?"

"I've reprogrammed it. I admit it's not very impressive, but this unit is all I have to work with. Do you collect antique machines?" he asked seriously. "I have known some to pursue this hobby."

So he thought this brand-new, state-of-the-art home computer, for which she had shelled out a huge chunk of her savings, was an antique! "No, this is one of the best computers out there for home use. In fact, I use it in my business."

His brow furrowed. "You earn your living with *this?*" He seemed surprised at the concept. "Such machines are just tools where I come from; I don't see how you could exchange money with it. What do you do?"

"I have a desktop publishing business. We—I mean, I—print technical manuals by contract. At least I used to." She sighed.

"What do you mean?"

"My partner, Mark, did all the graphics for the manuals; he was something of a genius with C.A.D., computer-aided design."

"He isn't doing this for you anymore?" He watched her intently.

"Mark . . ." She swallowed. "Mark left—so I think I'm going to have to return the contracts I have. I can't complete them, you see."

Trystan thought about it a moment. It was obvious to him that she did not want to return these "contracts" of hers. In fact, it seemed important to her not to do this. He didn't fully understand it, but if it was important to her, than it was important to him. After all, she was his One.

"I'll help you, Lois Ed. As you can see, such designs are a very simple thing for me to produce."

Lois started. He was right; it seemed like child's play to him. Could he help her? Just until she could find someone to replace Mark? It would mean the survival of her business. It would mean food in the refrigerator.

She flashed a warm smile at him. "Could you, Trystan?"

He believed his heart stopped for a moment.

It was something in the smile she had bestowed on him. Her lips were so soft looking and her mouth trembled ever so slightly when she mentioned the man, Mark. Had this man hurt her in some way? He hoped not.

She was leaning over him now, watching the screen. Unbidden, his eyes fell to her breasts. They were full, round, and womanly. He reflected on how nicely shaped they were.

Odd; he had never paid the slightest attention to a woman's breasts before. They were just there, a fact of the differences between the sexes; women had them, men did not. Why should he notice them now?

And last night, while she slept, he had noticed the shape of her legs, as well. They were smooth and tapered delicately to her small ankles. He thought them most alluring, even if he couldn't say why the shape pleased him so.

In fact, the sight pleased him so much, he could not resist stroking the flat of his palm down along the curve of her hip and thigh—just to see if the feel of her legs beneath his hand would please him as much as their visual shape. It had.

And it confused him.

More confusing still was the heavy sensation now concentrating in his groin. The weighted phenomenon seemed to accompany these bizarre thoughts about her. It was like a pressure, burning and swelling within him. It was very uncomfortable.

It was throbbing.

Chapter Seven

Once again, Trystan awoke in the middle of the night.

His head was resting comfortably on the flat plane of her stomach; his arms were wrapped securely around her waist. As it should be.

The tender skin of her abdomen was warm and soft against his face. He breathed deeply of her personal scent, letting it fill his lungs.

The sleep he experienced while touching her was a deep, comforting one; and yet . . .

He was strangely restless.

The unusual tingling sensation in his lower spine had returned. Only it was more insistent now. It hummed steadily along his spinal column. And the pressure in his groin had increased as well.

Was there something wrong with him? Perhaps he had contracted an unknown form of space illness, although he didn't feel sick . . . exactly.

Raising his head slightly from the region of her

belly, his sights were caught by the little pink nipple jutting close to his eye. The delicate feminine protuberance was . . . pretty.

For some reason, he suddenly wondered what it would taste like.

It was rather a foolish thought, but still . . .

Before he could analyze what he was thinking, he lifted his head further, lightly touching the tip of his tongue to the tip of her breast.

It was interesting.

He would try it again.

Trystan quickly flicked his damp tongue across the small pearly nub. It hardened instantly. *And so did he.*

Trystan glanced down at himself, amazed at what he saw.

His male member had swollen to an immense size! Not only that, it was stiff and hard, almost painful, jutting out at a strange angle from his body.

Earlier, when Lois Ed had smiled at him in that special way, a similar event had occurred, although he believed he was swelling even larger this time. It must be some unknown illness or perhaps it was a reaction peculiar to this planet. An allergy of some kind?

When it happened to him before, he had discovered that cold water alleviated first the burning sensation, then, eventually, the swelling.

Lois moaned.

Trystan's silvery blue eyes darted nervously to her face, noting her even breathing with relief. Thankfully, she was still asleep. How foolish he would have felt if she had awakened to his deviant behavior.

He rolled out of bed, quickly heading to the source of cool water.

When he turned the taps off and stepped out of the shower stall, his long hair dripping streams of water down his chest and back, he re-experienced in his mind the precise feel of that hardened little nub against his tongue.

Turning the cold water back on, he immediately stepped into the shower again.

Chapter Eight

"A man came by and corrected your sink. He left a note for you in your kitchen room."

The plumber—at last! God only knew what he charged her, but at least she had a working sink again.

"You just let him in?"

"Of course. Why should I not? He said you called him. I admit, at first I wondered why he thought you would call him when I am your One, but then I realized you did not call him in the same way."

"Huh?"

Trystan gave her a knowing look. "There is the one special thing between us, Lois Ed, that would bring *me* to you." His searing appraisal made her blush. She thought it best to change the subject.

"What are you working on?"

"I have finished the illustrations for this instructive book. Come, tell me if they are acceptable to you." Trystan spoke to her over his shoulder.

Lois put down the grocery bags in her arms and walked over to the computer station. "You've finished it already? The whole book? Let me see!" Trystan handed her a stack of pages.

Lois thumbed through them, amazed. "Trystan, these are wonderful! No, better than wonderful—they're brilliant!" She grabbed him around the neck, giving him a spontaneous hug. He placed his hands over hers, locking her arms around his neck.

He grinned up at her.

"It is so easy to please you, my One. I must try to think of something else I can do to bring this smile to your face." He winked at her, causing her to blush.

Lois was always surprised when he came out with one of his teasing innuendos. By this time, she realized that even though Trystan performed the actual mating act differently, he still behaved in a typically male fashion. He argued with her; he prodded her; he had a tendency to dominate.

In short, physical sexuality notwithstanding, he was very much like most men in the company of a woman they desired. He teased her; he made her laugh; he held her.

Trystan was proving himself a very enticing package of masculinity.

Lois decided she liked him. Very much.

Aside from his differences, Trystan had an engaging personality. He was smart and he learned quickly. Often, his silvery blue eyes would flash with humor. There was other evidence of his nature—just this morning when she was about to stomp on a spider in her kitchen, he had stopped her. Carefully lifting the spider onto a flat sheet of paper, he had gently deposited it outside.

And yet, he had told her he was a soldier of some kind.

A Patroller, he called it. He defended his home worlds against invasion, although he was very vague about just what or who would be invading them. When she asked him, he didn't seem to know the answer himself.

"Whosoever the Joint Council of Worlds deem as those we must have no contact with," he had finally replied.

"Do these Patrollers all have their own ships?"

"Not all. Only those who have proven their worth to our people. Some are gifted with better ships than others. The ship I have come to you in is of a superior design than most."

Lois raised her eyebrows. So, that meant he was probably the equivalent of a high-ranking officer. "Did you just . . . *leave* to come here?"

He seemed uncomfortable with the question, reminding her of a similar reaction he had when she had first questioned him. Now, as before, he answered, "You called me and I have come."

He was AWOL. She just knew it. How much trouble would he get into for it? Not too much, she prayed. Though misguided in coming here, he seemed to be such a caring, *decent* person.

"You know, Trystan, perhaps you should return to your home soon." Surely the longer he stayed away, the worse it would be for him.

"Not yet. It is not time." Then he smiled sweetly at her. "Besides, Lois Ed, I must help you with your desk–top–publishing–business." He spaced each word carefully, causing her to smile.

She glanced over the graphic sheets again, taking the stack to the couch with her. "These are so good . . ." she murmured absently.

Trystan came to sit by her, looking at them with her. "They are quite simple. I could do much better if you allow me to make further modifications to your machine.''

"No." All she needed was a manual with holographic illustrations jumping out of the page at poor, unsuspecting technicians. They would both be hauled away by government types. An X-File waiting to happen. "No, these will be just fine, Trystan."

"Is there anything else you require of me at the moment?" He leaned back against the sofa, raising a suggestive eyebrow at her.

Lois tried not to laugh. Trystan was not being very subtle.

"Well, there is one thing." He leaned forward, smoothing back a lock of hair from her face.

"Yes, my One?" His voice was a sultry purr.

"Why were you wearing that T-shirt when you first arrived?"

Her question was not what he expected or wanted to hear. "T-shirt? What T-shirt?"

"The one with the fuzzy teddy bears on it." She giggled, quickly covering her mouth with her hand.

Light dawned. "Ah, the shirt I copied from the small male. You did not like it? Everyone seemed to favor him greatly; he was touched and hugged by many in this shirt."

"And you thought I would touch and hug you in it?" Her eyes gleamed with mirth.

"Well . . ." He smiled back at her rather sheepishly.

"Why do you call him a 'small male'?"

"Because he was. I have never seen such a small one before. Only this high," he raised his hand a few feet off the floor to show her. "Perhaps he was a different species."

"He was a child, Trystan. Don't you know what a child is?"

He shrugged his shoulders. "I have never seen this life form before."

"*This life form?* How do you people reproduce, anyway?"

"What do you mean?"

Apparently, he had no idea what she was talking about. "How do you keep the species going?"

"Going where?"

Lois was getting exasperated. "Humans grow from children to adults. Don't tell me you were always the size you are now."

"Of course I was. How else would I be?"

"But how did you get to be ... *be?*"

Trystan looked puzzled. "I don't know," he finally said. "I never thought on it before. I remember my Waking, but not before."

"What is a Waking?"

"It is the beginning of an existence. That is all I remember, from that point on." *Why had he not thought on this before? Where had he come from? Where had they all come from?*

"So there are no children in your worlds? How sad."

"No, we do not have any of these children you speak of."

"Do you age?"

"Yes, we age. Although Patrollers take revitalization treatments to stay at optimum age for duty."

Lois gave him the once-over. "How old are you, anyway?"

"I have passed the equivalent of thirty of your years since my Waking."

But he was already an adult on his Waking. It was confusing. "How long is your life span?"

"I would normally live another seventy of your years, barring accident or other occurrences. I am still considered a young man in my worlds. Yet, I must continue my treatments or I will begin to age at a normal rate. If that occurs, I would eventually have to give up being a Patroller, which I would not want to do.''

"I understand. It must have taken a lot of training and hard work to have reached your position. It isn't so easy to give up something like that."

"You do understand. It is true I am very good at being a Patroller; it is why I was chosen for the position. It is something of an honor. One must have the proper balance of mental and physical attributes.'' He hesitated briefly. "But it is not all that I am, Lois Ed.''

She looked at him. "I understand that, too." She covered his hand where it rested on the sofa.

Trystan turned his palm up, clasping her hand in his.

Chapter Nine

Someone knocked insistently on the door.

Since Trystan was busy trying to figure out how to make some popcorn in the kitchen, Lois went to answer it. She was shocked to find Mark on the other side of the doorstep.

"Mark! Wh-what are you doing here?" She pushed a stray curl out of her face to gain a second to compose herself. This was the man she had spent the last four years of her life with. The man to whom she had given her love and innocence. The man who had run out on her.

"Lois. It's good to see you again." His dark brown eyes traveled over her form in possessive memory. "You're as beautiful as I remember. Can I come in for a few minutes?"

Lois looked over her shoulder in the direction of the kitchen. She heard a pan rattle on the stove, an "ouch," then a few muttered words in an alien tongue that sounded suspiciously like curses, followed by corn beginning to pop. "I—I suppose it would be okay for a few minutes, but I really don't think we have much to talk about, Mark."

"Just hear me out—that's all I ask." He looked at her beseechingly.

Despite being a rat of the first order, he was still a very good-looking man, she thought, holding the door open to let him in. It was amazing how none of the misery he caused showed on his face. *Maybe he has a special portrait in his attic that depicts the real Mark on canvas.*

There was only one thing she wanted to hear from the Dorian Gray of the desktop publishing world at this late date: why? Why, after four years, had he run out on her, leaving her in such dire straits?

Mark walked into the family room.

Lois closed the door, wasting no time in asking him, "Why did you do it, Mark?"

Mark opened his mouth to respond just as Trystan sauntered into the room carrying an overflowing bowl of popcorn. He stopped, staring at Mark curiously. Mark's return look was much more hostile.

"Who's he?" He jerked his thumb in Trystan's direction.

Trystan's nostrils flared slightly at the insulting gesture. "I am Trystan. You need but ask *me* if you wish to know."

Lois could see by the slight narrowing of Trystan's eyes that he did not cotton to Mark at all. She quickly stepped between the two men. The last thing she wanted right now was a scene. By the reddening of Mark's ears, it would behoove her to think of something to immediately diffuse the situation.

"Trystan is a . . . distant cousin. He's been helping me with the business"—she pierced Mark with a pointed look—"since you left." It worked; Mark turned away, uncomfortable with the blatant reminder of his deplorable behavior.

"Oh." Mark approached Trystan, extending his arm for the traditional handshake.

Trystan looked down at the proffered hand, then up to Mark's eyes. He studied him for several tension-fraught moments.

Trystan decided to ignore the man's gesture of false friendliness. Turning away from the annoying intruder, he plopped down into a club chair, put his feet up on a hassock, and started munching on his popcorn.

Lois hid her smile behind the back of her hand. Trystan was a very perceptive man.

Mark watched Trystan for a full minute in disbelief. Finally, he turned back to Lois. "Look, can we go somewhere to talk?"

"There is an empty chair here big enough for the both of you." Trystan curtly nodded in the direction of the couch while continuing to pop the popcorn into his mouth.

Mark gritted his teeth. "I meant, in private."

"This is private enough." Trystan sounded adamant. Lois swallowed.

"Why don't we sit here?" She sat quickly.

Having no choice, Mark joined her on the couch. "I wanted to try and explain to you . . . why I did what I did."

"What happened to you, Mark? How could you—" She stopped, unable to go on. Mark placed his hand on her arm, gently squeezing the soft skin in a gesture of feigned empathy.

Trystan watched them very carefully. For some reason, he did not like this man touching Lois Ed. It was not as if the man was being overly bold by attempting a prelude to *imbodying,* but still . . .

Mark's fingers stroked her arm as he began to speak.

Trystan observed the caressing motion. No, he did not like this at all! He leaned forward, shoving the bowl of popcorn under Mark's nose. "Try some."

Mark pushed the bowl away. "Do you mind? I'm trying to have a conversation here." He faced Lois again. "I had a problem, Lois. I wanted to tell you but couldn't bring myself to do it."

She never expected this type of a confession from him. Mark had always hated to have anyone think he was less than perfect. Which might mean he was telling the truth. "What type of problem?"

"Gambling. I—when it started out, it wasn't so bad. A few bets here and there, the horses, the dogs, you know how it is."

She didn't.

"Anyway, it sort of . . . got out of control. I started borrowing money from the business, but you never knew because I always paid it back before you found out. Then—"

"Then it reached the point where you couldn't do that anymore." She finished for him. No wonder, even with all their lucrative contracts, they never seemed to show a profit at the end of the month. "Oh, Mark, why didn't you tell me?"

"I . . . couldn't. I owed some guys money, a lot of money. I—ah, borrowed as much as I could from the bank books, then I hit the credit cards. I'm sorry, Lois. There was nothing else I could do."

"Mark . . ." Lois's eyes filled with tears.

Mark took her hands. "It's all behind me now, honey; I've paid them back and I—"

Trystan had heard enough. "This is the man who hurt you deeply, Lois Ed, is it not? The man who left you alone to fend for yourself? The one who never concerned himself with your welfare after he left you?''

Lois closed her eyes, then opened them. "He's right, Mark. Why didn't you—if you had problems you should have come to me, not shut me out."

"I couldn't do that. Lois, I want to come back—"

She shook her head. "It was over when you walked out that door, Mark."

"I still love you, Lois."

Trystan stood. He had definitely heard enough. "Then it is unfortunate for you. You lost your right to this happiness when you mistreated her. In any case, she does not love you; do you, my One?" He didn't even wait for her answer. "Nor has she ever truly loved you. You can go now."

Lois's mouth gaped. She wasn't sure whether she should berate Trystan for stepping in where he didn't belong or answer his accurate observation.

Trystan took her silence for all the confirmation he needed. He faced Mark again. "Perhaps you did not hear me—I said, *you can go now*."

Mark's focus shifted from one to the other. "Cousin," he spat out. "Yeah, right."

He stormed out, slamming the door behind him.

"There is a saying where I come from, Lois Ed: 'farewell to a dark wind'. I believe it applies here."

Lois reluctantly nodded her agreement. She picked up the popcorn bowl and flipped on the TV. Trystan sat beside her on the couch, reaching into the bowl every now and then for a handful of the snack. He maintained his silence on many levels.

Chapter Ten

It happened again in the middle of the night.

Worse this time.

They were lying side by side, curled into each other. As it should, the curve of her body fit perfectly to his own.

His arms were wrapped around her when he awakened. From the inside out, he burned. *He burned.*

His whole body was thrumming with an unknown energy sizzling, crackling through him. But it was at its worst in his male member.

He throbbed, swollen and pulsing. Would he die of this ghastly malady? He ached so. . . .

Lois muttered something incoherent in her sleep, leaning further back into him. The skin of her back and buttocks slid tightly against him. Trystan stifled his groan of agony.

He had faced down alien invaders, fought for his life and his people. He must remain strong. Vowing he would live through this, he tightly clenched his teeth together.

The night passed slowly for him, in excruciating torment.

By the time the first rays of light came through the bedroom window, Trystan was bathed in sweat. He was no better. If anything, he was in more pain.

A diversion.

He needed a diversion to take his mind from this affliction. Besides the monumental pain, this—this *thing* was making him irritated. He impatiently brushed aside the thick swath of Lois Ed's hair from where it had been tickling the front of his nose.

His sights fixated on the exposed nape of her neck. He wanted to press his lips against the vulnerable spot. *Glide them across the velvet expanse of exposed . . .*

Was he going mad?

Disgusted with himself, he jumped out of bed, wakening Lois in the process. She opened sleepy eyes to the sight of him standing right next to her by the bed. Her eyes widened at what was in front of her face. She sat up with a squeal, clutching the sheet to her.

"What is *that?*" She pointed an accusatory finger at the obvious swelling.

Trystan tried to pretend nothing was amiss. "What?"

"Don't be coy. What is that enormous erection for?" she demanded.

Trystan had no idea what she was talking about, but her attitude irritated him nonetheless. Could she not see he was ill?

"You are being argumentative and ridiculous," he bit out, stalking toward the bathroom.

Cold water would help him. Ice cold.

Lois remained in the bed, clutching the sheet in stunned silence. Trystan had become aroused.

Physically aroused.

Had it happened to him before? Did he know what it meant? Maybe he did.

Maybe it happened to his kind all the time, but they somehow ignored the implications.

Maybe that was why he seemed so testy when she pointed out the obvious.

Or maybe, just maybe, it had never happened to him before and he didn't know what to do about it.

A slow, impish smile inched across her face. She knew exactly what to do about it.

What would it be like with him? she wondered. She'd only ever been with Mark, but somehow she thought it might be different with Trystan—not for the obvious reasons, but by virtue of his heartfelt nature.

She believed Trystan would make the experience very special for her. He would cherish her and give completely of himself, she was sure.

Lois admitted to herself that she wanted him. The next time he found himself similarly indisposed, she intended to show him the prescribed treatment.

Chapter Eleven

He would live.

Apparently, whatever had him in its throes was not life-threatening. So far.

Trystan ran a shaky hand through his long hair. It seemed to come at him in a series of attacks. One minute he was fine, the next he was on fire. Perhaps he should go back to his ship to see if he could get the medi-program to search out an antidote for him.

No, he couldn't do that. He had calculated this trip so close to exhaust levels that he had to be very conservative with energy usage.

He had survived so far. In fact, between bouts, he seemed to recover completely—until the next attack seized him. This appeared to be a positive indication that his body was mastering the problem. Except that the attacks seemed to be coming more frequently.

He would give it one more day.

If he hadn't improved by the next morning, he

would have no choice but to seek aid from his ship.

Fortunately, for the rest of the day, he survived without a relapse. Lois Ed had gone into another room, which she called the den, to work on a different project. He stayed in the family room working graphics on her computer.

Chapter Twelve

His good fortune did not hold out.

Chapter Thirteen

Lois opened her eyes.

In the darkness of the night, moonlight filtered through the partially raised shade, falling across the bed. Illuminating Trystan.

Bronze and naked, he was sitting back on his haunches. The surrounding moon-aura made a pagan god out of him.

He was magnificent!

He was breathing raggedly; sweat beaded his upper lip and glistened on the perfectly delineated ridges of his sculpted chest. By his demeanor, she was not surprised to find that her hips had been lifted to rest atop his powerful thighs.

The tip of his throbbing manhood kissed the portal of her femininity.

Trystan saw that she was awake.

Their eyes locked for a timeless eternity.

Caught in his heated stare, Lois held her breath. *Would he?*

Trystan pushed forward slightly, never breaking eye contact with her. He barely entered her. Yes, she thought. *Yes . . .*

Trystan watched Lois's eyes widen, her pupils dilate. Then he felt fluid, thick and warm, surround the head of his manhood. He stopped, thought about it a moment, and decided he liked it.

More than liked it.

Slick, yet velvety, the unknown substance seemed to cool the fire in his man rod, yet ignite it at the same time. Sensually, he wondered how this rich juice would feel sliding against his mouth.

With a start, he realized the liquid was coming from deep inside her. Instantly, he wanted—needed—to immerse himself in more of this hot, viscous substance. And when he suddenly realized he was *causing* her to make this dewy wetness, he all but moaned.

He would have more of her.

Trystan pressed forward slowly, allowing himself the time to feel his body gradually sink into this wondrous liquid heat of hers. Inch by inch, he entered her, deeper and deeper. He slid in as far as he could go and wanted to go further still.

He clasped her hips in his strong hands, bringing her up tightly against him. The sensations flooding him caused him to close his eyes with an ecstatic joy he had previously experienced only in the throes of mind *imbodying*.

Only this was different. Less, and yet . . . more.

She surrounded him with herself—not just heat and liquid now, but *her,* caressing him, bringing him in, *imbodying* around him, until he was not sure where he ended and she began.

Shocking him, she caressed him inside.

A low sound growled from deep in his throat. The cords of his neck stood out as he threw his head back. A bead of sweat trickled down his brow.

"Kiss me." Her breathy voice caused him to open his eyes. She wanted something from him, but he knew not what. His mouth parted slightly as he watched her beneath him.

"Show me, my One," he rasped.

Her arm coiled around his neck, gently tugging him forward, urging him toward her mouth while the fingers of her other hand threaded through the long strands of his straight hair. His eyes widened momentarily as she placed her lips against his, then closed of their own accord when she moved those softest of lips against his, back and forth, in the most pleasing manner possible. She was beautiful.

He could taste her now. Taste her and drink of her.

She licked his upper lip. He licked her back and tickled the corners of her mouth with his tongue.

She nipped at him. He returned the favor by nipping back, then decided to gently suckle on her full lower lip.

Trystan did what he was good at; he took command. No longer content to follow her lead, his tongue began a foray of its own, teasing the little indentation above the bow of her mouth, laving across the seam of her lips, and, finally, doing what he had thought of doing the other night. He came into her completely with his tongue.

She was moist and hot there, too.

Leisurely, he explored her and stroked her and tasted her until he thought he would go mad from the feel, taste, scent of her against him, beneath him, in him, within him.

He was swelling and thickening inside her. But she did not seem to mind; on the contrary, she moaned and squirmed beneath him. He knew now what she wanted; Lois Ed wanted him to move within her the same way he had done in her mouth with his tongue.

But he would not. Not this first time.

His hands came down to anchor her hips, to prevent her movements.

"Trystan," she moaned. "Move inside—"

"No, my One," he answered her raggedly, "I want to feel you this way . . . I want you to feel me within you like this, *deep . . .*"

He throbbed inside her, felt her responding shudder. He started to bring his hands up to her face, to the base of her head, attempting even now to give her his mating embrace, but something was happening to both of them. Something powerful. Raw. Wild.

The fire in his body was out of his control. He felt a rushing, pounding surge from deep within him, building and building. He choked out her name, clutching her tighter to him. Could he die of this? *He didn't care!*

The same thing he was experiencing seemed to be happening to her. She embraced him, calling out her pleasure with his name.

"Trystan!"

It burst upon him, then.

An unbelievable rush of energy, life, and power. It surged from him, from that part of him connected to her, buried within her. It gushed on and on, seeming to come from his very soul.

He streamed into her. And she accepted it, absorbing him within her joyously, still coaxing yet more of this spurt of joining fluid from him with tiny contractions all along the shaft of his member.

It was his final undoing.

He was overcome by his soaring emotions. He sobbed her name in the throes of his passion. "I am yours," he whispered, falling unconscious in her arms.

Chapter Fourteen

"Trystan—Trystan, are you okay?"

Lois lightly tapped his face with the flat of her hand. He had scared her when he passed out at the culmination of the act. What did she really know of his alien physiology? What if, in her exuberance, she had damaged him in some way?

The silvery blue eyes opened slowly, looking slightly dazed. "I am alive?"

Lois couldn't help but smile. "Yes, you're alive." She smoothed a damp strand of silky hair off his forehead. "You're not hurt in any way, are you? How do you feel?"

His brow furrowed while he thought about his current state. "I feel . . . fine." That didn't seem to be the entire truth. "No, I feel very, very good, Lois Ed." He grinned at her.

"I think we know each other well enough now for you to drop the Ed part and just call me Lois."

His eyes took on a hazy light. "I will know you better, Lois." He eagerly rolled toward her, brushing his mouth across hers. "I like this new method of mating I have discovered." He captured her earlobe with his teeth.

"You've discovered? Trystan, I don't think you understand—"

"It is a wondrous expression of joining, unlike any I have experienced before. Was it the same for you? I can tell you what I am feeling without words and thoughts but with my physical body alone. It's most remarkable." He ran his palms down her backside, cupping her buttocks to him.

Unbelievably, he was hardening again!

His open lips fastened on the curve of her neck, drawing against the skin. Lois gasped. "Trystan, you—"

"It appears I am being afflicted again, Lois. Being the caring individual you are, I know you will help me to relieve this condition, my One." He seized her mouth in a heated kiss.

Whatever she had been about to say was lost when he captured the peak of her breast in his hot mouth.

"This time I will move for you," he whispered.

And did he ever.

Chapter Fifteen

"We've got to stop," she gasped.

"Why?" Trystan rotated his hips, causing a tiny moan to escape from Lois's lips.

"B-because I'm going to collapse. I can't move a muscle."

He smiled against her throat. "Surely you can move one muscle . . ." He flexed deep inside her.

"Oh, God . . ."

Trystan kissed her hungrily, his hands cupping the sides of her face. "Let me come inside you my way, Lois," he panted, his artistic, energetic movements below making both of them breathless.

Once again, she shook her head no.

It had been the same request repeatedly throughout their heated lovemaking of the past week. Once Trystan had tasted the joys of physical passion, there was no controlling him. He had been insatiable. In fact, they had barely left the bedroom for days.

Like a kid with a new toy, he wanted to try everything, in every conceivable way. He had loved her with his tongue, his mouth, his body, on the bed, the floor, the kitchen table, in the bathtub, and once, when they had failed to make the bedroom, on the stairs.

He was incredible. Once, he had inadvertently let it slip that he had something of a reputation amongst the Patrollers regarding his encounters with women. Lois suspected his natural inclinations toward "lustiness" spilled over into the physical realm as well.

The passionate side of his nature now had a new outlet, and it wasn't long before he was teaching her a thing or three. Where did he get his stamina? He had virtually exhausted her.

It had never been this way with Mark. Never.

In Trystan's arms, she felt totally beautiful—a sensuous, alluring lover. She had never considered herself overly passionate before—until he made a wild woman out of her, causing sounds to issue from her throat she had never even suspected she was capable of making.

When he loved her like that, she could deny him nothing.

Except his repeated plea to allow her to let him *imbody* with her.

She continued to refuse him on that score. It scared her, this alien communion of his. What would it do to her? How would it affect her? Would he actually come into her mind to join with her in some way?

From what she remembered of his first and only attempt at the alien mating, that was precisely what he intended to do.

No, she didn't think she could handle extraterrestrial sex just yet—if ever. Anyway, it hurt like the dickens! What pleasure was there in that?

He would just have to be satisfied with what she was giving him. And from the raw, gravelly little moans he was making, he was plenty satisfied.

Chapter Sixteen

Lois stretched her arms over her head.

She had been at the computer for hours. Her back was killing her. It was, unfortunately, one of the disadvantages of her chosen home job.

Trystan came up behind her, placing his large hands on her shoulders; he expertly massaged the stiff muscles in her neck with a rare skill.

"Oh, that feels so-o good."

"You might think I am physically mating with you by these sounds you are making," he observed.

She opened one eye to glare at him over her shoulder. "Very funny."

"Mmm." He rubbed his chin against the top of her head. "If I knew I could coax such sounds out of you by simply rubbing your shoulders like this, I would have tried it sooner. Think of all the time we would save."

"You think you're cute, don't you?"

He leaned down to place a kiss on the rounded curve of her arm. "Does it work on all women the same way, or are you especially sensitive to my touch?"

Instead of smiling, as he had anticipated, her shoulders drooped.

"I suppose you'd want to find that out, wouldn't you?"

His brow furrowed. "What are you talking about?"

She pivoted in the seat to face him. "Well, I mean, now that you've . . . tried it with me, I guess you want to see what it would be like with someone else." She didn't look at all happy about what she was saying.

Trystan was confused. "Why would I want another when I have claimed you?"

"*Claimed* me? We tussled in bed. It *was* your first experience. I'm sure you want to spread your wings—"

"My first experience?" He grinned at the very idea. Yes, the mechanics were different, but a comet was a comet. "I've been making love for—well, let's just say I am very experienced."

She stood. "You know what I mean, Trystan."

He ignored her words and began stalking her around the room and out into the hallway, a glint of sexual mischief lighting his silvery blue eyes. "As for spreading my wings—maybe I will spread yours instead." He lunged for her.

Lois shrieked and ran up the stairs.

Trystan strolled behind her until he got halfway up the staircase; then he bolted after her.

"Put me down, Trystan! Put me—" Lois's voice briefly filtered down the hallway before the bedroom door was slammed shut.

Chapter Seventeen

Trystan rolled off Lois, gathering her to him in the secure comfort of his embrace. Already she was fast asleep. He had exhausted her.

His conscience pricked him slightly. He had thought if he tired her enough, she might lower her adamant resistance to him. But it hadn't worked out that way.

Not that he wasn't sufficiently motivated within his own body to enthusiastically participate in their physical exchange; he was. In fact, he could have vigorously gone on all night long loving her in this new way they both so enjoyed. However, he wanted more.

He wanted to *imbody* with her.

Not just wanted . . . needed.

Being an innocent, she didn't understand a man's natural impulses. Every time he joined his flesh to hers, the desire rose fiercely within him to make her his completely.

My One

A few times, the longing had almost overwhelmed him. But he had fought it down. It would be unforgivable of him to enter her without her consent; to take what he so desperately craved.

He was known among his peers as a man of strong character, a man capable of total control. Lately, however, he wondered how much longer he could retain that control when every time they mated, he seemed less sure of his ability to obey her wishes not to *imbody*.

Trystan absently watched the window curtains fluttering in the night breeze. The light wind was welcome against the warmth of his naked flesh. There was nothing he could do except give her more time to accept him. Eventually, he hoped with all his heart, she would let him in.

Until that time, he could not even think of attempting the journey home. No, she must *imbody* with him before they approached his home worlds.

If not, under the best of circumstances, she would be considered an alien, subject to review or sanction by the Joint Councils. At the worst, she would be considered an invader. What she would be subject to should such be the case didn't bear thinking about.

Chapter Eighteen

The following month was an idyllic time for the two lovers.

They played together and worked together, following no pattern whatsoever, yet somehow managing to get both jobs done.

Trystan had devised a new desktop publishing program for the business, which worked like a dream. Specifically tailored to his own style of imaging, the work he produced was both timely and innovative.

As a result, Lois had managed to deliver most of her contracts on time, picking up several new ones as a result of the fine job they did.

While he was working on the new program, Lois had cautioned Trystan not to make too many improvements. He caught on quickly to what she meant, toning down what he really wanted to do by compromising on the final program. The end result was still yards better than anything out there on the market.

In the future, Lois thought maybe they could publish and sell the program. It could prove to be worth a small fortune. Come to think of it, with his superior ability, Trystan could start up his own programing development company.

Along with developing programs, Trystan had also developed a taste for the classic movie channel on cable. He especially seemed to favor musicals of the 1940s and '50s. She often caught him watching the television, a slight, bemused smile on his face as Fred Astaire tapped across the ceiling and walls or Gene Kelly pranced through the streets of Paris.

Once she saw him laugh out loud as Donald O'Connor bounced his way like a springy rabbit across the streets of a small town proclaiming his love for a woman in time to music. She wondered what interpretation he put on the lunacy of Hollywood. Lois was sure nothing across the galaxy could be so alien or bizarre as a movie director with carte blanche.

The intimate side of their relationship continued to deepen; Trystan avidly explored all the physical aspects of their alliance with passionate intensity. He was a bold, sexy lover. Tireless in his pursuit, erotically inventive with his desire, he kept her in a perpetual state of sensual haze.

It was a perfect interlude.

Until she began getting nauseated in the morning.

Chapter Nineteen

It couldn't be.

It just couldn't be! Lois wiped the sweat from her brow as she tried to master this latest bout of sickness. Trystan had told her . . .

Regardless of what Trystan had told her, all the signs were pointing in one inevitable direction. The late period. The tenderness in her breasts. Her tired feeling in the afternoon. The nausea.

She would kill him.

No, first, she was going to the drugstore to buy a home test. Then she would kill him.

She found him, later that day, sitting in front of the TV in his jeans and T-shirt, stockinged feet crossed on top of the coffee table. There was a boyishly innocent expression on his oh-so-handsome face as he watched the screen. Yes, she would definitely kill him.

Lola from *Damm Yankees* was asking, "who's got

the pain when they do the mambo?'' Lois thought she could answer that question with authority now. Grabbing the remote, she punched off the television. Trystan turned to her with a questioning look.

"I thought you said you couldn't have children." Her hands were at her hips, her foot tapping impatiently.

Trystan's silvery blue eyes widened. "We do not have children."

"Well, you're going to have one now!"

"You—you mean I have given you a child?" The corners of his lips lifted in a semblance of a smile. "I do not understand this, Lois, but it is most intriguing."

That did it. "Intriguing? Intriguing! You oversexed, ignorant space . . . dupe!" Lois started pacing, then stopped, slapping her forehead with her hand. "I don't believe I fell for that sweetly innocent approach of yours. What was I thinking of not to—"

When she made the next pass, Trystan calmly leaned forward, clasped her about the waist, and tumbled her across his lap. His eyes were twinkling with amusement as he gazed down at her shocked face.

Using her momentary astonishment to his advantage, he brushed his lips back and forth in a sensual slide across her own. "I like this idea of a child. It pleases me, my One."

Lois blinked up at him, still slightly dazed to find herself lying across his thighs, staring into those gorgeous sparkling eyes. Her fingers twined in the long strands of his black hair, which fell forward over his shoulders.

"You—you do?" she whispered against his mouth.

"Mmm. Very much." His mouth fastened on her own in a searing kiss.

Lois was never exactly sure what happened after that, but the next thing she knew they were both lying across the couch sans clothes, trying to regain their breath.

"You do realize this is what caused the trouble in the first place?"

"It is no trouble."

"Easy for you to say," she muttered.

Either he didn't hear or he wasn't paying attention; his mind seemed totally wrapped up in the prospect of being a father.

From that moment on, he bombarded her with endless questions.

When would the child come? How big would it be? Would it look like him? On and on the questions came until she was sorely tempted to conk him on the head. He was the most excited father-to-be she had ever seen.

Chapter Twenty

The next weekend, Lois took Trystan to a small shop a friend had told her about in the center of Wystershire, a nearby town which seemed to be a local mecca for artisans and craftpeople. The shop specialized in handmade baby clothes.

Trystan was amazed at the tiny outfits. He examined them very closely. Lois was wondering what he was thinking when he turned to her with a very serious demeanor.

"If the child is going to be so small," he said sincerely, "then we both are going to have to watch it very carefully so nothing bad happens to it."

He is so sweet. Smiling, Lois stood on tiptoe to kiss his cheek. "We will be very careful, Trystan; I promise."

They purchased several little outfits suitable for a newborn, Trystan being unclear as to why they could purchase none of the blue or pink outfits, saying it made no sense to him when a few of the blankets she bought had both colors in them. The saleswoman winked at her as they left the shop hand-in-hand.

On the way back to the car, Trystan was very quiet. Lois thought he was still trying to make sense of the blue and pink taboo. In actuality, his thoughts were going in a much more serious direction.

He had not realized the child would be so tiny. How could he take it on his spaceship? The rigors of space travel might prove too much for such a small life-form.

And what of Lois? How would she fare under these conditions? Would she be weak from having his child?

He didn't know a lot about the process, but what he did know made him concerned about the wisdom of subjecting them both to the journey any time soon.

Lois had never even experienced intersteller flight before. It was a long journey. Who knew how they both would react to it?

And Lois still refused to *imbody* with him. That alone precluded them from leaving. And now with the child . . .

He would just have to wait until the child arrived and they both seemed strong enough for the journey. By that time, Lois would have *imbodied* with him and the timing would be right.

Trystan sighed. He had so wanted to immediately present his child to the people of his home worlds, to show them what he had done. There was a pride in this accomplishment like none other in his past. No one else he was aware of had done such a thing.

Unfortunately, it would just have to wait.

After all, their welfare must be his first concern. Already, he could sense Lois looking to him for a certain protection. This natural expectation of the female to the male usually only occurred after a couple *imbodied* completely with a total mating.

It pleased him that she relied on him now in this manner, even if it was subconscious on her part. No, he would never let either her or their child down. The journey must be postponed.

They were passing a florist shop when he suddenly stopped. "What do you call these flowers?"

Lois looked to see what he was pointing at. "Pink tea roses. Why, do you like them?"

Trystan stared at them for several minutes. *There was something about them* . . . "I want you to have these, Lois."

He seemed so serious. "All right. Let's go get some. They are pretty; we'll put them on the kitchen table."

He paused, looking down at her, a loving expression crossing his face. His strong hand gently tightened his clasp on hers. "And we'll put more next to our bed so we can see them when we arise in the morning, my One."

"How romantic! What about on the table next to the computer? And the coffee table in the den?"

"Yes." He smiled broadly at her. "Let's fill the whole house with them. So everywhere we look we see a reminder of—" His brow furrowed.

"A reminder of what, Trystan?"

"I—I don't remember." He looked momentarily confused.

It doesn't matter; we'll do it anyway!" Taking his hand, she dragged him into the shop with her, where they purchased all the pink roses the florist had.

Chapter Twenty-one

The coffee machine dribbled dark brew into the pot.

Trystan was not overly fond of the stuff, but drank it on occasion. She, on the other hand, was a coffee-holic. At least, she was until her pregnancy.

Lois stared at the pot with a jaundiced eye, wondering if she was going to be able to handle it this morning. The kitchen door opened behind her, and she heard Trystan padding across the tile floor in bare feet. She turned to him, intending to ask him if he would like a cup, but the words never crossed her lips.

Something was wrong.

She could see it in his face.

Wearing nothing but a pair of jeans, he sank to his knees in front of her, burying his face against her midriff. He hugged her hard to him and when he pulled away, tears glistened on his eyelashes.

Oh God, not now. Not when everything is going so

well. Please don't let him tell me he has to leave. . . .

Placing a hand on the crown of his head, she let her fingers sink into his thick hair, wondering what she would do if she was never allowed to feel the silky mass beneath her hand again.

"What is it?" She could barely get the question out.

Trystan's palms cupped her elbows. His face held a monumental sadness. "My ship is gone. I can never return home."

Lois closed her eyes for a moment. It was selfish of her, she knew, but she could not help feeling relieved at the news. He couldn't leave now. "Why?"

Trystan couldn't speak; he hugged her to him again, burying his face against her. And Lois did feel terribly sorry for him. He had come to her, and now he had lost everything.

She suddenly knew why his ship was gone. "Because of what we did." Her voice was flat.

"Yes. I am the first in two thousand years to . . ." He raised his head to watch her. "You have awakened a pleasure center in me that has lain dormant in my people for millennia, Lois. It was feared, should I be allowed to return home, I would likewise contaminate others simply by my presence. My energies run high, you see."

How well she knew.

"I am now labeled an invader and can never approach any of the twenty-seven worlds ruled by the Joint Councils. To make sure of my compliance, my ship has been recalled."

"Oh, Trystan, I'm so sorry for you, but I'd be lying to you if I didn't tell you I was glad as well. Now you can't leave me to—"

"Leave you?" He looked stunned. "I would never

leave you, my One. Never. Why would you even think such a thing?"

"I thought you would return to your worlds—you said you would."

"Yes, but I intended to take you with me. The only reason I waited this long was because we have not *imbodied*. I wasn't sure about the effects of the journey on you and our child—I thought it best to wait until you were both strong enough. But leave you?" He embraced her around the waist, bringing her closer to him. "Could I leave a part of myself behind?"

"Oh, Trystan." Her arms went around his neck; she bowed over him, rubbing her chin against the top of his head.

Trystan stroked his cheek against her abdomen. "Perhaps it is for the best this way. The Joint Councils were right. I could never give up this physical pleasure I have found with you, my One."

"I know I couldn't." Lois tried to smile through her tears.

His clear eyes met hers. "What better way to tell you how I feel? When I touch you with this pleasure, you know. When my mouth begs to caress yours, you know. When my body presses hot against you, you know. And when I stroke inside you"—his eyes hazed over with remembered passion—"you know. Is it not so, my One?"

"Yes, Trystan. It is so."

He swung her up into his arms. "Then let me tell you now how it is for me, this minute, when I need you so much my heart pounds with it. I will show you my spirituality in this physical expression, this translation of One." He carried her up the stairs to the bedroom.

There, he gently placed on the bed.

He untied the belt of her robe, helping her to shrug

loose of it, then he unzipped his jeans, stepping from them into her arms. They lay side by side on top of the handmade quilt.

Lois wondered if her great-grandmother ever knew when she was lovingly piecing this quilt together, that one day she and Trystan would become a living part of the pattern of interwoven rings. It was a fanciful thought.

The back of Trystan's fingers lightly brushed the shape of her collarbone, trailing down to sweep the underside of her breast in a slow, back-and-forth motion.

"Your breasts are fuller. And these"—one lazy finger swirled around the nipple, causing it to instantly harden—"these are deeper in color now." His eyes darkened when the peak jutted into a nub. "Will you feed our child, Lois?" His voice was a husky purr.

"Yes," she breathed, running her hands down the strength of his arms.

His silvery blue eyes lifted slowly to hers. "And will you give sustenance to me as well, my One? Should I have a need of you?"

"Yes, Trystan, yes...."

He bent his head slowly to the distended nipple, his palm cupping the weight of her breast, lifting it to his descending mouth. "Then sustain me now," he whispered before his hot mouth covered the peak.

Lois clutched his powerful shoulders, crying out at the searing contact. He drew on her, taking her deep inside; the tugging, drawing motions set up an instant humming throughout her body. She always wanted him and, to his delight, was always ready for him. But when he set out to play with her like this, she knew he meant to take her at his leisure, driving her crazy into the bargain.

As if to prove her point, his tongue swirled around the nub now, teasing; the broad, wet surface glided across the tip in a drawling lick, scraping languidly across the beaded surface. In reaction, Lois delicately bit the curve of his neck. He chuckled low against her, the vibration further exciting the raw nerves of her skin.

While he continued his devastating ministrations at her breast, a lazy finger meandered its way across her rib cage, down the center line of her torso, to tease her sensitive little belly button. Lois jumped when the tip of his fingernail lightly scraped concentric circles around her navel.

Trystan acknowledged her response by returning the favor. He gently bit into the curve of *her* neck. His finger dipped lower. . . .

Twining the curls at the juncture of her thighs round and around, he lightly tugged against them just enough to cause a certain friction across a very sensitive spot. A taut pulse of longing rippled through her from that centralized location between her legs. At that exact moment, he recaptured her nipple with his teeth.

Lois uttered something inaudible and slid her palms down the curve of his back to cup his perfectly rounded buttocks. They were a nice, tight handful.

Lois tried unsuccessfully to bring him closer to her in an effort to speed him up.

Trystan smiled at Lois's obvious attempt to move him along. He had been the captain of his own ship; he was used to setting a course. It was no different here. He would guide this journey with her at his own pace. Next time, she could take the helm.

He moved his finger along her silken cleft, inserting it slightly in the dewy folds. Her liquid essence surrounded him. She was very wet. He knew exactly what this fluid was now, what it signified, the texture of it, the sweet, pungent taste. He felt himself get harder.

No, he would never willingly give up this pleasure he had found with her. Not for his ship. Not even for the Joint Councils.

He would sooner choose being labeled an outcast for the rest of his life, never to see his homeland again than to be forbidden to ever feel her sweet mouth beneath his own or hear the tiny sounds of pleasure she made just for him when he slipped full into her body.

Trystan pressed into her with just the tip of his finger. The velvety walls surrounded him. His finger rotated circular motions inside her, letting her know him all over again, preparing her for his eventual entry, letting her see how it was going to be between them. The masterful actions spoke to her with the special language of lovers.

"Trystan, that feels so, so good . . ."

"To me as well, my One. Do you want me to enter you now?" His mouth made a passionate sweep of her throat. "Should I come deep inside you now so that you can feel my man shaft throbbing for you as my heart beats?"

His words made her shiver. "Yes, Trystan, now . . ."

Lifting her leg up over his thigh, he entered her in a swift, steady thrust that took both their breaths away.

Capturing her mouth in a fiery blaze of desire, he moved in long, endless strokes. His skillful movements and heated caresses soon rendered both of them almost incoherent.

Disjointed, indecipherable words of endearment spilled from each of them, but they were not meaningless. On the contrary, both Trystan and Lois were very aware of what each was trying to say to the other and thought their sighs, moans, and guttural groans most eloquent under the circumstances.

Caught in the love tempest, Trystan feverishly rolled them over so Lois was beneath him. His arms encircled her, bringing her tight within his embrace. He thrust deep into her, pinning her to the mattress with a totally erotic movement of his hips.

He spoke low in her ear, his husky voice trembling seductively along the side of her throat.

"Let me come into you now, Lois. Completely. You know what I want."

Lois froze beneath him.

Trystan ran his hand lightly over the small swell of her stomach. "We have made a new life together. I will make more for you; but I want to know you in *my* way," he whispered. "I want to make you mine completely. Let me love you, my one . . . let me . . . let me . . ."

He punctuated each of his heartfelt pleas with his open mouth trailing wildly across her face, forehead, the line of her jaw. With slow, strong pushes into her body until she thought she would go mad.

She could deny him no longer.

She flung her arms around his neck, closing her eyes tightly. "Please don't hurt me too much, Trystan."

He stopped all movement, exhaling in disappointment at her misconception. Trystan cupped the back of her head in his hand. "Look at me, my One."

Lois opened her eyes warily. He cupped her face, gazing down at her with a tender expression.

"I would not hurt you willingly for anything in the universe. It is not what you think. I have tried to explain to you that I did not know you were untouched the last time, and so did not prepare you properly for my entry. It will be different this time, I promise.'' He hesitated, then continued.

''I will not be able to prevent all discomfort this first time, but my intention is to bring you only pleasure. I will try my best to ensure that it is the most enjoyable of experiences for you. You must trust me in this or I will not continue.''

His beautiful, sincere features watched her expectantly. She did trust him. It was odd, but now that she recalled, she had never fully trusted Mark before, had never felt completely sure with him. It had never felt right with Mark.

But it had not been that way with Trystan.

Almost from the beginning, she had felt a certain acceptance of him. Certainly, she had never felt threatened by him in any way, not even when she first found out that he was an alien. Oh, she had been shocked, certainly, but not scared. Never scared.

Lois relaxed in his arms. ''I do trust you, Trystan.'' She rested her forehead against his chin. ''Make me yours.''

His lips brushed her brow briefly; then he lifted her hair to place his fingers at the base of her head.

Lois fell into Trystan.

Light and color flashed before her eyes, and once again she was swirling amidst a riotous flow of interchanging patterns. Joy surrounded her and she knew it was Trystan. He was taking her on his personal magical mystery tour.

Lois laughed, but if pressed to put into words what was humorous, she would have been at a loss. It was as if she *felt* humor. And such happiness! She realized Trystan was conveying this to her, beginning his journey in his own special way.

Then the presence turned into a gentle pressure surrounding her. Only it wasn't like the last time. This time, Trystan came to her and retreated, came to her and retreated, in an easy back-and-forth flow.

His presence approached her in lapping waves.

Rolling against her, and back, he ebbed, he surged. Each time, he seemed to trickle into her a little more until, with the final wave, he flowed into her completely in a seamless, painless motion.

There was the briefest moment of discomfort. Then a sort of popping sensation. And he was in.

It was the most remarkable thing Lois had ever experienced. He was with her inside herself—she could sense it!

He began to love her in this strange new way.

It was unlike anything she had experienced before. Trystan twined himself around her in a dance of light. He coaxed and teased and stimulated senses she didn't even know she possessed. He led her with him on an inner adventure. And the pleasure he was giving her!

Even though she was a total novice in this realm, Lois more than suspected that Trystan was very gifted, indeed. Now she fully understood his well-deserved reputation in the art of this *imbodying,* for he took her with such exquisite finesse, highlighting every drop of sensation like a true artist.

Lois was mesmerized by him.

Then she felt something else. A physical sensation. *Trystan was moving in her.*

They were still joined physically—he was on top of her, moving seductively inside her even as he *imbodied* with her mind. Lois uttered an uninhibited cry of delight.

It was the most beautiful experience of her life.

To think she was afraid to let Trystan share this

utterly incredible joining with her! What a fool she had been.

Trystan sent her a ripple of his passion. It flamed about inside her in tones of red and purple, a heavy, humid impression. He followed it with a cool wash of green satisfaction licking at her reason.

He continued his expressions of affection, caressing her in heated rainbows, nestling within her his way and hers. Trystan coaxed every response he could from the experience.

Then he turned his sights to that special place that had called him from the beginning—an inner repository which must never be breached except by the One. A place where heart and spirit joined as One.

He faced the symbolic doorway. His heart beat to a steady thud; he could see the life flow around him in tones of pulse.

Breathing deeply, Trystan unlocked her doorway and opened his own, joining them together for all time.

And in that instant of eternity, they remembered . . .

Tristan, is it you, my love?

Yes, it is I. Wake up now, my sweet Isolde. Wake up . . .

For one brief, glorious moment, they knew. They clung to each other until the true vision of incarnation passed, fading forever from their minds back into the corridors of time.

Trystan trembled from the depth of the experience, taking Lois with him over the abyss.

Into union.

Epilogue

Lois peeked around the door frame.

Trystan was holding their infant daughter, walking back and forth across the nursery, gently patting her back. As he paced, he crooned in low, soothing tones to the baby.

"Did I say you would be no trouble? Hmm?"

A tiny fist smacked his chin.

"See? You are already arguing with me. What am I to do with you?" He caught the small fingers in his mouth, playfully teasing them.

"If you keep me up all night like this, how am I supposed to make more for your mother?" He kissed the fuzzy little head, gently rocking her.

Lois's eyes filled with tears as she watched the two of them. She recalled the first time Trystan had held his daughter in his arms shortly after her birth. Tears had tracked down his cheeks, he was so overcome by his emotions for the tiny life he had helped to create.

My One

Life was a continual surprise, she marveled. On the verge of losing all, she had, instead, found everything. On a lonely, desperate night, she had sent out a prayer to the cosmos and this man had heard her. *This man.*

He had turned his back on everything he knew, defied custom, and, probably, broken several of his laws to reach her.

Her Love.

Her One.

Her Trystan.

Taking one last look into the nursery to ensure that she would never forget this picture, Lois smiled to herself and quickly tiptoed back to bed. He would return to her soon.

He always had.

Author's note: As you've probably surmised, yes, Lois Ed's name is an anagram for Isolde. According to at least one version of the story of Tristan and Isolde from the Legends of the Round Table, Isolde's intended, Mark (Marc), King of Cornwall, killed Tristan in a jealous rage and Isolde died of a broken heart. The hapless lovers were buried together in a single grave where they slept in each other's arms for eternity. A white and a red rose bush grew by the gravesite. Over time, the white and red roses grew together, forming the pink rose, which forever symbolized their love.

I thought they deserved a better ending this time around.

Wild Desire

Phoebe Conn

Nineteen-year-old Eliza has run the Trinity Star Ranch since she was a mere child. Though she is every inch a lady, she has no trouble standing up to any man. That includes the tough-looking drifter she finds camping on Bendalin land. Little did she dream that Jonathan Blair was the friend who'd saved her uncle's life on the battlefield, or that his dark good looks and brash seduction will tempt her to forget both the rules of deportment and the duty she owes her family.

Jonathan takes what he wants from life. And he wants Eliza. Though she is already engaged to be married and far outclasses him, he will let nothing stand in his way.

The
Very Virile Viking
Sandra Hill

Magnus Ericsson is a simple man. He loves the smell of fresh-turned dirt after springtime plowing. He loves the heft of a good sword in his fighting arm. But, Holy Thor, what he does not relish is the bothersome brood of children he's been saddled with. Or the mysterious happenstance that strands him and his longship full of maddening offspring in a strange new land—the kingdom of *Holly Wood*. Here is a place where the blazing sun seems to bake his already befuddled brain, where the folks think he is an act-whore (whatever that is), and the woman of his dreams fails to accept that he is her soul mate . . . a man of exceptional talents, not to mention a very virile Viking.

MR. COMPLETE

SHERIDON SMYTHE

Lydia Carmichael is looking for proof that the drop-dead gorgeous date provided by Mr. Complete Escort Services is a gigolo. All she has to do is lure that bad boy into her bed and she could put the slimeballs out of business.

But Lydia soon learns she isn't cut out for this kind of under-the-covers work. Luke is not only Hot with a capital *H*, he is also a considerate, caring man. As she discovers there is a lot more beneath the surface than his sexy underwear, she finds herself wanting to leave her tidy white-cotton life behind. If her secret wishes could come true, their bought-and-paid-for beginning would lead to a happily-ever-after end that has nothing to do with money and everything to do with love.

Hot Number

SHERIDON SMYTHE

Jackpot! No one needs to win the lottery more than Ashley Kavanagh, and she plans to enjoy every penny of her unexpected windfall—starting with a seven-day cruise to the Caribbean. But it isn't until a ship mix-up pairs her with her ex-husband that things really start to heat up.

Michael Kavanagh hopes this cruise will help him relax, but when he walks in on his nearly naked ex-wife, everything suddenly becomes uncomfortably tight. Sharing a cabin with Ashley certainly isn't smooth sailing—but deep in his heart Michael knows love will be their lifesaver.

KATE ANGELL
DRIVE ME CRAZY

Cade Nyland doesn't think that anything good can come of the new dent in his classic black Sting Ray, even if it does happen at the hands of a sexy young woman. He is determined to win his twelfth road rally race of the year.

TZ Blake only enters Chugger Charlie's tight butt competition to win enough money to keep her auto repair shop open. What she ends up with is a position as navigator in a rally race. All she has to do is pretend she knows where she is going. All factors indicate that the unlikely duo is in for a bumpy ride . . . and each eagerly anticipates the jostling that will bring them closer together.
